Tenpenny Dreadfuls

Tales as Hard as Nails

J.K. Raymond, Brittany McMunn, Fatimah Jan

WILD INK PUBLISHING

Contents

1

A Bloody Dilemma

Tom Elmquist

Jamie had woken up after many nights of drinking since Chris died. Normally she expected the blinding headache and the general feeling of throwing up. She had come to welcome that feeling when she woke up because in her mind it meant she was still alive.

This morning was different. This morning, she woke up with no headache, the light wasn't causing her eyes to burn and generally, she felt better than she had in probably 20 years. She lay there for a few minutes trying to sort out this new feeling of wellness she was experiencing.

When she finally decided maybe it was a good thing to get motivated for her day, she got the shock of her life. When she looked down at her sheets, they were covered in dried blood, and to her further horror, she was covered in dried blood too.

She jumped from the bed and snatched the blanket and sheets. As she did, she heard one of them tear a little. She grabbed the goose-down mattress pad because it was stained with blood too. She shoved them all down the laundry chute and turned to see the bloody footprints leading to the bedroom from the bathroom.

She followed them to the claw foot tub that Chris installed for her. It was filled with blood which had started to coagulate. She quickly reached into the tub and pulled the plug.

When she pulled her hand from the tub and saw the blood on her arm, she immediately felt sick to her stomach. She ran to the toilet and dry-heaved for a few moments. Once she was done, she moved to the shower. It took almost an hour to wash all the blood from her hair and body.

As she got out of the shower and wrapped herself in a towel, she caught a glimpse of herself in the mirror. What she saw at first frightened her and then amazed her. She moved to the mirror to get a closer look. She dropped the towel as she went to touch her face and then realized she had the body of a young woman as opposed to the body of a forty-eight-year-old woman she went to bed with last night.

"What the hell?" Jamie asked out loud as she touched her face. She felt like she was in a dream and could wake up at any moment. This is impossible, she thought and moved even closer to the mirror to look for the crow's feet around her eyes. When she did, she bumped the glass on the edge of the sink. It fell to the tile floor and shattered. Some of the shards hit her foot and stuck.

"Damn it!" she screamed in pain.

Then she realized it wasn't a dream. She was twenty years younger or at least her physical body was. She still had all her thoughts and memories. She picked the shards from her foot.

She went back and marveled at herself in the mirror again. She started to think. If this is real, what could I do? Is this a second chance at life? How did this happen? Many other thoughts filled her mind. With each new thought, she became more excited. Until she looked at the tub and then reality struck.

She immediately returned to the toilet and began dry heaving again. When the bout of heaves was done, she thought. Did I kill someone? What the hell happened last night?

She began to panic. She knew she had to get rid of all the evidence. So, she quickly grabbed everything she needed to clean up all the blood from the linen closet and spent the next hour and a half cleaning. After she finished, she put everything away. Then she noticed the smell of coffee brewing from downstairs.

Before she walked into the kitchen, she put everything that needed to be washed into the washer. She finally walked into the kitchen to see not only coffee brewing but eggs, bacon, and toast waiting.

"What the fuck is going on?" she said out loud.

"Don't you remember last night, my dear?" a voice asked from behind her.

Jamie spun so fast she nearly fell to the floor. What she saw as she turned was a man dressed in a black linen shirt, blue jeans, and black cowboy boots. He looked almost identical to Chris. He had Chris's jawline and facial structure. He looked like Chris from when they had met. The only real differences were this man had deep, dark brown eyes and long jet-black hair pulled back into a ponytail. Chris's eyes were a pale blue, and he kept his hair cut short. This man also spoke with what she thought was a South African accent. He looked different enough that she knew it wasn't Chris. It couldn't be Chris anyway because Chris was dead.

"Who the fuck are you?" she screamed.

"Easy, Darlin'. I'm the guy who made sure you got home safe and sound," he said nonchalantly as he took a sip from one of the teacups from Jamie's fine China. "Why don't you sit down and start on breakfast? I'll pour you a cup of coffee and we can talk."

She had no clue why, but she did as she was told. When she sat down, she realized she was ravenously hungry. She felt like she hadn't eaten in a month. The man set a cup of coffee in her favorite mug before her. Just the aroma told her it was made just as she liked it with three teaspoons of sugar creamer and a dash of cinnamon. A sip from the mug confirmed her suspicion. It was perfect.

Calmly, she asked, "Now, who the fuck are you and how did I get home, and why was my tub filled with blood? Why were my sheets covered in blood and why was I covered in blood for that matter? I have about a thousand other questions but let's start there."

"My name is Godfrey, and I am a humble purveyor of dreams on demand," he said with a slight bow.

"What's that supposed to mean?" she asked.

"We will get to that. As to your second question, I simply put you in your car and drove you home from the bar. Don't you remember anything at all last night?" he asked.

Jamie shook her head and took a sip of her coffee.

"So maybe I should tell you the events last night," he said.

So, he began to tell her about the night and how things unfolded.

"You came into the bar apparently hell-bent, pardon the pun, on trying to find comfort at the bottom of the bottle, or at least trying to numb the pain." His voice was soft and steady. "I was looking to make a deal and maybe have some fun. I watched you for an hour or so. You really know how to put away your liquor, by the way. "

She remembered that much. She had 6 shots of whiskey within thirty minutes. Shortly after that, she wasn't feeling anything much after that.

He continued, "After watching you put away so much alcohol where most men would have been on the floor, I decided to talk to you. I introduced myself and you introduced yourself. I asked you what you were doing there, and you simply responded by saying that you were trying to feel younger. You wanted to feel young again. You wanted to feel young and powerful. You said you wanted to have the world at your feet like when you were younger, like before you met your husband."

He took a sip from his cup and continued. "I knew the story already, but I still asked anyway. Mainly because I like to listen to you and your type's stories. You told me all about Chris and how he was killed in a mugging gone wrong. Very sad way to go I might add."

Jamie became angry and snarled at Godfrey, "You don't have to sound so damn condescending."

"I wasn't trying to be condescending, I was actually trying to be sympathetic."

"It didn't sound that way," she said.

"My apologies. Would you like me to continue?" he asked.

Jamie nodded and took a bite of the bacon.

"So, I listened as you went on. We talked for a few hours, and I bought you drinks to keep your interest. I finally gave you my proposal. I asked, 'What if I could give you a way to recapture that youth you so long for?' and you almost physically jumped at the chance. You asked me with so much eagerness I thought I might be able to have you sign the deal right then and there. Then you became reluctant. You asked me how."

"I mean it is a valid question," Jamie remarked.

"And I told you it is as simple as taking a bath,"

"Wait a bath of blood?" she asked, feeling the panic creep up on her again.

Godfrey just nodded.

"Where did that blood come from?" she asked.

"A drug dealer from 'the wrong side of the tracks' as they say," he chuckled.

"Wait wait wait......Did I kill someone?"

Godfrey erupted with laughter, "Oh no darlin' I took care of that for you. I told you the first time is free. So, your hands are relatively clean." He then gestured with his head to the upstairs bathroom.

"Oh, haha," she said mocking the man.

"I found him peddling his wares just outside the bar. I rendered him unconscious and threw him in your trunk. Then I hung him over your tub and drained him dry. That's the key. The heart must still be beating and pumping the blood into your tub. You can't just let the blood drain out like you are trying to drain the blood from a deer that's already dead," he continued.

The horror was evident on Jamie's face. "So, what? I bathe in the blood? Why does this sound familiar?" she asked.

"Well, many years ago I made the same offer to a Countess, except she didn't follow the rules," he commented.

"How many years ago?"

"Let's just the sixteenth or seventeenth century," he said with a sly little grin.

"Elizabeth Bathory?" she exclaimed. "Wait, how old are you? Wait, what are you?"

"Ah, yes. That was her name. As for your questions, you shouldn't ask questions about things you really don't want to know the answers to."

"Tell me," she said.

"Just remember, you asked. I am a denizen of that place which you call hell. I live primarily on this plane of existence and as for how old I am, I have existed since before you humans crawled from the primordial ooze."

"So, you're a demon," she said plainly.

"We really hate being called that, but if it will make you feel better, yes, I am a demon. No, I don't have horns or wings. Even if I did, I wouldn't show them to you," he said with a petulant little pout.

"Ok. Wait! That's why everything was covered in Blood?" She asked.

"Mmmhmm. You were still drunk, and the magic hadn't fully taken hold. So, you walked like a zombie from the tub to the bed. I tucked you in and have been waiting for you to wake up since," he explained like he was reading stereo instructions.

So, you are offering immortality if I bathe in blood."

"Essentially yes. There is more to it but that's the basics," he answered.

"So, what are these rules?"

She didn't think she would actually consider doing it, but she had to admit to herself she was curious. What would it mean to be able to live forever? She and Chris never had kids so there was no one she would feel guilty about outliving. What would it mean to be able to see the entire world? She could read all the books she had ever dreamed of reading. She could see all those places she and Chris talked about seeing. She would even take his ashes and sprinkle some at each place so he could always be there. Again, she thought to herself, asking if she could really do it.

"Well, the rules are simple. First and foremost, everything must be low profile. You cannot bring undue attention to yourself for your sake and those of my kind. The second rule is you have to kill the donors by your own hand. I can give you a taste of the magic without you doing the deed, but for the magic to continue they must die by your own hand. The third rule is the truly innocent are off-limits. No children nor anyone who lives a pure life can be taken mainly because their blood won't work for the magic. You want the blood of the corrupt. The more corrupt the better," he began.

"Why did you call them donors instead of victims?" she asked.

"Do you really see an arsonist burning buildings and killing people across the city as a victim? What about a man who defiles a woman so badly that she takes her own life? Do you see him as a victim? What about the man who killed your dear husband, and got away with it? Do you see him as a victim?"

The last one hurt Jaime and shook her to the core. "That's why you took the drug dealer," she said.

"Exactly, his misdeeds gave potency to the magic. By killing the donor, you in essence take their life energy which has been corrupted because of their wrongdoings. And that resets your clock so to speak. I use the term donor very loosely though. Forced Donation is still donation," Godfrey said and chuckled.

"I see," she said

"The last rule is this, you have to agree the souls of those you kill are forfeit and belong to me and mine. I mean, they are mostly forfeit anyway, but we get the souls used for the magic."

"Ah, that's where you get something out of this," she said with a dawning understanding.

"Well, that and your soul becomes forfeit should you die," he said with a gleeful smile.

"Wait. I thought you said I would be immortal," she said with a question implied.

"You will be functionally immortal. As long as you bathe every few months you will stay this age. If you wanted to wait to bathe on your deathbed from cancer at ninety years old, you can and you will wake up at this age again and completely healthy. Poisons will have little to no effect on you. As long as you are bathing, disease will no longer bother you. You will also be able to heal from injuries quickly. There is a caveat to this. Should you be decapitated, blown up, shot fatally, burned alive, or anything like that you will die."

"So not like a vampire?"

"Not even close. Vampires are a race. You are still human with all the human limitations," he said with what sounded like a sneer in his voice.

"So, what would keep you or any of the others like you from just killing me for sport?" she asked indignantly

"Well, I wouldn't because you are kind of working for me. So why would I kill someone who makes my job easier,"

She saw the truth in that. "What about the others? I would want some kind of protection from them. I wouldn't agree to this knowing one could just kill me,"

"I can write it into the contract that no other denizens of what you call hell can touch you. If they do, they will immediately be destroyed, and the contract becomes void. In essence, giving you a morally clean slate." he said.

"What about your counterparts?" she asked.

"The ones you call Angels? You're doing them a favor. You know, smiting evil and all," he said shrugging.

"So let me make sure I have this right," she said while hearing her own voice in her head.

You aren't really considering this are you? Seriously, you can't do this. It's wrong.

She continued ignoring the voice for the moment, "I am functionally immortal as long as I bathe in the blood of the corrupt. It would be written in the contract that you all can't fuck with me, or I get a 'get out of jail free card'. Your counterparts won't mess with me because I'm doing their job for them. The only two downsides are that I have to kill the people myself and I can still be killed by severe trauma to my body. Am I right so far?"

Godfrey nodded.

"The only benefit to you as long as I keep bathing or get my 'get out of jail free card' is that you get to collect the souls of the corrupt that I kill," she continued.

"Yeah, that sums it up. Do you want to look at the contract?" he asked eagerly

"Sure, but I will not touch it in any way shape or form. I don't want you to try to trick me by getting my blood on it somehow and calling that binding," she retorted.

A scroll and quill appeared in Godfrey's hand. They read the contract and made revisions as they went. She had him add clauses and he would remove unnecessary clauses. All the while a new voice came into her mind. The voice was soft, comforting and familiar. It was Chris. You don't have to do this. If you do, you will never see me again. I promise to protect you forever. So let me do that now. Jamie, listen to me. You can't do this. This is not you.

Another voice in her head began to speak. This one was angry, bitter and almost seething to do something. It's the people that took you away from me that I would be killing. It would be those pieces of garbage I would be taking out of this world. They would never hurt anyone else again.

Chris's voice, but then you become no better than they are.

The new voice, So what? What if they decide I'm not worthy to see you again?

Jamie heard her voice in her head, and it sounded sane and logical. You need to think this through. You can't make any rash decisions.

Jamie slammed her fist down on the table hard enough to cause her excruciating pain as two of the bones in her hand snapped. The pain was enough to silence all the voices.

"Are you ok, Darlin'?" he asked politely.

"Nothing. I'm fine." She could feel the bones knitting themselves back together. "I'm perfectly fine."

"So do we have a deal?" Godfrey asked while holding the quill.

And that is the moment we are at now. So, let me ask you this. What would you do if given the chance for immortality? What would you do to make all your dreams come true? Would you sign your name and damn your soul? Or would you walk away clear of conscience?

What would you do?

2

BEYOND THE PINE CURTAIN

NEDAN RAMBO

JOEL BLOOM WAS A dead man, he just hadn't realized it yet. Bobby and I sat in Miguel's office, a small room in the back of a strip club that stank of cigars, sweat, and desperation. From this dimly lit room, the boss would issue his marching orders with a somber restraint that elicited trust from his men.

A fair man when offered respect and a deadly one when a boundary was crossed. That was the one rule in Arlington, and Joel's momentary lapse in judgment would cost him.

"We're on it," Bobby said with a laugh. "Chris and I will have it done before lunch." He elbowed me with a smile, but I didn't smile back.

Violence came easily to Bobby. Too easy for someone so young, but maybe that's the cost of growing up on these streets.

"Hang on a second," I said, still mulling over the sudden request. "We've known Joel forever. Whenever we need him, he's a solid earner."

"*Was* a solid earner." Bobby leaned back in his chair with a smug dismissiveness born of inexperience.

"We all appreciate your enthusiasm, Bobby, but I've known Joel since you were in diapers. In my day, that meant something." I turned to Miguel. "With all due respect, boss, if I'm killing an old friend, I think we should know why."

"The *why*'s not our department. When Miguel gives us a *what* and a *when*, our only business is the *how*." Bobby glanced at the boss like a puppy, eager for recognition. But Miguel only puffed his cigar in response.

"A bit of unsolicited advice, kid. One day, running into a situation without knowing the whole story is gonna get you killed." I said, earning an eye roll from the young man.

Miguel, a man who commanded a room even in silence, offered no support to either side. Instead, he pulled an expensive watch from his drawer and slid it across the table. I recognized it immediately, the result of a mugging gone deadly. Joel always had a violent temper and picked the wrong old man to rob a month ago. The old guy got indignant and refused to give up his watch on principal. Joel gave the rich prick two rounds to the face for his troubles and went underground.

"Last week, Joel sold this to us for three grand. Two days later, I hear he used a watch to buy his way into one of our poker games, getting another thousand from us." Miguel pulled out an identical watch and slid it across the table.

"Are they fakes?" I asked, inspecting the watches. If they were fake, it was the best I'd ever seen. The weight, polish, and sound told me it was authentic.

"Well, there's the question," Miguel said, pulling out a third identical watch. "I find out he sold another watch like this to a jeweler we own, getting four thousand for it this time."

"Wait, shouldn't the jeweler be able to spot a fake?" Bobby asked.

"Yeah, they put these watches through every test they had. The jeweler tells me every watch is genuine—all three of them. And the jeweler says they all have the same serial number. Even the scratches on the gears inside are the same. They're complete duplicates."

"So, how did he turn one watch into three? It's impossible to make fakes this good, especially that fast." I asked.

"That's what I want you to find out. And once you know how he's making these fakes, you either get me back our $8K or bring me his head."

"We can get you both," Bobby said with a wicked grin.

Miguel shrugged, leaned back in his chair, and turned away, signaling that this meeting was over.

Joel wasn't difficult to find. He only had a few haunts where he burned through his money on liquor and girls. We watched from a distance as he threw around more cash than a small-timer like him should have. Hard worker or not, everyone knew Joel wasn't a riser. His ambition only extended to his next drink. He was born with nothing and would likely die with the same.

Eventually, he left the city, driving down an unlisted dirt road toward the country. We followed him past the farmland and off into the rocky hills nearby—useless land unfit for farming or living. We observed from a distance, watching through binoculars as Joel continued into an endless expanse of nothing. Eventually, he parked where the path petered into sharp stones and uneven terrain. From there, he continued into the wilds on foot.

Bobby and I did our best to stay hidden, watching as he marched through the stony fields broken up by patches of tall, browned grass. The hike ended when he reached something I'd never seen before. Joel arrived at a timber wall of thick trees so tightly packed together that they looked like a fence. He found a gap in this fortress and squeezed between two massive trunks.

Once he disappeared from view, we hurried forward to catch up to him. As we approached this barrier of pine trees, I felt a subtle tug of discomfort. There was something unnatural about this wall of trees that spanned as far as I could see. Some prehistoric instinct warned me to stay away, to wait for Joel to come back out.

Before I could voice my concerns, Bobby, gun in hand, squeezed through the slight gap in this pine curtain. After a significant amount of swearing, I reluctantly followed him into the dark passage.

On the other side, there were no more of the massive pine trees that acted as a barrier or patches of tall grass clinging to life. Instead, endless rows of white birch trees stuck out of the stony dirt. But these trees were thick, and their trunks were twisted like they grew under some heavy wind that left them permanently crooked.

The air had a pervasive weight that made breathing difficult. Before we entered, the sun was melting into the red-orange horizon. Now, the sky seemed an odd yellow, and strange hues danced through the air like we were in some enormous crystal box, fracturing light like a prism. This area was also unnervingly silent aside from the breeze through the pines. No crickets chirped, no rodents scampered, no birds sang. Bobby and I seemed to be the only things moving through this remarkable forest. My unease with this setting grew tenfold.

"Where the hell are we?" I whispered. "Why does the sky look like that?"

But Bobby didn't share my concern. He folded his arms and spat. "I told you the '*why*' isn't our depart—"

CRASH

The sound of shattering glass rang through the rows of white trees that surrounded us. A few yards ahead, a glass bottle of coke lay cracked open, spraying fizzy brown water into the soil. It lay on a pile of other broken bottles.

Bobby swiveled, gun in hand, looking for anyone bold or foolish enough to throw something at them. But I tapped his shoulder and pointed upward where dozens, maybe hundreds, of glass bottles of coke hung from a tree.

"It's a bottle tree," I whispered. "But this tree looks like it's a couple hundred feet tall. How did he get them up so high?"

"A ladder," Bobby snapped. "We're wasting time. Come on."

He continued searching the secret garden, but I stopped to look closer at the tree. It's not uncommon to see empty bottles hanging from trees in Arlington, but they were never filled, and I'd never seen this many bottles in a single tree.

Something told me not to get any closer, but I plucked a bottle from a branch and found no string, twine, or glue holding it there. It seemed like the leaves themselves were gripping the bottle. Even stranger, the Coke was ice cold, condensation droplets running down its side in the warm evening air.

I wasn't sure if I was bothered more by the how or the why of this tree, but Bobby's insistence they press forward kept me from wondering long. He'd barged ahead, determined to find Joel first. He was so far away I couldn't see him anymore.

Just as I was about to call out to him, something caught my eye in another tree. Some strange fruit hung high and out of reach, the lower branches already picked clean. The smell was familiar but out of place in these woods.

My curiosity getting the better of me, I found a long stick and swatted at one of the round objects until it fell, nearly landing on my head. I caught it and realized immediately that the familiar but out-of-place scent was tomato sauce, cheese, and garlic. The object I knocked from the tree was a pizza. Once freed from the branch, it unrolled itself, a puff of steam rising from its melting cheese. This tree held hundreds of pizza balls, dripping oil into the dirt.

I rubbed the pie, shocked at its temperature. The pizza was as fresh as if it had just come out of the oven when it fell from the branch. While I wouldn't dare put a tree pizza in my mouth, I recognized the smell. Mario's on 7th Street sold this exact pizza. Joel and I had been eating there since we were kids. The scent was unmistakable.

The echo of a single gunshot brought me to attention. Crouching low, I followed the sound and found Bobby standing triumphantly over Joel, who cowered in a waist-deep hole holding a shovel. As Bobby sneered, Joel drunkenly kept his eyes on the gun. He raised his hands more in defense than surrender. If Bobby was foolish enough to get within arm's reach, Joel would surely lunge at him.

"The next one won't be another warning shot," Bobby threatened. "Don't lie to me again." He leaned against a tree while keeping the gun trained on Joel.

"I'm not lyin'. I'm tellin' you, I didn't make them watches. This place did," Joel said.

Bobby raised the gun again, but I placed my hand on his, lowering the gun. "What do you mean this place did it?"

"Chris, you gotta believe me. I don't know how this place works. After I shot that old man, I needed to lie low for a while. I thought I'd camp in the woods for a few weeks. And that's when I found this place. It's strange, right? The animals don't cross that tree line, not even the insects."

I wanted to hear more, but Bobby grew impatient. "We don't have time for this. Who's making these fake watches? If you have an operation in town, you need to be paying your dues."

"I know it sounds crazy, but... these woods do it. Anything you plant grows here. Anything."

"What do you mean, anything?" I asked.

"When I first got here, I hid the revolver with four bullets left in it. And I was nervous about dogs, so I buried my pizza crust and half-empty soda, too. Then I went to bed, and the next day, there was a tree where I buried the piece, just like these." Joel pointed at the crooked trees that surrounded them.

I pulled my coat a little tighter as I surveyed the odd trees that loomed over us. A silent arboreal panel, judging the men that played in the dirt.

Joel sat at the edge of the hole as he continued. "On that tree, I found hundreds of guns just like mine. Each one had exactly four bullets left. I even fired one, and it worked. The crust grew into a tree filled with whole pizzas, and the half-empty bottle of Coke grew new ones, ice cold."

Sensing the young man's impatience, Joel spoke faster. "So, I started burying other things, and a tree would grow every time. It only takes one night. Time works differently here, I guess. Eventually, I wanted to try something worth some money, so I put that expensive watch in the ground, and hundreds of them grew."

I stood in silence, contemplating the dissonance between the impossibility of Joel's words and the proof lying before me.

Bobby, however, was less receptive. A cruel chuckle preceded his response. "You expect us to believe that? Do we look stupid to you, Joel? If you don't want to slowly bleed out in these woods, tell us who's making these watches."

Joel shook his head. "Look, kid, believe what ya want, but I've got nothin' more to tell ya. It's like I said, I plant 'em, and hundreds grow. Try it yourself if ya don't believe me."

"Sure. Next, you're going to tell me that money grows on these trees." Bobby said with a laugh devoid of joy.

"Well, now that ya mention it..." Joel lifted a sack from the hole he was digging, cash spilling from the top.

"Is that all the money you got from our games and the pawn-shop?" I asked.

Joel nodded, "What's left of it? I spent more than I should on the girls."

"Well," Bobby said, raising the gun again. "That was a mistake."

"Wait! Don't—" I shouted, only to be cut off by the deafening scream of the gunshot and the blinding light of the muzzle flare as Bobby put a bullet directly into Joel's chest.

Joel stumbled backward into the dirt, staring upward in a murderous rage. He tried to mouth something foul, but his lungs deflated, his limbs went limp, and the light gently faded from his eyes. As he died, he took one final enraged glance at the both of us.

Bobby jumped into the hole and took the money bag, leaving Joel's body behind. He wiped his fingerprints off the gun and tossed it in with the corpse. "Come on, let's get this guy covered and get back to town."

"Why did you do that? I had more questions."

"What, are you buying this magic tree nonsense? I know you two old-timers go way back, but I never took you for the superstitious type. Besides, Miguel said, bring back all the money or his head. He didn't have the money, so..." Bobby shrugged his shoulders without weight or burden. To him, this was neither tragedy nor triumph, just another job.

With some reluctance, I joined him in the regretful act of burying an old friend. Joel wasn't a good man. He was a violently temperamental drunken gambler who would steal anything that wasn't nailed down. But we'd shared drinks, laughs, and a lot of good times over the years. While an end like this seemed fated for Joel the day he was born, I took no joy in witnessing it.

We covered what was Joel Bloom in a mound of soft soil, and then a strange thump made us both jump. I raised the shovel, and Bobby pulled a knife. Approaching the source of the noise, I stepped on something shiny and metallic. Another watch sat polished and ticking in the grass. Above, hundreds more hung from every branch of a tree.

"Joel was right; things are growing on trees here," I said, but Bobby simply groaned.

"Oh, give me a break. So, he threw some watches into the trees to hide them. We don't have time for this."

"That doesn't even make sense. Why hide something forty feet in the air? Hey, will you just stop for a second and look?"

With the money in hand, Bobby had already begun marching toward the car, refusing even a glance backward. "Don't need to look. Come on, let's get back and get paid before I have to tell Miguel you wanted to go on a nature walk instead of finishing the job. If we head back now, we can still catch the end of the game."

While I hesitated momentarily, I followed Bobby out of these woods, wondering what we'd stumbled upon and what price we'd pay for meddling in things we didn't understand. On that bumpy road, beginning our long drive home, I watched Bobby bouncing in his seat, singing along with the radio, eager to tell Miguel what he'd done. Bobby was obsessed with today, unconcerned with how it would ripple into tomorrow.

We left that valley with little knowledge of its workings. Perhaps its secrets were unknowable to man, and trying to forget about it was for the best. I suspected we'd know soon enough if this ugly day would stay buried in the past. Just as we left, I noticed a small sapling sprouting from that mound of dirt where we buried my old friend.

3

You Seen Our Girl

S.E. Reed

Even in late fall Cicadas cry and the air is swampy in the Florida Everglades. Sure, a few trees turn ruddy and amber up along Alligator Alley letting you know the season is changing. But for the most part, things don't change much for us. Been livin' in the same house since I was born seventeen years ago. Same house Mama grew up in. And her Mama before her.

All the same folks live in Jerome, off Highway 29.

That was until Old Bucky died.

And the *Devil Himself* moved in next door.

"I told ya, one of them snoots from the Atlantic side would be drivin' in their fancy, black SUV out here to buy Old Bucky's land when it went up for auction," Aunt Sis complains when a mysterious vehicle parks in the long, circular driveway at the end of the property next door.

"I tell you–the first time one of them nosey asses come tellin' me to quiet my kids or clean my yard I'm gonna have a real problem," Mama adds, waving her finger.

"Damn straight!" Aunt Sis replies and slams down her glass of sweet tea for effect.

I let out a laugh. Aunt Sis loves being dramatic. Probably one of her best qualities. Me and Kenzy sit on the porch playing with her kitten Grace and eating potato chips from the gas station.

"Why'd some snoot want to come live out here in the swamp anyhow?" I ask. "Don't they know this is panther territory?"

"Y'all don't know nothin, so don't get your feathers ruffled." Uncle Silas comes around the corner wiping motor oil off his hands with a blue rag.

"You for real, Silas? Look at you! You think some city folk gonna take kindly to your half-naked, skinny ass wandering around town hung over? Or pushing that fucking shopping cart down the highway with junk in it?" Mama chastises her younger brother.

She does have a point. Uncle Silas rarely puts on a shirt—and he does push a shopping cart around picking up stuff he finds people dumped by the burned-out sawmill.

"Don't be such a bitch all the time, Dee. I ain't had a hangover in weeks!" Uncle Silas sasses back as he snatches up a glass of sweet tea from the tray and drains it.

He lights up a cigarette and I watch as he squeezes the butt of it flat when he puts it to his sun-cracked lips to take a drag.

Kenzy tugs on my leg.

"What is it, little buggy?" I ask and lean in to tickle my younger sister.

She's only six and about the cutest thing these swamps have ever seen. I love her more than Mama, Aunt Sis, and Uncle Silas combined.

"Why'd Unky call Mama a bad word?" she asks sweetly and nuzzles her face into the gray kitten.

"Cause they all freakin out bout that black SUV parked down at Old Bucky's place. See, Mama's worried it's an uptight out-of-towner who's gonna judge her. And Uncle Silas thinks Mama's being foolish," I explain.

"You watch your mouth, Rae." Mama thumps me on the back of my head with the fly swatter as she walks by to go into the house.

"OUCH!" I shout dramatically. "I'm calling child welfare on you!" I holler.

Me and Kenzy and Aunt Sis all burst out laughing. It's not funny, not really. But 'round here, it is—cause it's the kind of thing people outside the swamp think—that we are all a bunch of backward hillbillies with Mamas who beat us and case workers threatening to haul us off.

But it ain't like that.

We ain't got no case worker. And Mama's never raised a hand to me or Kenzy. Neither did Daddy before he died. He was a lot older than Mama and had a heart attack a few years ago. That's when Aunt Sis moved in to help Mama with us kids. I got two brothers, besides Kenzy. They out someplace now, playing in the woods or the swamps. Getting dirty and playing with baby gators. And yeah, they've taken a spankin' a few times, but— they're wild!

"Hey look!" Kenzy points down the road at Old Bucky's place.

The black SUV backs out of the driveway and heads our direction. The main road is paved, but our driveway is long and gravel laid. The SUV slows way down, like it's thinking of coming this direction–the windows blacked out with tint. Unexpectedly, the window rolls down just enough, and arm sticks out and motions toward us.

I get up to go see what they want.

"Don't fucking move, girl," Uncle Silas says and puts his own arm out like when he slams on the breaks in his truck, like he's trying to protect me from flying out of my seat and going through the windshield.

"But they want someone to come say somethin," I whine.

"We ain't at their beck and call, fucking assholes," Uncle Silas snaps. The arm waves again, trying to lure me forward. I take one more step. Uncle Silas scares the piss out of me when he screams, "KEEP FUCKING DRIVING!"

Unphased by my uncle's outburst, the driver casually pulls his arm in and rolls up the window and drives away slowly.

"Well then Silas, you proud of yourself? Scaring off them folk? Prolly our new neighbors! What a way to introduce our- selves," Aunt Sis says and scoops my sister and her kitten to take them inside, barging right past Mama who's returned with a basket to pull the laundry off the line.

"I thought that's what you wanted!" Uncle Silas shouts after Aunt Sis.

"What the hell's goin on out here?" Mama asks.

"Nothin, just the prick in that SUV. They're gone now. But I'll stick around for a while longer," Uncle Silas says and gives Mama a look I don't recognize.

I shrug.

"Rae, go find your brothers and bring them home. Dinner's almost done anyhow– and everyone needs a bath. You've got that science report due tomorrow you better work on, and them boys got that online math stuff."

Mama isn't really asking me.

She's telling me.

———————

The next few weeks in the swamp amounts to a whole lot of nothing. Same as it ever was in Jerome. Still hot. Still humid and sticky even though it's almost Halloween.

No one else comes to see Old Bucky's place.

Then one night, just when my dream was getting good—

"Rae, wake up," Kenzy says softly. She puts her little hands on my cheeks and smooshes my face around.

"Go back to sleep." I roll over, ignoring her.

"But Raaaaeeee... Gracie is outside– I can hear her cryin. I don't want a panther to get her. You bring her inside for me?" Kenzy begs.

I sit up and rub my eyes. The light from the kitchen drifts into our shared room and illuminates my precious, perfect little sister. I see big crocodile tears streaming down her chubby cheeks and how can I deny her?

"Stay here. I'll go find the kitten."

I crawl out of bed and pull my hoodie over my nightgown to protect my arms and neck from mosquito bites. Kenzy crawls into my bed and pulls the covers up to wait for me. I tip-toe, knowing which floorboards creek, and go through the side door by the bathroom—the one that don't wake up Mama. This ain't my first time sneaking around.

"Pssss. Pssst, kitty," I hiss and whisper for the little furball.

I see that black SUV down at Old Bucky's place parked in the driveway. At least, it looks like the same one. It's so dark, it's hard tellin'. I wonder what the hell it's doin' out here this time of night.

A light turns on inside the house.

My heart pumps harder.

Maybe they really did buy the place at auction?

Mama never said nothin' about seein' anyone moving in while I was at school today. And why would they move into the house anyway? The SUV is worth more than Old Bucky's run-down house. It's the land, three hundred acres, that's the reason to buy the place– good for swamp logging old Cypress and growing sugar cane.

The light in the house blinks a few times.

I shiver.

"Meow." A little soft thing rubs on me, and I jump a foot in the air, I swear!

"Dang you, dummy," I scold Grace and lean down to pick her up.

I walk back around to the side door of the house when I hear something– voices, drifting through the thick night air, competing with the Cicadas. I strain to hear.

"No. Please, no... " a woman.

"Shut up," a man's voice.

The kitten squirms in my arms, anxious to get inside and curl up with Kenzy. I want to stay and see if I hear anything else, but I don't either—cause I'm sure I'm hearing some kind of marital woes from our new neighbors. Mama's gonna be so pissed off when she finds out some creepy wife beater has moved in next door!

I go back into the house, making sure I lock the chain before I walk right to the front door and lock it up too — ain't never had to lock our doors at night. Not out here where everyone in Jerome is a relative or friend.

But now—with new neighbors—seems kind of necessary.

"Mama, you know them folks moved in. Saw 'em last night with lights on in the house and everything. I bet they got a big old moving truck out there right now," I say at breakfast the next morning.

"Shut your mouth," Aunt Sis yells and jumps up from the table, knocking over her plate to run toward the door.

My brothers both tear out of their seats, always ready for some shit.

"Move," shouts Bud.

"Me first!" taunts Leo as he trips Bud who takes a nosedive onto the floor.

I shake my head at the chaos I caused and turn back to Mama who shoots me the evil eye.

"What?" I laugh.

DING DONG.

The doorbell rings just as Aunt Sis puts her hand on the knob to go outside and snoop.

She screams and backs up. "Oh Lordy, someone's at the door!"

She rushes back into the kitchen and my brothers are pushing and shoving to get at it first.

"I'm scared," Kenzy says and hides under the table.

Ain't no one 'round here ring the doorbell except after Daddy died, and the insurance man came for Mama to sign papers.

"STOP," Mama smacks the boys and shoos them back to finish breakfast.

We all hover like flies on honey when Mama opens the door. A nice-looking man in a fancy black suit with sharp features stands there waiting. He towers over Mama who's only five foot tall.

"Can I help you?" Mama asks.

We all snicker cause Mama's using her angry voice, the one when she tells people where to shove things– you know, where the sun don't shine.

"Morning, Ma'am," he nods. He looks into the house and makes eye contact with me. I cringe. "May I?" He takes a step forward, like he was invited to come inside our house.

My cheeks burn.

"I'm not interested in your church," Mama says and tries to shut the door.

"Oh, no. I'm not from the church. I'm your new neighbor. I purchased the Bucky Jameson property as—an investment. I won't be here much. I—"

"Fine. Thank you."

Mama cuts him off and closes the door. But the man is quick. He puts his foot in just before it latches, and he gives the heavy wood a quick shove forward.

Mama yelps.

We all freeze.

The man gets real close and says kind of quiet-like to Mama, "I put up cameras to keep an eye on the place when I'm not here. So, keep all your fucking welfare kids off my land." He leans back and adjusts his suit. "Thanks for the southern hospitality!" His tone, about as condescending as any prick I ever heard.

"Well, I'll be damned!" Mama slams the door as soon as the man turns to walk off the porch.

"Holy shit, Dee. What the fuck is that all about? Cameras? Keeping the kids off his land? What an asshole!" Aunt Sis says to Mama, and she ain't just being dramatic–this is serious.

"Call Silas. You four, get ready for school. Bus in fifteen minutes!" Mama is visibly shaking.

I want to give her a hug. But that's the last thing she wants right now. So instead, I help by scooting Kenzy, Bud, and Leo along to finish brushing their teeth and putting on their shoes.

All day at school I worry about the sharp-faced man.

I make myself sick and throw up during gym class.

"Is everything okay Rae?" Ms. Jenkins asks and hands me a plastic cup of water.

We are outside running laps which is always a total sweat-fest and at least one person pukes. It's never been me before...

"Yeah, I guess. Some man bought Old Bucky's place and came over to introduce himself this morning and was a real asshole to Mama. I'm just worried is all," I tell her.

No point in keeping it a secret. Everyone from Jerome to Everglades City, where we go to school, probably already knows about it. Mama runs the dispatch for Frank's Tow'N'Fix and stops at the gas station on her way to work for a Mountain Dew every morning to hear and spill the latest gossip.

Word spreads fast in the Everglades.

"Yeah, I heard some rich fella from one of them gated places in Palm Beach bought the land. Something about an investment. But it's hard work pulling up cypress logs from the swamp–seems kind of strange for an outsider to invest in that," Ms. Jenkins says. "Too bad too, you know my brother Pete and his wife Lisa were hoping to buy the place. Pete's getting out of the Marines soon and they've got four boys and another on the way."

"Awe, that sucks!" I reply.

"Here, drink one more cup. And remember, your Mama's a tough cookie–you don't need to worry about her. And I bet your new neighbor is going to figure out real fast it's hard work making money in the swamp. If it was that easy to turn these lands into an investment, well we'd all be rich!" Ms. Jenkins winks then fills up my cup as the bell rings for lunch.

I chug the water and race off toward the building.

I sure hope she's right.

The black SUV is gone when we get off the bus. Kenzy, Bud, and Leo all run for home. Aunt Sis is sitting on the porch waiting for us. Mama's car is gone– still at work or picking up groceries. Uncle Silas's truck is around the side of the house, and I can hear music coming from Daddy's garage where Uncle Silas spends most of his time now.

I don't know why, but I turn and walk towards Old Bucky's former house. I want to see the cameras. I want to flip off our new neighbor. I don't want him to think he can scare me or my Mama. Aunt Sis waits for a minute on the porch, but then goes inside with my siblings to make them a snack or get them started on homework, 'cause I make it look like I'm getting the mail from the box that sits a few hundred feet down from our driveway.

But I'm not getting the mail.

I'm looking.

There! Something shiny catches my eye from his porch.

A camera pointed this way– right at our mailbox! Why'd he want to watch us getting our mail? I see another shiny glint in the sun on the pitch of the roof. It's a camera, pointing at our house! What does it mean?

I count five cameras, all pointing in various directions at our house. Not the way you'd set up cameras to watch for people sneaking onto your property. The hair on the back of my neck stands and I feel nauseous again.

"Don't throw up," I whisper to myself.

I run with all my might down the road and turn up our driveway.

"Whoa, slow down girl." Uncle Silas comes around the corner and I nearly smack right into him. "Whatchu running from?" He looks left, then right, making sure I'm not actually being chased.

"The neighbor, did Mama tell you?" I'm panting, sweat coming down my face.

"Yeah, Rae, she told me. I hope that prick comes back again soon. I'll be ready."

Uncle Silas spits.

"Gross!" I step to one side. "But did you actually go look? There's cameras! Pointing all at our place! Why'd he go and do a thing like that?"

"You sure them cameras are pointed over here? I've set up trail cams out hunting deer–they span a wide area, so you gotta point them just right," Uncle Silas says.

I can't tell if he's angry or defending the creepy new neighbor.

"It looked like they were pointed this way. And they ain't like those stupid, square trail cams you hook on a tree. These were real cameras, expensive kind, mounted and pointed at the mailbox and our house and there's five of 'em!" The more I think about it, the more I'm angry. "I'll show you!" I start walking.

Uncle Silas walks with me to the mailbox so I can point out the cameras.

But when we stand at the mailbox, they aren't pointed at us anymore. They've moved.

"They must be the kind he can turn remotely. I swear to God, Uncle Silas. That one there, it was pointed right at me! And the one over there was aimed right at me and Kenzy's bedroom window!" But they are all pointed in opposite directions now, toward the front door, the shed, and the garage of Old Bucky's place.

Like you'd expect a security system to be.

"I believe you, Rae. I don't trust no prick in some fancy suit who comes over uninvited to scare a woman and her children in the early morning hours. I'll be watching him, don't you worry your pretty little head," Uncle Silas says.

The anger is radiating off Uncle Silas's bare chest. Just then, Mama pulls into the driveway, and I run over to help her unload the groceries I see sticking up in the back seat.

———————

Over dinner Uncle Silas tells Mama he thinks he should move in to protect us all from the new neighbor. But the house is already full, and Mama says no—unless he's parking an RV outside.

Come Saturday, Uncle Silas pulls up in a 1968 Winnebago he found at a scrap yard north of Immokalee and bought for $150. None of us are surprised. He's been sleeping on an abandoned pontoon boat behind the burned-up sawmill anyhow and already spends most of his time at our place.

"Park that behemoth on the side of the house—that way you can use the side door to come inside to use the bathroom. I don't want you pissing in the yard and ruining my grass. Leo and Bud, go find your uncle an extension cord to plug in his new place. Rae, go up to the attic and get the extra swamp cooler and some bed sheets. Kenzy, find your uncle a pillow," Mama barks orders at everyone, just like most days.

No one argues. We are happy Uncle Silas is going to be here.

———————

Tonight, there are new sounds.

The humming of Uncle Silas's new home–right outside me and Kenzy's window. He's got a TV plugged in and it's on loud. Mama ain't never let us kids have a TV in our rooms, said that's spoiled. I can hear Uncle Silas laughing through the crack in our bedroom window. It's finally cooler at night and there's a good cross breeze from the kitchen window through our room.

Kenzy snores in her bed across from mine. It's the cutest little sound in the entire universe. And I guess, I feel safe knowing all the folks I love the most are right here with me. I let my eyes sink closed and I drift into sleep.

Maybe it's Uncle Silas's TV that wakes me.

Maybe someone flushed a toilet.

I dunno.

But I sit up—it's two a.m.—and I feel it in my gut. Something is wrong.

I jump out of my bed and go for Kenzy. She's not in her bed. My heart thumps heavy and fast.

"Kenzy?" I say, thinking maybe she went to the bathroom and is just wandering outside the bedroom.

But there's no reply.

I run into the kitchen. I flip on the light and look around–no Kenzy. I check the living room. No Kenzy. I run to Mama's room, maybe she crawled in with her.

"Mama, is Kenzy in here with you?" I ask.

"No, she aint," Mama answers sleepily.

I run to Aunt Sis and the boys– *No Kenzy.*

"Kenzy! Little buggy" I shout. And now everyone is awake, and every light on. Mama runs out the side door and we hear her banging on Uncle Silas's trailer door. They both come back into the house.

"She ain't with me," his voice cracks.

"Oh my god." Aunt Sis plunks on the couch and starts to cry.

"Where's her kitten? Where's Grace?" I ask Leo and Bud.

They are silent and shake their heads.

Mama's already dressed and has a flashlight. "Well, what are you all fucking waiting for? Put on your clothes and get outside to look for Kenzy!"

Before any of us say a word, Mama's got the front door flung wide open, "KENZY! MACKENZIE MARIE!"

She's screaming as loud as she can. Her voice carries through the dark in the calm swamp air, no thunderstorm to muffle her calls. She's like one of the mother panthers who roams, crying into the night for its young to follow, to scare away the gators.

Panthers.

Gators.

Fucked up neighbors.

There is a world of terror outside our house at night...

Aunt Sis calls the Collier County Sheriff while Uncle Silas goes to check Daddy's garage.

"She ain't in the garage!" he yells.

We aren't gonna sit and wait for the Sheriff to show up before we search. Everyone is outside and we form a line with me and Uncle Silas on the ends, then Aunt Sis and Mama, and the boys in the middle. We each have a flashlight and do a sweep, up and down the yard and down the driveway out to the road.

No one even has to say it, we all automatically turn toward the neighbor's house. There's a light on in the kitchen window, but the black SUV isn't in the drive. My teeth start chattering, but it ain't cold out. Far from it.

I remember the night I came out lookin' for Kenzy's kitten.

The woman who cried for help.

I wonder if she's in the house now. Does she have Kenzy?

"KENZY!" We all take turns screaming as we sweep our lights right and left, back and forth, looking for signs of her. Like her little blue wubby blanket she still carries around at night. Or one of her stuffies, like the baby Zebra we got from the Miami Zoo. I should have looked to see if anything was missing from her room.

"Silas, get your ass up to that house and bang on the door," Mama shouts.

Uncle Silas don't gotta be told twice. He leaves his spot from our search party line and runs up to Old Bucky's place and bangs on the door.

"HEYO, WAKE UP!! YOU SEEN OUR GIRL? YOU SEEN OUR KENZY?" He screams and pounds loud enough to wake all of Jerome.

But no one answers.

We never see the man who bought Old Bucky's again.

No black SUV in the driveway.

No one comes to retrieve the cameras.

A few months later, the house goes up for auction and Ms. Jenkin's brother Pete and his wife Lisa buy it. The Sheriff says they ain't got cause to believe the neighbor had anything to do with Kenzy's disappearance. Say she must have gone out looking for her kitten Grace and got lost in the Everglades.

Could have been a panther.

Maybe a gator.

Even years later, I walk in the brush, tryin to calm my soul... I can't escape what happened that night. Don't matter if I close my eyes and wish it all away. Kenzy was an angel, our angel.

Sometimes I see a gray cat down at the old burned-up sawmill crying for attention.

Sometimes I see the sharp face of the devil.

4

You Belong Here

Amy Nielsen

A NOTIFICATION PINGED MICHELLE's cell. She stopped typing the dissertation for her Board-Certified Behavior Analyst program. It didn't matter if the notification was for a low-effort puzzle app or a text from her recent Made-It-Face-Book-Official boyfriend; she responded to each with equal urgency.

She tapped in her passcode and swiped on the notification—a request to join a group chat titled *You Belong Here*. "Weird."

Without another thought, she continued writing what she'd uncovered in her research on selective and restricted eating in children with autism. Her neck and back ached. A buzz on her phone offered the break she needed.

She stood, pressed her hand into her lower lumbar and stretched. She answered the number she'd already memorized. "Hello." She bit her lip in anticipation of his deep, sexy voice.

"Hey. Just called to say I'm missing you."

Her cheeks flushed. "Same. I wish this thing weren't due so soon."

"Come over and do it here, then we can do *it* after," he teased.

Her pulse quickened, remembering the last time they did *it*. "I wish I could. I really do. I just need to be here to focus. Only a few more days, maybe hours."

"You belong here," he said.

"Wait, what did you say?" Something about that phrase sounded familiar.

"I'll leave you alone—Scout's Honor—mostly."

"Jason, I can't. Maybe we can meet for a quick lunch over the weekend—and maybe throw in a *quickie* for good measure." God, she wanted him before then.

He chuckled. "The weekend it is. Don't work too hard."

She ended the call. The phone displayed 8:15 pm. Her stomach roared and she couldn't ignore the hunger any longer. She opened the fridge. "Leftover pizza it is."

While the microwave whirred, she scrolled through her phone. The notification from earlier was still there. She opened it again. *You Belong Here.*

"Weird, but fine. Let's see why I belong here?" She clicked on the notification which dropped her into a lively chat room. A prompt instructed her to choose a username. She typed in Mayflower.

A bunch of college-aged young professional women were introducing themselves—law school student RayRay, home stager Liv4, public defender LilNikX, trauma nurse Ali. From what she scanned of the conversation they were from different parts of southwest Florida, just like her.

"Am I really doing this?" she said aloud as she typed her introduction.

Mayflower: *Hi! I'm a student at the University of...*

She hesitated. She shouldn't tell strangers where she went to school.

Mayflower: *I'm a university student in the Tampa Bay area. Does anyone know how we ended up here LOL?*

Rapid fire welcomes followed.

RayRay: *Hi Mayflower! Just over the bridge in St. Pete.*

LilNikX: *Not sure. Probably an AI bot threw us together due to our proximity or something. Who knows these days?*

Mayflower: *Hey LilNikX, my dad was also a public defender. I read in the thread you are. Great work you're doing! Ali, I couldn't imagine the challenges of being a trauma nurse.*

Ali: *Working at the hospital sux! Trying to get into the Navy. We'll see!*

Liv4: *Welcome to the We Have No Idea Why We are Here Club!*

Before Michelle realized it, she'd been chatting with these women for more than an hour. She said goodbye and promised she'd check back in tomorrow.

She opened her Word doc. The phone rang. Jason. She'd wasted so much time chatting with strangers that she didn't have time to answer his call.

The sun tore into her small apartment, highlighting the stacks of papers, books, laundry, and pizza boxes littering the space. She didn't have a minute to deal with that. She peeled herself off the couch, showered and dressed in record time. Her classes were over, but this dissertation was the last piece of the puzzle to her getting that Master's.

She powered her computer and while it booted up, she checked her phone. There were seventeen alerts from the *You Belong Here* group chat. She clicked on it.

RayRay, LilNikX, and Liv4 were in mid-conversation about Ali. Apparently, Ali had gone on her lunch break during her shift and mentioned someone left a basket of plump strawberries tied with a huge bow and a caricature of her image. She figured it was from her ex.

Mayflower: *That's so sweet! Been hard-core working on my master's dissertation and foraging on old pizza. I'd kill for some fresh fruit. I mean not literally.*

The chatter that ensued agreed. Liv4 shared that her ex and her split in weird terms. She caught him messaging other girls. She was still hurt.

RayRay: *Girl, kick that dickhead to the curb. Don't give him another moment's thought. When I caught my guy messaging other women, it was OVER. Ain't nobody got time for that!*

Michelle left a thumbs-up emoji. She had to get back to her dissertation.

Before she'd typed one word on the section about her field research with her client BaNi about his eating restrictions, Jason's' number flashed across her phone. She could carve out at least five minutes for his call.

"What's up sexy?" he said.

Fuck me, she thought to herself, wishing she was fucking him. "I'm knee-deep in this dissertation. I promise if I can focus it'll be done by Friday."

"It seems so far away. I was hoping I could give you a full body massage while feeding you chocolate-covered strawberries."

She'd been craving savory berries since the convo with the girls. "Jason, please just a couple of a more days. That's all I need. Then I'm all yours." She meant and longed for every word.

An exhale filled her ear.

"Of course. I get it. You can be last."

"Excuse me?"

"Sorry. I totally respect you've got things going on."

"I gotta go." She hung up and went back to the group. Something felt off. She couldn't put her finger on it. She opened up the *You Belong Here* chat to ease her mind.

RayRay: *WTF! Ali's still MIA! Earlier Liv4 said something odd.*

LilNikX: *What do you mean, odd? Sorry, been in court all day.*

The group chat didn't ease her mind. Instead, the conversation sent it reeling.

RayRay: *Said she'd showed up at a house she was staging and there was a plate of fruit on the table including strawberries.*

Mayflower: *That's not odd. Maybe the realtor or the home-owner set it out for potential buyers.*

RayRay: *She asked everyone.*

LilNikX: *This is getting fucked up and I know fucked up. I'm a public defender.*

Mayflower: *Have you tried finding them on social media? I know we use nicknames. But we could try.*

LilNikX: *If any you bitches had half a brain you used nothing like your real name.*

RayRay: *Hey, who you calling a bitch?*

LilNikX: *Sorry. The language comes with the territory. Let me do some digging. Maybe check any missing persons. A nurse nicknamed Ali, and a home stager nicknamed Liv 4.*

Mayflower: *And probably nothing to do with it, but don't forget the possible strawberry connection. If that's even a thing.*

RayRay: *Down to 3. If you see any strawberries run for the hills!*

Mayflower: *Gotta go. You hear anything, please ping. I'll be checking notifications all night.*

Michelle had no idea why she was so invested in these strangers. Why did the mention of strawberries, a perfectly normal fruit, seemed odd. Probably stupid.

Before she picked back up on her research into the empirical evidence as to the correlation between autism spectrum disorder and selective eating in children, she called Jason.

"Hello, this is Jason. I'm probably too covered in paint to take your call. Please leave a voice mail and I'll get back as soon as possible."

"Hey, it's me. Can't wait til the weekend. Bye."

She tried to envision what his studio might look like. And old warehouse he'd converted—his canvases and paint everywhere. A date there sounded sexy.

Rather than get back to her dissertation, she took a bath. A full-on bubble bath. She put her teak tray across her small tub. Lit a candle. Poured a glass of Sauvignon Blanc and sank into the warm water. Her phone buzzed. She'd put it on the tray also just in case. She dried her right hand on the towel next to the tub.

"Hey Babe. Sorry. I was running an errand with a friend. What's up? You done yet?"

"No, I've got like eighteen hours of work to do. Best guess. Maybe Saturday instead of Friday. I'm tryin'." She took a huge gulp of the wine and wished he was staring at her from the other end of the tub.

A notification pinged on her phone from the *You Belong Here* group. Michelle wanted to know what was going on.

"Hey, can I call you tomorrow. I'll have a better idea after an all-nighter."

"Sure, no problem. Have a berry good night!"

Her mind was playing tricks on her for sure. He surely didn't say *have a berry good night.*

Before she got out of her happy place and back into the grind, she checked the *You Belong Here* notifications.

RayRay: *Mayflower, are you there. This is getting freaky!*

Mayflower: *I'm here. What's going on?*

RayRay: *LilNikX said that Plant City Strawberry Festival has been going on a few days. I forgot about it. Her friends wanted her to go. She was hesitant. She went. She messaged from a bathroom. She thought someone followed her. She hasn't messaged since.*

Mayflower: *So, let me get this straight. Since this group chat materialized. Someone left Nurse Ali strawberries and she went silent.*

Ray Ray: *Check*

Mayflower: *Liv4 found strawberries at a house she was staging, and she went silent.*

RayRay: *Check*

Mayflower: *LilNikX went to the strawberry festival and then went silent.*

RayRay: *Check*

Mayflower: *What the actual fuck! What's the connection between all of us and strawberries? This is ridiculous.*

RayRay: *Have you ever been to the Strawberry Festival?*

Mayflower: *Yes, multiple times.*

RayRay: *Do you remember anything odd. Anything?*

Mayflower: *I don't know. Maybe. This one girl wanted me to buy some expensive caricatures. She looked like some crackhead. I said, "Fuck no, I'm not buying you your next fix."*

RayRay: *Do you think she was able to get your contact info or anything?*

Mayflower: *What? No. Wait, I used my ID to get a drink after. Are those carnies in cahoots?*

RayRay: *Maybe.*

A buzz from her doorbell interrupted Michelle's irrational thoughts.

Mayflower: *WTF. I'm in the tub and someone just rang my doorbell.*

RayRay: *Put your robe on and go answer it.*

Michelle stepped out of the warm sudsy tub and wrapped herself in a white waffle-weave robe she'd stolen from a Westin on a trip with an old boyfriend.

The bell buzzed and buzzed. "Hold on, Asshole. I'm coming."

She opened the door. On the floor was a caricature portrait of her next to a plump basket of strawberries.

A card was nestled inside the basket of berries.

If you bitches had bought a caricature, this would have never happened. Welcome to the last Strawberry Festival you'll ever attend. Love RayRay

Michelle's knees buckled and the last thing she saw was a small-framed woman covered in paint coming at her with a knife. A man she recognized was behind her.

5

CAN YOU SEE IT TOO

NEDAN RAMBO

I'VE HAD NIGHTMARES FOR as long as I can remember, and I don't know if I'm dreaming right now. I lay in bed, telling myself to sleep, but something stirs in the house.

We squealed with joy when Pa first said he would build a spare room for Alice and me. But my brother's teasing was incessant.

"Don't put Mary Lou in her own room, she's still a bedwetter," they'd cruelly jeer.

How I hate their awful grins and finger-pointing.

Even my sister, Alice, would join the boys in mocking me. They ignored me when I told them I saw a goat-headed man with eyes like firelight dancing in our farm at night. They laughed when I mentioned the strange woman and her banshee-like screams in the woods.

Every time I see something in the dark, I scream, but when Pa comes with his lantern, the monsters are gone.

"It's just your imagination, Mary Lou. You need to grow up," Pa would say. Then he'd return to bed, annoyed, and my sibling's teasing would resume. Then I'd cry myself to sleep, ashamed of my foolishness.

Tonight is the first night Alice and I have our own room. This is my chance to prove that I'm no longer a child. But I'm awake while everyone else sleeps, and something stirs in the house.

Cough. Cough.

There it is again. Those hacking, aching sounds rouse painful memories I'd tried to bury. Pa never built that spare room because the consumption came for Nana this past summer. Her old bedroom sat empty for months before he finally fixed it up for Alice and me, though it only had one bed.

Nana was strong, beautiful, wise, and brave, yet that sickness, that evil, still ravaged her body leaving her crooked and deformed. Nana was kind once, but I barely remember those days. I only remember the hacking, groaning, bitter thing she became. Eventually, I couldn't recognize her, and later, I couldn't bear to look at her. Consumption took Nana almost a year to date after it took Ma.

Cough, cough.

The rasping, gagging, sickly wet coughs drift through the cabin. Each wheezing breath gets louder as it moves through the hall in our direction. Perhaps someone is just clearing their throat. But it doesn't sound like Pa's heavy footsteps toward the outhouse. And it also doesn't sound like the whispered tiptoeing of my brothers when they sneak a few swigs of Pa's applejack.

These footsteps are slow, hobbled, and dragging. Footsteps that keep creeping closer.

Desperately, I try to forget what my brothers told me. Trying to scare me, they said they saw Nana, crooked and slow, moving through the halls at night. They said that I'd better not look at her spirit, or I'd catch the consumption too.

The breaths, thick with illness, are right at the door, but I won't let my brothers scare me. They're fools and heathens, and I won't fall for their tricks. It's just my imagination, and I simply need to go to sleep. Pulling the covers over my head, I lie perfectly still, hoping that sleep takes me before my mind produces new manifestations from shadows.

CREAK

Rusted hinges moan as the door creeps open.

Cough. Hack.

The awful sound of someone coughing their life away echoes in the bedroom. It's inside, part of me moans while another part of me says that this is another manifestation of an overactive imagination. I should just look and confirm that my sister and I are alone.

I could check, I should, but I can't bring myself to pull the covers from my face. If something stands in this room, do I really want to see it? Would the thin fabric barrier of this comforter defend me from attack?

As I lay paralyzed with fear, a reeling terror rolls through me as I feel the mattress give near my feet. Something is on the bed. Something that coughed.

My stomach twists in knots and sweat dampens my brow as I lay unsure of what to do. Is this my brother here to play a prank on me? No, as rambunctious as my kin are, they'd never risk discipline from our father.

I glance under the covers at Alice as she snores gently. Should I wake her and ask if she sees it too?

My fingers tremble as I slowly peel the covers away, allowing me to peek into the bedroom, and something like ice drips down my spine when I see it. A looming silhouette sits at the edge of the bed, with its back facing us.

Before the consumption took Ma, she told me that children see things in the dark, but those things don't exist in the light because they aren't real.

I repeat that in my head, but it doesn't make this creature disappear.

The phantom has silver hair tied back in a taut bun, just as Nana used to put hers. It wears a nightgown of cascading shadows on its hunched form. The breaths it takes are heaving and labored as all lungs afflicted by consumption do. Before the bed sits a long dressing mirror, and in it, I see the creature's face.

It's not her, I know it's not her.

Staring back at me through the mirror is a blank, featureless void. No eyes or nose, just a porcelain face and the thin red line from a twisted smile. The skin shifts, changing like smoke as this creature tries to form a macabre semblance of Nana.

Please let this be a dream. Let this be fruit born from the seeds of dread my brothers planted. Sights and sounds could be imagined. Perhaps the feeling of the mattress bending under her weight was my imagination too. The mind is an unparalleled artist when given a canvas of shadows.

I won't scream or cry out, welcoming more mockery. I refuse to allow them that satisfaction. If I can just fall asleep, whatever this is will vanish.

However, before I shut my eyes and drown out the world, the shape jerks forward as it coughs, raising a hand to cover its mouth. In response to that sudden movement, I gasped. It wasn't a loud or distinct noise, but it was audible enough to get the attention of whatever sits at the edge of the bed.

Slowly and painfully, it turns its head to look at me. As it moves, a stench assaults my nostrils, watering my eyes. I remember this sickening and horrible musk. It was a mixture of sweat, decay, and the semisweet scent of rotting fruit. It's the smell of death that has so often visited our farm. The stink only grows worse as the eyeless face looks in my direction. Its thin, blood-spattered lips form a crimson smile before its sagging jaw falls open.

"Mary Lou..." a rasping voice hisses.

This isn't real. It can't be speaking. Its mouth isn't even moving.

"Mary Lou," I hear again and realize the sound is coming from Alice, who's staring at me wide-eyed.

Did I wake her?

Alice quickly strikes a match, lighting a lantern to illuminate the room. I glance back at the edge of the bed, but the shape is gone. It was another nightmare. I must have cried out and woke my sister. Come morning, she'll tell my brothers, and they'll mock my childishness for weeks. Perhaps they're right about me.

But I see no disdain, annoyance, or smugness in Alice's eyes. All I see is terror.

"Did you see her too?" Alice asks, and I nearly choke on those words.

I open my mouth to respond, but all that escapes my lips is a horrible retching cough.

6

DEMON ANTE PORTAS

DAVID RYDENBACKER

THEY HAVE ALWAYS BEEN there
There, just behind that door
I can feel them
I know what they want

There had been silence for years
But I had to open the door
Just a crack
Just to look

Now they scream at me
Desire floods my mind
They demand
They won't let go

I struggle against their pull I want to resist
I have to fight
I know the risks

I want the pleasure they bring
It's easy to lose myself
To give up
To give in

They scream, they rant
I want what they promise
I fight
I deny myself

The door closes
The noise quiets down
Silence
until the next time

7

WHISPERS

KIM PLASKET

I LOOK AT THE images before me and I can't figure out why they look so foreign. Almost as if the pictures were of someone else, that smiling face couldn't be me. I don't recall the last time I smiled, the darkness inside of me had taken its toll. You want me to tell you the story even though you say you won't believe me. You think that you have all the answers. Sometimes the answers to the questions only bring up more questions.

It started when I was a kid. It was very easy for me to know how others were feeling. If I was in a group of people who were feeling a certain way, it always made me feel the same way. It was a quirk back then which never bothered me much. I would find myself shying away from large groups for that reason only.

My mom told me that I would grow out of it, but it got worse. I didn't realize what it meant until I was in my late 30s. Up until then, I would do my best to be around positive people, but being a teenager was rough because who knew a teenager who was positive?

That is all I'm going to say about that time as it was rough. If it wasn't for books, I would have ended it all. I spent many hours with books because they were easy to figure out. I would go to the local library and spend hours lost in the worlds that books created.

When I was reading, I thought I would hear whispering but the fact I was in a library made me ignore it. I never gave it much thought until the whispering happened when I was home.

At first, I never could make out what they were saying so I would do my best to drown it out. After a while, that no longer worked. I started trying to understand what they were saying. It was louder in the library so when I was there, I would look around as I tried to find the origin.

I knew from books there was always an origin to every story. I felt as if I was living in a mystery novel, but the dead body would be mine if I hadn't figured it out. My imagination was active. I would start to imagine the whispering was the demons trying to get the strength to break out of hell and come after me. Once in a while, it would be angels but most of the time it was demons.

I could see them in my mind's eyes. Crouching down as they lie in wait to reach out and grab me. Their voices reached me from the depths of hell. The black ooze dripping from their eye sockets would kill me if it touched me. Their hands would lock onto me and pull me down.

There was one set of tables at the back of the library where not a single person would sit. When I was younger, I used to tell myself it was because that was where the God of the library sat. I did say I had a very active imagination if you recall.

It didn't matter what I told myself. Not a single person would sit there. As I tried to find the whispering it was near that table where it was the loudest. I was able to understand what they were saying.

"It must be opened so it can close."

I had no idea what it meant. I forced myself to sit down and as soon as I did, I realized the rest of the library seemed to fade. As if I was stepping into another dimension that coexisted with the one, I was used to. I wondered if I was the only one who could see this table, which could be why nobody ever sat there.

Was this what they meant by it having to open to close? But if it was, then why not let it close because it was open? I felt a cold chill coming upon me to the point I couldn't move. There was a fog swirling around my feet and every so often I felt something brush up against my leg.

It made me remember the demons, how they watched me from the shadows ready to pounce. The demons were the ones who were whispering, they wanted to peel the skin from my bones. They wanted to take my heart and rip it into shreds as if I never mattered.

They would leave my rotting carcass on this chair while everyone kept living. I could see people walking by this one spot never knowing there was a rotting corpse sitting on the chair.

My heart was ripped out of my chest with sharp dagger-like claws and left on the table like a leftover plaything of a bored child.

"It must open to close."

It made no sense to me, but I had to get away from where I was. I couldn't think about anything but what was swirling around my feet. I had no idea how I was going to get off the chair into my reality, but I had to try.

"It should be easy to get up. After all, it was easy for you to sit down," I muttered to myself as I started to stand. I expected something to try to drag me back onto the seat. It could also drag me under the table, but nothing happened so I was able to stand.

As soon as I stood up, I was standing close to the table but not actually at it. I knew if anyone was around me, they would wonder what was wrong with me. I rushed out the door, I had to get home before it got darker.

I got into my house and right away I went for the photo album. It was something that I knew could help me to recall my life before the whispers.

I opened my old photo album, the same one you looked at. I could see my image but behind me was a ghostly figure. I had never seen the image before, but it scared me. The image wasn't looking at the camera, instead, it was watching me.

The pictures that used to keep me grounded had been changed somehow. I knew then and there that nothing was going to be the same. It started when I heard the whispering as if the whispering was the start of the whole thing.

I had to find what needed to be opened so it could close. I knew something bad was trying to come through if it hadn't already.

The sky was dark as midnight, the thunder was rumbling in the sky, but the lightning hadn't started yet. As violent as the thunder sounded it was a matter of time before it began to flash across the sky.

"It must open to close."

The whispers came again on the wind that was picking up. It was loud enough that I could hear through the windows. It almost sounded as if the voices were right next to me.

"It must open to close."

I had no idea what they meant. If anyone else could hear them then they would be able to help me figure out what was going on. It was so many years ago that I started to hear them.

"You thought it was more recent?" I smiled as you tilted your head as if listening to something. I can see your hands moving as if you are opening something.

I know what you are going through but let me ask you something very important. Did you think that hearing my story would leave you untouched?

This is pure evil. When you come across this sort of evil it leaves you with a wound that can't be seen. It is subtle, something you can't feel until it is too late.

I used to think I would never be able to get over it, but I knew what I had to do. So, I set out to get it done. I thought I had to open a door and then allow it to be shut. While that is close to what must happen it's not exactly what must be. The library is where it must happen, but I need to find someone willing to help me. I have talked to others before but they all tell me I'm crazy and they ignore what they hear.

"It must open so it can close. The blood from the willing will allow the spirit to go free."

Finally, more of the story is heard. I heard this part years ago, but as I said, nobody was willing to help me. You told me that you wouldn't believe me, but I can see by the fear in your eyes, you can hear it.

The storm will rage on while we sit here. You can look in the photo albums and see what I'm talking about. Others in my pictures weren't there when they were taken.

I wonder why you stop and look at me with such a confused look on your face. Are there pictures of your own that you see another figure in?

It started when I heard something in a crowd of people. I would think it was directed at me, but there would be nobody speaking to me. The phone would ring but when I answered it all I could hear was static.

I found a book I thought would help but the only thing on its pages was, "The two must trade places for the pact to work. The story must be believed, or all will fail. It must open to close."

This was repeated on every page. So, I knew it meant something but still wasn't sure what.

I saw you and knew you would be the one who would help me figure this out. I know you are full of doubts but if you think about it you will come to the realization. This is something that has been happening for a long time.

You have heard the voices and seen pictures change. You have even heard the song that resonates from within you. I have been waiting for you, but I see you still need convincing.

Has there been a time when you lose track of time? You walk into a room and realize you can't remember why you went into that room. Your expression gives it away.

I can see the fear in your eyes and to be honest, that is good. The fear will cause you to lose the ability to disagree with me. I want you to be malleable to such an extent you hear my words and know they are right.

"The two must become one for the door to open. Once it is open then it will close."

I've heard this before but never understood what it meant until I was sitting here looking at you. I've had enough of this life so when I die before I am thrust into hell, we must become one.

You are going to kill me. I know this shocks you, but it has to be done. I have been on this planet long enough. When I die, I will be going to hell. I have taken the lives of those who didn't mesh well or understand what I was talking about.

Their blood is on my hands as my blood will be on yours. You tell me that you have never thought about killing anyone. I wonder if this is a match unless this is a dream. What if you aren't real?

I find myself backing away as I try to come to terms with the fact you might be another figment of my imagination. I step back and realize the mistake that I made as I start to fall.

As my broken body lies on the ground, my blood pouring out of me, the whispering starts once more.

"The door is open, let the demons of hell come forth."

8

WHERE VENGEANCE GROWS

ADELE LILES

THE BELL ABOVE THE door jingled as Nora walked in for her shift. She waved to the day waitress who sidled past her on her way out, muttering to herself about the weather. At the stove behind the counter, the cook saluted her with a greasy spatula.

"Hey, Joel," she called.

Nora tied on her apron and prepared for another long night at work. She and Joel exchanged tired smiles unaware of the horror about to blossom around them.

The diner sat on the corner of an abandoned street in the sleepy town of Misty Hollow, blanketed by silence, and edged with cracked pavement. The buildings, once teeming with life, now stood as withered husks scarred by neglect. The windows were boarded up or bleary with smudged dirt, their exteriors worn, their signs faded, paint flaking. Except for one—a relic that remained rooted in time and refused to succumb to the decay—The Strawberry Hill Cafe. Its neon sign flickered defiantly, humming and casting a soft glow onto the barren street, beckoning weary travelers passing through and loyal locals alike.

That night, a chilling fog engulfed Misty Hollow in a shroud of grey. It crept through the streets, clinging to buildings and twisting around lampposts. Nora and Joel didn't expect to have much business apart from the nightly regulars needing their coffee and homemade cherry pie fix.

As the night deepened, Nora noticed the fog inched closer to the cafe, *and* became even denser, obscuring the world outside. Unease settled in her stomach, and she glanced around the diner, seeking a distraction from the encroaching darkness. The few patrons seemed equally on edge, their eyes darting toward the fog-filled windows, and Joel rubbed the stubble on his chin, his brow wrinkling.

An elderly man named Jack sat at the counter, nursing a cup of coffee that grew colder with each passing minute. His hands trembled as he raised the mug from its saucer, the rattle of the porcelain echoing through the low hum of conversation and quiet strains from the jukebox in the corner.

Nora's comforting smile wavered for a moment before she said, "We'll be okay, Jack.

The fog will lift soon. It always does."

"Not this time," Jack replied. "I can feel it. This time it's coming."

"Don't be silly." She patted his hand. "Those are just campfire stories."

Misty Hollow had once been a lush valley blanketed in the vibrant hues of blooming plant life until developers cleared it out to build the little town. It got its name from the perpetual mist hanging over it, as if Nature herself had woven a veil to attempt to hide it from the world or play a whimsical game of hide and seek. Long before the town's inception, the valley thrived, a sanctuary of bountiful magnificence.

Legend told a curse had befallen the garden when the town was erected on top of it, washing a pall of malevolence over its streets. As the foundations were laid, the threatening influence grew, seeping through the cracks in the earth, as if pursuing retribution for the desecration of its sacred ground. Groundskeepers struggled to keep the growth at bay, and the more superstitious locals swore one day it would flourish again, come back and reclaim its land.

Sometimes–like tonight–the gentle mist morphed into a heavy fog. The older residents blamed the ghostly shroud for their dying town, their superstitions stemming from the knowledge that another business fought to survive every time the air thickened with the mystical cloak until it eventually closed for good. On the nights when it was especially heavy, the townsfolk retreated to their homes to hide behind locked doors and drawn curtains.

Despite her reassuring words, even Nora had seeds of doubt as the fog pressed against the windows, curling like icy fingers, eager to invade the refuge within. She rubbed her arms as anticipation fluttered through her.

The bell jingled and Nora's adrenaline spiked, her eyes rooted to the diner's murky entrance. Who would be out in this? A young woman with a silver cascade of hair and luminous skin entered, clutching a book to her chest. Nora didn't recognize her. Must be passing through and couldn't see well enough to go on, she thought. The woman slid into a booth near the entrance and laid the book on the table. The waitress grabbed the coffee pot and approached with her brightest smile.

"Hi there," she chirped. "Welcome to Strawberry Hill. You must not be from around here.

Fog get ya?" She poured a complimentary cup.

The stranger gazed at Nora, her eyes soft and dark like a black orchid. She nodded.

"Not to worry. It'll clear off in a bit. Always does. What can I get ya?"

The outsider shook her head. Nora flicked her gaze down at the book. Midnight Labyrinth. She lifted it, turning it over as the woman's eyes widened. She wrinkled her nose as she caught a whiff of something she couldn't quite place—honey and something. Sickly sweet, like a rotting peach.

"Don't think I've read this one. Looks like you picked the right night for it though," she grinned, returning the tome. The stranger pulled it closer toward herself. "I'll be around if you need anything."

"We're out of coffee," Jack announced when she got back to the counter.

"Then I guess we better make some more." She laughed and reached below for the canister. "Ope—can's almost empty. I'll have to get another from the back."

Nora scooted down the alcove at the back of the diner to the storage room but hesitated with her hand on the tarnished doorknob. Something didn't feel right. The smell hovered back there as well—stronger, fetid. She bet there was a dead rat or something in there. It wouldn't be the first time. She shuddered, bracing herself, and seized the knob again, giving it a quick turn. She pulled it open, revealing a black void. Running her hand along the wall, she searched for the switch.

Light flooded the room, and she stepped inside. She didn't see any animals, thank goodness. She hunted around for the coffee. Finding no canisters in the usual spot, she dug through things on the shelves and metal racks trying to find it, muttering about needing to organize in there one day soon. As she pushed aside boxes of napkins and cans of beans, she noticed water spots on a seam in the faded wallpaper behind the rack, and the paper bubbled under them.

"What's this?" She traced over it and discovered it was moist and spongy. Her finger poked through to a hole in the wall behind. She picked at it, easily pulling it away.

She knew she should have left it, but with the fascination of a child peeling dried glue from their hands or shedding skin after a sunburn, she could not resist the urge to keep peeling the paper. Once she stripped a large chunk of it away, she was shocked to find a cracked door beneath, with the hole where a doorknob would have gone. Putrid splinters of decay invaded her nose.

She heard a noise behind her. Turning, she found a figure standing in the doorway of the supply room, cradling her book.

"Wh-what are you doing back here?" Nora stammered.

"Open it." The voice was dry and brittle like parched leaves in autumn. She crossed into the room.

Nora wanted to protest, but the stranger's eyes seemed to pierce through her, seeing more than they should. She obeyed the command and turned back to the door. Hooking her fingers into the cavity, she tugged on the door. It groaned open, its hinges protesting. The mysterious woman stood beside her now, reeking of fermented sugar and damp soil. Darkness lay beyond the door, even from the light in the room. Without hesitation, the woman stepped into the space and disappeared into the blackness. Nora gasped and fumbled for her phone, pulling it from her apron pocket. She used the flashlight to illuminate the hidden room.

Inside stretched a maze of flora, with vines that writhed like serpents and flowers with a watchful stillness. The foliage crisscrossed in intricate patterns, forming a mesmerizing labyrinth that beckoned her further into its depths. She did not resist. Could not resist. Following the trail of dense undergrowth, she stared in wonder at the concealed lair. She thought it was a basement or cellar, but when a moon and stars rose overhead, bathing the path in light, she knew she *had* entered another world entirely—the world that had existed long before her time, the world when Misty Hollow remained a quiet secret of Nature.

A breeze tickled the leaves and blew the frogs full of life. The whip-poor-wills burst into song, their chirps punctuating the silence of the night. Her steps were hushed, barely audible against the symphony of nocturnal sounds.

The maze stretched endlessly before her. Goosebumps crawled over her arms, and she wanted to turn back, but she was hypnotized by the mysterious chamber. Ahead of her, the stranger floated along the path, stooping to touch the greenery, bringing it to life.

As Nora ventured deeper, the garden soon revealed its secrets as plants reacted to her presence, acknowledging her intrusion. One lunged toward her with gnashing teeth, narrowly missing her. Branches clawed at her clothing with thorny fingers. Trees towered like cathedral spires, their bark pulsating. Underfoot, the ground unfurled like a living carpet, tendrils reaching out to caress her feet. A yelp escaped her throat as she jumped away. With each step, she encountered new horrors—carnivorous blossoms, venomous thorns, and disquieting willows.

Her heart punched inside her chest as she trailed behind the woman.

Eventually, the ethereal beauty turned and returned to Nora. Taking her hand, she pulled her back *in* the other direction to the supply room. The path followed them, growing under their footsteps, escorting them to the dining room.

The lights flickered, casting shadows that climbed across the room. The jukebox crackled, and its music ceased. The patrons exchanged fearful glances, disturbed by the ominous events. Outside, the fog took on a life of its own, undulating and shifting, controlled by an unseen force.

Nora and the stranger emerged from the alcove, the latter's body now intertwined with shoots and leaves, her eyes glowing like moonlight. The aroma of damp earth and decaying petals—a haunting symphony of musky and sweet—per*meat*ed the air. Joel's spatula clattered to the countertop, Jack dropped his cup, which shattered on the floor, and Nora stumbled backward as she wrenched her hand free from the stranger's grasp, fear clawing its way down her throat.

The once-familiar *surroundings* of the diner ripened into a verdant, nightmare landscape, the air thick with pungent odor. The walls produced briars that snaked along the ceiling, tables sprouted grotesque blooms, and the linoleum squirmed with ivy creepers.

"It's come," Jack whispered as a peculiar plant with vibrant, hypnotic flowers caught his attention.

Mesmerized by its radiance and intoxicated by the fragrant buds, he stroked the delicate petals. Nora reached out to stop him, but she was too late. As his fingertips grazed the plant's surface, a grim energy surged through their bodies, a venomous toxin coursing through their veins.

They recoiled, grasping their arms in agony, only to find their flesh entwined with stems that snaked and twisted, constricting their limbs. They looked around and saw Joel and the others in similar predicaments. Terror squeezed their hearts as the coils wrestled, entangling them further, refusing to release their grip. Bark-like growths erupted, turning their skin to hardened, thorny armor. Their eyes turned black like polished river stones.

They screamed, trapped in the cursed botanical tableau. As the tendrils continued to spread, their minds deteriorated, their identities replaced with the dark essence.

The silver-haired woman opened the door to the diner, and the foliage expanded, spilling into the night. It persisted—alive and hungry—consuming everything in its path, cutting through the fog, wrapping Misty Hollow in an unholy metamorphosis. Mutated plants and abominations burst through the soil, their vines creeping along the avenues like the gnarled fingers of a vengeful deity. The town awoke to a nightmarish scene as the resurrected garden unleashed its wrath.

Horrific creatures, birthed from the corruption, prowled the darkened streets, searching for harvest. Fear slithered in the veins of the townsfolk as they fought to escape the clutches of this monstrous infestation. The night echoed with a cacophony of desperate pleas for salvation from the sinewy growth. They struggled in vain as the garden claimed them, its essence seeping into them, mingling with their energy and melding them to it. The suffocating grip of the overgrown vegetation silenced their cries of terror. Their bones crackled and stretched like branches while delicate buds sprouted from their skin, blossoming into sinister flowers. Their feet grew roots and fused with the earth, binding them to the garden as it accepted them, embracing them as its own.

It continued its insidious advance, sliding over every street and enveloping the town in herbage again, the patient mist draped over it like a gossamer veil. When the sun rose, it had transformed into a dreamscape of twisted forms and grotesque splendor. And the townspeople were part of it, living manifestations of its dark allure, their identity forever entwined with the malevolent flora. *Passersby* marveled at the beauty of Misty Hollow, unknowingly witnessing the tragic fate of those consumed by its secrets.

9

DIE PRETTY

RAVEN ELLIS

MAYRA SAT IN FRONT of the mirror removing her makeup and wondered who she would discover underneath. Grabbing a wet cloth off the table, she turned her chair away from the vanity, her evening ritual. She wasn't ready to reveal what lurked beneath the layers of foundation and concealer, the false eyelashes, and red lipstick. It all suited her in classical fashion, the way she liked. Although she doesn't recollect applying it. Things happened fast as of late. She couldn't keep up with all of it anymore.

It had been long since she faced a mirror. She didn't recall what she looked like without the coats that were her faux complexion. The paint made her appear prettier under all the bright lights, but she wondered if, beneath it, she was a monster. Taking her mask off, she chuckled to herself. What if she was a lizard? She could be a dragon or nymph. What if she had no features? The thickness of makeup is a second skin.

She looked down at the cloth she was using to take her lipstick off, *i*nspecting it intensely for any signs of flesh or scales. It looked like lipstick to her. She always considered herself to be the odd man out, set apart from the rest. She acted as though no one in the world understood her. When you are pretty and popular, you are not supposed to have problems; it made who she was invisible compared to her looks. People saw her dolled up and wanted her right away. They had no desire to know her, at least not in the manner she longed to be known. She wondered if she did not have the crowds of people surrounding her, painting her face and primping her for shows and appearances, would she cease to exist? She forgot herself somewhere during her career, a long time ago.

Whoever lived under the makeup was a total stranger. When she wasn't working, she was sleeping. She wished she had a friend or someone to love. Perhaps this emptiness that ate her away would disappear. If only she could recognize the woman in the mirror. She wondered what life would look like if she had made different choices. For her, that was unobtainable, the cost of it all. She was a toy, a fashion doll. People were always touching her. She was numb to it all, a car on autopilot with a distracted driver. Perhaps it was time to change. Could she transform?

Inhaling, she faced the mirror. Startled by the corpse of a person, she sees staring back at her. She gasps, leaving her lips frozen and cold. She examined her hollow cheeks that were sucked in, a skeleton with skin attached, muscles fading. Her eyes sank into her face. Had she fallen so far from herself that she was dying? Makeup has a way of making the impossible seem real. She eyed the box knife left on the corner of her vanity table. She picked it up to examine it with morbid curiosity.

Haunted by her reflection, gripping the knife in her hand until her knuckles turned white. She sliced away the pieces of herself that didn't fit. Layer by layer, she removed the ugly parts of herself until the blood poured down her chest. Shaken by the realization that she might disappear, confident that at least now she would die pretty. She collapsed to the ground; the blade falling from her hands. Drowning in a pool of her own blood, she surrendered to the blackness behind her eyelids as what she left of her lips curled upward in a smile. Peace at last. The final thought passed through her brain as she bled out on the dressing room floor.

10

FLORA'S HORA

TREVOR ATKINS

AWAKENED BY VIOLENT SHAKING, I try to make sense of what's happening. My awareness is blurry, fuzzy. I have vague feelings of movement nearby, next to me. There is vibration, sound, but I can't make out any meaning. I sense touching, along one of my limbs. A sudden piercing of my skin! The pain comes again, again, and again! At last, I'm left alone; bare, trembling, mutilated.

I next awake to a steady staccato drumming. Moisture drips along my healing body. It's refreshing; I soak up the feeling. I'm aware of others around me. Some are close, but all are alike, unable to move about or call out. I strain to reach them, to touch someone, anything. Sometimes I think I have, but nothing feels solid. I'm just brushing past.

It's been days, weeks, months maybe. I've only the warmth of the sun to track the days. With no way to record them, I can only guess at the number, at the passage of time. Past pain is a faded memory. I'm thinking only of the new life I will soon bring forth! It's growing quickly now.

I've been visited more frequently as of late. Around me now are many vibrations, the most yet! They are handling me roughly, prodding, pulling… They're tearing them from me! They're taking them!

I'm empty; empty and cold, inside and out. The cold makes me remember. This has happened before… Once I've rested, recovered, and forgotten, they will come again—for me, and the seeds of my children.

11

WAITING WITH BATED DEATH

GLENDA DARUSOW

THE DEPUTY DROVE UP onto the driveway of a walled residential compound. There was a fifteen-foot-tall black metal gate blocking her vehicle's path. She rolled down her driver's side window and pushed the button on the intercom system.

"Yes," crackled a reply.

"Hello. My name is Deputy Jaylen from the Nelson Ridge Sheriff's Department. I am here responding to a rabid animal complaint."

"Yes. The gate's a little slow so give it a minute before you proceed."

"Okay."

The dark metal gate slowly parted in two and rattled open for the deputy's Jeep. While she was waiting, she called in her position to her headquarters. She clicked her satellite phone into the, "on" position and then waited for the green light. She then spoke into the hand-held radio attachment.

"Dispatch. This is Victor One-Eight. Do you copy?"

"Copy One-Eight."

"Ten twenty-three Dispatch. Address is 101 North Trail, Terrance Canyon, New Mexico, 87310. Copy?"

"Ten-zero Victor One-Eight."

"Ten-four."

The deputy turned her satellite phone to the "ready" position so it would continually give off her position to headquarters. She drove her Jeep into the compound. The wall that surrounded the property was about twenty feet tall and five feet thick. The residence was constructed with an old Spanish motif. The place looked like an old presidio.

The deputy parked. She then did a routine check of the items in her police belt including a canteen and her backup pistol. She looked at her cell phone in its holster on the dashboard. No service. She thought for a moment and then just left it where it was.

As she exited her vehicle, she put on her hat, locked her Jeep, and walked toward the residence in the center of the compound. She was impressed the inner courtyard was paved with intricate new brickwork. The compound was alive with natural flora yet there were no weeds anywhere to be seen.

As the deputy approached the front door it opened and a middle-aged man with thick white hair emerged from the dwelling.

"I am looking for Theodore Mallory," said the deputy in a firm but friendly voice.

"I am Ted Mallory." The man said, "You must be Dr. Silvia Jaylen."

The man extended his left hand to shake her right hand. This caused momentarily awkwardness. He smiled and instinctively switched to his right hand to shake her right hand.

"I am Dr. Jaylen, and I am also Deputy Jaylen. Back at the station, they call me the Dep-Vet from Virginia Tech. How did you know?"

"You're the resident veterinarian and animal control officer for Nelson Ridge. Information like that moves quickly around in a small town. I'm sure your doubling up on two jobs, saves the taxpayers plenty."

Deputy Jaylen smiled and looked around the home. She noticed the many luxury items contained within Ted's residence. His house was orderly and stocked with polished marble, heavy oak furniture, and fine crystal. She also noticed a number of large fish that had been stuffed and mounted on the walls. The home was decorated with an omnipresent neo-bachelor flair.

"Your home is beautiful, Mr. Mallory. What do you do for a living if you don't mind me asking?"

"I deal in auto parts and auto accessories. Most people look at a car as a whole and say, 'It's a Toyota or a Ford or whatever.' I see all automobiles as the collective sum of their parts. Even older models can deliver relative value in various international markets depending upon the part's age its wear.

Most of my work I do here at home in my garages, but I do have an office up in Gallup. I make the trip a few times in a week. There's at least cell reception and a working internet connection there. Those are two commodities you won't find here in Terrance Canyon."

"Okay, Mr. Mallory. I am here as a result of your phone call to the Sherriff's Department. Before we continue, I need to ask you is this residence on tribal land or part of a tribal trust?"

"No ma'am. I pay my taxes to the County of McKinley and the state of New Mexico. I do pay some annual municipal fees to the municipality of Nelson Ridge, so I guess that makes me your problem."

"Where is the animal that you called us about? Your pet. The one that you suspect is rabid?"

"Well, calling him mine is kind of a stretch. It is mostly feral, but I do feed it every now and again. I guess that makes him mine.

Deputy Jaylen took out her police notebook and prepared to write down pertinent facts about her discourse with Mr. Mallory.

"So, your pet is a dog? What breed?"

"Ma'am. I don't rightly know."

"Is it a big dog? Small dog? Is it a mixed breed?"

"I don't know that I would call it a dog. I don't rightly know if I am qualified to answer that question."

"Is it a coydog? A coyote-dog hybrid?" The deputy was becoming intrigued by Mr. Mallory's non-answers.

"That's possible. I don't really know. I have never seen it in the daytime."

"You have never SEEN your pet?"

"No ma'am, not in the light of day. That's not unusual for desert creatures. Most critters out there in the canyon don't come out of hiding until after the sun goes down."

"Okay, can you describe your pet?"

"Not completely. I have only seen it in the dark. It just might be a coydog like you say or not. I am not really sure."

"Then what makes you think it's rabid?"

"I hear it howling in the daytime. Sometimes at mid-day. I have been told that it's a symptom of rabies. A night critter who is suddenly active during the heat of the day."

"I don't think we are dealing with a coydog then. Coyotes, are by nature, diurnal. Those that live near human habitation sometimes adopt temporary nocturnal habits to avoid humans, but that would seem unlikely behavioral trait this far from civilization."

"Again, I don't know anything about coyote hybrids. I do know that its howl is different than usual. Its behavior is very different. It sounds like it is ill or maybe injured."

"Is it possible we are talking about some kind of wild animal? Maybe a cougar or bobcat?"

"No ma'am. I was born in Gallup, New Mexico. I have lived here all my life with the exception of the eight years I spent in the Navy. This pet is something different."

"A strictly nocturnal coydog is not out of the realm of possibility. It is however exceedingly unlikely. If your pet is a wild

animal, I am afraid you are going to need to contact a park
ranger, or the county, not the Sheriff's office."

"Dr. Jaylen, it is November. God knows how many people
from God knows where will be wandering through Terrance
Canyon right in my backyard as the days get cooler. If one or
more of those hikers gets bit that could become a potentially
fatal problem for them. Somebody's life may depend upon your
response to my request to have you come out here today. Please
don't pass the buck Doctor. You need to terminate the damn
thing before it hurts or kills somebody."

The deputy thought for a moment and then said, "Okay Mr.
Mallory. Let's go find your pet or whatever it is, and I will try to
put it down for you."

"You won't need your catchpole or euthanasia solution. The
only safe solution to this problem will be your pistol.

Deputy Jaylen put her notebook away in her utility belt after
her final notation. She gave Ted a thin professional smile.

Ted looked at the Rolex on his right wrist, and said, "We need
to go now, or we may run out of daylight."

The two exited the home. They walked out past his swimming pool, hot tub, and gazebo. As they continued past one
of his open garages the deputy could see three mint-condition
vintage automobiles. As they approached the wall surrounding
the residential compound Ted took out an electric key fob and
used it to open a door concealed as part of the barrier. The two
walked through the door together and Ted stopped to shut it.

He gave Deputy Jaylen a wink as he took the lead hiking towards a path that went down to the basin floor of the canyon.

"Where are we going exactly?" Deputy Jaylen asked.

"There is a place down in the canyon where my pet normally sleeps during the day. It's not far doctor. We will be there soon."

"I noticed that you had a number of stuffed fish on your walls."

"Yes. I fish quite a bit. There are a surprising number of great spots here in New Mexico, Utah, and Arizona."

"Do you use lures or live bait?"

"Lures are just fine doctor, but I really do prefer to use live bait."

The pair made it down the hill and onto the floor of the canyon. The shadows cast by the afternoon sun seem to reach into infinity. The duo looked out of place walking about in this landscape of stone, sky, and twisted scrub.

"My brother and I used to camp down here when we were kids. This place is called 'Massacre Bluff' by the locals."

"That's a lovely title. Why do they call it that?"

"Well, as the story goes, there was a contingent of Spanish soldiers looking for gold out here back in the late 1700s. They had captured about fifty natives from various tribes with the intention of making them mine for it. Consumed by greed; they kept looking until their supplies ran low. The soldiers realized that there was no way they could make it back to their settlement on the Santa Cruz River toting fifty captive natives. So, to lighten their load they just garroted all of them right there in the basin. They were also low on gunpowder and shot, but they apparently had plenty of rope.

Now, a few days after the massacre, they ran into this Apache raiding party making their way across the desert. The Apache captured and then tortured all of these soldiers to death for what they had done. The only one they let go was a Jesuit friar who actually made it back to the settlement there on the Santa Cruz River in Arizona. He wrote down all of the events as a confessional before he expired from injuries he sustained during this ordeal.

This is an unforgiving land, Doctor. It's not like back East where you are from. In this land, death can be waiting for you just around the corner. This canyon has a LOT of horrible things happening in it. So much so my older brother used to call this place 'Terror Canyon' instead of Terrance Canyon."

Deputy Jaylen chuckled, "Older brothers can be the worst. My brothers used to try to scare me with..."

A howl roared out from somewhere in the canyon. It seemed to echo from the canyon walls and last for an eternity before it finally faded away. The deputy stopped talking and froze. She then made a visual check of her surroundings.

"That was my pet," said Ted cooly, stopping and looking back at Deputy Jaylen.

"That was no coydog," Deputy Jaylen whispered in the calmest voice she could manage.

"One thing is clear, Doctor. That animal, whatever it is, needs to be put down."

Deputy Jaylen nodded her head in agreement. She then pulled her sidearm out from its holster on her belt and racked the slide putting a bullet in the chamber. She engaged the safety with her thumb, and then held the pistol in her right hand and pointed it down toward the ground."

"Lead on, Mr. Mallory. Let's get this done."

The two continued hiking at the bottom of the canyon until they arrived at a stark windswept area containing hundreds of different pillars of sandstone. These pillars were anywhere from five feet to fifteen feet high. The area looked like some ancient graveyard with a myriad of giant headstones.

"The locals call this place 'The Maze'," said Ted. "It can get a little confusing once you are walking around inside there. Please just follow behind me."

"How do you know your pet is even in here?" asked the deputy sternly. "That howl could have come from anywhere in this canyon."

"I don't know for sure. Normally it would be hiding here until it gets dark. Since it got sick who knows, but I think it would be wise to check it out first. There is a place in, 'The Maze,' the locals call the 'Minecave'. It is a natural cave that was used by prospectors to mine for copper and tin. They didn't find anything of value, and it was abandoned over a hundred years ago. It's not far Doctor. We are almost there."

Ted looked again at his watch and walked into, "The Maze." Deputy Jaylen followed close behind. It was clear he knew exactly where he was going. There was no hesitation in his movements at all. After winding around and around, Ted finally stopped.

"We're here," he said. "I hope you brought a flashlight."

"It's standard issue," she said, attaching it to the top of her sidearm and turning the light on."

Deputy Jaylen directed her flashlight inside the cave. It was dark, but it didn't look that deep. The deputy looked at the sides of the cave. They were bone dry and dusty. There was no bat guano at all that she could see. She found this to be a bit peculiar.

Ted dug up a large spool of rope that was half buried in the sand near the opening of the cave. He ran one end of the rope through an old half-rusted pulley system and gestured it toward the deputy.

"This is your lifeline, Doctor. Wrap this rope around your waist as tight as you can. This cave is not very big, but it can be tricky. If my pet is in there you will see it right away. If it's not just tug on the rope and I will pull you back out."

"You are not going in for your pet?" she asked, looking at Ted in disbelief.

"Somebody's got to hold the rope to get you back out. Use your deputy training. You'll be fine. Trust me."

Deputy Jaylen said nothing. She just stared at Ted incredulously.

"We are running out of daylight, doctor," Ted said again, offering the rope to the deputy.

"Mr. Mallory, if you think I am going to tie a rope to my waist and let you lower me into an unknown hole in the ground that may or may not contain some wild, rabid animal without any safety gear or contact with my department, you are sadly mistaken. I have taken an oath to serve the public, but that is not going to happen.

There seemed like an eternity between the two as Deputy Jaylen's stern refusal seemed to just hang in the air.

"Okay Doctor, fair enough. You're in charge. I need to get some things while we are here and then we will go back to the house. You can radio into the station and get whatever tools you might need. This is clearly more than a one-deputy job. I'll be right back then we can go. Keep your eye on that opening."

Ted disappeared around one of the many pillars of sandstone while Deputy Jaylen kept focused on the opening but also kept looking behind her. She disengaged the safety on her pistol with her thumb. A rabid animal sick out of its mind could be anywhere. Even with her 9mm pistol at the ready she still felt a certain degree of trepidation. Mr. Mallory was right. They did need to call for backup on this one.

She thought for a moment she heard a noise down in the darkness of the cave like the rattle of stones. She set her focus on the opening when she heard a metal click behind her. It sounded like a bolt action rifle pushing a round into the barrel.

"Please, don't turn around, Doctor. I am armed with a 30-06 hunting rifle. This rifle is more than capable of blowing a large hole right through that Kevlar vest you wear underneath your uniform.

What I want you to do, without turning around, is slowly remove your flashlight from your pistol, and then toss your pistol over your right shoulder toward me as far as you can.

"Mr. Mallory, do you have any idea what you are doing!? Do you know how many laws you are breaking right now!?"

"At the moment I have a rifle aimed at your back and if you don't do as I tell you I will kill you. The only law out here is survival.

Let's try this again, doctor. Remove your flashlight from the top of your pistol and put it on the ground in front of you. Then slowly take your sidearm and toss it over your right shoulder. If you don't do that now I can promise you that your life will end right here with a bang!"

"Okay, Mr. Mallory! Okay! Let's just relax. I am following your instructions."

The deputy put the flashlight in front of her and tossed her 9mm pistol behind her.

"Now, using that same right hand of yours, detach the key ring from your utility belt, and toss it behind you the same way you tossed your pistol."

Deputy Jaylen did as Ted requested and tossed her keys behind her as well.

"Fantastic! Now, reach behind you and grab that rope. Tie it around your waste. Make sure that it is tight and secure."

The deputy reached behind her and grabbed the end of the rope. As she was tying it around her waist, she touched the handle of her backup pistol. She thought about covertly pulling it out while she was tying the rope around her waist, then turning around and firing. This idea lingered for a moment until she realized it might be safer to wait for a better opportunity.

"Thank you, Doctor. Now, please pick up your flashlight, and move forward past the opening and into the cave.

"Okay, Mr. Mallory. Let's talk about what we are doing here. Let's take a moment to..."

"Get down in that goddamn hole, lady!" Ted shouted behind her. "NOW!"

"Okay, Mr. Mallory, I am going."

Deputy Jaylen picked up her flashlight with her right hand and walked steadily into the opening of the cave. She walked down a steady incline about thirty feet. It was at that point the incline turned into a harsh, ninety-degree drop of about another twenty feet to a sandy ledge. The deputy turned, switched her flashlight to her left hand, and reached around to secure the rope. She then repelled backward down the twenty-foot incline to the sandy ledge. Just before she was able to stand on the sandy ledge Ted cut the rope. She fell on her back with a loud thud.

The deputy immediately got up and used her flashlight to look at her surroundings. She pushed her back flush against the ninety-degree incline and drew her back-up pistol. She racked a .380 round into the chamber still holding the flashlight upwards to study the incline. She did not bring an additional magazine so eight shots were going to be her limit.

The incline stood like a wall preventing the deputy from climbing back up to the opening of the cave. She could see that the afternoon light in the cave had started to fade.

Ten feet below the ledge there was a level tunnel that tapered off to her left and to her right. The tunnel was about seven feet high and bore the scars of once being a mined. She adjusted her flashlight to be more of a beam and focused it down the tunnel to her left and then to the right. There was only darkness. The only other light source was from the opening of the cave.

The deputy reckoned her best chance at escaping this was to start digging foot and hand holes into the ninety-degree incline. Once at the top of the incline, she would crawl toward the opening. She would be in a prone position, and she could wedge herself against the wall of the cave. She would have the advantage over Mr. Mallory if he tried to shoot her. Her pistol's rate of fire was also much faster than his rifle. She could fire off a number of shots before he fired one.

She tried to attach the flashlight to her pistol, but the barrel was much too small. She then pushed the butt of the flashlight into the sand on the ledge and adjusted the beam. She took a small lock knife out of her utility belt and started to use it to carve hand and foot holes into the incline so she could escape. As she began to chisel into the incline a roar came from one of the mining tunnels below her that made her heart stop cold.

Ted's voice called down from the entrance and it echoed about the walls of the cave. "The Cherokee called it a 'Uktena'. The Lakota called it a 'Miniwatu'. The Europeans called it a dragon. You asked me what my pet was. I still don't know what to tell you, Doctor. It has not been as yet classified by science, but it's evil and it's nasty. That much I can tell you.

"A dragon, Mr. Mallory?!" Deputy Jaylen yelled up toward the opening. "Really?! I thought they were going to be hauling you off to jail when this was all over. Now I think they're going to be hauling you to a psych-ward instead."

"That howl you've been hearing is real. They don't call New Mexico the 'Land of Enchantment' for nothing. This creature, whatever it is, communicates with me in my dreams. I have made a deal with it to feed it so it would leave me alone."

"That howl was probably just some bear that got stuck down here. As far as your dreams. It's just further proof that you clearly need some professional help," yelled the deputy upward still frantically chiseling the incline with her knife.

"I wouldn't be sacrificing you to some bear. You are about to meet a bona fide Native American deity. You might want to show some respect."

"Thank you, Mr. Mallory! I will be sure to be on my best behavior down here in the dark."

As Deputy Jaylen's words echoed through the darkness another howl roared out from below. This time the howl seemed much louder and closer.

The deputy dropped her knife in the sand, picked up the flashlight, and scanned into the darkness. There was nothing on her left, but on her right, she saw two red eyes flashing up at her. She fired her weapon down at them. The sound of the gun blasts was deafening as it rattled throughout the cave.

The creature climbed quickly to the ledge like a spider climbing a leaf. The speed at which this creature could move was stunning and it made the deputy momentarily freeze.

The deputy could see the creature in her flashlight beam. It was some kind of reptilian by its thick outer scales, but it didn't move like one. Its shoulder structure and hip structure were both high off the ground making it look like some hairless, scaly, mammal. It was the size of a large cougar. The creature kept its head low to the ground as it approached the deputy.

She fired her pistol again and again at the creature. It was about fifteen feet away from her and she could hear some of her bullets bouncing off its thick scales and ricocheting off into the darkness.

The creature opened its maul and blasted a stream of acid from one of its stomachs directly at the deputy. It was like she was being doused with burning napalm. The first stream hit the deputy in the face causing her to drop her gun and fall to her knees in excruciating pain. The creature then pounced upon her. The creature locked its jaws onto the top of the deputy's skull and shook it. Her tongue helplessly flapped around and poked through a hole in her face where her left cheek used to be. All her sensations ended as the creature bit cleanly through the middle of her skull.

Ted could hear the sounds of Deputy Jaylen's body being consumed by his pet and then realized his offering to this Native deity was complete.

He reached down and picked up the deputy's sidearm and secured it in his belt. He returned his rifle and bowie knife he used for cutting the rope back to their slim plastic container. He put the container back in its hiding place and covered it with a thick layer of sand.

"If they find it, I will say that it is my hunter's chest," Ted thought to himself.

Ted hiked back out of the canyon to his residential compound. He retrieved a pair of work gloves and a special toolbox from one of his garages. He unlocked the deputy's Jeep with her keys. He checked the vehicle over thoroughly making sure that there were no GPS tracking devices except the satellite phone. He put the toolbox on the passenger's side of the vehicle, put on his gloves, and started the engine.

He quickly checked his watch again and then drove the Jeep out of his residential compound and onto his private road. As he cruised up the hill to the lip of the canyon, he could see the sun going down. This prompted him to step on the gas and drive the Jeep as fast as it would go. When he got to the end of his private road, he turned onto NM Route 790 heading west toward the Arizona border.

After a few moments on the road, he pulled out a strong magnet from his toolbox and attached it to the side of the satellite phone. This caused the light to rapidly flash yellow. He then took out a special screwdriver from his toolbox and began to work on the satellite phone with his right hand while he steered the vehicle with his left. After a few moments, the satellite phone stopped sending out any signals at all. There was now no way to trace its location.

Ted drove the Jeep down a large dry wash off of NM Route 790 and continued off-road. He engaged the four-wheel drive on the Jeep and continued about another mile. Ted drove into an old mine used by smugglers and parked the Jeep there with the keys in it.

"By the time the Sheriff's office comes looking for Dr. Jaylen, this Jeep will be at some chop shop in Mexico," Ted thought smugly to himself.

He took her cell phone with no signal from its holster on the dashboard and tossed it in the back of the vehicle with her catch pole and mobile medicine box. Ted paused for a moment and slowly shook his head.

He took his tools out of the Jeep and headed home. He checked the deputy's sidearm to make sure it was secure in his belt and left the mine. There was a shortcut that bypassed all the winding canyon roads. He knew the path well even in the dark.

As he walked along, he thought, "That satellite signal started bouncing around when I put on that magnet. All they will know for sure is that the Jeep drove out of my compound and then into oblivion. They are never going to be able to prove a thing with no body and no vehicle. I am in the clear."

The moon was full and high in the sky by the time he could see the lights of his home.

"That took a lot longer than I thought, but at least I will be home soon," said Ted quietly to himself.

As he started on the trail that went back up the hill to his residence compound, he could hear heavy breathing. He stopped. The air was tense and smelled like ammonia. Then came a deep piercing howl that split open the calmness of the night. Ted found it difficult to breathe.

"I fed you!" Ted yelled into the darkness. "I made my sacrifice."

Ted took the deputy's sidearm from his belt and fired wildly into the darkness. He started running up the hill to his home. As he did, a stream of acid came from behind him soaking the back of his legs. It burned like fire and Ted struggled to keep his balance on the hilly terrain.

"We had a deal!" Ted screamed in a loud high-pitched voice.

Ted could feel the skin on his legs sloughing off his bones. Ted screamed in pain as he fell forward onto the ground unable to move. The creature launched itself on top of him accompanied by two smaller ones that looked just like it. They all tore into his flesh with reckless abandon. The last thing Ted felt was his head being jerked backward toward his shoulders and separating from his body.

12

Uncle Hollofax

J.K. Raymond

THE LITTLE HAIRS ON her arms started to stand from the chill in the air, but she didn't want her sweater. She always liked the goosebumps feeling of a chill dancing across her skin.

It was the first day of October, and fifteen-year-old Mia was slowly but surely slipping into life in Mozelle, Missouri, population nine.

"That's how everything was around here, 'slowly but surely'," she thought to herself as she took a jaywalker's shortcut through the tiny cemetery on the corner of the town's one and only four-way stop.

Some stones were so old you could only assume they were once headstones by their rough shape. But Hollofax, Uncle Hollofax, was a baller, the ten-foot, black polished tombstone called out to Mia's teenage heart in absolute irony. She'd never been emo, but her thoughts were turning darker by the day, and she had no one to blame but her mother for moving them to this one-horse, strike that, zero-horse, town. But she didn't blame Uncle Hollofax as she read his towering tombstone for the gazillionth time.

Remember friends as you pass by

As you are now, so once was I,

As I am now, so you must be,

Prepare for death and follow me

"'Chills', gets me every time, Uncle Hollofax," Mia said before fist bumping the headstone and turning to walk the twenty-seven feet it would take to finish crossing the tiny graveyard.

There was so much spooky shit in this little town that it all kinda rolled off your back after a month of seeing doors open that were closed, cackles from people in your house that weren't there, and of course, the one unused red balloon she found on her way to school in the darkness just before dawn every morning.

It lay there flat and innocuous enough that it didn't frighten Mia the first time she saw it. It was more of an intrigue than anything. Mia was the youngest in town and her balloon days had been long over by the time they moved to Mozelle.

Mia walked to the corner two blocks down Main Street and met an Uber driver who took her to school in Union, a few miles up the road. Technically, Mozelle was a no man's land, no buses had to come, but she could choose to be homeschooled or go to the nearest school upon procuring her own transportation, of course. It was anybody's guess why the Uber driver wouldn't come down two more blocks, but there was no way Mia was doing homeschooling. Hell, she even signed up for after-school activities and zero hours before school started as a study hall. Anything to get out and stay out of Mozelle.

All of that meant walking through no man's land in the dark to the Uber pick-up. Which so far hadn't come to much more than a handful of red balloons, and lately a few blue and yellow ones too.

The older kids were all in high school and had a two-hour later start time, staggered with the other schools in the district due to budget cuts. With less money, the school chose to stagger their opening and closing times and the start time for high school was two hours later than Mia's middle school.

"Fuckers," she thought about the boys and how the buses they didn't take because they shared a car were forcing Mia to start her day just before dawn as if she were in a really bad horror movie from the eighties.

The stripey green and burgundy sweater tied around her waist signified she was well aware of the joke her life had recently become. She originally had worn the thing ironically at an ugly Christmas sweater party last year, but upon unpacking it during the move, everything in her bones knew that this sweater was her first dip into the emo pool clothing department and the water felt just fine. And not to be too girly or anything, but a pair of combat boots covered in roses had already made its way to the top of her Christmas list.

So, her slightly spooky life went on and as the days passed Mia made a few friends at school who of course called her "Freddy" which she minded not one bit. I mean, if you're going to have a nickname in high school, you could do a lot worse than Freddy.

Around week two, Mia began to forgive her mother for moving them here. I mean she was still pissed but was old enough to understand that no money meant making serious sacrifices. In their case, it was a couple of deadbeat dads who never paid a dime in child support along with stagnant wages and unholy rent increases that landed them in this mess. It was a letter from a lawyer informing Mom she'd inherited a whole town from a long-lost family member that had them packed up and headed for Mozelle with Mom's best friend of course.

When they arrived they realized there wasn't another soul in town which gave them the pick of the litter in homes. The moms choose side-by-side white two stories with wrap-around porches. It was picturesque as long as you ignored the standard haunted house sounds and sightings, which when you had no money was a lot easier to do.

Business as usual until October twenty-fourth when Mia strode through the graveyard on the way home, stopping to have her usual talk with Uncle Hollofax. The poor man had become her therapist in the afterlife. He knew everything about her; good thing his lips were sealed. Anyway, Mia was just wrapping up her talk with Hollofax when she remembered the green apple jolly rancher in her back pocket and suddenly felt compelled to give it to him. So, she did.

And just as she was turning to leave, there came a very proper, "Thank you, Freddy, or would you prefer I call you Mia?"

Because Mia regularly had the shit scared out of her she didn't flip out as much as one might think and instead just turned her head back toward Hollofax's headstone. And there he stood, leaning against it, looking like a dapper young man from the 1940s.

"You look good for someone who is sixty-five... and dead," was all Mia could think to say.

"So, what's it to be? Mia or Freddy? Freddy or Mia?"

"I'll be Freddy and you'll be Hollofax. Now that we have the niceties out of the way, do you mind telling me how you're here and why you look twenty-seven?"

"Simple answers, because I liked the way I looked at this age, and because you gave me an offering when the veil was thin enough for me to cross over and say thank you."

"Veil?"

"Yes, Freddy, the veil. And you gave me that offering just in time. Living in a place like Mozelle and not knowing about the veil is like walking into a lion's den with a blindfold on. Honestly, both are dumb, but as you are a child and have little say as to where you live, I've decided you need a little education to survive the impending onslaught."

"Onslaught?" Freddy began to tremble.

"Let's start with Millicent. She's going to get closer and scarier until her story plays out. She's the one leaving the balloons."

"What's that all about anyway?"

"They are just little toys that came in loaves of Wonder Bread in a long bygone era. What's more important is that you picked up the balloons and kept them."

"Let me guess, that offering thing goes two ways?"

"Yes."

"Fuck."

"Exactly. Listen, Freddy. I can't leave the cemetery even if I wanted to, but I can see most everything from here on the corner and Millicent is up to no good.

"What exactly do you mean no good?"

"Take this," Hollofax said as he held out a necklace of gold with an H pendant the size of a dime on it. "It will show the others I look over you. It might help keep you safe as the veil continues to thin."

Freddy wasted no time putting the necklace around her neck while asking, "The veil? Tell me more about the veil, Hollofax." When she looked up he was gone.

"Guess that's all the help one jolly rancher gets ya," Freddy said as she looked around, finding no sign of Hollofax anywhere, with the exception of the marble slab in her face indicating his death decades before. She googled "The Veil".

Freddy reached to feel the little gold H on the necklace to remind herself she wasn't dreaming and found it there. The backside where it rested against her skin already warm to the touch, while the front of the pendant remained as cold as the grave.

Chills ran down her spine as the cold ran straight to her bones. It wasn't the kind of cold she liked, and it wasn't the kind of cold she'd ever known. Winter's cold came with a promise of springtime, this kind of cold held no promise at all.

The next few mornings she could feel Millicent watching her from behind this tree and that, as she made her way to the uber stop, the following days got even more interesting, with Millicent peeking around the trees and giggling.

Freddy's nerves could take it no more and the following morning, October thirty-first to be exact, Freddy made a peace offering and laid it by the first tree she knew Millicent frequented. A PB&J on Wonder Bread. After putting the offering near the tree, Freddy began to whistle as she sauntered on her way.

"He's no good, you know." Freddy heard from behind her. She knew exactly who Millicent meant.

"He hasn't caused me any harm," Freddy answered, her back still to Millicent.

"You're a little older than he usually likes, but left with no other choice, I suppose he was willing to alter his peccadillos to suit the situation. I used to walk this way to school too."

Freddy brought her fingers up to the pendant and felt the chill of the grave still present as she turned toward Millicent.

Millicent sort of floated there in front of her, a beautiful girl in 1930s clothing right down to little white lace socks and black patent leather shoes. But of all the things Millicent wore, it was the H pendant resting at her throat that took Freddy's breath away.

"Death cannot stop the kind of sickness Thomas Hollofax has. Stay out of that graveyard, Freddy." And with that, Millicent was gone.

Freddy spent the entire day at school trying, with no success, to remove the necklace Uncle Hollofax had given her. How could she have not seen it before? It was so fucking clear now, even the thought of Hollofax turned her stomach.

Freddy took a wide berth around the cemetery on her way home, but it was no use. The necklace pulled like a noose around her neck, closer and closer to the edge of the cemetery and the shadow of Uncle Hollofax leaning smugly against his grave. And just beyond that on the outskirts of the other side of the graveyard stood at least twenty little girls from the ages of eleven to sixteen, every last one wearing a little gold chain pendant.

"Oh my god," Freddy whispered as she struggled against the chain that pulled her by the neck toward the giant tombstone. "Help, Millicent, Help!" Freddy cried to the one young girl she recognized at the front of the pack as she was pulled across the cemetery grass and into Hollofax's arms.

"We can't go in there. We weren't buried on hallowed ground like Hollofax, we were buried wherever he left us. But don't worry, we won't let him use your life force to leave the cemetery and cause even more harm."

"Did you hear that, Hollofax? You take one step out of that cemetery and you're dead forever, we will capture your soul and never let it return to rest, Freddy will be your last victim, Uncle Hollofax."

"What? No! No, no, no." Freddy pleaded and cried as the girls outside the cemetery reassured her it would be ok, that she would be buried on hallowed ground, that her soul would go on, that she would be free, that it would all stop with her.

From her perch atop Hollofax's towering tombstone, the birdseye view of twenty little girls invoking a curse that sucked Hollofax's spirit into an old glass medicine bottle was the stuff of nightmares. Sounds from what could only be the pits of hell screamed across Mozelle as the ghost fought with all he had to remain free, but the girls were stronger, their power together was more than he could withstand on his own. Now it was Hollofax's turn to plead as he was sucked along with the sounds from Hell into the little glass prison in Millicent's hand.

Freddy looked down upon her lifeless body laying eyes wide open on Hollofax's grave.

"Millicent?" Freddy called out across the quiet graveyard. "Am I dead?"

"Very," Millicent answered as Freddy's pendant fell loose from her neck to be swallowed like rain by the ground below.

Sources:

http://www.vastpublicindifference.com/2010/02/remember-me-as-you-pass-by.html

13

GRIMM'S WOODS

LETA HAWK

A SOLITARY MAN, TALL and imposing in his heavy coat, separated from the group and turned to face the others. Their low, murmured conversations and nervous titters faded into silence as he stepped up onto the root of a gnarled, old oak tree. Leaning against the trunk for support, he raised his lantern to survey the faces before him, his eyes glittering in the yellow-orange light.

Eighteen, he thought with satisfaction. *My biggest tour yet.* However, getting a head count wasn't the only thing on the man's agenda. As his gaze landed on a fresh-faced coed, his lips parted in a sneer.

Bingo!

Curt Hampton had been a tour guide with Boos in the Burg for only a few months, but in that short time, he had gained a reputation of showing customers "a spooky good time." In addition to possessing a deep, resonant voice and natural story-telling ability, he prided himself on his powers of observation.

He had quickly learned every tour group was made up of three types of people: skeptics, scaredy-cats, and those who were just there for a good time. Those who were in it for fun were usually easy to please; as long as they got a good story, they were happy, and any unexplained noises or shadows they might experience along the way were just an added bonus.

The skeptics were an entirely different story. That lot was difficult, if not impossible, to please. He had learned almost immediately not to tangle with them or to attempt to sway their beliefs; nothing short of a flaming demon from hell would ever penetrate the walls of their cynicism and make them believe in the supernatural. It was best to give polite answers to their questions and to ignore their heckling.

It was the third group that was his bread and butter. Curt had built the bulk of his reputation by targeting the scaredy-cats. He had learned to pinpoint the most gullible attendees and play upon their obvious fear of the supernatural. By watching their facial expressions and body language, he could determine how to play upon their fears and phobias until their nervousness spilled over into the rest of the group, making them ripe and ready to be deliciously frightened. Judging by the too-wide eyes and hunched shoulders of the young woman clinging to her boyfriend near the front of the group, he had found his target for this evening's scare.

Evelyn Martin pressed closer to her boyfriend Sean, making it nearly impossible to walk without stumbling. When some fearsome creature with enormous wings appeared out of the darkness and fluttered past right in front of her face, she let out a loud squeal and jumped back, causing Sean to stagger and drop his flashlight. With a huff, he glared at his girlfriend as he bent down to snatch it up.

"Evelyn, would you chill?" he hissed, swatting at the insect that had sought the warmth of his flashlight beam. "It's a freakin' moth, not the Mothman."

"Sorry," Evelyn mumbled as she took a step away from him, embarrassed by the snickers that erupted around them. She couldn't help feeling jittery; for as long as she could remember, she'd heard her grandmother's stories about Grimm's Woods and the things that had happened there—things that *still* happened there. If she'd known before tonight that Grimm's Woods was on the itinerary, she never would have agreed to this, but it was too late to back out now.

As the group approached the edge of the woods, her eyes darted this way and that, trying to see—but hoping she wouldn't—what it was that had set her teeth on edge and made her insides turn to a quivering mass as soon as the trees had come into view. Was it just her own trepidation, fueled by her grandmother's stories, that was making her tense, or was there indeed something waiting in the woods?

She pressed close to Sean once more, scrunching down into her coat to make herself smaller, less visible to whatever might be lurking deep within the dense copse of trees. Despite keeping herself as close to the center of the group as possible to avoid lagging behind, she still felt exposed and conspicuous, as though someone—or some*thing*—had fixed evil eyes on her and was watching, waiting to catch her alone.

Trying to dispel the unsettling notion, Evelyn swallowed hard and turned her attention back to the tour guide, who had begun speaking.

"This is Grimm's Woods." Curt extinguished his lantern, and the rest of the group likewise switched off flashlights and cell phones, plunging them into an inky darkness that the dim glow of the harvest moon on the horizon could barely penetrate.

"The site gets its name not only from the Grimm family, who staked the first claim here in these woods" —He directed a laser pointer off into the woods behind him— "but also from the settlement's grim ending."

"So, what happened to them?"

Curt's eyes zeroed in on the silhouette of Brody, one of several skeptics in tonight's group. Even though darkness masked the older man's features, Curt could hear the smirk in his tone. Trying to keep his voice low and steady, he responded, "No one really knows."

Scoffing laughter and derisive murmurs rose like a cloud of biting mosquitoes from the crowd, shaking his confidence and making him curse his decision to throw out such a trite line. Glad for the shadows that hid the bob of his Adam's apple as he swallowed hard, Curt paused—he hoped—dramatically. *Just give it a minute*, he coached himself. *Don't get defensive, or you'll lose 'em.*

As he waited for the group to settle, his gaze rested once more on the young woman. In the dim light, he could just make out her mouth, darker against the fair skin of her face, set in a straight line that suggested that Brody's comment and the crowd's resulting cynicism had alleviated some of her anxiety.

However, before he gave in to the fear that tonight's tour was in danger of falling flat, he noticed that despite her outward expression of bravado, her eyes were still wide with apprehension. Certain he could bring her fear to the forefront once more and turn this crowd in his favor, he drew himself up taller and focused his attention on her as he continued his tale.

"No one really knows what happened to the Grimm family. Legend has it that the Carpenters, another family who'd settled nearby, about a quarter mile that way"—He directed his laser pointer behind him and off to his right—"came to call one morning and found the place abandoned. The cabin door stood wide open, and the ashes in the hearth were still warm as though a fire had been left to burn overnight. None of the family's belongings were missing, including their wagon and a pair of spooked horses in the barn, but there was no trace of the family."

Soft gasps and murmurs rose around Evelyn, and a shiver of fear raced down her spine, displacing her moment of skeptical disbelief. Her gaze once again drifted behind the tour guide, to the trees that hid... what? Again, she sensed some presence that watched and listened, waiting for someone foolish enough to enter the woods.

With some difficulty, she tore her gaze away from the woods and focused again on the tour guide's face... and immediately wished she hadn't. Milky moonlight shone on his visage, and she imagined for a moment that it was no longer the tour guide from Boos in the Burg who spoke, but rather one of the ill-fated members of the Grimm family come back from the grave to tell of his fate.

She gave her head a shake to banish both the image of a spectral storyteller and her urge to turn and run back toward town. Her scalp prickled as the tour guide glossed over the Carpenters' findings, leaving out the grisly details she'd overheard her grandmother sharing when she thought the children were asleep. Either he didn't know, or he simply chose not to share reports of the strange markings gouged into the door of the cabin, or the way the barn doors hung askew, as though someone or something had attempted to enter.[FJ1]

A woman in the back interrupted the narrative to ask sensibly, "Well, what did the Carpenters do? Did they go looking for the family?"

"Indeed, they did," the tour guide acknowledged, fixing his gaze once more on Evelyn. "They spent the better part of the day combing these woods, looking for any trace of the missing family, any clues to their whereabouts, but they found nothing."

Nothing but some blood-stained shreds of clothing and a single child's shoe, Evelyn thought, her eyes trained once more on the dark thicket behind the tour guide, where she was certain she had just seen a darker shadow pacing back and forth.

"Come nightfall, the Carpenter family locked themselves inside their own cabin, barricading the door and securing the shutters over their windows, fearful of whatever unseen evil had befallen their neighbors." As he spoke, the back of his neck began prickling as though he felt someone watching him, unseen, from the cover of the trees. His eyes sought the young woman whose fears he'd been provoking all evening, and he once again found her attention focused on the woods behind him, as though she saw something there. Beads of cold sweat formed on his forehead as it occurred to him that this didn't look like the run-of-the-mill, scared-by-a-ghost-story fear he was used to seeing. Running his tongue across lips that had gone suddenly dry, he rationalized that he'd done so good a job of scaring her that he'd made himself jumpy in the process... *Or else she knows something I don't.*

A jolt went through him as he recalled his boss' initial hesitation in allowing him to add Grimm's Woods to his rotation. In fact, he was well aware that the only reason she'd agreed at all was because he'd hinted, maybe a little less than truthfully, that their biggest competitor was already considering the location for Halloween. Eager to get the jump on her rival, she'd reluctantly given him the go-ahead. *I just hope this doesn't come back to bite me*, she'd said, giving him a pointed look. *Or you.*

Swallowing hard, he realized that in his haste to seal the deal and be the first guide to lead a ghost tour into Grimm's Woods, he had neglected to do his usual research on the location. What if there was more to the story than he'd heard from the local teens? What if the timid young woman in the tour group knew something about the family's fate that he didn't?

Suddenly, feeling threatened by the darkness, he picked up his lantern and relit it with trembling fingers. Tearing his eyes away from the nervous young woman before him, he rushed to conclude his story with a shaky voice.

"The story goes that many times that night, the Carpenters heard blood-curdling shrieks from deep within the woods. More than once, the doors and shutters banged and shook as though something was trying to get in. When morning came, the family scrambled to throw together their belongings and supplies, and they abandoned their cabin. When they stopped in the nearest town a couple hours east and related what had happened, many of the old-timers crossed themselves against the evil that inhabited Grimm's Woods. To this day, on a crisp, cold, autumn night, when the harvest moon is full, you can still hear the tortured cries of the Grimm family deep within this very wood."

Chancing a brief glance over his shoulder, Curt stepped down from the tree root and gave a tight smile to his audience. "I hope you've all enjoyed tonight's Boos in the Burg ghost tour. Please stay together as we make our way back to town."

That's it? As the tour guide held up his lantern and made his way back through the group, Evelyn's knees went weak with relief. She'd been certain that he'd take them into the woods to investigate whatever remained of the small settlement, but she'd been wrong, wonderfully wrong. The tour was over, and no evil had befallen them. She beamed up at Sean, about to tell him how much she'd enjoyed their spooky date night but froze at his expression.

"That's it?" Sean's words might have echoed her thoughts, but his attitude was decidedly different.

"I thought we were going to investigate in the woods," a woman behind Evelyn whined. "I bought a new voice recorder, especially for tonight."

"This is bogus."

"What a rip-off!"

"I told you we should have gone with Gary's Ghost Tours. They guarantee a ghost hunt."

As protests flew all around her, Evelyn met the tour guide's eyes. For the briefest instant, she was certain she saw a bit of her own dread reflected on his face, as though he, too, had sensed something sinister lurking just beyond the tree line. She held his gaze for a moment, silently pleading with him to ignore the jeers and take the group back to the safety of town. Just when she thought she'd convinced him, another voice spoke above the others.

"What'd I tell you?" Brody sneered. "All these ghost tour places are fake, and this guy and his company are the fakest of the fake. At least they got the name right—*Boos* in the Burg. *Boo! BOO!*"

When Evelyn saw the tour guide's jaw tighten amid the chorus of boos, she knew it was hopeless. With one final, apologetic glance in her direction, he forced out a laugh and turned back toward the woods. "Gotcha! Of course we're going to investigate the settlement. Follow me, but watch your step. The site is for the most part overgrown and hasn't been kept up or improved. There are roots, rocks, and branches everywhere."

Evelyn narrowed her eyes reproachfully as he pushed past her. "If you take this group into Grimm's Woods, you'll be sorry," she hissed. "We'll all be sorry."

A short time later, Curt sat on a log just off the narrow path, his lantern at his feet, questioning his decision to bring the tour group into the woods. With a shaking hand, he brought a cigarette to his lips and took a long drag. As he slowly exhaled a cloud of smoke, he listened to the voices coming from all directions.

"Hello? My name is Tina. Is there anyone here with us?"

"Did you live in this cabin? What happened the night you disappeared?"

"Did you see that? That was an EMF spike, right there!"

"If you're one of the Grimm family, make this flashlight turn on."

Curt shook his head at the stupidity. What were they playing at? What was *he* playing at? Who knew what kind of spirit would respond to their questions? He didn't know any more than they did what had really happened here. The only one who seemed to know anything was...

Evelyn sat on her own log a short distance away, hunched down in her coat, arms crossed tightly in front of her. What had started as a fun night out with Sean to celebrate their six-month anniversary had turned into a nightmare. After dinner at her favorite restaurant, he had surprised her with tickets to tonight's ghost tour. Even after learning that they would be going to Grimm's Woods, she had swallowed her objections and gamely agreed to go. However, she had drawn the line at accompanying the rest of the group into the woods for a ghost hunt, thinking Sean would give in and take her back to town. Instead, they'd gotten into a heated argument, during which he'd called her a wuss and then issued an ultimatum: either suck it up and stay with the group or walk back to town by herself.

Now here she sat in the heart of Grimm's Woods, cold and miserable and afraid, while Sean investigated with Brody and another young couple somewhere near the Carpenters' cabin. In the silent darkness, her heart pounded in her chest as her eyes darted in all directions, watching for the unsettled souls that she could sense, but not see. *Can't they feel it?* she wondered. *Aren't they afraid of what they might awaken?*

Suddenly, her gaze landed on the tour guide. In the dim light of his lantern, it was hard to read his expression, but she was sure he was pleased with himself. *Hoping for another five-star rating, Mr. Tour Guide?* She watched the tip of his cigarette glow a brighter orange as he took a drag. The wraithlike ribbon of smoke he blew out hid his face for a moment; when it cleared, he was looking directly at her. With a curl of her lip, she turned away.

Seeing the young woman's animosity directed at him, Curt made his move. He dropped his cigarette butt on the ground and crushed it with his heel, then got up and crunched through the leaves toward her.

Evelyn was on her feet before he even reached her, now more angry than afraid, and ready for a confrontation. "Why did you have to bring us out here? You could have just taken us back to town and let them investigate somewhere" —she was going to say *safer*— "else."

"Yeah, right, and miss out on leading the first ghost hunt in these woods?" He let out a short laugh, trying to convince himself, if not her, that he'd been justified in bringing the group here. "Listen to them. They're having a blast."

Her face contorted with disgust and disbelief. She'd certainly read him right, hadn't she? "Anything for a five-star review, right *Curt*?" She reached out to flick his nametag. "This should read *Curt the Creep*."

Just in time, he stopped himself from slapping her hand away. It wouldn't do to have it on record that he'd struck a customer, especially a female, even if it was justified. "What is with you anyway? Are you just a wuss, like your boyfriend said, or do you know something about this place that I don't?"

As soon as the words left his lips, her demeanor went from combative to apprehensive, as though he'd just reminded her where she was. She took a step back and began looking around wildly, as though she'd heard something. Meeting his eyes again, she asked low, "You mean, you really don't know?"

"Know what?" Curt exploded, throwing his arms wide. "For God's sake, woman, if you know something about this place, then tell me! What happened out her that has you so scared?"

"No one really knows," she said, mocking his earlier line. When he glared at her, she elaborated. "No, Curt, no one knows what happened to the Grimm family, but it's well documented that the Carpenters found more than an abandoned homestead that morning."

The sensation of ice water being poured down his back made Curt shiver. "What...what did they—"

A scream from the direction of the Carpenters' cabin cut him off. "What was that? Did you see that?"

"That wasn't human," another voice answered. "I don't know what it was."

Curt had just snatched up his lantern and bolted into the trees toward the first scream when another cry came from a different direction, further off. Then a third voice cried out from the vicinity of the Grimm's homestead. "Something scratched me!" Soon, screams—both human and non-human—came from every direction, along with the sound of crashing trees, snapping branches, and bodies being struck by...by what?

With the light from Curt's lantern gone, Evelyn was left alone in the pitch-black woods. She stood frozen, listening to the horrific sounds all around her, too frightened to even switch on her flashlight. *Is that a wise thing to do anyway? I don't really want to draw attention to myself*—she swallowed hard—*or see what's out there.*

As she stood contemplating whether she should stay where she was or strike out on her own to find Sean, she realized that everything had gone eerily, deathly silent. The screams and shouts had ceased, along with the sounds of death and destruction. Not even a breath of wind stirred the leaves that still clung to the branches.

"H-hello?" Though her voice came out as little more than a whisper, it was loud in her ears, and she shrank back, startled.

There was no answer.

Just as she opened her mouth to call out again, something in the trees caught her eye. She took a step forward and squinted to see what it was. A tiny, yellow point of light winked on and then off. A moment later, it winked again, a few feet further away, and then again.

A firefly, Evelyn realized. *It's a firefly.*

Forgetting her fear and whatever had just happened in the woods, she hurried after it, hoping against hope that maybe it would make its way out of the woods and into the field beyond. Then she could run back to Boos in the Burg and call for help, even though she was certain that Sean, Curt, and all the others were beyond help.

Inexperienced in running through thickly wooded deer paths in the dark, Evelyn was soon winded, and her face and hands bore scratches from branches and thorns she'd encountered, but still she doggedly followed the tiny beacon that continued to flash every few seconds. At times she'd lose sight of it, and then stand looking around wildly, uttering tearful prayers under her breath. When at last it appeared again, she'd resume the chase, seemingly always getting closer, but never able to catch up to it.

After what seemed like hours, she saw what appeared to be moonlight shining through a break in the trees up ahead. With renewed strength, she ran ahead even faster, heedless of the branches that snagged her clothes and her hair as though trying to keep her from reaching her destination. When at last she shoved her way through the remaining brush, she found herself not in the field close to town, but instead in a place where the trees had thinned just enough to allow the moon to shine through the branches.

As she looked around to get her bearings, she had the distinct feeling that she wasn't alone. For the first time since she'd burst into the clearing, she saw the flashing yellow point of light that had led her here. Something about the light didn't seem quite right, and she took a step back as her thoughts cleared. It suddenly occurred to her that it was the end of September, and the weather was too cold for fireflies. *Then what is it?*

Fear rose into her throat, threatening to choke her, as she sensed some sinister force gathering around her like a storm. All at once, the yellow light vanished, and in its place stood a dark, faceless form. It slipped out of the trees on the opposite side of the clearing and started toward her at an impossible speed.

She screamed and turned to run back into the trees. The moon suddenly disappeared behind a cloud, as though it couldn't bear to watch the fate of the young woman who tried desperately to escape an unspeakable horror.

———

Curt thundered through the trees, oblivious to the searing pain in his twisted ankle and the blood that kept trickling into his eye from a gash on his forehead. His mind was singularly focused on getting out of these demon-infested woods and finding the others. A glimpse of moonlight through the trees up ahead renewed his strength, and he pushed forward toward his goal. As he burst out of the woods and into the field, he came to an abrupt halt, bewildered, unable for a moment to get his bearings.

"There he is! Curt! Over here!"

Relief surged through his veins as he spotted his group in the middle of the field. Some lay sprawled on their backs, while others sat half-upright in the grass. All were breathing heavily, as though they'd been running for their lives, just as Curt had. It was obvious, even at first glance, that none had come out of their ordeal completely unscathed, but from what he could gather, no one was seriously injured.

Curt barely made it to the others before collapsing in a heap, his lungs burning, and his ankle throbbing unbearably. For a moment, he lay with his eyes squeezed shut, clutching his ankle and replaying in his mind the horrific events he'd just endured. When he could bear the memories no longer, he rolled onto his back and opened his eyes to stare up at the harvest moon, which had just peeked through the clouds almost directly overhead. He blinked in disbelief, recalling that the moon had just risen when they'd arrived at the edge of Grimm's Woods. *Dear God, how long were we in there?*

Sitting up, he turned his attention to the others. He shuddered as he listened to their broken narratives of the terrors they'd experienced—glowing red eyes in the trees, the growls of some unknown beast, inhuman screams and tortured human cries, shadows roaming in and around the ruined foundation of the Grimm's cabin...

He shook his head and squeezed his eyes shut once more, trying to banish the remembered image of the tall, hooded figure that had pursued him as he tried to escape the woods. Time and time again, it had fallen behind him only to reappear again in front of him, forcing him to change direction again and again until he was utterly lost and had given up hope of ever finding his way out.

"Where's Evelyn?"

It took a moment for the voice to break through his mental torment. "Wha...what?"

"Where is she? Where's my girlfriend?" Sean had made his way on hands and knees over to Curt.

"I... I don't know. I left her... by the log on the path..." Curt gestured helplessly toward the woods. He hadn't given the timid young woman a thought since grabbing the lantern and running toward the ghost hunters' screams.

"What do you mean you left her?" His glassy eyes blazed with worry, fear, and anger as he seized Curt by the throat and brought his face dangerously close. "You said you'd stay with her. *You were supposed to keep her safe!*"

Too exhausted and weak to even raise his hands to defend himself, Curt choked out, "I... I'm... sorry. I..."

"*Evelyn!*"

Sean released the tour guide, letting him drop to the ground like a sack of potatoes. With a grief-stricken howl, he got to his feet and began half-staggering, half-sprinting toward the woods. Before he could make it ten yards, Brody and two other men had raced after him and wrestled him to the ground. Still struggling to free himself, Sean extended a hand toward the trees, screaming his girlfriend's name over and over.

Curt lay on the ground in a daze, watching the scene before him, yet feeling it was all a dream, a horrible, far-away dream. The only thing that was real at that moment was the young woman's voice echoing in his head. *I...told...you...you'd...be...sorry...*

14

HIGH HEELS AND SNOW BLOWERS

REBECCA LINAM

"I'VE HAD ENOUGH!" KATRIN shouted with a dangerous gleam in her eyes. "I swear it will be a cold day in Hades before I buy a pair of high heels!"

Philipp, her boyfriend, sat in the obligatory men's waiting chair at the shoe store flipping through the news feed on his phone. "Tell that to Anastasia."

Katrin ripped the pair of high heels from her feet and waved them at his head like a ninja's sword. "And risk having your sister turn into a bridezilla? I don't think so."

Anastasia, Philipp's sister, had ended up a bridesmaid short and that was when Katrin was drafted. The past three months had been a series of one shoe shop after the other. At first, Anastasia accompanied Katrin to what seemed like every shoe store in Rhode Island. Then they moved on to Connecticut.

After that, Anastasia left Katrin on her own because she was too busy arranging the perfect wedding.

"Forest green high heels with silver trim," Philipp said, shaking his head. "Why does it matter what type of shoes you wear?"

Katrin shrugged. She had been living in the United States of America for almost a year and still didn't understand the whole wedding phenomenon. In her homeland of Germany, most people got married at the Standesamt, the equivalent of a courthouse, and had money left over for more important things, like a house. High heels had never been a big deal.

Speaking of high heels, here it was, the day before Anastasia's wedding, and Katrin still hadn't found the perfect pair to meet Anastasia's expectations. To make matters worse, it was the first week of December, and everyone and his mother-in-law was out shopping.

"Mama, ich habe Hunger," a small voice said behind Katrin.

Katrin turned to see her six-year-old daughter, Jana, looking up at her with large eyes. "I'm hungry, too. Let's go get something to eat. The shoes can wait."

Philipp stood, stretched, and headed for the exit. "See you tonight, Katrin. I'll stop by after work. Good luck with the shoes."

———————

Later that afternoon, Philipp had finished up his shift at the hardware store when he smelled smoke. Looking around, he saw no sign of fire, and the usually over-sensitive fire alarm was strangely silent.

"Might as well check it out," he said out loud.

The store was empty except for a tall man in a long, dark trench coat near aisle seven eyeballing an expensive snow blower. Philipp cruised each aisle checking any wall outlets for possible electrical fires. So far, nothing looked suspicious, yet the fiery smell had gotten stronger. Now it had an additional odor of sulfur.

Upon entering aisle seven, Philipp bit his tongue to keep from gagging. There stood the same tall man in a dark coat looking at snow blowers.

"How can I help you, sir?"

The man had dark skin and a black beard, and his head was surrounded *by* a black turban of thick cloth.

Probably some religious thing, Philipp thought. Best not to ask.

He wore long, rubber boots similar to those of the volunteer fire department down the road and a pair of dark sunglasses. However, the most peculiar thing was the man's aftershave; he positively reeked of a forest fire gone wrong.

"Ja," the man said with a heavy accent. "I vant someting to remove snow."

German, Phillip thought.

"Well, you've come to the right place," he answered, coughing away at least two years of his life. "This is our best model. Out of all other models, it tested the best in—"

"I vill take it," the man said.

Grabbing the heavy box, he clomped his way to the nearest checkout counter in his long, rubber boots and paid for the snow blower with a fistful of sooty hundreds.

"Thank you, sir," Philipp said, smiling broadly at the man. Eighteen hundred dollars at *a* five percent commission meant he would earn ninety dollars on the sale.

The man turned to give him a crooked smile. "No. Thank you."

Philipp took a double look, but the man had disappeared into the dark parking lot. He could have sworn he had seen the man's tongue flick out, forked like a snake. Then again, it wasn't every day a clone of Lucifer himself showed up at the hardware store to buy a snow blower. Never mind there wasn't a millimeter of snow outside nor a snowball's chance for a freeze in the long-term forecast.

"I bought some high heels," Katrin told Philipp later that night at supper. He often stopped by her apartment for one of her tasty German meals. "Jana and I found some like Anastasia wanted after lunch."

Philipp laughed so hard he almost choked on his bratwurst.

Katrin glared at him. "What's so funny?"

"That explains why I saw Lucifer buying a snow blower today at work!"

"Huh?" Katrin looked confused.

"Didn't you say it would be a cold day in Hades before you bought—"

"Yeah," Katrin cut him off. "Something like that."

Philipp put down his fork, grinning. "Well, today, some strange-looking dude with a forked tongue walked in smelling like fire and brimstone and bought the biggest snow blower in stock."

Six-year-old Jana looked up in surprise. "Did he have long horns and hoofs like a goat?" she asked in almost flawless English.

Philipp laughed again. "No clue, but he did have on a dark turban, rubber boots, and walked kind of weird."

"Krampus," Jana said with a straight face. "You met Krampus, and I bet he was hiding his horns under the turban and his cloven hooves with the boots. Was he carrying a large basket on his back with naughty kids in it?"

"Who? What?!" Philipp almost choked on his spätzle.

Katrin laughed, "It's an old German tradition. Krampus is to bad kids what St. Nikolaus is to good kids."

"And he drags you down to hell in a basket if you're bad," Jana finished. "If you're good, St. Nikolaus fills your shoes with goodies. That's tomorrow night, you know." Suddenly, she turned to Katrin with worry written all over her face. "Mama, does St. Nikolaus come to kids in America."

"Ja, natürlich. He knows whether or not you've been good, so don't you think he knows we moved to America?"

Jana returned to her spätzle. "Well, yes. And besides, if Philipp saw Krampus today, then St. Nikolaus must be here in Rhode Island too."

Philipp laughed, "Krampus can't be worse than a bridezilla who doesn't have every bridesmaid in the right shade of high heel."

"Anastasia's not that bad," Katrin replied with a roll of her eyes. "Then again, if I sprain my ankle walking down the aisle, she might turn into something worse than Krampus."

———————

Before leaving for Anastasia's wedding, Katrin made sure to fill Jana's shoes with the usual goodies for St. Nikolaus Day—nuts, small chocolates, and a few tiny toys. She hid them in the kitchen cupboard where they would be ready to sit outside after the wedding. It was reassuring to have these old customs to fall back on in another country. Katrin remembered fondly all the years of running out to the doorstep early on the morning of December sixth to see whether or not St. Nikolaus had left her something. There was always the fear in the back of her mind that maybe Krampus would be waiting there on the doorstep for her instead, but no one really believed it; it was just an old superstition.

Philipp came to pick up Katrin and Jana in his classic, red Mustang.

"Because we're going to arrive in style at Anastasia's wedding," he said, raising his eyebrows. "No girlfriend of mine is going to disgrace the bride by arriving in a sub-par car."

Katrin gave him a pointed look but gave him a kiss on the cheek. "At least it will be over in a few hours. Then I can get out of these cursed high heels."

"And I'll get something from St. Nikolaus!" Jana added, waving her basket of flowers around. Anastasia had insisted Jana be one of her three flower girls.

They arrived two hours early and went through the usual American customs: hiding the bride from the groom, making sure the bride's veil wasn't crooked, *and* rearranging the bride's twenty-foot train. By the time the ceremony started, Katrin was ready to give up the idea of marriage forever and join the nearest nunnery.

"Remember, pace yourself," the wedding planner kept telling Katrin. The shriveled, raspy-voiced lady of at least ninety had coached her up and down the church aisle in high heels for a solid hour. "Stand up straight. No, pull your shoulders back. Good. No, don't stick your bottom out. Yes, that's it. No, don't waddle like a duck. Slower. No, faster. Just... just... walk!"

Katrin was the last bridesmaid to walk down the aisle. Every girl before her had managed to do it effortlessly. Katrin just wanted to make it through the ceremony without a broken ankle.

"Breathe, Katrin," the wedding planner whispered, sending her down the aisle.

Katrin took a breath. She counted the steps—one, two, three, wobble, four.

To her left, she passed Philipp sitting next to the aisle giving her a thumbs-up sign. So far, so good. She looked straight ahead to where Jana stood with the other flower girls.

Then Katrin fell flat on her face.

"Mama!" Jana cried out, and a gasp went up from the audience.

At the back of the church, Katrin heard Anastasia screaming bloody murder.

I can't be the only bridesmaid in history who's ever tripped over her own two feet in a wedding.

"It's—it's a monster!" the wedding planner's raspy voice croaked.

Out of the corner of her eye, Katrin saw Philipp stand up and wave toward the commotion. "Hey, mister! Aren't you the guy who bought the snow blower yesterday?"

Meanwhile, a pair of cloven hooves stomped down the aisle. Katrin managed to get back on her feet and found herself face to face with the biggest, smelliest creature ever to crawl out of German folklore.

"You belong to me!" the red-eyed man growled, two curvy horns poking out of his head.

It didn't occur to Katrin until a few seconds later the man was speaking German. Then she gagged; he smelled like ten bonfires of sulfur and brimstone wrapped in one.

"Who—who are you?" she choked out, eyeballing the basket he carried on his back.

"You know who I am, Katrin," the man spat. "You feared every year I would come for you instead of St. Nikolaus, and now I'm here."

"Krampus!" Jana screamed from her place among the flower girls. "Krampus, why are you here? I've been good, and so has Mama!"

Katrin gawked at him in disbelief. "Krampus? But you're just a legend!"

With a backdrop of screams and cell phone videos, the man pulled a chain from the basket on his back and pulled it taut. "You swore an oath on my homeland and then broke it. You've created all sorts of problems for my boss, not to mention *keeping* me from my duties. I'm supposed to be out snatching up little kids tonight, but instead, I'm stuck buying snow blowers and salt to get rid of the snow down in hell."

Suddenly, she remembered.

I swear it will be a cold day in Hades before I buy a pair of high heels!

"And if you don't take it back, I will personally drag you down to pay for your careless oath, snow or not."

Katrin felt like kicking herself. Not only had she ruined Anastasia's wedding over a pair of high heels, but she was about to be dragged off into the pits of hell right in front of two hundred wedding guests and her own child—not to mention it was probably already major news on Facebook.

"Anastasia will never forgive me for this," she muttered. Speaking of Anastasia, it looked like she had fainted in her father's arms at the back of the church. "Fine!" Katrin spat. She ripped the forest green high heels from her feet and tossed them at Krampus' head. "Take them! I never wanted to wear high heels anyway!"

The next few things happened all at once. Philipp burst out of the pew toward Krampus in a tackle worthy of Sunday-night football. Krampus ducked, and the high heels sailed over his head. The pointy end of both heels flew straight into Philipp's forehead and knocked him out cold.

"Great," Katrin muttered.

"Take them back," Krampus growled, his forked tongue flickering like a whip.

Katrin blinked at him. "Take them back?"

Suddenly, Katrin found Jana at her side. "Take them back to the store, Mama," Jana whispered. "You said you'd never buy high heels, so now you have to take them back to reverse it."

The scowl on Krampus's face slowly molded into a smile full of sharp, pointy teeth similar to a shark. "The child speaks the truth. You have exactly one hour before I have St. Nikolaus duty, and if you're not back by then, you belong to me!"

Snatching up Jana and the high heels, Katrin fished Philipp's car keys out of his pocket, and darted down the aisle toward the exit. A smoky fog of sulfur had enveloped the parking lot.

"Jones' Shoe Company," Katrin muttered, jumping into the driver's side of the car. "Buckle up, Jana. It's going to be a wild ride."

Katrin put the Mustang into reverse, backed out of the parking place, and kicked it into first gear. She tore out of the parking lot slinging gravel, dirt, and anything else in her way. Once she reached the interstate, she shifted gears faster than a Formula One driver; it was just like being at home on the Autobahn. Even more impressive was the fact she managed to do it all barefoot while wearing a long, tight-fitting bridesmaid's dress.

"There's the exit, Mama!"

Katrin sped away from Interstate 95 and straight toward Jones' Shoe Company so fast she left a Lamborghini behind in a cloud of dust. Two more traffic lights and they turned into the strip mall where Jones' Shoe Company was located. The clock in the Mustang read 8:01 p.m.

"Let's go!" Katrin yelled. She and Jana raced from the car only to see a blonde *salesclerk* locking the front door.

Katrin recognized the clerk from yesterday, who had been only too happy to sell a pair of eighty-five-dollar high heels on commission. She probably wouldn't be eager to hear they hadn't worked out.

"Sorry, we're closed," the lady said, not sounding the least bit sorry. She gave the keys one last twist and headed toward the parking lot.

"But you don't understand!" Katrin said. "I have to return these shoes right now."

"Please!" Jana piped up. "It's an emergency, or Krampus is going to drag my Mama down to hell!"

The clerk gave them a bored look and said, "We open tomorrow at 9:00 a.m."

Finally, Katrin had no other choice but to use the super-weapon all Germans ha*d* at their disposal. Glaring at the clerk, she took a deep breath and let it out in her loudest voice.

"Mach doch endlich mal die Tür auf, du blöde Kuh! Schnell!"

Jana's eyes grew twice as large, and the salesclerk took the shoes back with no problem despite the fact Katrin didn't have her original sales receipt or the box.

"W—would you like to trade them in for another p-pair?"

"No, that's okay," Katrin said, cringing. She hadn't wanted to call the lady a stupid cow, but it was her last hope. Fortunately, anything shouted in German, whether it be a declaration of love or war, was just plain scary. "We have to be going now. Goodbye and thank you."

"One more minute," Krampus snorted.

The front door to the church burst open, and Katrin and Jana raced inside. Nothing had really changed since they left. Anastasia was still lying in her father's arms in a faint. The audience was still taking cell phone videos of Krampus as if he were, well, a living German legend. No one had moved from the pews, and Katrin found the lack of police surprising. She wondered if the sulfur fog outside had anything to do with that.

"We're back!" Jana sang triumphantly. "Krampus, we returned the shoes!"

The smoky fog slowly dispersed. Krampus narrowed his eyes at Katrin. "Let that be a lesson to you. Never toy with things you don't understand."

He turned to Philipp who had just regained consciousness and was holding his head as if he had a migraine.

"I vill return ze snow blower tomorrow," Krampus told him in English.

Philipp looked up at him in a daze. "Dang. There goes my commission."

Two hours later, it was all over. Philipp drove Katrin and Jana back home. As soon as they got inside, the three of them collapsed at the kitchen table.

Katrin sighed, "I've had it up to here with weddings! It'll be a cold day in—"

"Mama!" Jana squealed, plastering her hands over her mother's mouth. "Not again!"

Philipp agreed with a weary nod of his head. "Yeah, we've had enough excitement for one day."

He fingered the diamond ring he had been carrying in his pocket for the last two weeks. It could wait. New Year's Eve might be better anyway, and besides, a courthouse wedding would be just fine.

And Katrin would be free to wear whatever shoes she wanted.

15

THE WHISKEY VOICE

MELISSA ROTERT

A VELVET VOICE WHISPERS through the half fog of my mind. *My e*yes flutter trying to shake the sleep from my lashes. The dream fades to finality, but the smooth, deep, drawl can still be heard. My husband sounds gravelly with a low growl, but the vibrations in my ears are whiskey in my throat, warming me through to my center and down into my toes.

I roll to the left, draping an arm where John should be, but the bed is cold beneath my flesh and a hollow dent on the pillow is the only sign he was here at all. Gone to work at four, I missed my goodbye kiss. Strange he would not wake me. My eyelids finally part*ed*, searching for the light of the alarm clock. It's darker than it should be. The digital numbers read two in the morning. My brow crinkles in confusion. But John? He should still be here.

A gentle pressure on my back eases my concern. He's come back to bed. But the voice, butter in a hot pan, tickles the small hairs in my ear, stretching my spine reflexively and triggering goosebumps on my neck. Not John. My breath catches in my clenched chest, afraid to release, hoping it's only a dream. Icy fingers trace the ridges down my back. Not cold like the exhilaration of a first touch, but sharp like frostbite. A scalpel carving me as it glides toward my tailbone. I try to turn around, but my frame is frozen in place. Welts spring up on my skin from a scratch I did not see or feel. I wince in delayed pain.

"John," I cry out. "John, help!"

The whiskey voice laughs, deep and demonic. Fear cuts into me like a serrated knife. The jagged teeth bite in with each sound.

"John!" I call again.

Two hands like shackles clasp my bare ankles. So tight, I already feel the finger-shaped bruises I know will form. I grab at the headboard as a tug of strength that I've never experienced rips me from the bed. I fly with a thump to the floor, landing so hard it knocks the air from my lungs. I wheeze and gasp, sputtering when I feel the grip release. My eyes search the darkness for answers, finding only more horror. I spot John sprawled out on the floor beside me. His eyes stare into nothing, his skin blue and coated in a fine frost.

I know he is gone.

I scramble to a sitting position, back pressed to the foot of the bed, desperate to avoid the same fate. But the monster is gone. The voice is silenced. A warmth returns to the room leaving just a set of melting footprints retreating to the window—wide open, curtain blowing in the wind.

16

THE OLD LADY AND THE DEVIL

REBECCA LINAM

LONG AGO, IN WHAT is today Germany, there lived an old lady who owned a small farm in the countryside. Every morning, Sieglinde would pack up the vegetables from her garden and go to the marketplace in the city of Aachen to sell them.

The year was 814. Emperor Charlemagne had just built a cathedral in Aachen. It was the most majestic cathedral for miles around and everyone loved it—everyone, that is, but the devil.

The devil hated it. He had made a deal with the people of Aachen. They had run out of money to build their cathedral, and he had given them money to finish it. Unfortunately, he had disguised himself as a rich man from out of town, and the people hadn't realized it until after they had made the deal. In exchange for helping them, the devil demanded the life of the first person to enter the new cathedral. The people had outwitted the devil by sending a wolf into the cathedral first.

Sieglinde had seen the whole thing unfold before her eyes. She had been there in the marketplace selling vegetables when it happened. She still remembered the way the devil's two cloven hooves clip-clopped out of the city. She especially couldn't forget his last words.

"I'll get even with you! You'll be sorry you tricked the devil!"

Since then, Sieglinde had gone to the marketplace every day to sell her vegetables. She often wondered when the devil would return to get his revenge. The rumors said he had gone up north, so Sieglinde was quite surprised when she ran into the devil on the way home from the marketplace one September evening.

"Guten Abend, Fräulein," the devil said, wishing Sieglinde a good evening.

He bowed with a smirk around the corners of his mouth. Even though he wore the clothes and hat of a traveling peddler, Sieglinde recognized the devil immediately from his two cloven hooves. Two large sacks were perched on his shoulders, and smudges of dirt lined his face.

"Guten Abend," Sieglinde replied, wondering what nasty plan the devil had up his sleeve today.

"Pray tell, good lady," the devil continued. "I am but a humble peddler. I have journeyed selling my wares, and these sacks are heavy. Can you tell me how much further it is to Aachen?"

The city of Aachen lay in sight right behind Sieglinde.

"Well," Sieglinde said, sniffing the air. The devil had dirt in his peddler's sacks. She recognized the earthy smell from her own vegetable garden. "I've just come from Aachen."

"Really?" The devil grinned. "Then it's not very far from here!"

Sieglinde shook her head and pointed to her shoes. "See my shoes? You can tell how far it is to Aachen just by looking at them."

The devil looked down at her tattered shoes. One of them was held together by a bit of old string and beeswax. The other had at least three holes and Sieglinde's toes wriggled through one of them.

"I bought these shoes new in Aachen in the marketplace," Sieglinde said. "I've worn them to pieces on the journey home."

The devil's face turned bright red. "That's too far away! At this rate I'll never get to Aachen!" he roared. "And I'm tired of carrying these heavy sacks!"

With that, the devil threw down his sacks of dirt and stomped away.

Sieglinde smiled and continued home. Not only had the devil been outsmarted twice, but she had also saved Aachen's beautiful new cathedral.

The local people say the dirt from the devil's bags became the small mountain just north of Aachen and can still be seen today. They call it Lousberg, or Lous Mountain, from the old Aachen word 'lous,' which means 'clever'.

17

I SCARE MYSELF

NICOLE SMITH

When I was little
I don't remember if I
was scared of the dark or
the monsters
living under my bed.
As an adult, the
thing I fear most
is the darkness in my head.
The depression that keeps me
weighted down,
the endless anxiety
running non-stop loops,
emotionally exhausted.
With intrusive thoughts
wiggling in,
burrowing deep,

making me believe
I'm not needed,
not wanted,
unloved.
The imposter syndrome
reminding me of
how worthless I
actually am.
Demons, monsters, poltergeists
might bring relief
to the living nightmare
of being trapped in here
with me.

18

JACK

JESSICA SCOTT

IT'S DANGEROUS TO LEAVE them unattended.

A chill runs through me. I walk a little faster.

I feel their eyes follow me. The screaming intensifies as I pass, but I dare not look. I mustn't.

If I acknowledge them, they'll see me.

I can't save them.

I release the breath I unknowingly held as the darkest light and quietest screams fade behind me.

Mustn't look back, can't look back. They'll see me.

19

THE FALL

ADELE LILES

IN THIS DISMAL AUTUMN, I stand.
Singularly dreary, a silent stone.
A spectator to horrors.
In this desolate landscape, I crumble, aware.

In my chambers, secrets sleep.
Gothic specter, a haunted shrine.
A witness to suffering.
Through soundless days, I keep them close.

In my walls, I cradle them.
Melancholy mansion, a family tomb.
A guardian of their legacy.
Under skies of insufferable gloom, I hide sorrow, guilt, and shame.

In my halls, play discordant melodies.

Time-worn tales, a cursed estate.

A watcher to agony.

Behind my vacant and eye-like windows, I smother them.

In my timbers, madness thrives.

Crumbling lineage, a cracked facade.

A sentinel over the fragments of their tragic life.

In the sullen waters of the tarn, our twisted souls are mirrored.

In my dungeon, choices are made.

Sad demise, final resting place.

An observer of misfortune.

Beneath the floor, beyond the copper archway, I cannot hold her.

In my sky, a tempest rises.

Terrible influence, destinies molded.

An orchestrator of Roderick's fear, of Madeline's plight.

Through each gust and shiver, I feel their torment.

The darkness zigzags through us. Claims us.

Sullenly.
Silently.

20

THE EYE OF SUCURI

CHRISTOPHER DEWITT

THE IMMENSE CREATURE LAY in the cool of the jungle, ancient and constant as the rotting loam through the ages, looking, to the naked eye, as if it were not moving at all.

It lay there, though coiled, its scales moving, overlapping each other in a tiny, whispering dance. The massive muscle that is its body slowly contracts and expands in a deadly, unstoppable rhythm.

The great sinuous reptile could feel a thumping against its millions of scales—the rapid, panicked beating of its prey's heart, struggling within and against its own fear. The prey's hope for escape has long fled. The thumping becomes weaker.

The scaled coils continue to squeeze onto the ever-fainter tapping of the victim's heart, feeding the great python's senses with soft, delicate brushes. The snake feels the deliberate, soft crunching of the bones of its prey, comforting it with their plentiful, gentle snapping. A sizzling tingle goes down the length of the python as it anticipates the fullness it will soon feel, and the weight of it that will leave it relatively helpless for a time. Yet it will be satisfied for a long while.

The beating of the prey's heart dwindles to the faintest tapping against the snake's cold, smooth skin. It is near the time, and the serpent feels a sudden, sharp heat at the hinges of its huge jaws. It feels them come loose of their own accord. Its fangs are quite ready to be on with it, ready to pull its prey deep into itself.

The tapping rain against the interior of the snake's coils ceases forever.

The hinges of its jaws widen impossibly, the serpent's green-prismed eyes now clouded with growing, impatient hunger. Its maw is now grotesquely agape and blinds the beast to all except what must be consumed. The lifeless thing is drawn into the python, the muscles still working, its fangs puncturing its flesh as it does, adding its warm life juices to its feast.

The reptile's breathing stops, only for a moment, then begins again, issuing from another place in its body, deep in its gullet, fetid and horrible, a place it comes from only when it feeds.

The snake does not understand it but welcomes it as it does its growing. The green-prismed eyes close a little, their transparent scales coming down to protect them as the prey moves inexorably further down, and it knows it will consume, rest, and sleep.

The great python's mind swims up from the place it thinks of as the Dark Quiet, and it knows it was only while it dreams its serpent dreams, a recent memory, and one of many. It remembers it last fed on a fat four-leg, heavy and hairy and coarse. It does not think to thank the four-leg in any way except to know that it had fed its beautiful coils and green-prismed eyes, fueling it for its next hunt. It enjoys, in its reptilian way, the dreams of the prey's heart racing, its dwindling repetition, its own powerful, relentless coils crushing life itself.

Now it can move its length with greater ease to the shade of the low bushes, to the dark coolness of the water. The water welcomes the snake with its black embrace. In this place, there is safety, the leaves and the vines lay on the surface and the python becomes one with it and disappears.

It moves here as effortlessly as the winged things move in the place the snake thinks of as the Far Above. The green-prismed eyes look just above the surface of the coolness. There is a winged thing just at the edge. Why they do not stay in the Far Above is a puzzlement to the reptile. There is safety there for them, just as there is for it in the coolness and the dark leaves. The winged things have fed its coils many times, in small measure, but they do not interest the snake now and it does not know why.

Has the four legs ruined its coils forever for a larger hunger? Many of the winged things were now at the edge of the coolness. The reptile can seize one with predatory, blinding speed.

The snake does not ponder this long and continues silently at the edge of the water, gliding easily under the leaf and the green, something forever and inexorable pulling it on. The serpent does not travel during the day, when what it thinks of as the Great Light shines so brightly high in the Far Above. It is compelled now to move and knew not why.

The sinuous creature travels through the coolness of the water farther than it has in a very long while. It eases the bottom of the coolness to rest. The green prisms atop its head fall into a watchful stillness. The bright glow of the Far Above barely pierces through the surface of the coolness.

The great snake finally, after a while, moves on, its energy is restored.

The Great Light descends, nearer the horizon, its glow now a muted orange, and the creature knows it's time is near. The time for the hunt. It lays still as Death in the coolness and the leaf and the green and it waits. It knows that in time they will come, the four legs, their thirst bringing them after feeding on the leaf of the forest.

True darkness finally befalls the tall trees surrounding the water and the python sees all.

It sees the prey's heat, great and small, between the trees. Sound means nothing to the snake.

At last, a four-leg approaches the edge of the coolness. The serpent lays still as a stone. It knows the four-leg sees it without seeing it, hiding in the mottling of the shadows cast from the surface of the coolness. It is merely another irregular shape of rotting dark green.

It waits with primordial patience.

The four-leg trots closer, its blunt-ended nose quivering, sensing. The snake watches through its unmoving green prisms not with hunger's lust, nor malice, but with infinite time, waiting.

The four-leg edges closer. The green prism sees the hairs on its back limned in the light of the moon, what the serpent knows as the Cold Eye in the now black Far Above.

Now the four-leg is within easy reach. It would take nothing for the python – in a blink of the green prism – to launch its length to it, pull it into its coils in a blur, fangs sprouting, stabbing mercilessly into it, beginning to sense-touch the terrified thumping, feel the ecstasy of the four-legs bone's soft, slow crunching beneath its skin.

It would take but an instant to begin this dance.

But beyond the heat of the four-leg is another.

A wavering blossom of heat in the distance draws the attention of the green prisms, turning the serpent from the hunger within its coils.

The four-leg moves on now, quickly, as if startled. The snake does not care. The blossom of wavering light draws it still but has not yet moved.

The four-leg is gone, now. No others are among the trees. They appear to have been warned by something, their instinct moving them away.

The blossom pulls at the python, drawing it, something within its memories, from its serpent dreams, its hunger dreams, the Dark Quiet.

It moves from the coolness of the mottled water to the hard shore. This is something rare for the great snake. It does not move as swiftly as it does in the coolness.

The wavering light and the heat of the strange blossom pulls it, and it sees another, smaller one, perhaps more distant. It does not know why, but it is pulled to them.

Then the creature sees them. The Tall Walkers. They move as the four-legs do, but instead are on two, not four. The snake thinks it strange, unnatural. To it, they are indeed bizarre creatures, but the green prism tells it that it has beheld them before, somewhere, at another time.

Oddly, they are not covered by hair. They are smooth things, like the snake, but have no scales, and sometimes have on their bodies things that are also from the forest, sometimes made from other creatures, with which they cover their hideous smoothness.

The great snake now remembers that the Dark Quiet has shown it that these Tall Walkers even cover their smoothness with the skin and the hair of once-alive fanged beasts. Beasts like the python, those that prey. The image surfaces from the Dark Quiet of one fanged beast that it has encountered. The memory brings the great snake a cold amusement. This fanged creature deigns to think the mighty python to be its prey. It ponders this for a moment. Very amusing indeed.

There are many of the Tall Walkers now. The snake watches as they slowly approach, gathering among the fiery blossoms. The heat of the blossoms is almost too much for the green prisms, but they cannot stop watching.

It pulls itself to one place among the leaves and the green of the forest. It knows the Tall Walkers cannot see it, would never see it. They are almost blind, unlike the others of the jungle. Even after the Cold Eye goes to its home and the Great Light emerges and begins its journey across the Far Above, they would not see the python in the shades of the forest.

It watches this place of the Tall Walkers carefully as the Cold Eye completes its path. It watches them even as it pulls itself up into a mighty tree that is able to support its great coils.

Just before the Great Light shows itself, it is well above the Tall Walkers.

It waits.

———————

The Great Light has completed another of its countless arcs. Throughout its journey, the serpent has slept. The Dark Quiet again showed it this place of the Tall Walkers, from a time in the very distant past. In the memory, the place is filled with many more Tall Walkers. On the far end of this place of gathering is an edifice of stone. It is lit with many more wavering blossoms of fire than before. The Dark Quiet shows the snake a table, also of stone, large and heavy. On it, lying down is a Tall Walker, its body covered with odd symbols and figures, painted on its smoothness.

Its eyes are closed.

The snake feels the familiar thumping against its skin, but it cannot be from the body of the Tall Walker on the table. The green prism shows the python that the thumping comes from the other Tall Walkers, feathers on their heads and bodies, gathered about and using sticks on hollow round things. The hollow round things are covered on one end with the skins of forest animals. The snake thinks this very strange and yet very wonderful, and the sound beckons it.

There is a huge tree with a large, thick branch reaching over the edifice. It is as large—larger—than the one in which the great snake now sleeps. The branch extends over the stone table, over the Tall Walker lying upon it.

Something forms on the branch, a shape, a black shadow, moving, long, and sleek. It is beautiful. Tremendous, powerful coils reach endlessly back into the darkness of the tree's branches.

The shape gathers itself over the stone table. The thumping from the surrounding Tall Walkers beating the round things has somehow become muted, and distorted. Their ugly, smooth-skinned faces are slackened with awe, their eyes shining in primal anticipation.

The shape uncoils itself and its head extends, green prisms of its own riding atop it, glistening with their own anticipation. That of hunger.

Down and down it goes, a steady and deliberate river of scales and muscle and Death. It slowly and carefully encircles the unmoving Tall Walker. The pounding and thumping from before has dwindled to nothing. A dark hush drapes over the edifice. Some of the surrounding Tall Walkers stare raptly, their hollow things and their sticks forgotten in their hands.

The Tall Walker on the table moves, but not of its own accord. The coils move it, closing, squeezing, tightening.

Slowly, almost reluctantly, the thumping of the sticks on the round things resumes.

Some of the Tall Walkers have fallen to their knees, touching their feathered heads to the stone floor.

The body of the Tall Walker is unseen now, engulfed in the lovely coils of the great python.

The serpent emerges from the Dark Quiet. It feels as if it had been the one that felt the bones of the Tall Walker beginning their tiny shattering, as if through its own scales and skin. It had felt the wonderful sting of the heat in its own jaws opening to receive the Tall Walker into its coils.

It envied the dream snake its feast.

The Great Light had receded and the Cold Eye glided slowly above the forest. The reptile had been in the Dark Quiet for a long time.

The gathering place of the Tall Walkers was bathed in the Cold Eye's stark light.

The great snake moves toward the edifice, reluctantly leaving the comfortable tree branches, descending its coils to the soft loam below.

It moves, as silent as the air, toward the gigantic tree looming over the edifice, and grasps the trunk with the muscle of its body, creeping ever up into the dappled shadows cast by the jungle canopy.

The serpent watches with the cautious eyes of the hunter as the Tall Walkers begin to gather in numbers, their faces painted, their heads adorned with the feathers of the winged things, carrying sticks with the fiery blossoms atop them, just as the great snake had seen in the Dark Quiet. They hold the blossoms to the various bowls that encircle the stones, the edifice gradually being bathed in their soft orange glow.

There is something else here, though, the serpent noted with its green prisms. Another Tall Walker, seeming of greater stature than the others. Its headdress rose higher, its bearing regal and commanding. The other walkers moved carefully around this one, their eyes careful not to gaze too long in its direction. The snake marks this one as their master.

The milling Tall Walkers suddenly part and step aside, making way for a small group of them carrying another of their kind, moving slowly toward the table. The form they carry appears lifeless at first, but the great python knows it is not, sensing its heat.

The snake at last reaches its final perch over the stone table as the Tall Walkers lay the motionless being onto it.

The Tall Walkers begin their thumping of the round things. It is much louder here than it was in the serpent dream. The python feels their vibrations against its scales, and it is at once soothing and electric.

The serpent's coils gather, waiting to embrace this gift. For it knows, by some ancient instinct, that this is indeed an offering. An offering to it, the Great Python.

The green prisms turn to show the Great Python the image engraved into the stone of the edifice. It is an image of endless, perfect coils, a magnificent, tapered head, jaws open wide to swallow a sphere covered mostly with the coolness of large bodies of water. The coolness is broken here and there by irregular shapes. The sphere itself is surrounded by an even greater circle, making the sphere its pupil. The eye is in the same shape as the Great Python's own green prisms

The great snake knows this eye sees all things, for it is its own.

It is the Eye of Sucuri.

The Great Python—Sucuri—Fragrant Flower of the Forest, lowers its mighty head over the offering, turning slightly, the green prisms connecting with the eyes of the master of the Tall Walkers. The eyes of this one glow with an intensity the Great Python has never before seen in any other Tall Walker.

Sucuri, god of all gods, blood of all bloods, embrace what is yours only.

The words merge into the mind of the Great Python as serpent-speak, and they are at once strange and familiar to it.

Consume of your kind, ancient Sucuri, named before time.

Its head still fixed in position, Sucuri's mighty coils entwine against each other, moving in a sinuous dance of muscle and scale and power, gleaming in the fiery light.

All is Sucuri, forever. We are Sucuri, forever.

The green prisms do not leave the master of the Tall Walker's. The Great Python remembers now that these Tall Walkers belong solely to it, that they will be everywhere and forever, and the sphere is the world that belongs to it, and they, the Sucuri, will consume it utterly.

Their eyes locked, the Great Python remembers that it was once this very priest, this master of the Tall Walkers, countless eons before, and had been transformed to perfection. Its coils are infinite and flawless, always hungering for more, their endless perfection exalted since the dawn of centuries.

The pounding of the drums is everywhere now, ceaseless in their earnest, worshipful noise, as deafening as the crashing from the black Far Above in a terrifying jungle storm.

Sucuri descends.

21

LITTLE BEAR

AMY NIELSEN

"DAMN. I'M GONNA BE late again." I rapid-fire my horn. "Move over!" I yell at the mud-caked, forest-green John Deer. The fast-paced Orlando traffic is nothing compared to the frustration of crawling behind an overgrown tortoise. I'd much rather race a hare down I-4.

I dig my cell phone out of my corduroy knapsack and call the school to tell them I'll be late. Thank God I have first-period planning. Although I still expect Principal Sanders, AKA The Sarge, armed and ready for an ambush outside the door of my sixth-grade classroom.

After calling the school, I hit play on my audiobook, a steamy, new contemporary romance. It's the only thing I look forward to on this commute from my boyfriend's house to rural North Lake. But before I can settle into the cringy love scenes that make me wish I was back in bed with Brandon, something ahead catches my attention.

A plump, medium-sized, brown teddy bear wearing a bright blue bow sits at the base of a large pine tree. Other than the tractor, there's not another vehicle, nor house, in sight.

Weird.

As my Honda Civic inches past the black-eyed stuffed animal, the tractor pulls over.

Finally!

I offer a courtesy wave. The driver, a scrawny old man in dirt-streaked overalls and a weathered baseball cap grins, exposing a missing front tooth. A shiver surges down my spine.

"You're one creepy dude," I whisper and fake a smile.

My eyes dart back and forth from the empty road to the rearview mirror. I turn a sharp corner, and finally, both *the* creepy tractor dude and the bear are out of view.

I park next to a jacked-up truck belonging to some redneck P.E. teacher. I'm pretty sure he's the one who left the love note on my car my first day that read, "Nobody in North Lake likes granola." Classy. As soon as I have some teaching experience under my belt, I'm outta here.

My racing heart slows when The Sarge isn't lurking near my classroom door to slap my wrist for being late again. But even though I dodged his bullet, I still feel—off.

Throughout the day, students come and go, bells ring, and I fake teaching. I can't shake an increasing curiosity about that damn bear and why someone placed it at the base of a tree in the middle of nowhere. It had to be intentional. By day's end, driven by a now-consuming curiosity, I dash out of the campus as soon as my last student leaves.

I don't bother turning on my audiobook. I won't be able to concentrate on it anyway. Instead, I hypothesize about the bear. Is it a memorial? A secret message to someone? A prank?

My pulse quickens when I spot him at the same tree. His bright blue bow sits in stark contrast to the pine's dark brown bark.

"Hello, there, Little Bear. Who put you there and why?"

I brake to get a better look at him. There isn't anything unusual except his large, dark eyes seemed to have, I don't know—depth. There are no signs of anything odd around him. No footprints or notes.

A horn honks. Oh shit! A car whips around me.

"Bye, Little Bear. Let's see if you're here in the morning."

I keep an eye on him in my rearview mirror until he disappears.

"Hey, Hon. How was work?" Brandon asks when I walk through the door.

"Exhausting. Is it Friday yet?"

He comes up behind me and wraps his arms around my waist, kissing my neck. "I know why you're exhausted, and it has nothing to do with teaching."

Brandon and I are still in the honeymoon phase of our relationship, and often, the nights are long. But as I lay in his bed tonight, the only thing on my mind is that damn teddy bear.

I wake early the next day, curious to see if he's still there. As I speed down the road and near the spot, I wipe sweaty palms on my long skirt.

Yesterday, he was fresh and plump, but now he's weathered from the overnight dewy mist. I stop in front of him.

"Good morning, Little Bear."

I want to get out and save him from the elements. Someone put him here. But why? That question bores into me as if the answer is as significant as the meaning of life.

For weeks this has been my routine. I stop in front of Little Bear each morning, say hello, and study his degrading appearance. The first time I'd seen him, he looked like he'd just come off an F.A.O. Schwarz shelf. Now his once fluffy fur is matted. Instead of sitting erect, he slumps to one side. I don't know why, but this makes me sad.

I leave the school for Brandon's as quickly as possible to visit Little Bear in the afternoons. Each time, I want to get out of my car, take him home, and clean him. I think about him at night. I wonder if whoever put him there ever visits him. Or, worse, if they've forgotten about him.

After school, as I pack my bags, the intercom startles me. "Ms. Hawkins, Mr. Sanders would like to see you in his office."

"Oh, shit," I say out loud. "I'm sure Mr. Sanders's secretary heard me. "Sure, I'll be right there."

"Ms. Hawkins, please have a seat." Mr. Sanders adjusts his tie and crosses one leg over the other from behind his enormous desk.

I wrap my long skirt around my legs, pull my hair to one side, and crouch into the tiny chair in front of him.

"Can you explain this?" He unclasps his fingers and slides a document toward me.

At the top, it reads **Employee Attendance Log**. I recognize it immediately. It's the sheet he requires us to sign each day when we arrive and out as we leave. So old-school. This must have been a copy because everyone's name is struck through except mine, which is highlighted in bright neon yellow.

"Nearly every day for the last two weeks, you've arrived late and left early. I've also received several phone calls from parents you were a no-show to conferences. You also were absent from the last two Wednesday afternoon staff meetings. Is there something you need to tell me?"

I twirl my long curly brown hair around my finger as he goes through the checklist of my offenses. I'm a criminal in front of Bad Cop sans Good Cop. But I can't tell him the real reason. Sorry, Sergeant Sanders, I'm obsessed with this stuffed teddy bear by a tree on my drive. I know it sounds crazy.

But it doesn't just sound crazy—it is crazy.

"I don't know what to say. I've not been myself lately. It won't happen again."

"Ms. Hawkins, you know I run a tight ship around here. And if we hadn't been in the middle of 8th-grade testing, we would've had this conversation days ago. Consider this your first and last warning. The next time it's an official insubordinate write-up."

He peers at me with spectacled eyes. Gray, neatly trimmed brows are barely visible above the frames.

I exhale a sigh of relief. "I understand, sir. I appreciate the leniency."

When I return to my classroom, I call Brandon.

He answers, "Hey, Gorgeous. I can't wait to celebrate our six-month anniversary tonight. I'm making that vegan pizza you love."

I hate doing this to him, but I can't go. I can't drive past that bear again. Not yet. "That sounds delicious, but I'm sorry. Something's come up, and I won't be able to make it." I hold my breath and wait for his reply.

"Well, that's disappointing. I guess it's just me and my teddy bear tonight."

His comment startles me. "What did you just say?"

"Nothing, just being funny. You know, like if I don't have you to squeeze, I'll have to squeeze my teddy bear. It was a joke."

My irrational thoughts are overwhelming. "That wasn't funny. Not even a little bit."

"You're acting weird. You have been for the last few weeks. I don't know what's going on and apparently you aren't going to tell me. But it's like you're hiding something. I care about you, but I really don't want to play games. I gotta go. Give me a call when the real Naomi comes back."

"Brandon, wait."

A dial tone tells me it's too late. I collapse into my swivel chair. Everything's falling apart. I haven't updated my classroom calendar. Stacks of ungraded papers cover my desk. School's only been in session for six weeks, and I'm off to a rocky start. If I ever want to transfer out of this rural hell, I need to leave behind a clean resume. Things must change.

By the hour's end, every paper is graded, each mark recorded in the grade book, and the chairs neatly stacked. The last thing to do is update the bulletin board. Sixth-grade social studies had just started a unit on U.S. presidents.

As I aim to put a staple through the face of the twenty-sixth leader of the United States, I freeze. Theodore "Teddy" Roosevelt. I rub my hand across his bespeckled image. I remember hearing somewhere that the teddy bear was created in his honor. I drop the items in my hand and dart to my computer.

In about five minutes, Google delivers. I learned in 1902, President Roosevelt took a bear-hunting trip to Mississippi. I shudder, thinking of a group of men with rifles hunting bears. So barbaric.

Days into the trip, Roosevelt still hadn't tracked and shot a bear. Some men cornered one on his behalf, bashed in its skull, and tied the poor creature to a tree, proud to deliver the prize to their leader.

But the president believed shooting the captured bear was non-sportsman-like. The papers called him a hero. The real story was he refused to shoot the bear not out of compassion but because it lacked the thrill of the hunt. Although he tried to proclaim himself as a conservationist, he'd killed more animals than any other president in history.

Instead of aiming his gun at the bear, he ordered others in his party to stab it to death. A political cartoon captioned Drawing the Line in Mississippi depicted a hunter tying a cute bear to a tree with Roosevelt walking away. Not long after, a Russian immigrant family in Brooklyn, inspired by the cartoon, made a stuffed bear they called Teddy's Bear. The rest is history.

My heart sinks. Little Bear is helplessly at the base of that tree. It's getting dark and has started to rain, but I must see him. I have to save Little Bear. I grab my umbrella, rush to my car, and speed toward the tree.

I reach into my bag for my phone to call Brandon. I need to tell someone about Little Bear. But he'll think I'm crazy. Maybe I am. But I don't care anymore. I just want to save Little Bear.

Heavy raindrops pelt my windshield. My wipers can't go fast enough. It's getting hard to see. I turn on my brights and scan the tree line looking for him.

"Dammit," I passed him.

I try turning my wheel, but the car hydroplanes and spins. I clench the steering wheel and try to regain control. But it's no use. The last thing I see is my car crashing into Little Bear's tree. Then everything goes black.

A blaring horn won't stop—raindrops splatter on glass. I open my eyes. The crushed car engulfs my contorted body. A warm liquid gurgles up my throat into my mouth and fills it with a copper taste. I try to swallow it back, but there's so much of it. I can't squeeze my arms free to try and unbuckle. But even if I could, I wouldn't be able to open the door because the car is so mangled.

Headlights shine in my rear window. Thank God! Maybe it's the police, an ambulance, or a passerby with a cell phone who can call 911.

"Help! Help!" I weakly cry as I choke on the blood filling my mouth.

But even through the deafening blare of the horn and torrential rain hitting my car, I know the sound—a tractor. Help is here. The machine stops behind my car. My rearview mirror shows a blurred image of an old man in overalls and a dingy yellow raincoat.

He shuffles in front of my car. "Help. Help." I think I'm screaming. But no sound is coming out. My headlights shine on the tree where Little Bear sits. The man smiles, revealing that missing tooth. He then picks up Little Bear and walks away. I can't hold my eyes open any longer. Horn, rain, and a tractor's rumble blend into a peaceful medley. The last sounds I'll ever hear.

———————

"Mom, it's fine! I'm not going to be late for school. I promise. I like staying with Dad on weekends. It's not too far."

Ugh. I hang up on her. No use continuing to argue. It's not my fault she and Dad divorced, and she moved to the middle of nowhere, forcing me to switch schools from Orlando High to BFE, North Lake.

I open my visor and check my newest piercing in the mirror. The septum bar is the seventh piercing to my face. That meant I had five more than any other student at North Lake High. And I'm perfectly content being that girl.

I shut the visor before almost rear-ending a tractor. "Seriously!"

The freakin' slow-ass machine crawls at a snail's pace ahead of me. I slow down and slam my hands against the steering wheel. If I'm late, Mom won't let me stay with Dad on a Sunday night again.

But on this windy two-lane road, there's no way I can pass. I beep my horn, "Pull over, asshole!"

He ignores me. I'm about to gun it and risk my fate. My Dad's old BMW can certainly whip around this hick in no time. But before I gas it, something catches my eye.

At the base of a pine tree ahead, something looks like it doesn't belong. As I creep at a pace I could probably walk, I see a fluffy teddy bear with a blue bow around its neck. That's freakin' weird.

Focusing again on my task at hand, I gun the gas about the same time the tractor pulls over. I look over at the driver. A gray-haired man in dirt-streaked overalls smiles at me, revealing a missing tooth. I flick him off and then speed toward Hicksville, USA.

22

LITTLE RED CUPCAKE

SHEELAGH ASTON

A RED DROPLET OOZED from the small cut on Helena's left thumb. Under the ochre light of the gas lamps, the blood dripped onto the cupcake, turning its spongy surface a dark plum colour, which matched the other cakes in the box. With the cakes decorated, she sealed the box resting on the side table in the lounge, careful not to press too hard. She had sat in the leather armchair beside the table waiting for the cakes to cool before adding the final touch.

She pressed her thumb with her index finger to stem the blood and slipped the box into the wicker basket at her feet against a posy of sunburst marigolds and white calla lilies: Grandma's favourite.

Helena buttoned her red coat and pulled the hood over her head. She lifted the basket, looping an arm through its handle. A high-pitched scream shattered the quiet of the room. Helena started, hurried over to the window, and peered between the velvet curtains. Outside, the reflections of the streetlights shimmered in the puddles along the pavement. The first threads of dawn peeped through the night sky. She dashed out of the room and down the hallway.

Have they caught her? Helena wondered as she pulled the wrought-iron handle to open the front door. Has the girl gotten away or has the pack claimed another feast?

Opposite, the shadows roamed. She caught flashes of silhouetted figures darting in and out of the alleys. When they ventured too close to the hazy glow of the streetlights, she spied glimpses of their rough, hairy faces before they disappeared back into the dark to wait for sunset to arrive again. The sound of her rapid heartbeats filled her ears as Helena stepped down the stone steps of the apartment block onto the pavement.

Checking no one was in sight, Helena rushed across the street. Slumped against one streetlight, a man sat, a blood-stained hand clutching his stomach. Around his neck hung a skull on a chain.

"Be careful, Helena," Helena recalled, her mother warning her many times when they watched from the window at night. "Remember to go straight to your grandma's house. Don't get distracted. Don't draw attention to yourself or talk to anyone. Timing is everything. Too much daylight and all will be lost."

The previous evening, when they had watched, Mother's lips had curled back, forming a snarl at the lone figure standing on the street below. The young man had stared up at them and licked his bottom lip. 'Especially him.'

"Yes, Mother," she replied, trying to ignore the fluttery sensation that crept into her stomach. He eyed her with a wolfish grin.

Mother drew the curtains and picked up a folded newspaper from the table. She let out a soft cry as she stared at the front-page photo. Above it read, **Missing Young Woman Found Dead.**

Mother traced a thin finger over the photo. Her black fingernail paused somewhere amid the girl's long raven mane of hair.

"Be careful, Helena," Mother said. "I could not bear to lose you like Hecate."

Helena glanced at the photo. The young woman shared her own dark hair, snub nose, and dark eyes, but not the widow's peak or the plump cheeks.

"I promise," she had replied, sealing her words with a kiss on her mother's pale cheek.

Reminded of the warning, Helena quickened her pace. Soon the streetlights would turn off and the shadows would disappear until sunset. Grandma would not be pleased, Helena fretted. Their chance would be lost. She had to reach Grandma's house by dawn, as promised.

Helena brushed the memory and her mother's warning from her mind. She ignored the rumbling of soft howls and headed to the stone pillars that marked the entrance to the park, keeping her face hidden under the coat's hood.

She turned into the park and on to a path lined with trees on either side. They stood like soldiers guarding the dense woodland.

"What're you doing out here, hon?" a smooth voice murmured beside her.

She smelt him before he fell into step beside her. A rich musky scent, similar to a bear or dog. She tilted her head, tugging back the edge of her hood to view him. The leather jacket he wore hung loosely from his broad shoulders over a grubby white vest. Patches of hairy skin were visible through the holes and tears down the legs of his stained jeans.

"I've heard of young girls disappearing when walking through here." He drew close to her, pressed his face near, and sniffed. "You smell nice. Too nice to disappear."

His lupine eyes set underneath a pair of heavy eyebrows met hers. Up close, his dark hair, combed back from his forehead, appeared less midnight and more a tawny tone. Sideburns covered his cheeks, leaving his chin and upper lip with a light stubble. The lobes of his ears poked through his mass of hair.

He drew away and asked, "Where are you going?"

"To visit my grandma, who lives on the other side of the park."

Helena would have explained how the path led to her house, but the young man sprang behind a nearby tree. She looked around. Two police officers walked towards them.

"Be careful, young lady," one of them called on their way to the entrance. "There are bad people about."

She thanked the officer, promising to go as fast as she could, and went on her way at a brisk pace.

The youth reappeared by her side, along with his smell.

Helena slowed down. He swept his tongue over his bottom lip and adjusted the scarf wrapped around his neck. "I know a shortcut." He pointed to the woodland on their left.

"Oh, but Grandma's house is at the end of this path by the park's exit." She pointed straight ahead. In the distance, smoke billowed into the air. "See, that's her chimney."

The young man peered into the woods. With a fleeting glance back the way they had come, he reached out to grab her.

At the ting-ting of a bicycle's bell, he dropped it and turned away. An elderly man cycled past, doffing his hat with a cheery Good Morning to them.

The young man looked up at the fading moon and lightening sky. "I should go."

"Oh, please don't," Helena pleaded. "It's not far to Grandma's."

"Ok, but let's hurry."

Helena did not quicken her pace when he increased his. She meandered along the path and picked some daffodils sprouting in the flower beds between the trees. When she heard the dawn chorus of the birds, she stopped and listened with a smile as though enjoying music.

Halfway along the path, they passed a large stone building. Helena threw her hood over her face. On top of the building's tower, two pieces of wood were nailed together, one vertical and one horizontal. Scattered amongst the grass were headstones.

"Wot's the matter? Scared of the zombies and vampires?" the young man teased. With a swipe of his hand, he knocked her hood back from her face.

Flustered, Helena pulled it back over her and marched ahead but halted at the sound of a series of ping-pongs. She glanced over her shoulder to see the lamps along the path's edge switch off one by one. Helena glanced at her watch. Gathering up her long skirt, she broke into a run. "Gosh, I'm going to be late for breakfast."

"Hey," he shouted as she headed down the path to the chimney. "I'll go this way and let your grandma know you're coming. I'm sure she will be worried about you."

Helena spun around to see him pointing to the trees again. Shreds of pale light broke through the branches. Its rays crept across the grass turning its night-time seaweed-green carpet to lush emerald shade. When she smiled at him, the young man released the familiar wolfish grin, revealing a set of pointy, yellow teeth. With a snap of his mouth, he bounded off and disappeared into the forest, leaving Helena to make her way to Grandma's. Which she did at a leisurely pace, humming to herself and thinking how pleased Grandma would be.

What have I got to do to get fed around here? The young man ran, weaving his way through the thickets of trees till he reached a side exit that brought him out the other side of the park, a short distance from the house with the smoking chimney. If only she'd gone into the woods, like the others did, instead of dawdling down the path. I should've grabbed her sooner. Too light. Too many people. If only she'd gone into the trees. Things would have been so much simpler.

He wiped the trickle of saliva from his lips, thinking of the juicy, fresh meat of the girl's petite frame. After days of roaming around famished it made his stomach muscles twist in anticipation. He panted and leapt up the steps of the tall Gothic house to the black-painted door. He grabbed the large brass knocker and rapped.

Tap, tap.

"Who's there?" crackled a weak voice through the intercom.

The young man coughed and licked his lips "It's me, Grandma," he replied in a sweet, light voice. "Your granddaughter."

"Push the door, my dear," Grandma croaked.

At the loud click, he pushed it open and stepped inside the house.

"In here, dear," Grandma's voice echoed from down the hallway.

The young man padded along the dim hall. He halted at the foot of the stairs transfixed by the wooden baluster carved in the shape of a woman. Coils of long hair fell over her bare shoulders and down the flowing dress she wore. In one hand, she held a lit torch high, and with the other she held a thin knife across her front. Curled around her feet, a greyhound stood and stared at him. Below the animal, engraved into the baluster's based the word **HACATE**. The young man edged past the statue, averting his gaze, half convinced she might turn him into stone if he lingered.

Resisting the temptation to look at the Medusa-like figure, he scampered down the hall to the stream of light that formed a small pool beyond the open. He sniffed the air and breathed in the warm moist air as he entered the dark room.

"I see the goddess let you pass," the old woman said from the brass bed piled with blankets. "Did Hecate give you the evil eye like your sister used to?"

"Yes."

He remembered in time to change his deep voice to the sing-song tones of the girl's.

"That's why we called her after our goddess." The old woman beamed. "You sound a little hoarse today, my dear."

"I have a sore throat, Grandma," he replied, and his eyes adjusted to the faint glow of the lamp on the dresser by the door.

"Of course. It is winter still." Grandma patted the covers of her bed. "Come, bring the lamp nearer so I can see you, my dear."

His stomach rumbled as he lifted it, shedding its light over the bed. A withered old woman in a nightgown and cotton cap sat upright, staring straight ahead. Curled on the floor between the bed and the open fire lay a black greyhound, fast asleep.

He followed her gaze to the large oil painting that hung above the fireplace.

"Beautiful, isn't it?" Grandma sighed.

The young man gripped the lamp's handle tighter and clamped a hand over his mouth, wishing he could tear his eyes away from the sight before him.

An inferno dominated the painting's background. Around it, the artist had painted flames dancing high in the tangerine sky. Contorted figures were being thrown into the fire by faceless demonic figures. Below it, discarded, bleeding limbs lay scattered on the ground. Some demons thrust spears into the bellies of their captives while others devoured the living dead.

His gaze drifted across the scene to a young man withering on the ground screaming as his tormentor feasted on his body. A skull hung from his neck.

High above the inferno, on a hill, stood a giant with a pair of twisted horns. Beside him, a raven-haired woman robed like the statue stood watching the banquet.

The young man placed the lamp on the bedside cabinet.

Grandma thrust an arm out to him, with no more flesh on it than a sparrow. Its bones pushed through the thin layer of skin as blood-filled veins bulged through it like tunnels. Blood. The young man smacked his lips.

He waved a hand in front of her eyes. Blind as a bat. How fortunate. An easy kill.

The room smelt of stale air and, most of all, warm, moist meat. Not much, but enough. A snack before the main course.

His nose twitched and his mouth salivated. Sometimes you have to eat the crusty bits before the tasty ones.

He leaned over her, his mouth opened wide. An acidic stench burned the lining of his nostrils. With a howl, he snapped his mouth shut and reeled back.

The old hag's body's as rotten as a tomato left out in the desert sun. Gut rot I do not need with such a prize coming to me. What to do? He lifted his scarf to his face.

The greyhound stirred. The young man knelt, reaching for the animal.

"Good doggy."

The greyhound's whimper ceased before the animal's breath left its body. The sound of crunching teeth on bone and tearing of flesh filled the room.

"You brought Cerberus a bone. Oh, wonderful." Grandma clapped her hands with glee.

"Why thank you, Grandma," the young man replied, wiping his bloody mouth with his scarf. He untied it from his neck and held it in his hands.

"Come closer, my dear," Grandma beckoned.

"Why of course, Grandma," he whispered with a satisfied burp, holding the scarf tight as he approached the blind old woman with a wolfish grin.

With her hood still up, Helena pressed the intercom.

"Yesss?" came a feeble voice.

"It's me, Grandma. Helena." She pulled back her hood. "I've brought you cupcakes and flowers and a bone for Cerberus."

"Come in, child."

Helena entered the house. She kissed the statue's face and skipped down the hallway to the room at the end.

"Hello, Grandma." She placed the box on Grandma's lap and removed its lid.

"What delicious cakes, my dear," Grandma said, picking one up and opening her mouth wide. In one gulp, she consumed the cake. "Hmm. Lovely," she mumbled, grabbing another one.

"Why, Grandma, what thick arms you have," Helena said.

"All the better to hug you, my dear." Grandma leaned her head back so far to eat another cake, her nightcap slipped a little way from her forehead.

"Grandma, what large ears you have."

"All the better to hear you with." The old woman splattered bits of cake as she wolfed another down.

"Grandma, what funny-shaped eyes you have." Helena gasped as Grandma scoffed the last of the cakes. "They look like almonds."

"All the better to see you, child." Grandma licked her fingertips. "Delicious."

With a terrifying howl, Grandma pulled off her cap and leapt from the bed, no longer the shriveled old woman. The box fell to the floor. The young man crouched, opened his mouth, and bared his teeth, ready to lunge. His shadow loomed over her. He froze, eyeing the wall.

Helena's emerald gaze danced back at him as if reading his mind.

She held a hand up and formed a rabbit's head with her fingers. The green wallpaper remained unblemished where her hand's shadow should have been.

He gripped his stomach and winched with in pain, as though he had swallowed a lump of burning coal. With a groan he fell on his hands. A stream of bile volleyed out of his mouth. The spongy mixture of the cakes he had gobbled up spread out, now a pinkish-yellow mess.

Helena licked her thumb and turned to the painting on the wall.

The young man followed her gaze to the painting, which was no longer still and silent. From it, agonizing cries rose as though coming from the tormented beings within, louder and louder, filling the room. The inferno's flames grew and extended beyond the painting's gilded frame. They flickered across the walls. From the hill, the raven-haired woman began to stroll down past the inferno and through the sea of writhing bodies. A greyhound trotted beside her.

An old woman stepped out of the painting near the bottom frame's edge. Her long, grey hair fell over her skeletal body and covered the flimsy nightdress.

"You got him then, my dear," The old woman cackled, approaching the bed. She stood by its foot. "A tad late, given that dawn had come. He must have been ravenous to take such a risk as to eat you in the daylight, my dear."

The young man whined as he clawed to the door on his hands and knees.

Helena slammed it shut. 'As we predicted, Grandma.'

He reared up and toppled backwards. Helena stepped closer to him. The young man scuttled away from her and collided with the bedside cabinet.

Behind Helena, the furnace's flames covered the wall. Sweat poured down his face and dampened his hair.

A soft thud-thud drew his attention back to the painting. The raven-haired woman and the greyhound stood by the old woman.

"Welcome Hecate, dear granddaughter," Grandma said.

Hecate kissed the older woman.

"Thank you, sister." She looked at Helena. From within a face paler than a death mask, Hecate's lips formed a grateful smile. Below her face, torn flesh marred her swan-like neck.

Helena sucked her thumb as several demons climbed out of the painting and into the room Hecate's smile disappeared as she stared down at the young man.

"You remember me, don't you?" Hecate stroked the greyhound. "Your kill."

The young man raised a hand, his fingers curled as though gripping something tight. "But, but you're dead."

"And you are not," Hecate replied with an eerie smile. "Did you enjoy the cupcakes?" Grandma chuckled.

Helena held her thumb up. The one from which droplets of blood had stained the cakes. A slight cut was visible on its smooth surface.

"Just as those who eat of the Lamb will live, you shall live too. Forever." Helena gloated at him with a devilish glint in her eyes. "But you have eaten not of the Lamb, but of the Beast."

The demons flicked their tails like whips and stretched out their talon-shaped hands to the screaming young man. Grabbing hold of his limbs, they carried him like a trussed-up pig to the painting, Hecate leading them.

The greyhound jumped into the painting after her.

"Well done, my dear. Perhaps we should have named you after our goddess of evil instead of your sister." Grandma smiled at Helena, then turned and serenely followed them.

With them, the flames retreated from the walls into the painting as the cries of the damned faded.

Helena stood alone in the room. The lamp's pale glow stretched over the floor before her.

On the wall, the painting hung static once more.

Helena pulled up her hood and picked up the box by her feet. With a sigh, she licked her thumb and ate up the cupcake crumbs.

23

THE CORRIDOR

JESSICA SCOTT

IT'S COLD.

It's always so bloody cold here.

I can't figure it out. My skin prickles and I feel the need to pull my cardigan tighter. Not just for the warmth, but as if a threadbare cardigan might offer any protection at all from anything. Still, I wrap myself tight, tamping down the irrational fear (it is irrational, isn't it?), and force myself into the corridor every morning and evening, just to prove to myself that I can.

Nothing ever happens.

Yet my fear grows. Why? There is absolutely nothing strange about this narrow alley. No dark figures in the shadows or on the rooftops.

Wait.

Was there someone on that roof?

Well, if there was, it's none of my business.

But why is it so damn cold?

My mates refuse to walk this way with me anymore. *So,* I walk alone. At least, I don't see anyone else. And I'm not afraid! I'm not. What is there to be afraid—

24

THE CATHEDRAL

TOM ELMQUIST

"THE FACT THAT YOU think you really have a choice in whatever happens next is funny," the man said.

Not even thirty seconds ago this was the caretaker of the cathedral. He appeared weak and frail. Now he was young vibrant and most importantly strong. His eyes were an impossible green and they stared deeply into hers. They held her will just as strong as the hand that held her neck. She couldn't even imagine breaking either grip.

"What the hell are you and what the fuck do you want?" Carrie asked.

"Oh, my dear, I have exactly what I want and my will is going to be done despite your foolish hope. So let me introduce myself," the man's American accent faded away and a genuine Irish accent took its place. "I am Jameson Grady and what I am is hungry."

Carrie whispered, pleading, "You can let me go, I'll forget everything that happened tonight."

"First you came to my home and insulted me by taking videos of my home without my permission. Then your little friend shoved his little legal paper and money in my face. As I said I'm all too happy to take your coin if you are willing to give it," his voice trailed off as the gray of faintness crept into her vision as his grip tightened.

She thought to herself as she began to pass out, How the hell did this happen? Her mind started to roll back to where everything began tonight.

Carrie was an internet influencer who dreamed of having her own TV show one day. She wanted to be the next big Ghost-hunting or Paranormal Investigating show.

She was pretty blonde, had bright blue eyes, and had curves in all the right places. *So,* she knew people would watch for that, if for no other reason but she had intelligence too. She had two degrees, one in parapsychology and paranormal science.

She loved all things spooky and unexplained. She loved Ghost stories and Gothic tales. She had loved all of it from a young age when she saw her grandmother walking in her home weeks after the funeral.

She loved everything except the name of her internet show. Her self-appointed producer came up with Carrie's Creepy Corpse and Catacomb Show for her. The thing she hated the most hated the most, was the alliteration. It seemed tacky, cliche, and way over the top. The show had a modest following of three hundred and fifty thousand followers, but she still hated the name.

She was getting prepared for her next show. She wanted to know everything there was to know about the Rose Cathedral. It sat on a huge piece of land compared to the rest of the city and was rumored to have miles of catacombs beneath it.

The Rose Cathedral was once owned and run by the Catholic Church. It was abandoned in the early 1800s when several prominent families disappeared from the church or disappeared on church grounds. Before being abandoned, the Catholic Church tried to reconsecrate the Cathedral many times.

It was finally abandoned in the early 1800s, but the disappearances continued despite falling into disrepair. Hundreds of people disappeared from the Cathedral over the years.

Finally, it was declared a historical landmark in 1980. At which point it was fully restored. During the restoration nearly a dozen men disappeared or died in mysterious ways. The restoration brought back to its former glory and most of the catacombs were sealed off. A few were kept *open*, so people got an idea of what they were like.

Nowadays it is bright and shiny. There are guided tours and there is a fantastic Halloween haunted house, boasting chills for young and old.

Only one caretaker lives on the grounds in one of the former priest's living spaces, but the city takes care of most of the upkeep.

After reading her notes on the Rose Cathedral for the thousandth she felt like she was ready for the night she had planned. She wasn't ready for the events that followed. Nothing could have prepared her for what happened next.

James, her self-appointed producer and tech guru, Alica, his girlfriend and Lydia, Carrie's best friend were all waiting in the van. They all worked together chasing ghosts and had been friends since they were all in elementary school together.

"Come on, we are losing the dark," James yelled and beckoned her to the van.

"I'm coming, I'm coming. I had to get a few notes to go over," Carrie yelled back.

"Yeah for like the millionth time?" Lydia asked.

As she got into the passenger seat of the van, "Oh shush", she said to Lydia with a smile. There is nothing wrong with being prepared"

"You mean obsessively prepared," Lydia commented while rolling her eyes.

Carrie looked at James, "Do you have the liability waivers and cash?"

"Of course. What do you think I am stupid?"

Alicia and Lydia giggled. In unison, they said, "No comment."

James frowned and looked back at them as to say "Really?" but he said, "What are you? Five."

He looked back at Carrie, Are we good?"

"Yeah we're good," she replied with an excited sigh.

About thirty minutes later they were standing at the Cathedral. James looked at his watch and whispered to himself, "Three hours until the witching hour."

"Huh?" Lydia asked. It was cold enough to see her breath when she said the word.

"Ignore him. He's being all spooky and broody," Alicia said as she kissed his cheek. "Aren't you baby?"

"Yeah, anyway let's do this."

They shot all the outside shots and the introduction to the segment. While they were doing that Carrie felt as if she were being watched. When they finished they walked to the side entrance where the caretaker lived.

James knocked on the door hard. No answer. He knocked again even harder. No answer. As he knocked even harder for the third time a voice came from behind the door.

"Christ! Impatient son of a bitch!" the voice yelled to no one.

The big oak door *opened,* and an old man stepped through the door. "What in the ever-loving hell do you want?" he asked looking at the quartet.

Carrie stepped forward and said, "Hi my name is *Carrie,* and these are my friends. We were hoping that you would let us film a show here on the Internet. It's about the history and,"

"And the scary factor," the man said cutting her off. "I've seen your show. It's cute maybe a little naive, but still cute. I'm sure you give a good scare to the little kiddies."

"I hope we do but I also like the dark history of places like this," she said while trying to bite her tongue at the cute comment.

"Why didn't you set it up earlier? I mean I'm sure the city would love the publicity," the old man said.

"True, but sometimes it's easier to ask for forgiveness,"

"*Then* permission. Yeah, yeah I know my dear old dad said that a lot," he said cutting her off.

James cut them both off, "Look uh," he said holding out his hand and trying to get the old man to say his name.

"Max, just call me Max," the old man said and shook James's hand.

"Ok, Max. I have signed waivers of liability for all of us," begins by handing the signed forms. "These absolve you and the city if anything bad happens, or one of us gets hurt, *y*a know the unforeseen."

"Mmmhmm, I get it you realize you are invading my home. Right?" Max said.

"I have something for your trouble too," James said as he held out an envelope with cash in it. "It's five thousand dollars and no one needs to know we gave it to you."

Max's face brightens and he begins to speak in a very fake Irish accent. "If they be excited and willing to part with their coin, you be just as excited and willing to take it." Then his voice returned to normal. "That's what my grandfather would say at a moment like this."

"So do we have a deal?" James asked trying to hurry an answer from the man.

"We have a deal. You better be staying away from my quarters, I don't want you filming anything in there."

Carrie quickly took over to soothe Max, "Of course not. Would you mind staying in there until we are done?"

"*Sure,* I will. I don't want to be seen on video either. Oh, and by the way you have until sunrise to be done. The first tour starts just after dawn and I want you gone by before that," Max said in a gruff voice. He shook each of their hands while looking each in the eye and then nodded. "I'll be upstairs if you need anything." He tossed James a big ring with an almost impossible set of keys on it. "You might need these. They are all marked so you shouldn't have too much trouble."

That was it they had their way in. James set up the camera and the electronic equipment in the room where Max walked up the stairs to his room.

Carrie jerked James by the arm, "Five thousand dollars are you insane?"

"It worked. Didn't it?" asked with a sarcastic tone.

"That's not what we agreed on. It was supposed to be a maximum of a thousand. What the fuck are you thinking?" she said almost screaming.

"You ladies go on. I'll monitor from here," James said as he sat down and tested all the equipment.

The three ladies looked at each other and then at James as if to ask a question.

"Just go, I have sound checks to run on everything. I want to be out of here by dawn," he said sounding almost exactly like Max.

So, the three would-be paranormal investigators split up and began to search the cathedral. Lydia searched the offices and storage areas where many of the disappearances over the years had happened. Alicia explored the bell tower, where a young man was reported to have hung himself due to a love affair gone wrong. Carrie explored the main hall.

Over the next few hours, The Rose Cathedral seemed lifeless. There was no activity and Carrie began to give up hope of getting any evidence. That's when she heard Alica scream in the bell tower. It was faint but she definitely heard it.

"Guys, do you hear that?" she *asked,* keying the mic on her headset.

There was no response.

"Guys?" she asked again.

In the distance, Carrie heard Alicia's voice again, "Carrie? Help me! Noooooo!"

Carrie ran up the nearly three hundred steps to the bell tower. What she saw horrified her. Alicia hung upside down from some scaffolding her feet bound together her arms hung lifeless. Her throat and wrists had been cut and her blood was draining into a fifty-gallon drum.

Carrie, still horrified, moved closer to Alicia. She reached out a hand and touched the body. "Oh God. What the hell? Who did this to you?"

The lifeless eyes stared back as if to blame Carrie. She ran down the stairs to the control area to find James. What she found made her scream out loud. She found James face down on the floor but the only way she knew it was James was by his class ring on his right hand. His head had been beaten so badly, there was no discernible skull left. A case from one of the instruments lay nearby. Carrie could see blood, brain flesh, and bone clinging to it.

Another thought immediately came to her *mind,* and she ran from the office. She said with a gasp "Lydia" as she ran.

Lydia was Carrie's best friend, and they had known each other since preschool. Lydia was the sister that Carrie never *had,* and Carrie was fiercely protective because of that.

She searched for what felt like an eternity. Another horror show greeted Carrie as she reached the lower library that led to the catacombs. She found her best friend lying face up on the top of a bookshelf. It looked as though she had been thrown from one of the upper levels. Her accusing eyes stared at Carrie as if to say, "This is all your fault."

Carrie ran back to Max's apartment and banged on the door. He slowly answered the door, "I told you, that I didn't want to be a part of your little show."

"You have to help me," she said while gasping for air.

"What do you mean?" he asked and then a stunned look came to his face. It was the kind of look you see on someone when they see something horrific but can't comprehend what they are looking at. "What did you do?"

"What do you mean?" she asked back and then she saw her reflection in a mirror nearby. She was nearly covered in blood and her clothes were torn as if she had been fighting with a wild animal. "Oh my god"

"Calm down, tell me what happened," Max said.

"Wait, I can show you," she said and dragged him. Down the stairs to the recording equipment. She pressed play on the multicamera feed. She wasn't ready for what she saw next.

"You two go ahead. I'll catch up I have to talk to James," Carrie's voice said but she didn't remember saying it. "James told us to go on. Not Me."

The scene that unfolded was one of predator-like behavior. They talked for a few minutes and Carrie seemed to be lulling James into a sense of calm. That calm was broken when the playback showed Carrie raising the case over her head and bashing him in the head. She did this over and over while saying "I hate the name of this show." Each word was punctuated by a blow from a case.

"Wait, I didn't," Carries voice cut off as she continued to watch.

The next scene unfolded even more horrifying than the last. She could see herself creeping up the stairs to the bell tower. The night vision showed in perfect clarity what happened next. Carrie threw a large piece of cinder to startle Alicia causing her to scream. Carrie snuck up behind Alicia on the scaffolding and pushed her over the rail.

As she fell Alicia saw who pushed her and screamed, "Carrie? Help me! Noooooo!"

Alicia's feet became entangled in some ropes causing hang rather than fall to her death.

"Hmm, even better," Carrie said.

She climbed down the scaffolding and pushed the empty fifty-gallon drum under where Alicia's semi-conscious body hung. She grabbed a box cutter from one of the nearby crates.

"My grandfather how to drain deer so that the blood doesn't spoil the meat. I've always wondered what would it be like to do it to a human and if it would keep the meat from spoiling," Carrie said as if she was talking to no one.

"No, please. Don't," Alicia whispered so weakly that Carrie barely registered it.

Carrie then cut Alicia's throat. The arterial spurt covered Carrie in blood, but she didn't seem to notice. She then made two long cuts down the arms, making sure to hit all the major blood vessels.

When she was done she stood there admiring her handy work. The body drained in mere moments or so it seemed to Carrie.

Both body cameras stared at each other as Carrie watched. Carrie's showed a beautifully horrific cascade of blood flowing from Alicia's body. Alicia's camera showed a picture of Carrie upside down, grinning like one of those crazy people you see in horror movies. She was covered in blood and there was a haze on the image from the blood that made the night vision image even more horrific.

"I guess you shouldn't have stolen Lydia's man," Carrie said as she turned and walked away.

About ten minutes later Carrie saw Lydia appear in her camera image. She was on one of the walkways of the library filming the stained glass windows.

"The light creates some interesting optical illusions in the dark. There seem to be moving shadows everywhere," Lydia was saying trying to sound like a real journalist.

"Lydia, help me," Carrie said in a weak voice.

"Carrie? What happened?"

"They're dead. Both of them are dead," Carrie said but to her own ears, her voice sounded stiff almost robotic.

"What? Why? How? Tell me what happened."

Again, in the robotic voice, "I killed them because of what they did to you," she said.

"For me? What do you mean? Because they're together?" Lydia asked.

"Yes."

"I told them to be together because I was in love with someone else," Lydia said.

The robotic voice became enraged, "What? I killed them because he cheated on you with her. I did it for you!"

"Honey, I never asked you to. I never wanted that,"

What the body cam showed next broke Carrie's heart even more. She saw herself go insane and threw her best friend over the stone rail. Lydia's back made a sickening crunch as she hit the stone bookshelf. Her body twitched several times and as she died Carrie heard her voice whisper, "I love you, Honey. I wanted us to be together."

The video played for a few minutes and showed Carrie coming to the base camp and stopping the video.

"I never did those things," Carrie said.

"I think the courts will see it differently," Max said.

"I've got to get out of here," Carrie whispered and tried to for the door. An iron grip on the back of her neck stopped her.

"No no no. It's not going to be that easy," Max said turning Carrie to face him and switching hands so he could hold her by the throat. "One of three things is going to happen next. One, you will be my next meal, two, you will be my next progeny, or three, I am going to muddle your mind so badly that when your kind finds you, they will have no choice but to lock you away for the rest of your natural life."

"Maybe you could let me go."

The form of the old man seemed to shimmer and change to a tall black-haired man.

A blinding pain and sudden movement cleared her head.

Jameson gave her a shake to snap her back to the moment. "As I said it's quite comical to think you have a choice in any of this. No matter what I choose, I win. Why? You might ask?"

He gave her a little shake to prod her into asking, "Why?"

"Glad you decided to rejoin the conversation. That little tape that you made tonight will bring so many new people to this place. It will add to the mystery and make more people curious. Thus, giving me a veritable buffet of people to dine on."

"How?" she asked, only able to utter a single word.

"Oh, that was easy I simply controlled your mind when I looked into your eyes. You were easily played and bent to my will. So yes I made you kill your little friends," He said with an air of glee. "Now what to do with you?"

In a flash, Carrie felt an excruciating pain and literally felt the life drain from her. Suddenly she was dropped to the ground. As the gray of unconsciousness started to take hold at the corners of her vision, she saw Jameson say, "Maybe you'll learn something from this for your next life."

⤛⤜

25

LOVE WITH A NARCICCIST

NICOLE SMITH

When was the exact moment I became a victim of a narcissist?
Was it when he told me he loved me,
but in the same breath asked if that's what I was going to wear?
Or maybe the first time he asked me to skip girls' night?
Maybe when it escalated into him asking me why I ALWAYS
chose them over him?
Fights ensued and I started staying home to keep the peace.
Was I a victim of abuse as soon as I had to keep my mouth shut
to "avoid trouble?"
He feasts on my insecurity.
He points out my every flaw.
Until him, I didn't realize I had quite so many.
I am lucky someone like him could manage to love me.
Really, that anyone could manage to love me.
Right?

I can't talk to my family because I didn't want to bad mouth
him.
They never seem to understand, he does love me.
They don't like him, and I don't know why.
Besides, it's not like he hits me!
When we drink, the ugliness bubbles up to the surface.
I get brave.
He doesn't like it when I talk back.
If he hits me, I'll leave.
But he doesn't.
He never would, he's not THAT kind of man.
He never leaves marks anyone can see.
He texts me the sweetest things.
I cringe when my phone dings wondering what I did wrong.
I'm in too deep.
Is this what love is supposed to feel like, a mixture of fear, shame,
and loneliness?
When did I become this person?
How do I escape?
Maybe this is what I deserve.

26

DINNER WITH MRS. ANNABELLE

LINDSAY SCHRAAD KEELING

I had a girl over for dinner.

She was about seven or eight.

She was very nice and polite,

Her smile thin and straight.

It was a new recipe,

So I was a little wary

As eating new things

Is often pretty scary.

Supper was delicious though,

As the story goes,

But what do I do now

With her fingers and toes?

27

THAT ONE STORMY NIGHT

N.M. LAMBERT

THE SILHOUETTE OF A knife sweeps across my vision in a cold and calculating manner. For a moment, I watch it in stunned silence against the melting, bloody background. Soon, a face appears, belonging to a girl who at one point had been beautiful but is now reduced to ashes. Her face is charred, and as she smiles, there is a gaping hole where her two tops and front teeth used to be. Her grip on the knife tightens, white splitting her knuckles, as she turns the blade toward me.

"Come play, Elizabeth. Come play with me."

I wake up with a start, breathing heavily and covered in sweat. One glance at my phone tells me it's two a.m. Lightning soon flashes outside my window, temporarily illuminating my entire room, followed by the boom of thunder. I roll over onto my side and pull the comforter tighter around me as I fight to go back to sleep.

Something soft and wet grazes past my cheek, and the girl whispers, "Come play with me, Elizabeth."

I recoil from the voice and shoot up in bed, sweat coating my forehead. I glance around the dark room, but I'm alone. Another flash of lightning strikes and rain violently pummels the roof. I jump at the onslaught of sound, paralyzing fear clawing its way up my throat.

I reach for my bedside lamp, but nothing happens. Goosebumps pepper my skin. The power's out. My heart sinks at this realization, my body trembling with dread. I curl up into a ball, pulling the covers even tighter around me and wishing that whatever's here with me is just my imagination.

My door slams open, jolting me toward the sudden sound. I give a startled cry and pick up my phone with shaking hands. I shine the flashlight toward the entrance. Once again, nothing's there.

The fear is palpable, a tangible mass coiling around my throat like a serpent. I can't think. I can't even breathe. All I can do is make myself as small as possible and hope that whoever—or whatever—is there with me w*ill* leave.

Then, that same damn voice says, "Come find me, Elizabeth. Come play with me."

Only this time it seems to be coming from every direction, the walls vibrating with the onslaught.

Before I know what I'm doing, I'm out of my bed with the flashlight still illuminating my doorway. There's a pause before moving again, my feet gliding toward the distant voice. What appears after my door is a seemingly endless, narrow hallway that leaves me horrendously confused. My house doesn't have a hallway, especially one this long, and I carefully move further down. Various unfamiliar pictures line the walls like a museum, each one depicting the same young girl in different scenarios.

A girl who looks oddly, terribly familiar.

There she is at a dance recital, beaming widely at the audience, as she performs a croisé. There she is at a birthday party in someone's backyard, surrounded by other smiling individuals as another girl forms a pair of bunny ears behind her head. And there she is at her elementary school, mounted on top of a marvelous black stallion, her hands on the reigns but her eyes staring triumphantly at the camera.

There she is on the day of her death, her face bloodied and mangled beyond recognition, as the seatbelt strangles her alive. Blonde curls spill from her head, mixing with the blood that stains the concrete.

I stumble backward from the last picture as my vision temporarily darkens. Why is this here? I wonder, my body fighting to catch up to my frightened mind. But I know why this is here. I know why all of this is here.

The girl pictured in each of the photos was my younger sister, Mariette. And the last photo depicts the day she died, a day that will haunt me for the rest of my life.

I remember the screeching tires and the crunching of metal as my mother swerved to try to avoid the other driver. I remember my sister screaming, followed by me, and then, my mother as we were sent tumbling into oncoming traffic. And then...complete and utter silence as I was pulled into unconsciousness.

When I woke a few days later, my mother and I were in the hospital. And my sister was gone, having been pronounced dead at the scene.

"Come find me, Elizabeth. You are so close."

The same eerie voice from before jolts me back to the present, and my heart lodges in my throat. Because now, the voice is familiar too, all the pieces finally clicking into place.

I follow the voice into an empty room, or at least at first glance, it seems like it's empty. Soon, the girl with the same charred face materializes before me, only this time, the details are clearer. I back away slowly as the dead face of my sister stares back at me with a knowing grin on her lips and the same knife outstretched in her hands.

Acceptance flows through me, chasing away the fear as I take a single step toward her. In the months that followed the accident, all I knew was guilt. Because despite being right next to her, I had survived the accident, and she had not. Half of my soul died that day as she was wrenched from me.

But now, we can be together again. We can be complete. Whole.

"Join me, Elizabeth. We can be together again," Mariette murmurs, parroting my thoughts. A small, wistful smile appears on her lips.

And then, she plunges the knife into my chest.

I wake up once again, only this time, its morning, and the storm has all but faded away. My hands go right to my chest as I try to ground myself and breathe. When I no longer feel the crushing weight of my newest nightmare, I think back to the night before, to the game my sister played with me.

Was it truly all a dream?

A huge dull ache then slams into me, starting in my chest and soon spreading throughout my entire body as if I were still in the throes of sleep. An ache that conveniently starts where my sister stabbed me.

I instantly rip the covers off and stare, horrified, at what I saw.

There is now an angry, swollen welt where the knife had slid into me. My hands reach for the spot just below my jawline, and I feel the familiar thrumming of my heartbeat. I'm still alive, even though the dream seemed to suggest otherwise. But I've had dreams like this before, and I know they are not just dreams. They are windows to wherever my sister is, a tether she uses to reach me.

Then, I hear the voice again, though this time, it's faint. And the cycle continues.

"Until tonight, Elizabeth. Until tonight."

28

STIGMATA

RILEY KILMORE

I POWERED DOWN THE laptop and set it aside, my palms aching.

They'd been hurting a lot lately, and I wondered if I was getting carpal tunnel syndrome from typing too much. After all, I was finally living the writer's dream, so there had to be some downside, no? Every dream has a downside.

Still, I'd navigated the path toward independence through considerable sacrifice and had made it out alive, left with both sufficient means to live off of and ample time to write without distraction. Granted, my needs were few, which helped—the isolated mountainside cabin where I'd taken up residence in Pennsylvania, basic but adequate.

The only thing I hadn't really factored in was the loneliness.

Like a lot of writers, I'd always been an introvert. I grew up loving nothing better than the hushed sanctuary of a public library surrounded by shelves of books looming over me like rock cliffs I longed to scale. Sometimes I got a sick feeling in the pit of my stomach knowing I'd never read them all.

Books aside, I'd forgotten one vital factor: other people. Sure, they were all quietly reading, lost to their own fictional adventures with their noses buried in books, but they were present. Breath, pheromones, micro noises in the background, that invisible way yet to be explained by science that lets one silent mind touch another.

When my youngest was in preschool, his teacher told me about *parallel play* and how it's developmentally appropriate until about the age of three. Once I heard about it, I thought maybe that was wrong—the age range, I mean. After living five months alone in that cabin I knew adults needed parallel play, too. Parallel lives. It was why most people chose to live in neighborhoods whether they ever got to know their neighbors or not.

In youth, I'd read the Little House books by Laura Ingalls Wilder and was struck by her mention of Pa's growing discomfort anytime he could see the smoke of another chimney. That was when he usually picked up the family and moved, a worldview I could understand even at the tender age of ten.

After my typical bedtime routine, I crawled beneath my worn-down comforter and added one thing more: a heavy dose of Aspercreme massaged into my palms. I preferred it to other topical analgesics because it had no smell. *Scent-sitivity*, as I'd come to call it, was another reason crowds had never been my thing. Sometimes it seemed I was allergic to everything. Well, every man-made scent, at least. And crowds were filled with a nearly unimaginable array of things to set me off: deodorants, shampoos, and body wash; perfumes and aftershave; makeup, face creams, mouthwash, and laundry detergents. I swear I was kin to that bubble boy they'd done a TV special on back when I was in high school.

More tired than I'd realized, I fell asleep quickly—the Aspercreme tube still open on my lap. The disturbing dream that followed blossomed almost as quickly.

I'd been raised Catholic, so disturbing dreams were kind of par for the course to begin with, but the ache in my hands made this one almost amusing. I dreamed I was a stigmatic. Me. *Right*. Still, I startled awake—probably that intransient Catholic guilt filling my brain with shame for the sin of imagining myself within the circle of St. Francis, Padre Pio, St. Gemma.

The fog of slumber lifted, and I realized what had startled me awake was in fact a physical sensation. And there it was again.

For a few moments, I lay frozen, uncertain if I was really awake or not. A shaft of moonlight slanting through the window drew a blazing slash across the bed, illuminating my upturned hand, and I blinked to clear my vision as I stared at it. Then, once more, I felt it.

Only, this time, I *saw* it, too. I bolted upright, reached for the lamp.

A circle of blood the size of a nickel glistened in the center of my right palm.

Jesus Fucking Christ.

And as if to answer, *no, of course not, you pompous wastrel*, a fourth plop landed where my hand had been, leaving a red blotch on the white comforter. It looked like a bullet hole.

Plop. Again, *plop!*

That was when the sound of rain soaked into my sleep- and guilt-addled mind, offering absolution. A leak. That had to be it. Rain had found its way through the old, corrugated roof and was leaving a rusty reminder for me to add a patch job to tomorrow's to-do list.

I grabbed a sock off the floor, wiped my palm, and pulled back the comforter, placing an empty mug from my bedside table on the mattress to catch the drips while I went upstairs to assess the extent of the damage.

The stairway was of stacked, half-hewn logs, their rounded bottoms facing down but their tread surfaces polished to a honeyed hue. I'd always loved cabins, sure one day I'd live in one, and rustic features like those log stairs were one reason why.

Livin' the dream, I had to remind myself as I grabbed the flashlight off the landing and headed up the steps.

The stairs opened into one of two second-story rooms, that first one, above the kitchen and dining room. I made my way through it to the other, the one above the living room and the bedroom where the leak was besmirching my mattress in rusty signs of sainthood.

The flashlight flickered, refusing to offer more than the failing yellowed glow of well-drained batteries, and I smacked it on my palm, trying to coax a few more minutes of light from it. *Ouch. Dammit.*

At least the pain reminded me to stay in the center of the attic; I'd smacked my skull enough for one lifetime on those steeply angled rafters when I'd moved in. I'd stored the cardboard boxes filled with my life's detritus up there, unsure if I'd ever go through them but unwilling to part with what few good memories their contents might one day provide in my dotage.

I shone the light across rafters, boxes, and exposed floor, but nothing seemed wet. *What the actual hell?* I just wanted to go back to sleep.

I made a quick run back downstairs to find the ceiling still leaking over my bed, the mug already a third full. But it didn't look like rusty rainwater anymore, no sir. It looked like blood.

A sudden urge to get the hell out of that cabin gripped me like Stephen King was up in New England or down in the Florida Keys typing my name in some half-written manuscript, and I didn't want to wait around to read the rest of the story.

My heart drummed so hard it drowned out the sound of rain on the metal roof.

Rain. Did I really want to go out there?

I started talking to myself as I moved about, turning on every light in the cabin. "Get a grip. You been here nearly half a year." *Click.* "There's no goddamned body buried in the floorboards upstairs courtesy Vincent Price or Rod Serling." *Click.* "And even if there was, it'd be a dried up bag of bones and couldn't bleed, right?" *Click. Click.*

My pulse settled.

That was it! *A body*. But of some woodland critter that'd crawled into the attic somehow and gotten between the floors, probably built a nest there, then got stuck and died. I didn't cherish the thought of that cleanup detail but could deal with it. If I didn't, the stench in store for me would be worse than disposing of a squirrel or possum corpse that'd started to decompose.

When I went back to the bedroom to get dressed, the mug was three-quarters full.

I retrieved a pan from the kitchen and set the *mug 'o vile* inside it before heading back upstairs with a crowbar, a pair of work gloves, a garbage bag, and the reluctant flashlight. I guestimated the area above my bed, but before prying up any floorboards I put my ear to them. What if something *alive* was in there, had merely dragged dinner home and was devouring it?

Convinced the only noise was the patter of rain above me, I took the crowbar in hand.

Okay, then. Here we go.

The end of one floorboard was almost exactly where I wanted to pull up the floor, so I pried there, and with a squeal of old nails that end of it came right up. The rest of its length retreated beneath a bevy of boxes I didn't want to waste time moving, so I slaved and grunted till the old wood snapped in half and sent me reeling. The board flew from my grip. I backpedaled into the boxes, landed on my ass, and a second later the board came down like a propeller dislodged from a plane and smacked me in the knee.

Jesus—

The flashlight rolled off the box, where I'd left it propped, and whacked me in the head.

—Fucking Christ Almighty!

At that point, I was just plain pissed. I snatched up the light and aimed it in the hole beside me. The floorboards were mixed sizes, but the one I'd pried was wide, a good ten-incher, leaving plenty of room to see in, but also plenty of room for anything to come flying out.

The dull light glinted off something, and I jerked, thinking the light had reflected off the eyes of some critter staring back at me. But no. It was something metallic. A piece of sculptured metal. Sculptured metal nailed to wood.

A crucifix.

It lay in a puddle of blood the size of a dinner plate, sourced from tiny rivulets pulsing from the five wounds of Christ.

I think that must have been the moment my mind congealed into a blob of useless grey matter. It was either that moment or the next—when that goddamned thing opened its eyes and looked at me.

The next few minutes remain only as clips from some time-lapse captcha of panic: me lying at the bottom of those log stairs, having fallen part way down; me, pacing by the car, cursing the keys for not jumping into my hand on my way out the door; me in the shed, my grip closing on a shovel.

I considered a lot of possibilities over the next hour while I dug the hole. I was soaked as a rat that jumped ship as soon as I'd run from the cabin but had no plan to ever go back inside—at first. Then anger overtook fear. *This is my home, goddammit.*

Some of the possibilities I considered? Maybe I'd been dreaming. More likely, I'd let my imagination run away with me—fueled by the stress of isolation, the rusty rainwater dripping on my bed, and my stupid catechismal (cate-*dismal*!) thoughts the evening before about carpel tunnel stigmata syndrome. Then there was the possibility what I'd seen was what I'd seen. *Ok. Fine.* Not the eyes part, though. That, I'd definitely imagined.

But maybe there really was a crucifix stashed between my cabin floors, which meant someone put it there. *Some asshole.*

Being a basically logical person, I knew there was an explanation for everything, and the next possibility I considered was scientific. I realized the crucifix was just like the one that hung in our dining room when I was growing up. I must've been ten before discovering its secret, amazed at the hidden space behind Jesus that housed two small candles, a wee bottle of holy water so yellowed by time it looked like piss, and a tiny scroll of paper printed with a prayer. The crucifix, my mother told me, was for the rite of extreme unction—one of the seven sacraments.

That cavity could certainly have held chemicals, ones that might react over time to bubble up, overflow. That had to be it, right? Some flaming prankster leaving a timebomb howdy-do for a future tenant—some jerkoff with an unhealthy Halloween obsession and way too much time on their hands.

I got angrier and angrier as I dug, planning to look up the chemical possibilities online as soon as I buried that accursed thing. Reason repossessed me.

Shovel in hand, I returned to the cabin, surprised now that I'd run a good three hundred yards into the woods alone at night. I realized there was a hierarchy to everything, even fear. I strung two extension cords together, attached a lamp, tucked a garbage bag under my arm, and went upstairs with the shovel and makeshift lighting. I walked fast and bold, refusing to be cowed, cursing everyone who'd ever written a horror story, everyone who'd ever put a ridiculous notion in my head.

I stood over that broken floorboard and angled in the lamplight. Definitely a crucifix; I hadn't been dreaming. But now it looked innocuous enough, whatever had served as blood rapidly drying and turning crusty, separated into layers of maroon and mauve and make-believe. I scooped up the offensive thing with the shovel and bagged it, carried it at arm's length outside. For a moment I thought to just leave it till morning. It was still raining, I was suddenly feeling exhausted, and I didn't want to traipse back up into the woods at night.

No. Determined to see it through, I did the deed. I marched into the woods and buried Jesus, rolled a rock overtop the muddy tomb after walloping dirt and leaves with the shovel.

When I returned to the cabin the rain was little more than a light mist, hints of dawn overtaking the somber stillness of night: birds exchanging their first, tentative wake-up calls; a crease of paler darkness outlining the crest of the mountains. Finally, I could get some sleep.

I went upstairs to turn off the lamp, planning to leave it up there so I could see to clean up the remaining mess later. Someday this would just be a funny story I could tell to entertain others. I topped the log stairs, crossed to the back room, stepped to the broken floorboard, and reached for the switch.

Then I was running, running, moments flipping past again like time-lapse photography till I was in my car, this time with keys in hand and the image of what I saw as big and clear as a neon sign in my mind: that goddammed crucifix. It was back. Back in the floor. But that wasn't all. It opened its eyes, began rising up out of the hole like some levitating parlor trick.

My car skidded on the dirt of the steep, rain-slick driveway leading down the mountain. I didn't remember turning the key, backing up. A deer darted out near the bottom and I braked hard, the car slipping broadside onto the roadway and snapping off the mailbox. It hit the ground with a wet *thwap*. The impact drove the little you-got-mail flag to attention, punched open the hinged door. That crucifix was inside.

It stared at me, rising from that mailbox tomb like it had the floor, like it must have the grave I'd dug for it in the woods.

I gunned the car, but it was hung up on the broken post.

Then that abomination was at the passenger window, tapping against it as if trying to get inside. It opened its mouth, vomiting blood onto the glass.

I floored the pedal, the car tore loose, and I was careening away through morning mist, its filmy fingers clinging to the sharp curves of my remote mountain road. I knew it was following, flying after me like the demon it was, but my eyes were fixed on escape.

And escape, I did.

———————

"Good evening from WWSB Channel 7 News, Sarasota. I'm Nerissa Lamison." The anchor turned to another camera and continued. "Strange news from rural Pennsylvania tonight of a tragic accident resulting in a local woman's death. The victim's name has not been released, pending notification to relatives."

Pictures of a demolished car crumpled among trees played across the screen.

"Hikers in the area discovered the wreckage of the woman's vehicle in a remote ravine a few miles from her residence. It was unclear if she'd been thrown from the car, her remains reported to have been found in repose nearby but without any sign of injury."

A newsclip played of a lightly bearded man in his twenties wearing a red plaid jacket and speaking into a hand-held microphone. "It was weird, man. I mean, really weird. It freaked us out. She looked like she'd just gone to sleep, or was laid out for a funeral or something. There was no blood. Nothing. She was just lying on her back in the leaves with her hands resting on the crucifix that was on her chest."

The screen split, Lamison now side-by-side with a still shot of the apparent crucifix in question. It was hard to tell the background, but the photo appeared to have been taken on the hood of a squad car.

Lamison looked into the camera, her practiced reporter's expression inscrutable. "The hikers who claimed to have found the woman's body are under investigation for tampering with evidence and may face second-degree misdemeanor charges under Pennsylvania penal code 5510, Abuse of Corpse."

Stephen King clicked off the livestream broadcast and went into his office. He slid his fountain pen aside and picked up the notebook containing his latest half-written story, one about a bloody crucifix cached beneath an old cabin's floorboards.

He tore out the pages, crumpled them, and threw them away.

29

NIGHT OUT, LIGHTS OUT

ALEX HEROD

I CAN SMELL YOU on the rim of the whisky glass. Smoky, acrid, and very, very bitter. I was outside when the bell rang its last call, smoking one cigarette after another, crushing the end of each between my fingers until the filter was puckered and brown. I need to make this drink last until the blonde comes back from wherever the hell she went. I turn the glass on the table, running my finger around the smooth lip, watching how the light dances on the amber liquid before disappearing below the surface. I lean forward, placing my nose and mouth into the glass, inhaling you. My hands squeeze the sides of the wooden *table,* and it creaks under the pressure. I could snap it.

There's a cough to my right. Without moving my head, I shift my eyes to meet a milky pair that belongs to a man with spit beading the hairs around his mouth. His face is creased, the hairs white, red, and dirt, a patchy beard surrounding a mouth that is jagged and missing at least three teeth.

Not now, grandad. Where's the blonde? I hear a noise to my left. My hands clench the wood. About time. I swing my eyes to the left, expecting curves and scuffed heels, not too trashy, not too nice. Instead, I see furred paws and the curl of a tail. A fucking cat? It's all bottle-green eyes and twitching ears. I glance at Grandad who is lost in his pint.

The cat lifts a paw, gently places it on top of my hand, and embeds a single claw in a gap between *my* knuckles. I try to yank my hand back, but this thing is strong, and somehow the claw keeps my hand pinned. Glancing around, everyone is going about their business, but you can guarantee they will look up if I give it a swipe. The cat doesn't hiss, just stares at me, the stabbing pressure on my hand even and firm. I feel hot breath as the man leans in and slurs something. Without turning I tell him to back the fuck off, that he doesn't want to get into it with me.

The cat bares its teeth like I couldn't crush its skull with my bare hand, and I snarl, raising my lip to show it mine. We tilt our heads to one side. The cat starts to move, a slow weave and wave from its neck, rippling fur down its body and off the tail tip like a rattlesnake. The lights flicker for kicking out time and my glass is empty and I'm not entirely sure how long I've been eye-locked with this mangy visitor.

I turn and find that Grandad didn't heed my warning and is still there, slobbering away to himself, and as he shifts in his seat, a piece of something chewed falls out of his mouth and lands on my shoe under the table. The whisky repeats in the back of my throat and I taste you, bile and disgust.

The door to the toilet cracks the tiles as I burst through it. I throw cold water onto my face, leaving the tap running to cover a guttural noise escaping from my chest. I grip the sink unit and piece my face together in the mosaic of a broken and graffitied mirror. I ball up a paper towel, scrub at my tongue, and jab a soap-covered wad up my nose until it burns. I want no trace of you left. I walk back out to a near-empty room, the landlord sweeping up and the lights showcasing every cigarette burn and blood spatter on the faded floor. The blonde is there, in the doorway, holding the door open, hips forward, head tilted back and lolling slightly on the stalk of her neck. I loop an arm around her waist, and we stumble out into the daylight and—wait...

Daylight?

I swing around and look back at the pub. The wooden door is closed, the windows dark and empty, the stinking bin bags are piled high at the corner ready for collection, and a puddle of piss has almost evaporated in the morning sun. I hear a shuffle behind me and turn just as the man from the pub—toothless McFuck—tries to grab my arm and I dodge, leaving him to crumble to the floor. Pathetic. I crack my knuckles and flex my neck ready for him to get up but he stays on the ground, a breeze swirling up dust around him and sticking gritty in my eyes.

I feel my back pocket for my phone. *Ano*ther pocket for *my* wallet. Empty. My skin itches with uncertainty as I try to piece it together.

I do still have my lighter so I pick up a handful of butts and couldn't give a shit who sees me sucking the last bit of nicotine out of them. I remember to check my inside pocket. I reach in my jacket and my fingers tangle in a matted ball of–Jesus–fur, a nest of fur, sticky, soft, inside my damn jacket. My heart rate is not *ok*.

In the alleyway next to the pub I hide in the shade and lean against the reassuring solidity of the brick wall. I need a plan, some story for your stupid head, a drink. There's a metallic taste in my mouth like I have bitten my tongue or chewed my own cheek to bleed. Nothing hurts, so I wipe a finger on my jeans and run it *a*round the inside of my mouth. I don't feel any damage, but the finger comes out slick with bloody saliva. There's a pain in my chest. I slump to the floor, head between my knees and force myself to breathe.

A foot kicks mine, a voice says he's wasted mate and laughs, and as my eyes come to focus it is night and the alleyway is full of people passing rolled cigarettes, crunching on broken glass, vomiting behind stacks of wood pallets.

It's... night. I swallow, and the blood is still there but as an aftertaste. You are back in my throat, burning and attention-seeking. Get out. I stand and weave between pairs of boots and sharp elbows and cheap perfume, ignoring the shouts of the redhead in the ripped camo who I don't know but is gesturing at me like I do.

I swing open the doors and the tables have all moved, the bar is now lined with ripped flyers, not chipped commemorative plates. Gone is the tobacco-coloured lighting and stained carpet, replaced with a strobe that casts twisted shadows and a sticky, black floor that holds my soles in place like tar. The flashing lights and the heat and the floor and the glass in my hand that wasn't there before...

I hit the deck.

Fur brushes my face, then a spiked tongue grazes my cheek and I feel the sharp needling of a claw piercing the flesh just below my eyeball, in the dip of the socket. I try to move and to touch the *softness,* but the claw digs deeper so I lie still and keep my eyes closed tight. The music has *stopped,* and the floor is no longer sticky–it is wet and moves. My hands slide in the mud beneath *me,* and I try to roll onto my back but I'm choking on something that sticks under my tongue and to my lips as I try to spit. It's half down my throat and half twisted between my teeth. I claw at my face, pulling and clearing as much as I can.

Sodden fur, clumps of it, and as I start to pull on one of the longer pieces I retch, feeling my stomach and chest lurch. I retch again, convulsing, pulling on the thread of twisted hairs, feeling something dislodge and work its way up my gullet. One last shudder and it's out—a tightly packed wet cylinder, matted and slick with mucus. A splatter of dark blood follows, speckled with clots and a singular claw.

Screw you. I don't deserve this. I can fix it. My feet stumble their way to a junction and I try to feel my way back. I press my face against a lamppost, rubbing against the cool, textured metal. The bulb is too bright, and I shield my eyes. I don't recognise this street that I have seen a thousand times. A rat emerges from the drain and stops in my path. It approaches, sniffs the frayed and sodden bottom of my jeans, and starts to climb. I shake my leg, and then swing for it, watching it clatter against the post then turn to face me again, undeterred. Gooseflesh bumps my entire body, and I can smell myself, *the* rotten and oozing stench from my pores. Another, larger rat approaches and I don't stop this one, feeling it scale my back and start to gnaw on the lobe of my ear. Blood is dripping down onto my jacket, pooling where fabric meets flesh.

The streetlight flickers, day into night into day again, and as I open my mouth to scream my jaw cracks, dropping my lower teeth against my chest. Unhinged, tongue long and loose as my maw opens for the rodent, welcoming. I think maybe, just maybe, this will get rid of the taste of you. I watch the narrow, hairless tail disappear from *view,* and I take my mandible in one hand, lifting it back into place. I walk like that, holding my face together, to the end of the street where one more corner brings me home.

There is a car in the driveway and with one hand cradling my hanging jaw I can't resist touching the hood to see if the engine is warm, something to singe and burn me. The windows are dark and configured differently *from* how I remember—everything is on the front of the house, the walls all facing forward, facing me, like it's made of an unfolded card with just nothingness behind it. I reach out with both hands, to feel if it's real, my dangling face clicking and catching my tattered tongue. I slam my fists against the door just as it changes from purple to red and a spy hole replacing *the* stained glass. Then it is a brown and peeling door and I'm sure there's someone just behind the pane of frosted glass, so I extend my arms again and the bronze sphere handle becomes a knocker that becomes broken, split wood, and yellow tape.

One of the windows is open an inch but I can see nothing beyond it and nothing reflected in it. I support my lower teeth on the sill, pushing my upper teeth over the lip of the pane, and expel a black cloud of flies into the house–my house–our house–beyond, coating every surface and shedding shit and eggs. I feel a tear escape my left eye, which is now bloodshot from the effort. I feel so very tired. I gather wet, slimy leaves from the floor and stuff up the crack in the window because I can't pull it shut. I stagger backwards and admire my work, my hands coated in sodden decay.

The house has shifted again, it's not where I belong. The flies have gone. The windows are smashed. The car is on fire. There is rain, so much rain, but the fire doesn't even flicker, resolute in its destruction. I shove my hands into it and watch as the skin tears, the soft tissue contracting, fat melting away, flesh falling to the floor leaving bone and charred nails that embed themselves in my hair. I tangle these bony fingers in my curls and shake the strands free of ash and matter. I laugh from the hollow that is my mouth, a shapeless and formless laugh, but one that no longer tastes of you.

⸻ ⟨↬⟩ ⸻

30

SOUL OF THE DOLL

KIM PLASKET

THIS STORY MAY SOUND confusing and made up. I swear it's as real as the burn scars you see on my face and arms from the final confrontation.

The first time I saw the doll, I cried and told my mom I wanted to go home. I didn't want to play with her, which is all my Aunt Virginia, wanted me to do. She kept telling my mom that I had to play with the doll. She even told my mom that I had to at least touch the doll and then see what happened. Each time the doll got close I'd get as far away as I could. Even if I had to pull away from my mom and head for the door I would.

Her dress was old and torn but my Aunt did sew it up to make it look pretty. The tears were almost gone but they were still there if one looked closely enough. The stains on the dress looked like old blood to me. The arms and legs had to be manip- ulated in the direction you wanted them to go. Aunt Virginia preferred to have the arms reaching out to her intended victim, normally me.

"Agnes, you know she needs to play with her." She glared at my mother as she tried to put the doll into my arms.

The doll's dead eyes made me shiver, it was as if she could pull my soul out and eat it. It was only in the past few years that I was able to tell what I felt. I guess maturity helps even when dealing with fear.

When I was little I was unable to voice this, all I told my mom was "The doll is creepy, Mommy. I want to go home". My mom would agree with *me*, and we would leave. It was odd we would be at my Aunt's home most of the day, but as the day turned into evening, out would come the doll.

It was as if the evening made her want to pull out the doll. I had heard all my life how evil came out at night so it made sense that such a thing would happen. I also noticed that my mom would seem to want to leave as soon as the sun began to set.

As I got older, it dawned on me that my cousins and Uncle were also gone from the house. When I asked my mom she told me "They left" and of course I never questioned it. I did recall that they hated the doll more than I did which was saying a lot. My dad left when I was a *baby*, so I never knew him.

It seemed as if my mom and my Aunt were the only family I ever knew. My mom worked at the local high school. While she had a decent schedule she had to go to work one day early. *So*, I got left off at my Aunt's house, my school closed due to an electrical issue.

The sky had been dark all day, the clouds were grey and foreboding. I hoped whatever storm was brewing would wait until my mom came. I hated being in my Aunt's house during storms. It was so dark. Even the brightest of lights couldn't pierce the shadows. The night was bad enough, during storms, it was worse.

Halfway through the day, my mom called me. She didn't say much only that something bad had happened at the school and she had to be there until it was resolved. I was okay as long as she got to the house before evening.

"Was that your mother?" my aunt asked me as if she was waiting.

"It doesn't matter" I tried to play tough. I hated how anxious I was feeling but it made me feel tougher.

"She's leaving you here for a reason. She knows what has to happen." She sounded so sure of herself and the way she was looking at me.

If I had to describe how she looked at me it would be feral. As if she was a wild animal who was waiting until it was time to strike. She went into the back bedroom, I knew the damn doll was back there. I waited until she was gone for a while, I knew she would be back there for at least an hour or more.

I decided to see what went on. You see most of the time when she was with the doll. I would be in the living room watching T.V. or reading a book but this day I had to see what was up with that doll. I wanted to be able to tell my mom something wasn't normal.

"Valerie, we almost have her." I could imagine her stroking the hair of the doll as she spoke to her. I wanted to call my mom and insist she pick me up.

I wondered what my Aunt would do if I grabbed the fireplace poker, stormed in there, and stabbed the doll in the head. I had a feeling the woman was *insane,* and I would end up in the fireplace instead of the doll.

I walked back into the living room, praying to God my mom would come before the sun began to go down. The afternoon stretched on and on, I knew if I touched the doll something bad would happen.

The shadows began to gather outside, and I heard the back bedroom door open. The song began, it was something I forgot. Before she would bring the doll out there was a strange song that could be heard. When I was little there was no way I could understand the words, but this time I heard them and they made my blood run cold.

"She will be mine, one last time as I took the ones before. They are powerless to stop me. Their souls are mine to devour, one last minute. one last hour." the voice sounded like a small *child,* but I knew it was the doll.

"Fate has chosen, the others were simply there I was waiting for this girl. She is special, she will free me"

The voice sounded like nothing I ever heard before.

"My mother will be here very soon." My voice was loud in the silence that came after the song. I am not sure why I was so sure of this. I knew I wanted nothing to do with my Aunt or her doll.

"You are here until she comes back." My Aunt came around the corner. The doll was held in her arms. The painted smile reminded me of blood, I wondered when the mouth would open so she could bite me. I knew evil when I saw it, in the darkened shadows this doll was evil incarnate.

"I refuse." I was hoping, like a horror movie, if I refused then I would be safe. I didn't have any holy water or even a wooden *stake,* but I was determined to fight to the death, be it mine or hers.

"You are my family, thus Valerie decides who she wants. Where do you think your cousins, uncle, and even your father have gone? Valerie decided she wanted *playmates,* but they were unable to live." My aunt looked like some sort of wild thing.

I had seen movies where someone loses their *mind,* but I wondered if she lost her soul. The eyes of the doll no longer seemed dead. In fact, I never saw a doll look so alive. My Aunt on the other hand looked dead. A corpse walking, talking, breathing but still dead.

"Aunt, Valerie seems to have chosen you not me." I wondered what *I was* doing. My Aunt was still bringing the doll towards me. The arms on the doll were outstretched as if she was reaching for me.

"She takes all she wants. She is the one who decides." My Aunt placed the doll lovingly on the chair. I stood up and slowly headed towards the door, I didn't give a damn if I was supposed to leave or not. My chest hurt, it was hard to catch my breath. I knew it was from *fear,* but I tried not *to* let it show. After all, when you see a wild animal it is better to hide your *fear,* so they won't know when to attack.

"Aunt Virginia, you have to wait a moment. You told me when I was younger I had to accept Valerie. I don't accept her. She is nothing to me. As far as I am concerned she is nothing but a piece of trash that needs to be thrown in the fire." Those were big words coming from me especially since she never said such a *thing,* but I was desperate.

"No," her voice was loud but didn't seem as confident as she did at first. I may have been *fourteen,* but I felt so much older.

"This doll has been in our family for a very long time. Your mom knew what was going to happen" She seemed to get some of her bravado back.

"My mom was the one who took me home each time I asked. If she was accepting this do you think she would have told me the one secret neither of you thought about." I had no idea what I was going to say but I saw headlights outside and could only pray my mom was there to rescue me.

"There is no secret, there is only Valerie." She held the doll out once more. I could feel the doll pulling me towards her, I thought it may be a *dream,* so I started to think, "God wake me up now."

I heard a door slam. Footsteps racing toward the door. I reached out to grab the *handle,* but my Aunt grabbed my hand as if to prevent me from getting it open.

"You are not going anywhere," she snarled at me spittle dripping from her lips. It felt like acid when it hit my skin

"You cannot keep me here." I shoved her back making sure she landed hard and not close enough to touch the doll.

She fell back her head hitting the floor. She was moaning as if I injured her and while I felt bad, I had no choice.

I ran outside, my mom was racing up the steps. I saw the panic on her face as if she was terrified at what she would see.

"Honey, are you okay?" She glanced at the front door as if expecting something.

"I'm fine Mom but we need to go." I could see Valerie at the front window. She stared at me as if she hated me.

"We need to get rid of that doll," she glared at the house. "Where is your Aunt?" She noticed the doll in the window.

"I knocked her down, I had no choice." I was shaking. "Mom, there was nothing of Aunt Virginia left. Valerie took her soul!" I knew how strange it sounded especially since I screamed the last word, but it was how I felt.

"I can only pray something happens." My mom looked at the sky which somehow chose that moment to open up.

A streak of lightning arced towards the ground, it lit up the evening sky. As it got closer, my mom grabbed me and threw me in the car. She seemed to time it so, it made me wonder if she planned this for a while and was waiting for the right time.

The streak hit the house, causing it to burst into flames, and pieces of burning house made their way into the car. Landing on me, it hurt but I was still concerned for Aunt Virginia.

I heard her and I would have gone into the house but there was another voice screaming as well. As I heard that one I guess I passed out from pain and knowing that I caused my Aunt to die even though I was sure she was already dead.

The last thing I remember seeing was my mother standing there, rubbing her hands together. Fear for me and what just happened etched on her face.

"It is finally done, one day I will forgive myself."

31

NOT YET

TREVOR ATKINS

A SILVER PIECE OF eight spun, flickering in the moonlight, before landing flat, face down in the wet sand.

"Just like 'im."

The body lay next to the coin, also face down. Its back bare and scabrous, the body was clad in only a pair of trousers with rough-cut legs, bound with a scarred leather belt.

A circle of four others stood close, half-ringed around. Fog trailed along the short stretch of beach and wove among their bare feet.

Interrupting the path of moonlight on the quiet water, the skeletal silhouette of their two-masted brigantine sat at anchor, sails furled. The ship's rowboat, abandoned in the shallows, rocked gently as wavelets lapped at its side.

"Git on with it then." A shovel blade sank into the sand next to the body and coin.

"Not I."

"Nor I."

"I'll not be taking charge of 'im. Alive or dead. Coin or no."

As they stood together, a breeze rose and stirred the fog.

"If 'e wanted someone to take care of 'im like this, 'e'd have showed a greater kindness afore now."

"Greater kindness?" A gobbet of spittle decorated the sand.

"Like you, or I?"

"Or any of us?"

Their laughter brayed harshly, self-reproachfully.

"A shock to 'im it was, this end of 'is. Laid low by a rutting fever. Not by pistol, nor blade or pike."

"Or overboard in a storm."

"Or by kicking the bucket with ole Jack Ketch." An imaginary noose was yanked tight.

"Aye. But 'e's finished now... all the same."

Another moment passed. They stared at the back of the body, at the shovel, and the coin.

"I'll still not be taking 'is charge. 'E was the worst of us. 'Is debauchery, 'is hate, 'is greed. Especially 'is unnatural greed."

"Leave 'im 'ere, then."

"Leave 'im and 'is soul to rot."

"Leave 'im fer the Devil's vultures to collect." A cross of protection was pantomimed.

Feet shuffled across the sand and into the surf. Oars creaked and faded. Faintly shouted orders for sails to be set signaled their final departure.

On the beach, hours passed, the sky brightened, and the tide crawled up the sand. Wavelets now lapped at the body's feet. The scent of warming flesh rose along with the sun of a new day.

Before overlong, the vultures arrived, the first landing awkwardly and hissing in its eagerness. It hopped close and offered a first tentative peck. Satisfied, it then delivered a more forceful stab.

A spray of sand scattered the raptor back.

A bony hand, skin taut and sickly, lifted free and reached.

The head turned, patchy dark hair screening hollow milky eyes, seeking.

Fingers grasped at the piece of eight.

"...I'm not finished yet..."

32

OUPIRE

LINDAANN LOSCHIAVO

DESPAIR FOUND ME A dozen steps from the hangman's tree dazed by pre-dawn hush, squinting at the bark's myriad imperfections and odd notches, some similar to letters. Wait. Did someone carve oupire? Impossible. Yet the word broke through the bastion of my thoughts, its sinister meaning slipping into my awareness like a skilled burglar. My attraction to broken wings, broken men, generated a low drone of dread, my lips parched with dry gloom and unuttered yearning. A moral failing.

A shadow bewitched the branches, thrilling me with a swoop of dark energy. Large footprints impressed the damp turf, great ghost ships of shoes. A tall, lean figure moved towards me, skullish in his gauntness and unworldly pallor, attire too formal for a forest trek. Rivulets of red streaked his stare, eyes all undimmed shock as if staring into questions that are invisible to mortals. Could he detect my goosebumps from my silhouette in poisoned starlight?

Suddenly, he covered my bare shoulders – with the plushest cashmere scarf or cape –saying that we must not keep friends waiting, urgency whispered with a heavy accent, betraying the lisp of a secret woe or ill-fitting dentures.

As my free hand clasped the fabric, my coil of rope slid to the ground. Untethered, I let the stranger usher me through the red moon's mist onto a gravel path as if we'd both made a bargain under our shared sky.

Note: Oupire is the Polish word for vampire.

33

PREVIOUSLY LOVED

DANIELLE RUESS

IT ALL STARTED WITH the ring.

My soon-to-be husband, Dante, knew I loved 'slightly-used', or as I say, 'previously loved', items. From shopping at vintage consignment shops for clothes and handbags to checking estate sales for that perfect accessory or unique piece of jewelry. I definitely wasn't a regular consumer in loving shiny, new things.

When he proposed six weeks ago, he did so with a tiny gold ring that belonged to his grandmother. He said that it was a 'placeholder' and he wanted to find the perfect ring with me, that it had to have history and be something I would love to wear for the rest of my life. Although I am a cynic about a lot of things, Dante is not one of them. I love this man.

We were walking down the street of a small town that we discovered on our way home from my cousin's wedding when Dante stopped in his tracks.

"Nat, check it out," he pointed at a display window.

I turned my head to see what had him mesmerized and that's when I saw it. It was perfect... small, *and* elegant, the stones so beautiful they seemed to glow.

I dropped his hand and walked closer, placing my face almost against the glass.

"Babe, it's... well, it's so... me," I said excitedly.

He looked a little smug and pleased with himself for a second and then laughed, "Yep, I know my woman!"

I started into the store and then turned with my hand on the door.

"What if it's too expensive? I'm almost afraid to go in there."

Dante took my hand, and without a word, opened the door and we strolled in.

Surprisingly, it wasn't an actual jewelry store. There was also furniture, tapestries, and a variety of art, all of the things you would expect to find in a second-hand shop.

"Hello darling," said a kind voice. "How can I help you to-day?"

I turned to find a woman, appearing to be in her early 70's, walking towards us.

"Hi, I'm Natalie and this is my boy... um... fiancé, Dante," I said and smiled.

Dante laughed and said, "Newly engaged, obviously, as she is trying to keep me in 'boyfriend' status."

She smiled and took my hand and then her eyes *widened,* and her mouth opened in shock, so briefly, that I must've imagined it because in the next second, she was smiling again.

"Then, you must be here for the ring," she said and began to lead me toward the display window.

"Yes, I saw it and, well, Dante saw it, and I like well-loved items; the history of items, the people that wore them or owned them, it's so interesting," I was babbling to the back of her head as she leaned over and took the ring out of the display.

I could see the ring was even more beautiful up close and my heart began to race. I knew before I even slipped it onto my finger that I wanted it. Gold, with intricate tiny vines, inlaid with opals, and petals, ending in tiny red rubies, wrapping beautifully around the three small, raised diamonds that finished the design.

She motioned for Dante to come stand next to us and she placed my left hand in his. "Well, go on, put it on her," she said.

Dante took the ring from her and looked into my eyes.

"I don't even have to ask you if this is the ring because it's all over your face," he said sweetly.

"Once again, Natalie, will you be my partner in this crazy life?"

He slipped the ring *on*, and it fit, perfectly, like it was made for me. I laughed softly and said," Like I would let you go on this trip on your own."

I held the ring closer to my face and realized the red rubies were actually tourmaline, more pink*ish* red, with tiny flecks of green, giving them a cat's eye appearance. It was stunning.

"Before I wear it out of here, I need to know the price..." I started.

"It's $500," she cut me off quickly. "But I can see how much you love it so I can work on the price."

My eyes widened. "It can't be only $500, are these real diamonds? Real gold?"

She smiled and said, "Yes, I have the certificate."

Dante said, "We don't need the box. Here's my credit card."

As I was leaving, the woman took my left hand and looked me in the eye. "This ring is special, it has a *history*, and it belongs to you, you are the keeper of the trinity now."

I was so enamored with the ring, and walking out to celebrate with Dante that I didn't even really hear what she said. Later, I would replay that last sentence over and over in my mind.

But, at that time, we walked out of the shop, up the street and celebrated with a glass of wine.

TWO WEEKS LATER

I wish I knew what was causing these headaches. I never suffered from migraines in my life and last week I had one for an hour. Now, I felt another coming on. The nausea, the fuzzy aura that seemed to emanate from every object I looked at, it was awful.

Dante was at *work*, and I was able to work from home three days a week so I was sitting at my desk, trying hard to focus. I felt like I was going to throw up again.

At 4 pm, I couldn't take it anymore so I let my team know that I would need to get off my laptop to go lie down.

I closed the blinds and crawled miserably into bed. I must have dozed off as the next thing I knew, it was pitch black in the room.

"Dante?" I called. I didn't hear him moving around our apartment, but figured he may have been purposely quiet since I texted him about the migraine.

I swung my legs onto the floor and shuffled into the bathroom. We kept a small night light plugged in so there was a soft glow to guide me. I didn't dare turn on the lights for fear of setting the migraine off again. As I walked past the mirror, I caught something out of the corner of my eye and looked at my reflection. For a second, I was sure I was dreaming. It wasn't me in the mirror. Although her movements mirrored mine, the face I was looking into was very different. I have mid-length dark hair, dark eyes and pale skin; the woman staring back at me had long, glossy black hair, greenish gold eyes and olive skin.

I walked closer, heart pounding, mouth dry but still moving towards the mirror. My mind was screaming at me to run but I couldn't control my movements.

The image smiled at me kindly. I could feel that I was not smiling. I felt goosebumps rise on my arms.

Suddenly, the image changed. Her eyes appeared to be filled with flames and her kind features twisted into a snarl. She lunged towards me and I heard glass crack.

At that very moment, the door swung *open,* and Dante flipped the light switch, and said, "Nat? Are you ok?"

I tried to say something... anything... but weirdly I just burst into tears.

"Oh, babe, does it hurt that much?" He reached back to turn off the lights.

"No," I screamed. "Leave the light on."

I tried to explain what happened. I know it sounds crazy. Dante chalked it up to the migraine and me being half *asleep,* but I know, with my entire being, that I didn't imagine that woman.

THREE WEEKS LATER

I don't know what's happening to me. I've never been truly sick a day in my life, other than the occasional cold and a few bouts of flu, but I can't seem to kick these migraines. Dante took me to the doctor, fearing that I had a brain tumor or something, but after an MRI and blood tests, the doctor said it could be a hormone shift since I was in my mid-30s, but there was nothing life-threatening that they could find.

I had vacation time saved up and decided to take a week off. I could let my body and mind rest while I started planning our wedding.

"Nat, that venue is perfect!" squealed my sister, Katy.

"Yes!," said my best friend, Julie. "It's surrounded by a forest, which takes care of a lot of costs for foliage. Since you didn't want traditional flowers and it feels... very you."

I had them on a video call, sharing my screen with them while I sat up on my couch showing them three venues I had found.

"How are the headaches, sis," Katy asked sympathetically.

"Ah, it comes and goes. Apparently, getting older sucks. Anyway, thanks for helping me choose. Next week, we'll tackle some dress shopping," I laughed softly, trying to veer the conversation back to the wedding.

"Sounds great, Nat! Take care of yourself and call me, day or night, if you need anything. I know Dante has been amazing, as usual, but I can always come over and help," said Julie. "Love you guys, I have to run." She blew a few kisses and disappeared from the screen.

"Everything is going to be ok, Nat," sighed Katy. "All your tests came back clear so, as painful as the headaches are, hopefully, it's just something that will pass."

"I know, but it's frustrating," I said. "And... well, um..."

Katy's eyes narrowed, "What aren't you telling me?"

"Um... well, it sounds ridiculous but Dante has pretty much tuned me out so I'll run it by *you,* and you can tell me I'm crazy too. I keep seeing things. Or, specifically, a woman. Sometimes in the mirror, sometimes in my dreams, and it's so real that I'm either suffering from hallucinations or something really weird is going on."

Katy didn't look at me like I was crazy, nor did she laugh. "Did you mention this to the doctor?"

"Of course! That's why Dante was so scared that I had a brain tumor, he is convinced I'm hallucinating. The doctor said that people with severe migraines can sometimes have hallucinations briefly, but when I tried to explain how long these go on, he seemed kind of dismissive," I sighed and rubbed my face. "Kat, you know I've never had anything like this happen to me and our family has no history of mental illness so..."

"Nat, you aren't crazy, sweetheart," Katy said gently. "You are under a lot of stress right now. As exciting as the wedding planning is, it's just one more thing. I know you have been killing yourself to get that promotion at work too, so that you can buy a house. Give yourself a break. Get some real rest this week, binge bad TV, and eat whatever you want. I'm also happy to come over and hang out after work."

"Thanks," I said. "I really appreciate it. I might take you up on that in a few days. Especially if I get another banger. I love you, sis."

"Love you too!" And the screen went blank.

In the black reflection of my screen, I could see the mirror behind me and that's when I noticed. There was an outline of a person. I frantically glanced in front of me, but of course, no one was there. I put the laptop down, got off the couch and looked into the mirror.

Again, it wasn't my reflection.. The woman was back. Smiling at me kindly.

"What are you? What do you want from me?" This time I felt less fear and more anger. Whatever this was, I felt that confronting it might get it out of my head, where I was sure it was living.

She beckoned me forward and, again, it was like I had no control over my movements. As I approached the mirror, I felt a sharp pain *i*n my left hand. I looked down and gasped.

My beautiful ring... it looked... alive. The vines were twisting painfully up my finger, small thorns were appearing and drawing blood. I looked back into the mirror and opened my mouth to scream and that's when her arm shot through the glass and things went dark.

LATER THAT NIGHT

I hum to myself as I finish setting the table. The silk camisole feels incredibly good on my *body,* and I run my hand down the length, enjoying the feel of it and my skin. It's been so long since I felt... like myself.

I catch my reflection in the mirror and smile seductively. After a shower, some artistic cosmetics, and hair styling... well, I feel incredible.

I open the wine and glance down at the glowing screen again. So strange that this is how we communicate, but it also makes things much more efficient. I reached most of them and they would arrive later tonight, for the ceremony.

It was almost time. He said he would be home by 7 pm, and that he was so excited that I was feeling so much better. I hinted that I needed him, needed his body...well, that did the trick and he said he would finish up early and be home by 6:30.

I made sure the blinds were closed, turned the lights down, lit the candles, and positioned myself close to the door. I heard footsteps, then the key turned in the lock.

"Nat?" Dante said softly. "Wow..." he turned his head back and forth. "Babe, we did pay the electric bill, didn't we?" He laughed to himself and then saw me, a dark silhouette in the doorway leading to the bedroom.

I motioned him forward and he walked quickly towards me. I grabbed his face and began kissing him, passionately. Walking slowly backwards towards the bed.

At the moment my legs touched the end of the bed, I switched places with him and fell on top of him.

"Whoa, no wine? Nothing? You must be feeling much better," he laughed again softly.

And that's when he looked up into my face. He really looked at me and his face twisted in confusion.

"What the f... wait... get off of me! What the fuck is going on? Who are you? Nat? *Nat* where are you?" he yelled, the words tumbling over each other.

I smiled, gently, as you would at a scared animal or child and placed my hand over his mouth.

"Natalie is here, with us," as I spoke, I pulled the serum out from under the pillow, and in one quick motion, I moved my hand away and pushed the opening of the bottle between his lips. His eyes opened in surprise, and with his mouth full, I replaced my hand and covered his nose and mouth. He couldn't spit it *out,* so his only choice was to swallow.

THE NEXT MORNING

I rolled over in bed, wondering how long I had been asleep. I remember talking to my sister and best friend and then, well, I must've just fallen into a coma. I don't remember doing anything after that...as I try to sit up, a sharp pain in my head stops me.

"Natalie... close your eyes... you are dreaming," says a soft voice. And when I close my eyes, the pain starts to *fade,* and flashes of memory begin to play across my closed eyes.

Dante *was* unconscious, tied up, strangers entering our apartment, a glimpse of myself in the mirror...but wait, she resembles me but her movements are different and...the eyes...the eyes...and then muffled screaming.

Blood... so much blood... on my hands, in a cup, and Dante, he's in pain! I have to save him, I have to do something. And who are these people?

And... wait... the woman from the secondhand shop, the one who sold me the ring. She turns to me, smiling, and says, "Welcome back, Persephone. We have waited for so long to find the vessel, the one who would bring you home." Her eyes flash with the same green gold as the woman I saw in my mirror.

And then, an understanding washes over me and I hear a voice. "Natalie, we must share this body, this mind, for now. You have given me, and the world, the greatest gift, and you will be rewarded."

Images of death and destruction, screaming and crying fill my vision, and then, everything goes black.

34

LADY, I AM IMPRESSED

S.E. REED

"ARE YOU SAYING HE'S stuck?"

Margaret Sutherland pushed open her pink, lace parasol and held it above her head to block the blazing Arizona sun. She waved a small, silk kerchief with her free hand to swat the incessant buzzing of horse flies.

"Ma'am, I'm saying he's underneath a toppled minecart full a'rock. Yeah, I'd say Prescott's stuck. I'd say he's dead too," Arnie McGavish, the copper mine foreman replied.

He was covered in red dust like all the men in Tombstone. His cracked lips pursed with exasperation. Ms. Sutherland's line of idiotic questioning was more than he could bear without a whiskey.

"Well, that's a tragedy now, isn't it? I rather needed Mr. Prescott," Margaret said woefully. "Now who is going to help me procure the item in question?"

"I don't rightly know, Ma'am, but if you don't mind I'd like to get something to drink," Arnie said with a lick of his dry lips.

He reached to the brim of his dirty hat and tugged it in a courteous nod. His boots clacked on the plank sidewalk as he made his way toward the local drinking establishment, glad to be done with that particular conversation.

"Yes, a drink! That does sound pleasant, Mr. McGavish. I shall join you at the saloon."

Margaret, oblivious to the man's social cue, followed closely behind with a quick trot as if she was a young filly ready for a ride in the desert.

Arnie slowed his pace and let out a long sigh. He wasn't one to turn down a free drink, knowing full well the lady would be paying their tab, but still—

"You sure you want to drink with the likes of me? I ain't really your breed," he said as he held open the swinging door to the Rusty Spur Saloon for Ms. Sutherland to enter.

"Why of course I shall drink with you, Mr. McGavish. They do have whiskey here, don't they?" She said loudly as they entered the room full of filthy cowboys and hardened miners.

The piano played brightly and scantily clad girls with gobs of rouge and lip stain danced on a stage in the back, a far cry from the finery she was donned in.

Arnie practically choked when he realized Ms. Sutherland was serious as she sat at a table and flagged down the barkeep, ordering a full bottle of whiskey and two glasses.

"I, uh, never drank with a real lady before. I mean, not like you," he said, meaning it as a compliment.

She took it as such and smiled before tipping back a shot of the harsh, brown liquor.

"If I was a real lady I wouldn't be out here in this nightmare of a place hunting a forbidden treasure, now would I?" Margaret asked.

The noise in the saloon gave them anonymity while she spoke.

"I'm not sure I should answer that," Arnie replied and took a shot. He poured them both another round then leaned in closer. "I don't really know what Mr. Prescott was supposed to be searching for down there in the mine, Ma'am. But if I'm being honest with you, he wasn't very good at anything 'cept getting in the way."

Margaret frowned. She lifted the glass to her lips, but held it for a few seconds, remembering the wild account from Mr. Prescott over the dinner they'd shared last night at the Westmore Hotel.

"My oh me, Margaret, you should see it down there! I've been excavating new tunnels and discovering hidden chambers using the drawing you made. I've found hieroglyphs and they are simply spectacular! I am sure we are mere days away from finding the item," Mr. Prescott said with a mouthful of thick angus steak.

He washed it down with the finest port wine in all of Tombstone. Of course, the meal was on her tab at the Hotel. As was Mr. Prescott's accommodations and his other bills around town.

"Everything all right?" Arnie asked, snapping Margaret out of her memory.

She drank the shot at her lips and set down the glass carefully, rolling it from side to side in her delicate hands. Arnie tried not to stare, but he couldn't help himself. Margaret Southerland wasn't so much a pristine flower as he'd originally suspected. There was something mysterious about her.

"Yes, yes. I just—" she paused, choosing her next words carefully. "I think I've been trusting others to do the thing I should be doing myself. Tomorrow, I shall join you in the mine," she said to Arnie with firm conviction and stood up. "I rather hate the red dust and the dirt, but if that's what it's going to take, well, then I'll just have to do it. Father always said a woman could do a man's job if she must. And it seems that I must be the one to do this job."

"But, wait, Ms. Sutherland, please sit," Arnie stood.

He hated to think of this fine creature down in the mine with the other men.

"Mr. McGavish... Arnie, may I call you Arnie?" Margaret sat back down. "I suppose I should be forthright with you. I hired you and your men as a ruse. I'm not here searching for a fortune in copper. I'm searching for something much more valuable. Mr. Prescott was one of the men my Mother wanted with me on this adventure since he was her brother's nephew by marriage—but truthfully, I never trusted him." She poured them both another shot.

"A ruse?" Arnie took the drink and swallowed it in a hard gulp. Now this was getting good!

"Yes. A ruse. A falsehood. A lie. A misdirection," she said and pushed a strand of her dark hair behind her ear. "I traveled abroad a few years ago and happened to fall in possession of a strange, ancient map. It gave very specific directions for finding something buried out here in the desert. Something with great power."

Arnie stuck his pointer finger in his ear and gave it a good swirl.

He wanted to make sure he had heard the lady right. "Say that again, an ancient map, from abroad? Like Europe? And something buried way out here in Arizona territory? But how them folks know 'bout this place?" He shook his head.

"No, not Europe. Egypt. But, that doesn't matter, does it? What matters is that so far, everything has been correct. The rock formations, the copper mine, it all matches what I found. Now Arnie– I think I can trust you... Can I trust you?" She asked and narrowed her green eyes on the mine foreman. If he was cleaned up, with a shave and some new clothes, he might actually be handsome, in a very tanned and rugged sort of way. For a moment she imagined what it might feel like to reach out and stroke his bearded face, the scruff against her fingers. It was probably the whiskey giving her such impure thoughts. A very bad habit, her mother would say. A very real necessity in a place like Tombstone, she would retort.

He looked at her, and for a brief second, he thought he saw a longing in her eyes, a tremble in her lip, desire welling up in her chest. His face felt flush. His legs twitched.

"You can trust me," he grumbled.

He needed this job—the pay was double any other mining operation had offered. And now, knowing it was a ruse, just a cover-up to dig for some ancient, buried treasure, there really was no pressure. If he didn't find a big haul of copper it didn't matter a lick!

"Good. Now, if you'd be so kind as to walk me back to my hotel I'd like to take a bath," she stood again, this time walking toward the door.

She waited for Arnie to come and hold it open for her. Thankfully, the air was beginning to cool as the sun sank down behind the open desert.

"You sure you want to go into the mine? I'm worried that–" Arnie said as they walked.

But Margaret cut him off swiftly, "Yes, I'm quite sure! I'm far sturdier than I look, Arnie. Like I said, I've been on adventures before. Now, if we plan on having any success tomorrow I'll need a few capable persons with me. Of course, I'll be bringing Sophie. She's the girl who manages my horses, and you. But I believe a fourth should accompany us. Do you have anyone you can trust?" She walked briskly toward the Westmore Hotel. Arnie took long strides to keep up with her clicking heels.

"Uh, you wanna bring your stable girl?" he asked, puzzled by the choice.

"Sophie has been with me for years. I trust her implicitly," Margaret replied. "Don't worry about her. What I want is for you to choose a man of your own, someone who can assist with anything difficult we might encounter."

"Difficult? Ms. Sutherland, Margaret– what exactly do you think is down in the copper mine? It's a tunnel, some rail cars, and a bunch of men with pickaxes. We chisel away in the tunnel, hunting the vein of copper, then fill up the carts with the rubble and send it out. Ain't nothing down there but dark tunnels." Arnie stopped walking.

They were directly across the street from the grand Westmore Hotel, the kind of place he'd never consider entering for fear of being laughed out of the lobby.

"I told you. There is something with great power in that mine. I'll know it when I see it. I'll need you and your man to help me with navigating and some excavating," she said, and reached for his hand. "Now, if you don't mind, I'd like to cross the road and I am not going to do it alone. Please escort me safely, sir."

Without any further argument, Arnie McGavish took Margaret Sutherland by the hand and gently guided her across the main Tombstone thoroughfare to the front of her hotel.

"I'll bring my brother Sam. He's the only person I trust– he's been working at the blacksmithing shop, but I'm sure he can take one day off to come down the mine and help you find what you're looking for."

The liquor had started to wear off– he'd need to go back to the saloon for a few more drinks before looking for Sam. They weren't exactly on the best of terms these days, but he'd convince him to join this silly treasure hunt if it meant keeping his job.

Margaret stepped up to the grand entrance of the Westmore Hotel. "Shall we meet at the stables tomorrow morning, let's say nine a.m.?" she *asked* and turned to head inside the opulent lobby. "Oh, and Arnie, make sure you bring a knife."

With that final request, she went in to bathe and contemplate on the dead Mr. Prescott and his complete ineptitude. She planned on sending her mother a very stern I told you so letter when this was all over.

"Sophie, now when we find the statue, remember to place the burlap sack over its face as soon as possible. Do not look into its eyes," Margaret reminded the girl.

"Margaret, I'm not dumb. I've read the map a thousand times! I know what happens if you look at it," Sophie complained.

She was sitting atop a chestnut brown mare and wore riding pants and a button-up cowboy shirt. Her long hair was in two braids, and she had on a wide-brimmed hat.

She looked like a true cowgirl.

"I'd prefer if you called me Ms. Sutherland when the McGavish brothers arrive," Margaret chastised her ward.

The girl was ornery and small for a seventeen-year-old. Much more like a child than a woman. Much more like a wild horse content with roaming and bucking than a handmaid. Sophie looked at Margaret and stuck her tongue out just as Arnie and Sam came walking around the edge of the stables. Margaret hissed at Sophie to behave and sauntered over to her hired men.

"Good morning, McGavish brothers! We have horses saddled and watered. We are anxious to reach the mine as quickly as possible. I'm not made for this heat, as you can imagine, my skin is far too fair," Margaret said and waved her hand in front of her face.

She too had on a wide-brimmed hat to block the sun. She was wearing riding pants and a blouse with a blue velvet jacket. Sweat pooled in her armpits, but it would be very unladylike to remove the jacket in town. Once they reached the mine she might remove it for the ease of digging and crawling around in the tunnels.

Arnie was hung over and a bit bruised.

It took a bottle of whiskey and a scuffle in the dirt before his brother Sam agreed to forgive him and join on Ms. Sutherland's treasure hunting mission.

"A temporary truce, you son of a bitch," Sam pointed a finger at Arnie.

There was a sheepish smile on his face and an eagerness in his voice. They were always feuding and making up, neither brother really remembering the reason for the gaff in the first place.

"Well then, if you ladies are ready, we should get a move on. Long ride ahead of us."

Arnie put a foot in the saddle stirrup of the gray spotted mare and hoisted himself up. He clicked his tongue and guided the horse toward the trail behind the stables in the opposite direction of the copper mines. The particular mine Ms. Sutherland owned was located in the exact wrong spot for mining copper. Which was probably why *Arnie* and his men hadn't found any strong veins after a full month of blasting and digging. But, they'd been paid to keep going, so that's what they did.

They rode in silence for several hours, passing giant thorned saguaro cactus and jagged agave plants. Tumbleweeds blew across the trail, reminding them there was a breeze, even if it was sweltering.

"I'm hot, Margaret," Sophie whined.

"Tsk!"

"I mean, I'm hot Ms. Sutherland. Are we almost there?" Sophie adjusted her complaint.

"Arnie dear, are we nearly there?" Margaret asked dryly.

She too was hot and exhausted from the two-hour ride. Her throat was parched from inhaling the sand and dust of the Sonoran Desert. She had no idea it would be this far from town! Come to think of it, Mr. Prescott must not have spent much time on site– considering he had breakfast with her every morning at nine and was back by five for drinks in the parlor before supper. She shook her head.

"Look, there," Arnie pointed.

An outcropping of rocks seemed to appear from thin air and at the top was the symbol that she'd seen on the ancient map. A huge jetting boulder with a hole carved in the middle in the shape of an eye.

"The eye of the Golem!" Sophie squealed with delight, perking right up.

"Yes, Sophie. It seems at least Mr. Prescott got that part right," Margaret replied as they steered the horses toward the many tents bubbling from the mirage along the horizon.

As they approached, men poured forth from their canvased lean-tos. A few at first like a trickle, then more and more, like a raging river. They didn't just look like a bunch of scruffy men on a work site as Margaret might imagine, no, these men looked angry.

"Fellas." Arnie sat up taller in his saddle.

"What's happening? Shouldn't they be working?" Margaret asked.

There had to be a hundred miners roaming the camp. And none down inside the mine.

"Stay here while I find out what's going on. Sam, keep an eye on the ladies," Arnie barked at his brother and rode his horse through the sea of laborers toward a big fella near the entrance of the mine.

Sam pulled his horse sideways, blocking Sophie and Margaret from riding further ahead. They watched as Arnie jumped down and began shouting at the big man. His arms flailed about, and his voice was stern, but the words were lost to the wind.

"Ooooh, look how mad he is. What do you suppose he's saying to them?" Sophie leaned forward and asked Margaret.

"I'm sure he's telling the men they've all lost a day's wages! They should be down in the mine digging," Margaret replied sharply.

"Nah, Ma'am. That fella's Mitch Dorset. A real SOB if you know what I mean. Arnie said he's been causing trouble. If I know my brother, he's telling Mitch he's fired. He don't like to look bad, 'specially in front of a fine lady as yourself," Sam suggested.

"Hmmm... well, that could take some time. I'm anxious to get into the mine and search—" Margaret said and clicked her tongue. Her horse began moving forward before Sam could stop her and she was able to ride past him with Sophie hot on her heels. They raced right past Arnie and Mitch, towards the entrance of the mine. "Hurry, Sophie, let's get in there and begin our search. I know it must be close. The Eye of the Golem, it's the sign."

"Wait for me!" Sophie yelled as she jumped off her horse to chase after Margaret, who was already running at full speed into the mine shaft.

"GOD DAMNIT MARGARET!" Arnie was screaming and running on foot after them. "Sam you worthless piece of shit, I told you to watch them!"

"Don't scream at me. I don't even know what the fuck I'm doing out here," Sam shouted back at his brother.

They chased after Margaret and Sophie who'd run deep into the rocky mine shaft.

"MARGARET! There's trouble, you hear me. There's trouble!" Arnie cupped his hands around his mouth and bellowed into the cavernous tunnel.

The word trouble echoed and was loud enough to cause her to slow her pace. She paused, as did Sophie, who was only running because irritating the mine foreman and his brother was more fun than she'd had in a long time.

"Mr. McGavish, I'm not sure what argument you have with your men, but it does not concern me. I need to find the statue! Don't you understand The Eye of the Golem, the rock outside the mine! It was on my map. This is the location of the Statue of Tor; and once it's taken back to its temple in Egypt it will change the world!"

Margaret's eyes were huge. She was overcome by the excitement of being so close to the thing she'd been dreaming of and searching for years.

"Ms. Sutherland, I think your passion is commendable. But, the men, they've seen something in one of the caves further down in the mine– we need to turn back right now!" Arnie took a few cautious steps forward towards Margaret. He reached out his hand towards her.

"What could your men have seen that would deter me from finding the statue?" She asked.

She was very annoyed that her mission was being halted. Her blue jacket felt like it was choking her, and she wriggled herself to get some breathing room.

"Well, Ma'am, it seems Mr. Prescott might not be stuck," he replied slowly.

"Stuck?" Sophie laughed. "Margaret said he was dead and under a cart!"

"Uh, Arnie," Sam's voice trembled.

"What exactly do you mean not stuck?" Margaret asked, her eyes shifting from wide as dinner plates to narrow like a snake.

"Arnie— there's—" Sam stuttered.

"Damnit Sam, be quiet!" Arnie snapped.

"THERE'S A FUCKING DEAD MAN WALKING!" Sam screamed.

Sophie shrieked.

Arnie yowled.

"Mister Prescott!" Margaret hissed. "You are supposed to be dead!" She wagged a finger at the rotting corpse limping in their direction. His face was contorted, and he held a golden statue in his outstretched hand. It was the treasure she had been looking for, the Statue of Tor. "Oh my! Look what you have. Sophie dear, do you have the burlap sack? Arnie, Sam, I'd advise you to turn around and avert your gaze."

"What the fuck is going on," Sam muttered when Arnie grabbed him by the shoulder and spun him around.

"Margaret, here." Sophie threw the burlap sack which Margaret caught one-handed. She gave her ward a stern look. "I mean, Ms. Sutherland, Ma'am."

Sophie stuck out her tongue again. Margaret would have to deal with that nonsense when they returned to the hotel later. But for now, she had to deal with the dead Mr. Prescott.

"You actually found it. I'm pleasantly surprised, William," Margaret used the corpse's first name. He continued to take shuttered steps toward her, slowly raising his arms. But she refused to let her eyes be drawn to the golden statue in his hands. "You know, I was beginning to think you were only here to take advantage of my generous nature. I mean, the tab at the brothel, you can imagine what I thought when I saw it!"

"Mmmmm... Mmmmm..."

"Mister Prescott! You are perverse and I disapprove of such contemptuous sounds!" Margaret shouted.

"I'll shoot him dead."

Arnie wasn't about to let this dead prick assault Margaret and her ward Sophie with his foul moaning. He pulled his pistol and cocked it.

"Put the gun away," Margaret chided. "A pistol will have no effect. May I have the knife please, Arnie."

She reached her hand out and took the knife from Arnie. Then, without warning or any hesitation, Margaret rushed at Mr. Prescott and leapt into the air.

"To hell with you!" she yelled.

Her arm swung back, not hindered by the tight-fitting jacket, and came forward with such power and force she slit dead Mr. Prescott's throat in one swift movement; all while maneuvering the burlap sack over the golden statue.

"Holy shit," Sophie and Sam gasped in unison, having both turned around just in time to see the action.

"Lady, I am impressed. You have killed a dead man," Arnie said, looking at the crumpled pile of dead flesh lying on the floor of the mine.

"Fuck, he stinks," Sam coughed and waved his hat in front of his face.

The entire mine shaft took on the tangy putrid stench of death.

"Oh no, Samuel. I imagine it's the statue. It's trying to scare us away—"

Margaret stepped over dead Mr. Prescott, to pick up the sack that held the Statue of Tor. A sulfurous odor wafted from the sack as Margaret wandered toward the front of the mine shaft.

"Ms. Sutherland, should you really be that close to it?" Arnie raced after her. "I mean, look what it did to your man Prescott."

"Yes, it's quite safe in this sack, tell them Sophie," Margaret replied.

"It's quite safe in the sack," Sophie mimicked.

Arnie placed a hand on the girl's shoulder, stopping her in her tracks.

"You see the treasure map she's got. You sure that thing ain't gonna turn her into a dead person," Arnie asked in a harsh whisper.

"Gah, get off me," Sophie pulled her shoulder from the mine boss. She wasn't particularly fond of men, let alone one touching her. "And yes, I've seen it. It says don't look the statue in the eyes. Sooooo, if it's in a sack you can't look it in the eyes, can you? Now, if you don't mind, me and Margaret need to go back to the hotel."

Sophie rushed from the tunnel into the bright light of the midday sun. The men had formed a crowd around the entrance to the mine, blocking Margaret from reaching her horse. The hair on the back of Sophie's neck stood up.

"Now what the fuck is this?" Arnie announced loudly.

"Looks like your men are getting ready to do something stupid," Sam said under his breath when he walked up behind Arnie.

"It seems these men are unhappy, Mr. McGavish. Please instruct them to let me and Sophie pass and I will make sure they are paid a full week's wages. They all look able-bodied and can find work at other mines." Margaret held up the smelly sack, letting its fumes drift in the dry wind towards the men, using it as a form of crowd disbursement. "Our work here is done. Go on now, shoo."

Half the men screamed and ran off when the smell hit their noses.

The other half looked wild-eyed and ready for blood. That's when the screaming and fighting broke out. They were shoving and pushing to get at Margaret and Sophie. Sam lunged in front of them to block the angry mob.

BANG!

Arnie McGavish fired his pistol in the air. The pushing stopped, but the jeering and shouting continued until he fired another bullet into the sky.

"GOD DAMMIT, WHAT'S WRONG WITH YOU AR-SES?"

"They're reacting to the statue, Arnie. Its presence can make some men with weak dispositions—oh never mind that. You may want to close your eyes." To which Sophie, Sam, and even Arnie kindly obliged and closed their eyes tightly.

"ARGH!"

"BITCH!"

The wails were quick. The statue was already back in the sack by the time the bodies started falling. Man after man, dropping to their knees and slumping over onto the desert floor.

"Ms. Sutherland, I will only ask you this once. Have you just killed all of these men?" Arnie's voice was thick with rage when he saw the carnage.

"Mr. McGavish, what kind of woman do you take me for?" Margaret huffed. "Sophie, please, the horses. I'd like to get back to our hotel and bathe before supper. Sam, would you care to join us for steak? We can discuss our next trip and what sort of accommodations you and your brother would prefer."

Sam nodded and rushed off to help Sophie with the horses.

Arnie paced back and forth in front of the piles of inca-pacitated men, finally throwing his hat in the dirt. Sweat was beading down his forehead and his chest heaved up and down. He had no idea what in God's name was happening, but so help him, if Margaret just killed all these men, he was going to have to take matters into his own hands. He leaned down to Mitch who was face down in the hot sand. He flipped over his body, expecting him to be as dead as Mr. Prescott.

"Ugh, that uppity bitch tried to kill me," Mitch groaned and put his hand to his head.

"Arnie dear, are you ready? We really should be on our way before all of the men wake up. I will send them two weeks' wages for the trouble. I think that should be sufficient. What say you?" Margaret was standing next to her horse. Sophie and Sam were already galloping on the trail, headed back toward the safety of the Westmore hotel with orders to prepare the special trunk that would be carrying the Statue of Tor to its next destination.

"I, uh, yes. Yes. Two weeks' wages will settle them," Arnie stammered. He looked around and saw more men moving and holding their heads with agony. Well, at least they weren't dead. Just stunned somehow by the statue. He reached down to the ground and picked up his hat, letting out a long, exasperated sigh before mounting his horse. "Ms. Sutherland, I expect some answers."

"And you shall have them." Her eyes glimmered in the after-noon sun.

Something in their sparkle made Arnie feel, well hell, he felt uneasy as shit! Margaret had just used some magic statue to render a rowdy crowd of men unconscious, not to mention she'd had the wherewithal to stay calm enough to slit a dead man's throat in the mine shaft. But, beyond that, the shine in those eyes was alluring. He felt, for a moment, that he might follow her anywhere– searching for adventure, maybe a little love, he wasn't sure yet.

"Mr. McGavish, are you coming? I'd like to freshen up before dinner. I generally don't wear pants this long and my legs are chafing in this heat."

"Yes, Ma'am." Arnie smiled.

35

SOMETHING IN THE WATER

DANIELLE RUESS

WE THINK WE KNOW how we'll react in a crisis. How many times have you talked back to a newscaster on the TV and commented how you would've done XYZ differently? How you would keep your cool, even if your brain couldn't comprehend what it was seeing. Or, you yelled at the person in a horror movie for being stupid.

We all think we know what we would do... we would do the smart thing... we would be the final girl, guy, person... the survivor... but to what end? We all think we know. But we don't... until we do.

AND SO, IT BEGINS

I sigh softly as I turn on my blinker signal. I have so many deadlines at work that it's been hard to switch to 'girl's weekend' mode. But, as I pull into Noelle's driveway and see her and Keeley clapping and jumping up and down next to their suitcases, the deadlines start to roll to the back of my mind.

"PB!" yells Keeley like we are eight years old again. I would die if anyone heard my childhood nickname, but with these two, there's a certain comfort to it.

"PB is my name. If you know me and call me Phoebe..." I say dramatically as Noelle and Kelley join in to finish the quote.

"Then you don't really know me at all."

"Yeah, ok Lady Gaga... if you are done with your pop quotes, can we get our cute selves into the convertible we rented and get on the road?" Noelle sang. "We could still be in time to catch some late afternoon sun."

With that, we loaded our bags, queued our first playlist, and started our two-hour road trip to Lake White Rock. Those two hours were filled with laughter, reminiscing, teasing, and confessing.

Later, I'll look back on those two hours as the last happy hours of my life.

WHAT LURKS BENEATH?

"This one... or this one?" Keeley asks, holding up two swim-suits.

"Honestly, Keels, you can wear anything and turn heads," I say, as I pack the last of our lake bag and cooler. Keeley is an absolute stunner; perfect cocoa skin, great bone structure, and the most intense golden-brown eyes I've ever seen.

She laughs and runs back into her bedroom in our three-bedroom cottage rental, to hopefully change so we can leave. Noelle is getting testy about the sun. Although she is pale beyond belief with natural light blonde hair and will not allow direct sunlight to touch her skin, she still claims that sitting under an umbrella while 'being outside while it's sunny' is healthy for her skin.

We walk down to the shore and are amazed at the number of people all around the lake. Besides many families, and groups of teens, we see groups of people that appear to be in our early 30's range. After setting up our umbrellas and towels, we walk down to the water's edge up to our ankles.

"That's strange," I muse. "I don't remember the water being so murky and greenish-yellow." "I was just thinking the same thing," replies Keeley while wrinkling her nose.

"We haven't been here at this time of year before," says Noelle. "Now, come on already."

We walk into the water waist-deep and that's when I see something. My eyes and brain are misfiring, they have to be. What I just saw in the murky water looked like a baby dinosaur, almost like a tiny, deformed triceratops. I blink and look again, and nothing is there. I shake my head and swim out to Noelle and Keeley. I decide not to say anything. Why? Later, I'll ask myself this question over and over.

After hanging out in the water for a bit, we return to our towels, pour our mixed drinks, and sit back to relax.

"So, Keels, any new updates on how the research is going on your newest franken food?" asks Noelle, trying to seem innocent but I already know what's coming. Keeley is a product manager for a bioengineered food manufacturer, while Noelle has always been our 'vegetarian, only eats organic, reads every label, works for a natural skincare company' friend. Keeley has worked extremely hard to get promoted at this company, and her leadership team is supportive, so she has a bright future there. I know she wants to celebrate her accomplishments, and she does, with me, but I get frustrated that these two can't just put this one thing aside.

"Elle," says Keeley exasperatedly, "I thought we agreed not to bring this up again. I know you don't like what my employer does, but the planet is overcrowded, and we have to feed the masses, so..."

"I'm not saying you are doing anything wrong," says Noelle. "I'm just curious about what's next on the list. I just wonder how you are doing with the lobbyists."

"You know I'm not involved on that side of the business," says Keeley, less exasperated but still guarded. "Right now, we have three more species of apples that have stabilized and should be ready to deploy, also a variety of peppers. They are still fine-tuning the protein programs, but anyway, work talk is so boring. What we really should be talking about is PB's hot new crush."

I bat my blue eyes dramatically and say with flair, "Oh, my love life, such a boring topic." "Spill. Now." says Noelle.

"Ok... ok," I replied. "There's nothing crazy to report, one of my clients is getting sued and one of the lawyers on his team came in to pull all the financial documents they need for the case. We had a long night in the office and ended up chatting the entire time we worked. He asked me out the next day and

I've been seeing him for a few weeks. It's easy, not serious and he is hella easy on the eyes so I'm good."

We continued to catch up on things and drink. I laid back on my towel, smiling and listening to the voices of my best friends, and I must've dozed off because the next thing I remember is being aware of a terrible, cloying smell; like bad eggs, bleach, and rotten fish. I sit up, gagging, trying to figure out if this is a bad dream.

THIS IS THE END, MY FRIEND

"Keeley, Noelle!" I say loudly as I look out to the water and see it 'breathing', there is no other way to describe it. Some bubbles were the size of a ship, others were the size of a beach umbrella, as if the lake were a giant witches' caldron, they grew, then receded, then grew again. My brain finally caught up to my body and I scrambled to my feet. I looked around wildly and realized that Keeley and Noelle weren't there.

"They went to grab food," yells a woman a few towels over and she turns her attention back to the lake. People are also staring so I must not be dreaming. "They told me to tell you if you woke up. They said you needed the rest."

I don't even thank her because I'm feeling panicked; the hair on my arms is actually standing up, and it feels like hundreds of tiny bugs are marching across my scalp. If we haven't ever experienced true terror, do we know what our brain and body are trying to tell us? Thousands of evolutionary years and we are still basic mammals when it comes to survival.

The air feels charged... something isn't right... and at that very moment, the largest of those bubbles rises hundreds of feet into the air and then it bursts, creating an almost tsunami effect on the beach. One second, I'm standing, and the next, I'm plunged into the water. I have no choice but to open my eyes to see which way is up.

And when I do, I think I must still be sleeping. This is a bad dream. It has to be. There is something directly in front of me; if I'm forced to describe it, it looks like a cross between a basset hound dog and some sort of platypus, with webbed feet and a nightmare octopus-like mouth. And trapped in its mouth is a small child. I push down the urge to scream. This cannot be happening.

I turn my head quickly and realize that the 'baby triceratops' that I thought I saw earlier is way too close to me. It's calmly staring at me and then tentacles make their way out of its mouth towards me. Now my brain fires my muscles and I feel myself push up with all my strength and as I break the surface, I can hear screaming and see people trying to get out of the water. Some people are standing higher up on what were cliffs surrounding the lake, but now the water surges upward. A guy screams 'grab my hand' and I do. Everything in my body wants to get out of the water and find Noelle and Keeley.

As I scramble to my feet, the guy begins screaming a few names and looking frantically at the water. "What are they? What the fuck are they?" he screams at no one in particular.

I don't pause or look back, I run, as fast as I possibly can, back towards the cottage and hope I find Keeley and Noelle. My heart is pounding out of my chest and I'm still trying to digest what I just saw.

I don't have the lay of the place since we just arrived and I can't take the path from the beach, so I stop, amid the orchestra of screams and the sound of running, to get my bearings. I'm terrible with directions but do a quick calculation and start running parallel to where the beach is. Now another, horrific sound fills the air, like a sound-barrier breaking foghorn. I clutch my ears and see water rushing into the trees. I run faster now and can see the tops of some of the cottages coming into view.

As I frantically look from cottage to cottage, I hear my name.

"Over here—PB! Now! Hurry!," Keeley is waving like she's trying to land a jet airplane.

I'm trying to catch my breath and speak at the same time.

"Where... is... Noelle?" I gasp.

Keeley immediately begins sobbing. "We were standing over by the lifeguard stand, where the food trucks are and one minute, she was there, and then this water rushed up. I grabbed onto the food truck, but Noelle was swept out with the water."

Now she's full-blown hysterical. "Oh god... oh... something grabbed her leg, and she started screaming and I tried to grab her hand, but something bit me." With that, she shows me her calf, which is missing a chunk of flesh and muscle.

I don't know what to do. I always thought I would be the one who performed well in a crisis. I can't move as chaos erupts around us and water continues to creep up toward the cottages.

Keeley begins shaking me hard. "Phoebe, we have to go. Now, fucking right now. Where are the keys?"

I stand there, completely paralyzed. Unable to comprehend what is happening around me. A man runs by us, screaming in agony, with some sort of baby chimp crossed with an octopus, clinging to his face, taking hearty bites.

Keeley begins crying harder. "Phoebe, my leg is killing me. Please, I need your help to find a doctor." Then she whispers in my ear, "Please PB, I don't want to die here."

Her pleas finally reach my brain, which engages my body to find the keys. I run into the cottage with Keeley limping in behind me and start dumping things out of my purse.

"Keys... keys," I start whimpering, thinking that calling them will somehow materialize them faster.

The ear-shattering foghorn sounds again. And a fresh stream of water surges into the cottage now.

"Keels, listen to me. I can't find the keys, but we have to get out of here. Can you walk until we can find a car that has the keys in it or someone to give us a ride?"

Keeley is staring strangely at the door, head cocked like the ear-splitting noise is not repelling her but captivating her.

"Keels..." and at that moment, Keeley, Keels...one of my best friends since grade school, turns her face to me and I scream.

Her eyes are a murky yellow, the shape of her head doesn't look right, and there is something wiggly it's way between her lips.

She's standing too close to the front door for me to run outside.

"Keeley, can you hear me?" I ask softly. "Keels... are you in there?"

Whatever this thing is, wearing the shell of my friend, doesn't react. Not a movement, not a twitch. Just stands, staring at me as the tentacles reach out farther from her mouth. The chaos outside continues and, as I quickly look over my shoulder, I realize there is a sliding door in Noelle's bedroom leading to a deck.

I leap through the bedroom room door, slamming and locking it. I unlock the slider and jump onto the deck, looking around frantically. There are some creatures who seemed to escape the lake by holding onto people but I see the nightmare chimp from earlier and it's barely moving, lying still on the ground.

I figure someone must have injured or killed it and I want to get a better look at one of these things but Keeley, or what used to be Keeley, will come for me so I can't hesitate. I run towards the creature and, as I look down onto it, I see what appears to be gills on each side of its body.

Opening and closing, seeking water where there is none. And then it stops moving all together. Perhaps this means that they can only survive in water.

I begin to run again. I have to find a car because, even if the creatures eventually die on land, I'm not sure what kind of infections they are passing on, given what I saw happen to Keeley. I start crying again as the realization hits that I will never see my friends again.

"Hey," screams a man, running towards me. "We have to get away from here. Something is wrong with my kids, and they just killed my wife."

He is hysterical and bloody.

"Did you get bit? Did they bite you?" I yell and take a step back.

He falters for one second before yelling back, "No. This blood is my wife's. I slipped trying to get away from..."

A chorus of the most unholy screeches erupts behind him and as I peer in the direction, I suddenly know why they say that your bodily functions can fail when you are truly terrified. Three children, all under the age of five, are coming towards us, faces deformed, tentacles escaping their mouths.

The man whips his head around and begins wailing. He seems to make a decision and looks at me and yells, "Take my car. The black SUV right there... I can't leave them like this." He throws his keys at me.

"They will kill you. They aren't your children anymore," I scream and start to take a step towards him.

"You need to go. Now. Save yourself and find help. Call the government, the police, everyone... this is the end of the world."

With that, the children are almost on him, and one turns its attention to me. With his screams surrounding me, I run to his SUV, jump in, lock the doors, and tear out of the parking lot. As I'm leaving the lake area, I see many cars still on the road, but many on the side of the road. I start to see people walking, slowly, on the side or the road and only when I'm close enough do I realize that they look like Keeley and those children. It's straight out of a horror movie. But it's real.

"This is really fucking happening. This is really happening," I chant to myself. I need a phone. I need to find a phone. Right now.

I remember that we passed a gas station about five miles from the lake and I headed in that direction. I see some people getting attacked, I even have a woman run after my car, begging for help. But there is already a creature attached to her back. I can't help her.

I see the gas station and barely stop the car before opening the door. The man inside looked startled as I burst through the door.

"Call the police, the National Guard!" I scream at him. "Something has happened at White Rock Lake. Hundreds of people are dead. Call them now!"

I guess he doesn't argue because I am completely unhinged. He picks up the phone and that's when I see the people outside.

"Do you have a room with a locking door?" I scream.

He pulls the phone away from his ear and says, "It's just a busy signal... what? A room?"

"We have to hide now... I'll explain but those people may be infected and..."

"Infected?" He looks like he might laugh. "Lady, you need to calm down right now, or I'll escort you out."

I don't have time to argue so I run for the back of the store. He's surprisingly fast and the next thing I feel is a sharp pain on my head and my vision goes dark.

WHAT IS HAPPENING?

I wake with a start.

"Whoa, it's ok, young lady. No one is going to hurt you," says the man from the gas station. "I'm so sorry that I knocked you out, you were not making any sense. I left you in here to keep trying to get the police on the phone and that's when I saw them...about eight people...and something was wrong with them...I don't know what's going on but they looked like something out of a horror movie. So, I brought you back here to the safe room and locked up the store. We have a signal back here so we should be alerted when the police do arrive." "How long ago was that?" I croak.

"Three hours ago," he replies.

"No one is coming," I say softly. "The world is ending."

"Now, come on," he softly chuckles. "I'm sure everything is going to be ok. The authorities will get it sorted."

He has no clue what's happening. "Can I use your phone?"

He hands me his phone, unlocked, and I dial my parents. Surprisingly, the phone call goes through, and my mother picks up. It's hard to hear her but I need to try.

"Mom! Mom, if you can hear me, just listen. I can't hear you very well but you need to pay attention. Stay away from water - they are in the water - creatures. And if they bite you, you will turn into something else- one of them I guess. Mom? Mom? Did you get that?" I'm sobbing again.

"Phoebe, Phoebe?" I hear my Mom shouting into the phone. Then she's speaking softer, I assume my Dad. "I don't know, she's hysterical, screaming about the water." then louder, "Phoebe, what's happened? Are you alright?"

I keep repeating my message but I'm still not sure she is getting it.

"Mom, I don't think you can hear me but I'm going to try and get to your house. Stay inside! I love you both very much."

The guy looks at me as I hang up.

"I'm real sorry, sweetheart, I really am, but you can't go out there. The parking lot may have more now. And I don't know if they know we're in here so I don't think you should try to leave right now."

I try to keep my cool. I'm locked in here with a strange man who has no idea 'what' those people are, what has happened, or the significance.

"I'm sorry," I start softly. "I didn't get a chance to thank you for saving me. My name is Phoebe. What is yours?"

"I'm Joe," he says, equally soft. "Born and raised in this town. My family has owned this station for three generations... and we've seen our fair share of crazy events. What did you see when you were out there?"

"That's what I wanted to talk to you about, Joe," I say and then pause. How in the hell am I going to explain what I've just seen?

"I was at White Rock Lake with two friends," my throat seizes up and a shockingly loud sob escapes me. "My best friends... and the water exploded, and flooded the beach, and there were creatures in the water, and people started dying..."

"Whoa, wait a second," says Joe with a strange look on his face. "Let's back up here... creatures? People are dying?"

"Yes, I know how it sounds to you but when you saw my face when I ran into your shop, what did I look like? Was that mental illness or true terror?"

Joe looks away from me and then back. "I don't think you are mentally ill, and I believe you think you saw something..."

"Joe," I say.

"...and you were hurt and scared and your brain just..."

"Joe," I scream.

He stops abruptly, probably rethinking his earlier diagnosis.

"I watched a woman that I've known since I was in fifth grade, turn into something... else... after being bit by one of those creatures. Her eyes were dead, and she had tentacles growing out of her mouth. And a few minutes later, I watched three children tear into their father like a pack of wolves."

Joe stares at the wall over my head.

"You don't have to believe me. But you have to let me go as I have to get to my parents before... well, before whatever this is, spreads too far. I take full responsibility for myself and will sneak away quietly so no one knows you are here."

He shakes his head. Mumbles to himself and moves towards the door.

He doesn't look at me. Doesn't tell me 'good luck' or 'goodbye'. He hands me the keys and whispers. "Out the back door, there is a small, fenced-in courtyard. In the detached garage, take the F150." And without another word, gently pushed me out of the safe room and into a dark hallway, shutting it quickly behind me.

I hesitate, only for a minute, and wonder if I will regret this moment. And then I quietly move to the back door. I lay my head up against it and listen for any sound, anything to tip me off that one of those things is outside. I don't hear anything so try to make the least amount of noise as I put pressure on the push bar. The metal door creaks as I ease myself out. I still hear nothing.

I step away from the building. My heart is pounding so loud in my ears that I am sure anything within 500 feet of me can hear it. I see the detached garage and head towards it. I keep looking everywhere, all at once, taking great care to watch my step and make as little noise as possible.

As I reach the door to the garage, I hear a sliding noise. Like something being dragged. I turn quickly and try my hardest not to scream or even move.

There is a man, or at least it used to be a man, he now appears to be melting, like his bones are becoming softer and he is turning into something that resembles a bell-shaped octopus. And he is... I don't know what he is doing. At first, it appears that he's eating another man. But the other man is not screaming in pain, I can see his eyes are open and the other thing is slowly moving tentacles into his mouth and ears. Luckily, it is so focused on its activity that it hasn't noticed me yet. I turn back quickly to the door and click the remote for the truck. It's quiet outside but inside the garage, I see a dome light come on so I know the door is unlocked. I'm going to run for it.

I push the door gently and then take off. Keeping my eyes aware of the dome light but checking my surroundings as fast as I can.

I make it to the truck and as I pull myself into the driver's seat, the outer door swings open and I see Joe. His face is an orchestra of terror, confusion, and resignation. He looks towards me in the truck and races to the passenger side.

"What is happening? What is that thing? I just don't know..." The words tumble together, and his voice is getting louder and louder.

"Joe... Joe, look at me," I say gently. His wild eyes meet mine. "Lock your door and once we are safely out of here, we can freak out. Right now, you have to tell me the best way to get out of here without raising the garage door."

He seems to come back to himself for a moment. "Just back straight out and give it a lot of gas. Those are breakaway aluminum walls so we should be able to just keep going."

I look over my shoulder, take a deep breath, put it in reverse and floor the gas. It's surprisingly easy and I see the street as soon as the aluminum slides off the hood of the truck. Then I see that there are more of those things on the street.

I don't bother to slow down or try to figure out what they are. I've seen enough to know that we have to keep moving and can't get near them.

Joe and I don't speak as I find the turnoff to the rural highway, driving away from White Rock Lake, and heading towards my parents. I glance at the gas gauge and figure we will stop every time we see a safe gas station, just to make sure we don't run out of gas.

AND NOW FOR THE FINAL NUMBER

I guess I'll just keep driving until I run out of gas...it's been five weeks now and I'm tired, so very tired. I made it to my parent's house the day after leaving White Rock Lake. The neighborhood was practically empty. One of my parent's cars was gone so I can only hope they made it to safety...somewhere.

I lost Joe about two weeks after that. All TV networks crashed, and internet service was hit or miss. We were relying on the radio for news, but it was also spotty and we hadn't heard much. Finally, a stronger signal came through.

"Turn it up! Turn it up!" I scream.

"It's unlike anything we've ever seen before," says the male reporter. "We have reports coming in from around the country. We thought the first few reports were a hoax but now we've seen the footage."

At that moment, the audio cuts to what sounds like a video, screaming, the fog-horn noise blaring in the background.

"We've just learned that reports of this phenomenon are being reported in Europe... oh no... I mean, I guess this really is the end..." The transmission fades to static.

The enormity of what this means crashes down on my shoulders and I let myself sob and scream. The grief I feel is like a horrible weight, crushing me. I pull over and allow Joe to hold me as he silently cries.

The next day, Joe and I followed directions to a town that had sent a transmission to the radio station that we had tuned to shortly after crossing into Iowa. We took shelter in one of the towns for a few days and that's when the first military group arrived. They seemed helpful, even calm, in the beginning. I felt a tiny spark of hope. And then, everyone was separated into groups and sent for medical testing.

No matter how many questions I asked, or how much I begged, our guests remained silent about anything they knew. They took blood and saliva samples and asked everyone where they were when it happened. But no one in the town was able to get any information from them.

And then, one morning, I woke to chaos. I'm ashamed to admit that, as I heard the door burst open below and gunfire erupt, that I ran into the hallway, passing children, up the stairs to the third floor and pulled the chain for the attic. People were running down the stairs, towards the chaos, I just wanted to get away. I hid in the attic, in a steamer trunk. No one opened the attic door and the gunfire and screaming continued for what felt like hours. And then there was silence. And then the sound of trucks driving away. I was afraid to move. Then I smelled the smoke.

I couldn't find Joe, or anyone else, alive. All of the buildings in the town were on fire and bodies were strewn everywhere.

So... here I am. Alone. I guess I'll keep driving. Is it possible to find a place without water? I laugh out loud... isn't over 70% of the Earth covered in water? I don't know what to do. I can't stop for too long. I don't trust anyone. I should just end myself...but the human psyche is built for survival and every time I think about how I'll do it, my mind whispers 'not yet'. But what good is being a survivor if everyone else is either dead, infected, or trying to kill you? So... I guess I'll keep driving.

36

A Life

David Rydenbacker

His death had been as violent as his life. He had been a fighter, a General of the IV Legion, and he fought hard for his last breath.

The Gods had not granted him the easy death that finds you in the night. The death they had bestowed on his wife years ago. Instead, they had smitten him with the pestilence that was sweeping this land clean. A slow, painful death. A death not worthy for a man like him.

I had been there for him all these years until his last breath took him from me. He had bought me on the market. I had been nothing but a shadow, forgotten by the Gods, tossed around in a war-torn land. Only foggy images remain of my life before him.

He had given me food and drink. He had been cruel to me. He had given me a sanctuary. He had made me cry. He had taught me to love. He had not been my first. Others had taken me before. But he had been my last.

The Gods had cursed him. No woman could bear him children that lived. There was no one left to carry on his line, no one to light a candle under his image. I was the only one alive to have known him.

I cleaned his body from the sweat and filth of his last hours, wrapped him in his best toga, and laid him out in the great room. I finally shed the tears I had held back until the night found me still lying next to him.

He had freed me with his death. He had told me so. I was free, no longer his Slave. I could now follow my own mind. My mind only wanted to remember him.

I bathed in the last hot water and lavished myself with the sweet Egyptian oils. The good Iberian wine soothed my aching soul and gave me courage. I dressed in the fine white toga he had given me and kissed him one last time.

I set up the candle and oil that will light the funeral pyre.

My step finds the empty air. The rope pulls tight.

I will be with you in a moment, Master.

Villa near Naissus, Eastern Roman Empire 168AD.

Context: The Plague of Antonine ravaged Europe between 165 and 180 AD, like the black plague centuries later, leaving whole villages dead in its path.

37

A Return of Peter as a Monster

Binod Dawadi

Peter wants to save the people,
As well as his world,
He already becomes a monster so,
By not wanting also he kills people,
He destroys the things,
He can't control himself,
He can't control all his angers,
Peter thinks from his all stories,

And imaginations,
Such kinds of pandemic is occurring,
He has travelled before many years,
He goes to another world,
He regrets also,

From his creation such things happen,
And he is searching for answers to solve,
The people and world.

38

⋘⋙

ACROSS THE BLADE

LORIE WACKWITZ

THE GATHERING ON THE porch did not deter him; this would be his last attempt.

Martin joined the group. He tried the magic words, hardly noticing the simultaneous cries of the others. "Trick or treat!" Someone shoved cubes in his hand. *Where was she*? He sniffed. Was that caramel? Chocolate?

The door opened. *Mom*? The word unuttered choked his throat. Shoved from behind, he looked up. The creature before him had a singular nose. Not his own kind, then. He sighed. The light went out, hope its hostage.

He thrust the gob of candy into his mouth. Carmel, not chocolate, with an undertone of marshmallow.

Alone on the porch, he scanned for his ship. *Where was it*?

Not marshmallow after all. Metal. Blood oozed out the side of his face. Red and sugary sweet, it stained the collar below.

He'd come to find his mother but had found pain instead. *Typical*. He turned to leave, seeking shelter.

At steps end, he stumbled and felt his childhood as it left his body. Mother and ship forgotten, Martin vowed to build a new life. One that began and ended with razorblades—razorblades in the candy.

39

THE IMPOSTER'S GAME

EMILIA THORNROSE

I KNOW AS WE age, we grow into new people. We like things we didn't before or behave in ways we never thought we would. My question is, could someone truly change all that much in so little time? Am I overthinking or should I pay it no mind? He won't entertain my worries. He says I'm being silly. Though, my husband isn't the same. He made his coffee this morning. He added cream even though he'd taken his coffee black with sugar for seventeen years. He never liked kids but now he volunteers to watch the neighbor's children while she struggles with three jobs.

His entire personality seems brighter, softer. He is always smiling. He wasn't like that before. He spends so much time in his office that it is unusual. He even locks it now so I can't go in. Something is wrong, but I don't know what it is. It's like I don't know who I married anymore. And nothing is "wrong".

Nothing harmful is happening that made it urgent. He's just... different.

This has been happening for months. For the most part, I don't think it is something to notice, but it keeps happening. I can't keep ignoring it. So, what can I do? How do I prove it isn't him? I need to get into that office. Though, I can't make it obvious. I still have to pretend everything is okay.

So, I continue with my day as normal. I do the laundry, fold it, put it away, and then move on to cleaning up the house while he cooks dinner. He never knew how to cook, but now says he has been taking lessons. I just can't understand why all of the changes so suddenly.

I finish cleaning the living room and set the table. I pause, my mind riddled with worry that he has put something in the food. I know he hasn't technically done anything hurtful or even wrong. He is changing positively but generally wasn't like this at all before. My husband can be a bit recluse and grumpy, but I love him. However, this... this isn't him and although he hasn't done anything harmful yet, it didn't mean that this wasn't leading to that. Maybe he is covering something up. Maybe he is just making up for something. I don't know. Though, I want to find out. I look over his shoulder as he cooks and hums a song I don't recognize. I hear him chuckle as I watch him.

"It won't be long now, love. Go ahead and finish setting the table. It should be done by the time you finish," he told me.

I know it might be suspicious if I don't respond happily, so I did. I smiled and nodded, going to finish setting the table.

"Alright," I say softly, trying not to raise too much attention.

I go back to setting the table and seem to zone out most of the dinner. He doesn't notice. He seems as happy as ever, like nothing is wrong. I never understood how some people seem to pretend so easily. He is pretending to be someone he wasn't. My husband has always been the opposite of this upbeat and positive man in front of me. The worst part is I don't know why he has changed all of a sudden. Things haven't changed in fifteen years, not even our daily routines.

I wait until he is asleep, climb out of bed, and look for the key to the office. It isn't in his nightstand drawer or in the jacket he used that day.

Where else could it be?

Then I relax. It has to be on his person, in his pockets, something. Of course, it would be on him. He doesn't want me to have it so he would protect it as much as he could and what better place to keep it than with him? I go back to the bedroom and look over his sleeping body. At first, I see nothing, but then a gleam of light catches my eye. It sits loosely in his pocket. It must have wiggled out a bit as he often moves in his sleep. I slowly reach and manage to grab the key without the situation going sideways.

I quickly, but softly, go to the office. I have to be quick. I don't want him catching me in here. I unlock the door and push it open. The place used to be a mess with papers strewn everywhere but this... The place is in absolute pristine condition. I sigh and push the thought away. I have much more important things to focus on right now. He would not have locked it and cleaned papers off the floor if he wasn't hiding something. I am determined to find it.

I go to his computer, but it is locked. I try my birthday, 0204, for the month and the day. It doesn't work. Of course, it doesn't. I knew there would be something on his computer he is hiding if he changed the password. For what seems like forever, I go through files and papers in his cabinets looking for something from recent months. I only find one paper. It's dated a couple of months ago, the day it all started. There it a code on it, 0213.

I enter the code on the computer, and it works. I look for a bit but quickly notice a whole new folder. I open it. It is filled with pictures, videos, information, all of me. Wait... I scroll down to the bottom and there is a picture of the local park at night. There is loose dirt in the shape of a grave. No... My hands tremble as I look through more of the pictures. A bloody hammer, black gloves in a zip lock bag, a stack of one-hundred-dollar bills, and a grave that appears to be filled with... body parts.

What is this? What has he done? This can't be what it looks like...

It looks like a paid deal on the outside. Like someone had been hired to do this and provide evidence of the job with the pictures. Maybe if I keep digging I can find out if they were sent to anyone and, if so, who.

Then the office phone rings. I quickly pick it up not wanting to wake my husband.

"Hello?" I whisper as quietly as I can while making sure the person on the other side can hear me.

"Yes. Is this Marianne Singer?" the man asks.

His voice is low and sorrowful.

I am confused. "Yes. Who is this?"

I need to know what is going on and something in my bones tells me this man is linked to everything.

"My name is Christian Brown. Ma'am, I'm a detective and we believe we've found your husband's body..."

As he says this, everything spins. I feel dizzy and I put my hand to the desk for support. I feel sick. So many questions fill my head, and I don't like any of them. I ask the biggest one I was afraid to ask.

"How... How did he die?" My hands shake.

"We won't know the official cause of death until forensics gets in touch with us but, well, his body was bludgeoned, dismembered, and buried."

As he describes the state of the body, I remember the pictures. I hope it isn't real, but I have to find out.

"Does the body have a birthmark at the base of its hairline on the back of the neck?" I ask, hoping I am wrong. While I ask, I look back at the pictures, no matter how much, it just increases my nausea and I search until I find the angle I need to see the back of the head. I find one and zoom in the best I can. That's when I see it, the birthmark. As soon as I see the birthmark in the picture, the detective gets back on the phone.

"Yeah, kinda shaped like Australia?"

My heart sinks. Tears fill my eyes.

"Yeah..." I say softly, almost in a whisper because in an instant it feel like everything is drained from me. The pictures aren't because my husband has killed somebody. Someone killed my husband and is pretending to be him, in my house, and my bed. But that couldn't be right, right? I so badly don't want to believe it. I just want my husband back and for things to be how they were.

Why would someone do that? There's no way that's true.

"But that's not possible. He's in bed. He—"

I hear a creak in the flooring near the doorway to the office. I look over and see the same man I've been sharing my life with for months. We stare at each other in silence as the man on the phone explains where they found my husband and the awful shape he was in when they did. My eyes burn as more tears stream down my cheeks.

His face... He has a wide, unsettling smile as the skin around his eye and cheek seems to peel off and reveal the man underneath. I can see both his eye and eyebrow are a different colors than my husband's and the mask he is wearing, it is like special effects makeup, something detailed I didn't to notice before. His lovely husband act is slipping as he knows the jig is up. Something far more sinister is underneath the facade as he steps closer to me.

"Put the phone down, love."

I am in complete shock but manage to move enough to hang up the phone. In the moment, I know he is going to hurt me the same way he did my husband.

I haven't heard from my neighbors, Mr. and Mrs. Singer, in a few days. The fact a couple of police cars, a firetruck, and an ambulance all crowd in their driveway only makes my worry grow. What could have happened?

"Oh, dear me. I hope they're okay," I say as I look through the blinds of the window at the scene while I sip my morning coffee.

"Oh, they'll be fine, Ophelia. Come and eat already so we can hurry to the football game," my husband says to me.

I look at him suspiciously.

"You've always hated sports, Michael."

Why would he want to go now? He hasn't gone to a game since our son was in high school twenty-two years ago.

"People can change, love," he tells me.

I nod, accepting his answer. Maybe he is nostalgic for the old days.

"I guess they can, dear."

40

MORTAL MEMORY

JINXIE R. THORNE

HE WAS CALLED 'THE shadow' – that's what he felt like. Abel peered up from the brim of his hood. "Another gloomy day." he noted. The silence was deafening. Densely weighted clouds packed an overcast sky. Shriveled leaves littered the cold Earth. Most of the trees had lost their leaves by now. Scrawny branches stretched their massive claws skyward.

"Fuck," he muttered.

An empty bench taunted him from afar. Abel was ready to go home. The assignment was late! 'This was supposed to be an easy job.' He thought. 'Show up, collect, and go home. Simple right? Yeah, WRONG!'

The shadow figure knelt down on the ground. Assignments were easy. It was 'the waiting' that was killer. He let out an exasperated sigh. Might as well make himself useful. He found a stick and began to draw in the dirt. Anything to kill the boredom.

Time passed, always passed so slowly. All he could do was wait. When Abel finally finished doodling, his gaze returned to the bench. Amid his absent-minded work, the empty bench had become occupied. A homeless man now lain curled up and gasping for breath.

'This must be the assignment.' Abel thought.

Tattered clothes hung from the homeless man's malnourished figure. Dirt smudged their face. The putrid smell of body odor was like a smack in the face.

"*GROSS!*" Shadow whispered.

He wanted to cover his nose, but that would've made it obvious.

Shadow stood, then crossed the yard toward the man.

'Am I the hero.... or the villain?' He thought. This job definitely wasn't for the faint-hearted. Someone had to do it. When shadow neared the man's side, gentle pitter patters were growing weak. *Thud... Thud... Thud.* Every beat of the heart stretched further apart than the last. The homeless man drew breathe. *Thud*.

Silence.

"I'm sorry my friend," Abel said.

Remorse was beyond him, yet Shadow felt guilty. He swept a gloved hand over the eyes of the deceased. "May your next life be better." Shadow truly hoped someone would find the man. They deserved a proper burial.

As Shadow turned on his heel, he nodded. The mission was complete.

While walking away from the homeless man, a woman walked into view from across the park. Shadow watched her thoughtfully. She appeared lost in thought. Her quickened pace noted slight aggravation. There was something about her that fascinated him. Although, he couldn't pinpoint exactly what it was. Maybe he could stay here– if only for a little while longer. A wicked grin crept across his face. His curiosity peaked.

'Maybe I got the wrong one.'

"This assignment," he said darkly.

"Just got interesting."

Shadow disappeared among the trees. The hunt was on.

Willow was at her limit. Fuck everything and everyone! Mercury must've been in retrograde again. *Damn Planet!* Everything was fine for one minute, and then people started acting like assholes. Why couldn't the universe get its shit straight?! Willow was going insane!

Sunlight sleepily peeked through the gray. *'its gonna be ok'* they seemed to say. Rustling leaves danced around her walking feet. The park was peaceful.

"It's nice to get outta the house for a while," Willow said softly.

A walk was exactly what she needed. People were dancing on her last ever lovin' nerve. This week had been absolute shit! Everyone treated her as if she didn't exist. It wasn't uncommon for the family to completely dismiss her. She was the 'black sheep' after all, but it was harsher if everyone cold-shouldered her. If people were going to ignore her, so be it.

Willow was determined to enjoy Halloween unbothered.

She inhaled deeply, taking in the breathtaking beauty that was Mother Nature. The air was cool, faintly riddled with the aroma of fresh pine and dewdrops. Smoke rolled over the majestic mountain peaks, barely hiding them from eye view. Trees closest to the mountain always lost their leaves last. Vibrant shimmering gold and ruby red gleamed from the towering distant maples. Willow loved the colors that Autumn brought. She wished it could stay this way year-round.

"Maybe one day," she began. "I can buy some land and a small cottage." Living peacefully within nature without cares or worries sounded like Heaven on Earth.

The sun descended on the horizon. To Willows' dismay, it was time to go home. On the other hand, there was a silver lining— tomorrow was Halloween! Literally, the BEST day of the year! *Eeek!* She'd prepped for months on a special project. All that was left was sewing the final touches for her costume.

Willow walked the winding hill toward home. Another silver lining– home was just around the corner. The pumpkins gave her away. Three orange Jack-o-lanterns sat lonely on a windowsill.

She expected to see happy smiles glowing from her apartment window. Alas, every window was dark. Three orange gourds sat lonely in a row. Their candles snuffed out. All three faces eerily reflected gloom.

'Silly goose.' the realization dawned on her.

She forgot to leave the TV on. Normally, the TV was left playing for her cat, Nova, to watch. Cartoons kept the lil' fluffer out of mischief while she was gone.

Cigarette smoke irritated her nose. Willow rolled her eyes. *Like clockwork.* Aubrey and Samuel were outside smoking. Bean pole figures slumped against the concrete stairwell.

"Just fuckin' great," Willow swore under her breath.

Sam and Aubrey were the narrow-minded type. The type that thought their 'shit didn't stink.'

Sam destroyed her artwork last week. Willow spent months painting her Autumn Square canvas– and what did that asshole do to it? He smeared dog shit on it! There was no saving the canvas. It was ruined.

Aubrey— that woman made it her personal mission to be a petty bitch. Willow could practically hear Aubrey's stifled laughter. "Still believe in a magic pumpkin?" the blonde twig always teased. Blah, blah, blah. Entertaining their antics was wasted energy. Willow would simply turn the other cheek. She didn't have time for bullshit today.

Shadow kept his distance, watching the woman like a hawk. The pumpkins in the window were a dead giveaway.

"So, this is where you live." He muttered.

That answers one question. One question remained: 'Why was she alone?' If he continued to follow, Shadow knew that he'd get his answer. He vanished into the wind.

Willow rounded the corner expecting the worst. To her surprise, Aubrey absent-mindedly puffed her cigarette. Samuel, on the other hand, was ghastly pale. Any other day, he would've roasted her.

"Did I grow a second head or something?" Willow asked.

Silence.

She tossed a quick glance over her shoulder. Nothing was behind her or beside her. Odd.

Dark bags under Samuel's eyes suggested he hadn't slept for days. Notably, the man looked directly at her. Willow felt cold-shouldered again. Maybe the graveyard shifts were taking their toll on him. Either way, Sam looked horrible. Willow started to approach the couple when she felt a cold hand tap her shoulder.

"Huh?" she said.

Were they messing with her? She turned around to face them. The apartment assholes were still turned away. Billowing smoke rolled into the air.

Willow lingered for a minute. "Should I be neighborly? - or mind my business?" She let out an exasperated sigh. Willow chose the latter.

"Hey Sam!" Willow cheerfully greeted. "You ok?" She asked out of genuine concern.

Samuel only shook his head. Damn, it must've been worse than she thought. Willow shrugged. Well, at least she tried to be neighborly. She walked passed the couple

Her azure gaze reluctantly drifted up the endless stairwell.

"This is gonna suck." she groaned.

Willow *hated* the stairs, and the landlord sure had some sick jokes about putting certain tenants on the higher levels. She trudged her way up, huffing all the way.

She reached the top flight, gasping for air. *Damn!* These apartments were cheap, but they *really* needed an elevator! Her lungs felt like they were on fire! She paused to rest. If only to catch her wind. The mesh material of her backpack slid down her shoulders. Almost home. Willow gathered herself, then continued down the hall.

Three sets of doors lined the walls on either side. Large gold letters labeled A through F clearly notated the individual units. She stopped at the door and labeled the letter C.

Across the hall, lighthearted music notes bounced from apartment B. Willow smiled. Her friend Alex must've been building model references on *'The Sims'* for her next Wild Ink novel; She'd check on her later, no need to disturb the author hard at work.

Willow pat her sides in search of her apartment key. Smooth cotton fabric brushed underneath her fingers. No key.

That would just be the icing on the fuckin' cake. 'The damn key has to be somewhere. It's not like keys just grew legs and walked off— right?' she thought. 'Right.'

Maybe it was in her backpack. That's where the key normally was. She slung her backpack around. The metal along the track sounded with its familiar *zip*. No key. The backpack was completely empty.

"Damn it, *Please* don't tell me I locked myself out," she said.

The lock clicked once, but she noticed the door was left unlocked.

"Shit," she swore.

Willow hurried inside locking the door behind her. She breathed a sigh of relief. At least no one barged in. It wasn't the first time she left doors unlocked. Once inside, Willow looked forward to Nova's chipper meow.

Silence.

Hmm, Baby Fluff must've been hiding. Poor baby was scared of everything.

"Nova?" She called. "Kitty Kitty! Momma's home!"

Willow quickly glanced around. Strange. That would've called her out. Fluff would practically prance into the living room like the pageant princess that she was. Willow let out a sigh. *'Oh well'* Nova had to emerge sometime.

The apartments at Maplegate Complex were simple. They each had their own design but were the same layout wise. Willow's den, and kitchen were wide open. The main dividing point was marked by two shades of linoleum tile: canary yellow and dulled out eggshell. A small hallway branched from the den. There were three main doors. Bathroom on the left, The master bedroom straight down the center, and spare room on the right.

Willow turned to the kitchen. A large cauldron sat center display. The vessel brimmed 'bubbling over' with treats. There was a little something for all the trick or treaters that she'd see tonight. Silver keys dangled from the table in plain view. *Figures.*

No surprise that she left them there for the millionth time. A small jack-o-lantern sat beside the key. Willow gently picked it up to observe the carving. The pumpkins' crescent moon eyes and goofy grin stared at her. Willow smiled. All it needed was the candle.

"Sweet Munchkin." She said to the pumpkin.

Her fingers prodded the rind for soft spots. 'So far, so good.' Willow thought. Her gaze traveled over the gourde. It's good that she found the pumpkin when she did. Elkston's pumpkin patches were harvested clean. This little one was the last of its vine.

Her smile sank. The vine had been cut too close. Fleshy rind sunk under slight pressure round the stem. The lantern may be semi-squishy, but it'd be fine.

"You'll still make a fine Jack-O-lantern." She said to the gourd.

Willow set the pumpkin back on the table. She was satisfied with her work, but her night wasn't over yet.

Weathered floorboards creaked as she walked to her work room. A dark figure zoomed passed the line of sight. Willow blinked at that. Eh, it was just her being tired. It'd been a long day. She turned right, now standing in the doorframe.

"FUCK!" Willow screeched. She felt her body jump. Goosebumps trailed down her arms. The hairs on the back of her neck stood straight on end. Every single nerve in her body signaled for fight or flight.

The dressmakers form stood on the center floor. Yards of midnight velvet lay draped over the mannequin. Her heart pattered. Damn jump scare nearly gave her a heart attack! Honestly, she felt like a scaredy cat. Leave it to her to forget the damn dummy sitting there.

Willow stepped across the threshold. Fine needlepoints jabbed at the soles of her feet. "Ow!" Willow lifted her foot. Crimson droplets dotted the floor. If the dress form didn't give her a heart attack, then she'd be stabbed to death. Spare straight-pins were scattered across the room.

"Damn it, Nova!" The fuckin' cat dumped the pins. This was *exactly* what she was trying to avoid. "Curiosity will literally kill this cat! "

Glitzy tulle peeked through wooden slats. Sliding doors concealed several ornate costumes from view. She really needed to do a closet clean out. The cosplay closet barely closed. Crumpled sketches littered the desk along the wall. How many drafts did she make for this character? Willow shook her head. At this point, she lost track. It took weeks to write up a concept– let alone design it.

A pencil sketch proudly hung above her desk. Willow wanted something whimsical yet dark. She was inspired by the many 'women of the dark.' yet Morticia Addams stood out among the rest. "Grimly Reaper the Pumpkin Keeper" was neatly printed above her sketch. The drawn image depicted a feminine figure. This woman was elegantly draped in black lace and soft velvet.

In the crook of her arms, a bright orange pumpkin cheekily grinned.

Mechanical rattling sounded through the night. Poor sewing machine, it was always working overtime. Willow was so excited! This costume was different than any character she'd previously created. Her closet was stuffed with fairy costumes, vampires, and Gods knew what else—and enough glitter to cover the entire apartment.

The Shadow reappeared. Spying the candy cauldron, he dove his hand into the pot.

"C'mon, peanut butter cups!!" He said.

Colorful crinkly wrappers rattled around. Kit Kats? Maybe. Sour worms? No. popcorn ball? *Ew.* Sour Zombies? Who ate those nasty things? Dang it! Where were Reeses in this thing? He gave the cauldron a good shake. *Nothing.* Not even a Nutty Buddy! Shadow felt defeated. Of course, his most favorite of candies- and this chick ate 'em all!

"Phooey." He muttered under his breath.

Well, at least he could take something for the road. Some candy was better than no candy. The sheen from something in the cauldron caught his eye. Crystalized sugar formed around a dark braided rope. If it weren't for the light, he might have thought it was part of the bowl. Shadow gleefully pried the candy from its sticky prison.

"All right, black licorice!"

Score! Shadow *loved* licorice! Screw saving it for later! He was eating it now! The shadow greedily stuffed the candy into his mouth like a greedy raccoon. surrounded Abel found the woman busily sewing away. Dark circles rimmed her eyes. Her focus never left the dark fabric. 'Poor thing.' He thought. She looked so tired. What was she making? He slowly observed the room. The drawing on the wall wasn't bad. It was certainly better than his stick figures. Stick pins were littered across the floor. Flimsy white plastic– of all things caught his attention.

The plastic barely hung from a doorknob. He picked it up to observe. Well, well, a little mask! Dark splotches riddled across its smooth surface. The rubber band tying it together looked rather thin. Abel could tell this mask was quite old.

"I'll hang on to this." He said. With that, Shadow stuffed the mask into his pocket.

Time ticked away. The weary seamstress rubbed her eyes, then clipped the last loose threads. Her costume was finally complete. *Bedtime*. She had a long day ahead of her. Willow shakily stood. Her hands ached as she draped a garment onto the mannequin. Popping snaps painfully ricocheted through her spinal cord.

"Fuck" she groaned.

Willow faceplanted into a sea of plushy pillows. She couldn't wait to sleep. Her body welcomed the comfort like a long-lost friend. She hoped sleep would find her soon. Insomnia was the bane of her existence. Her gaze drifted to the medication bottles and half-drunk water bottle on her nightstand. 'Did I take my medicine?' she thought while laying her head down. The early hours were eerily silent, yet Willow still tossed and turned.

A glowing ember flickered, casting shadows along the wall. The person in question was lost in their writing. They paused in a moment of thought. Their movements froze as the joints stiffened. A body slumped to the floor with a deep THUD. The world faded black.

Ugh, she thought after waking up from another. More strange dreams. Geez, that was the fifth one this week! Willow sat up and trudged to the bathroom. She took a long look in the mirror. These dreams never made sense. It was like some sorta fucked up morse code. Willow turned the water spigot– making sure it was on the coldest setting possible. A cold splash always woke her up. She sputtered under the icy touch. After drying her face, she shuffled back to bed.

Reality hazed into a dreamy fog. Dappled colors splotched over her line of sight. Drudge riddled her limbs, making Willow feel sluggish. Gravity packed down into the center of her chest. Breathing felt like lifting cement blocks. Willow tried to move yet felt herself confined. Grinning pumpkins danced round n' round. Heavy weight slowly lifted. She felt as if she were floating. Novas' face shimmered in a cloud of stardust. The world slowly disappeared.

Willow jolted upward in a cold sweat. Silver strands clung to her face "The fuck?" She sputtered n' spat. Her lungs begged for fresh air. The pressure of sleeping on her back made breathing difficult.

"Well, that was a strange dream," she muttered. Reality slowly moved into clarity from the morning haze. What time was it anyway? Sapphire hues drifted toward the alarm clock. 1:00 p.m. glowed cybertronic green.

'I must've needed the sleep." She said. Willow slowly edged to the side of her bed. "Alright, better feed the fur child."

Morning drudge was the hardest part of the day. Her movements were slowed as she shuffled into the kitchen. Willow glanced around. Everything within line was sight splotched into color. *Great*, Her vision was fucking up on the absolute worst day to fuck up! The house was silent. What was stranger—Nova never came to greet her.

'*Where is that cat?*' She thought. Come to think of it, she didn't see Nova eat dinner. A little blue bowl lay nestled in the corner of the pantry. Wet tuna chunks had gone as dry as the dehydrated kitty kibble.

Willow arched a confused brow. Fluff never missed a meal! She couldn't fill the bowl fast enough without that lil' butter ball meowing her tail off! Now it's untouched?

It was fun watching her. He l chuckled while watching the woman. Low baritone laughter drifted through the air.

'Hm?' Willow jerked her head around. Now she was hearing voices?

Halloween always had a certain strangeness to it, but this was wrong. Fluff was M.I.A, and Willow felt watched. It made her feel uneasy. Part of her expected to find Nova (God forbid) gutted and hanging from the shower. She shook her head. *No-and doubly Hell no!* She did *not* want to imagine that! A sharp pang slammed her chest. Oh fuck, who was she kidding?!.

Willow rushed into the bathroom. Plastic crinkled under her death grip. Shower rings snapped in two. When Willow ripped back the curtain– she found nothing. The porcelain tub was pristine.

'No murderer here!' She took a deep breath. Everything was fine. Nova was just hiding. For the next hour, Willow took her time and dressed.

The cloak was soft as the material draped over her skin. The crimson blouse had her feeling *fabulous*. She appreciated the black lace. It offered the blouse an elegant touch. Black dress pants comfortably hugged her form. Overall, she was happy.

Last thing before she left– makeup check. She leaned close to the mirror. All color drained from her face– she was white as a ghost. 'Huh?' Was she getting sick? She didn't feel shaky. No cold sweats. It wasn't her blood sugar. 'Hm.' Willow twirled one last time, letting the cloak brush over her skin. When facing the mirror, She was mortified by the image reflected back at her. No eyes, nose, or mouth. Her face was completely gone!

Stabbing pain punched her chest. Willow was certain in that moment that she was having a heart attack. Frantic hands desperately prodded her features. Velvet smooth flesh met her fingertips. Nothing more. She wanted to scream. She *couldn't* scream. The absence of a mouth only resulted in muffled 'Mm.' 'Mm.' noises.

Shadow roared in laughter. He reveled in her reaction.

Terrified, Willow grasped the countertop edge. She kept her head down for the fear of seeing the 'monster in the mirror'.

First, she was hearing voices. Now, HER FACE WAS GONE?!
What else could go wrong?! Scratch that; Willow didn't want
to know. The Jello feeling in her legs made her unstable. As
badly as she wanted to curl in a ball– Willow knew that she
couldn't couldn't stay like this. If she was gonna be a freak...
well, welcome to the freak show!

"On three 1-.2–2 and a half— 3!"

Willow moved to witness the monster she'd become. Her
face......was unscathed? Shaking palms flew to her face. The
bumps and ridges were welcomed under her touch. Two eyes,
one nose, a pair of lips. *What the Hell*? Did she not just see?
Willow waved her hand in dismissal. Whatever, at least her face
was back!

"I gotta get outta here."

That afternoon, It was off to the local cemetery. The pumpkin was ready and waiting. Willow went to grab her mask. When
she checked the workroom door–. no mask. '*Well, shit*!' That
was the last place she left it. She could have sworn that she left
it here. *Oh well*. It wasn't needed.

She left the TV playing before walking out the door. A joyful
fanfare of Lala's welcomed Nova's favorite TV show. Willow
was just glad it kept lil' furball quiet.

"I'll be back, Fluff! Watch Smurfs and stay outta trouble!"
She called.

The lock clicked behind her.

Redwood Grove wasn't far from home. A mile at best. The
jack-o-lantern nestled safely in her arm. She didn't have all night.

Willows' mission was simple: Offer the jack-o lantern to a grave–then go home. That candy cauldron was calling her name.

The roads stretched for miles. Not a car in sight. She followed the path down Maplegate Hill and turned right Walking Elkingston was always lonely. By this time of day, everyone was home. The cemetery lot was fenced by a wrought iron gate

"Redwood Grove Cemetery" stretched across the arch overhead. Etched tombstones lined the grounds for miles. A mourning angel offered their blessing for the sleeping souls. Stone wings spanned outward as the angel prayed.

Willow continued on the concrete pathway until she reached an old sugar gum tree. Earthy wafts of soil filled her nose. Redwood's dividing point was an old sugar gum tree. While other trees were vibrant with fall color– Ole Sugar gum could tell horror stories.

Moss riddled weeds grew around the trunk. Gnarly roots twisted, and splintered as they embedded deep within the Earth. Brittle bark slowly chipped away at the slightest touch. Decayed foliage littered the ground, leaving branches gaunt.

She had two options: The left turn would circle around back toward the cemetery entrance. Marble walls of a solitary building veered to the right. Pillar columns made barriers equal height of the Angel. A raven crowed as it reached its peak atop the vaulted roof. Two stone doors were sealed tighter than a drum. *'Redwood Mausoleum.'* She shuddered. Just the sight of it made her cringe.

Willow turned her gaze straight ahead. Essence of decay turned her stomach. Cool wind brushed Willow's cheek.; as she passed the other tombstones– she quickly glanced over her shoulders.

Weird. She shook her head in dismissal and kept going. An unfamiliar aura lurked around the yard. It didn't bother her; however, it was uncomfortably close. Prickling pins crawled along her skin *Great, here we go again*.

Shadow perched among the tombstones. Abel was having fun watching her, but time was of the essence. She'd notice him soon enough.

Dark figures zoomed past her line of sight. "It's just the grounds keeper," Willow told herself. She tried to calm her nerves. A little scare was good, but this was ridiculous.

"*Grimly....* " a raspy voice hissed in the wind.

"Huh?" Hearing 'Grimly.' set Willow on edge. That voice was clear as day. She knew that she wasn't hearing things.

'Just offer the pumpkin, then leave.'

Willow couldn't explain why– call it intuition or a hunch; something told her to walk the left path. A chill crept down her back. Her original plan was to offer the pumpkin to an older grave, but given her current *'watched'* status– she figured that leaving was best. She turned onto the left pathway.

She counted two rows from the main gate. That way if Willow needed to make a quick escape– it was a straight shot out. "Eeeny, Meeny, Miney. MO!"

Her index finger pointed to the second row from the main entrance. A tombstone was barely there. Willow slowly approached the plot.

'This is the one.' Her stomach twisted into knots. Willow didn't like this. This grave made her nervous. Unsteady hands caused the pumpkin's tealight to rattle. Intuition screamed to run, yet her feet compelled her forward.

She approached a marble plaque. The scent of freshly dug soil flooded her nose. This resident hadn't been buried for very long. Her trembling hands set the glowing pumpkin down.

Willow Rose
October 1st 1992- October 24th 2022.
Beloved Wife and Mother.

In that moment, Willow felt her heart stop.

"It's... me." Her voice was barely a whisper.

"There's nothing left for you here." A grave voice hissed.

Ice flowed through her veins rendering her body stiff. The deep laughter and voice that called her name. It made her blood run cold. Memories of her childhood flashed before her eyes. Beautiful memories faded into the dark. Willow stood still as stone- speechless. All of her memories...her life. Gone. Ashes to ashes.

Rotten fodder smothered the fresh Autumn air. Clouds of the vile fumes permeated the premises, leaving Willow choked.

GROSS. Jiminy land of the living! Her hands flew upwards to cover her face. Talk about a rude wakeup call! She'd never smelled something so nasty in her life!

The towering shadow materialized before her eyes. Head to foot, it was at least seven feet tall. Ominous black robes concealed his identity. Beyond the hood was void. Willow couldn't see hide or hair of a face. What first appeared as robes gradually clarified. This shadow wore jeans, and hoodie like any normal person. Was this death? Willow couldn't help wonder. If it was death, then they certainly look the part. It definitely wasn't human

Willow snapped her attention from the shadow back to the grave.

"This isn't real." She said shakily.

Everyone treated her as a ghost... because she was one? No.J ust NO! How?! Why? So many questions ran through her head. Heartbroken tears welled in her baby-blue eyes. Her gaze drifted to the Shadow, hoping for answers.

"I'm sorry you died." He spoke in finality.

This was a joke, right? A bad fucking joke! Willow stared at the figure completely lost for words. Based on this shadow's solemn stance- something told her that he wasn't joking.

To prove a point, Shadow dug into his pocket. From it, he pulled the crumpled skull mask. Bright green leaves poked out from under his sleeve. The woman couldn't see it, but he was embarrassed.

That's where her mask went! Willow reluctantly reached to touch it. The moment her hand meant to brush the plastic. Her hand phased right through it! It was like watching smoke. The palm of her hand melded perfectly around the mask. Willow wiggled her fingers. They moved like free-flowing water. Every pin prick, and tingle confirmed what Shadow said to be true. Willow was dead.

Somber realization hit like a thousand bricks.

"What happens next?"

Abel plucked a pumpkin seed from his pocket. He tossed it by the gate and waited.

"What are you doing?" Willow asked.

He smirked. "Just be still and watch."

Awkward silence filled the air. Lattice cracks chipped away the fragile shell as roots burrowed into the soil. Shifting masses below the surface caused rifts. Faint rumbling riddled the land. Every rift grew at an exponential rate. Within mere moments, pounding hammered the ground like giants stomping their goliath feet. Body rocking tremors pulsed through the Earth. Willows' feet struggled to balance, but attempts were futile. She went flailing onto dry dirt. Abel stood firm— grinning mad as a hatter.

The wrought iron gate acted as a trellis. Twisting vines burst forward, greedily clawing the archway. Leafy brambles nudged their way skyward; They intertwined around the sturdy metal. Golden blossoms opened their starry petals, releasing pollen into the air. Mana brimmed through every pore of the blooms.

Static energy crackled to life, buzzing with anticipation. Collective particles from the air fused with pollen.

Golden dust swirled. The reaction of mana to pollen sparked crackling bursts of light. *Zip! Zipp! Zip!* Luminous threads curled and unfurled as they climbed the fence pillars. Pulsating bolts melded as one to strengthen the current. Gleaming loops circled around the arch. Finally, blinding light exploded from the gate's focal point center.

Willow's hands flew to her eyes. These beams were enough to wake the dead! She waited a minute, then slowly lowered her hands. It. was. beautiful! Amber waves rippled outward. Even from a distance, Willow could feel warmth that radiated from the portal. She stood slack-jawed and stared in awe. She'd never seen anything like it. Willow tried to hide her excitement, but giddiness betrayed her.

She quickly straightened up.

"So, there *is* a light at the end of the tunnel." Sarcasm dripped in her voice.

"What happens now?" She asked.

"Well, you *could* cross over... or you could go through the portal. The choice is yours. As for me, I'm going home." Shadow picked up the mask. "And I'm takin' this with me."

Home? Where was home? It made Grimly wonder. The portals' gentle hum whispered secrets–tempting with knowledge of the unknown. She took a minute to consider his offer. The idea was sketchy at best. Sure, she could stay on Earth. Scaring the shit outta the living would be fun, however *otherworldly possibilities* intrigued her.

. "And you are?" Willow asked.

"My name's Abel." He said.

Shadows' eyesight drifted to the headstone "And, you're Willow."

"Or should I call you Grimly?" He said, returning his gaze to her.

Well, Willow was already dead. What else did she have to lose? A mischievous grin widened across her lips.

"Call me Grimly." She said. "Grimly Reaper."

Abel chuckled. "Then, from here forward, you'll be known as Grimly Reaper the Pumpkin Keeper." The Shadow slightly lowered his hood. A cheeky pumpkin grin peeked beneath the brim.

A curious calico perked its ears up. It stretched, slinking its flexible body from behind a tombstone. Toe beans kneaded into the ground The dirt felt soft beneath sharp claws. Seeing the humans, the fluffers' head tilted sideways. Maybe one of them would give it head pats. It pranced over in their direction. The cat rolled at the woman's feet. Tiny toe beans pawed at the corner of velvety fabric.

Grimly immediately turned her gaze down. Jade green eyes and a cheshire grin was there to greet her. It was Nova. The fluff gently mewed while nudging Grimlys' foot.

"I've been wondering where you were!" She said warmly.

Nova swished her tail, stirring a few dead leaves. Grimly knelt down to fluffs level. Nova tried to nudge Grimlys' palm, but it phased through her momma's hand. The cat scrunched her nose. She was *not* pleased.

Grimly chuckled at her furry friend. In that moment, she realized everything fell into place. Deep in her heart, she knew. This life wasn't meant for her. Somewhere better was within reach. Peace washed over her like a wave. Lost in thought, Grimly turned her attention to Nova. The silly cat was busy eyeing the portal.

"Well, Fluff, you comin'? or stayin'?" she asked.

Grimly nodded to Abel. It was time to go. She stood and cast Nova one last glance.

"I mean it, Fluff. Last call."

Together, Grimly and Abel stepped into the portal. Warmth enveloped their bodies as they glided through time and space. What lay on the other side? Who knew? Grimly was determined to find out.

Nova watched Grimly fade into the light. The felines' wide pupils narrowed into angry slits. Her perky ears flicked before completely flattening. No one was leaving her behind! Fluff waddled after Grimly with her tail held high. As Nova padded her last toe bean through the portal, the archway faded.

A new life — or afterlife awaited on the horizon.

41

GOIN' TO NEW ORLEANS

WILLIAM J. CONNELL

PETER TENPENNY STROLLED ALONG the side of Route 129. Gazing into the night, he could see the Ozark Mountains rise along the entire horizon.

"Kind of a barren view," he thought. *"Like always."*

Peter felt a sense of satisfaction. Behind him to the north, the town of Mystic Missouri had pretty much been depopulated, erased from the face of the earth, and there was no one left who could explain it. Oh, a handful had gotten away. There was that Jeannie girl—a camp counselor, no less—who'd escaped by sneaking through Overland State Park and dragging some counselors along with her. She should have been taken care of in the park, but how could Peter foresee one of his agents of destruction actually helping out that girl? Hard to find reliable people today. It angered Peter a bit. Still, the girl kept her head under pressure, so he could respect that. Maybe a couple of others also slipped from town. Other than those few, it was mission accomplished. Now it was time to head elsewhere. New Orleans seemed like a good place to begin again. His kind of people there. His kind of place.

He pulled up his coat collar. Even in the late summer, the vast flatlands of Missouri could get very cool at night, like now. Route 129 was a two-lane highway that ran north and south through what had to be the emptiest stretch of the flat, never-ending plain that was the Springfield Plateau. Except, of course, for the even more immense, more empty, and more flat Salem Plateau just to the south. Of course, Peter was heading due south. He might not see a motor vehicle for some time. But one would come. They always did, eventually. Wearing his tattered jacket and newspaper boy cap, and with a full moon tonight, he forced a smile. Had to look good. He might not be able to catch a ride for a while. But someone would stop. They always did, eventually.

Time passed. Peter Tenpenny kept walking. Tonight, there was a lot of light from the moon, one of those "blue super-moons" as his uncle, Talbert Tenpenny, used to call it. Peter felt sad for a moment and thought it was disappointing to have had to kill Talbert at the end. Then again, one of them had to go, and Uncle Talbert had outlived his usefulness.

Peter saw lights shining beside him on the gravel. Something large was coming up fast from the north. Peter stopped walking, turned, put on his most forlorn look, and held out his hand, thumbing for a ride. The round headlights grew larger. Peter leaned into the road and moved his hand back and forth. It was a large tank truck, and from the rumble it made on the road, it was pulling or carrying something heavy. As the truck approached, Peter heard the blare of a horn, but he stayed in position. It was a fuel tanker, and it ran right by him, coming so close to his nose that Peter could read the lettering on the fuel tank. The "Texas Oil Company." Peter watched it pass out of sight down Route 129.

He sighed and resumed walking. He'd remember the truck. And the driver. Time continued. Once a truck came from the south. Peter thought of trying to wave that one down, but by the time he decided to do so, it was too close for him to cross the road. Other than those two vehicles, Peter was the only presence on Route 129 for the next few hours.

Based on the position of the moon, he guessed it was around two AM. He could lie down by the highway for a couple of hours before the sun rose, but he still felt "up" from the adventures of the past month. He walked on.

Another vehicle was approaching from the north. Peter stopped and turned. Based on the headlights, he guessed it was an automobile. From the sound of the motor, it must have been a well-made one. Peter assumed his hitchhiker stance. Even before the light beams from the headlamps reached him, he saw the vehicle slowing. And what a vehicle it was.

Long. Sleek. Black. A big fin and a sloping shell on top. A fancy hood ornament on the front. The driver was sitting on the right-hand side of the car.

"*English-made*," Peter thought.

The car stopped, with the engine still running. Peter saw a smartly dressed woman behind the wheel, who rolled her window down. Keeping his head just outside the door, he pointed to the silver hood ornament, a female spirit in a flowing gown, leaning out from the front of the car.

"The Spirit of Ecstasy," Peter observed. "Not too often I get a Rolls Royce at this point in the evening."

The woman feigned surprise and said, "Really, I would have thought it was quite common out here. But I *am* impressed that you know cars."

Peter smiled and said, "You spend enough time on these roads, you pick up a thing or two." He looked directly into her eyes and asked, "Give a guy a lift?"

The woman smiled and waved him around, saying, "Why not. Too dangerous to be out walking out here at this time of night. No bags?"

"I believe in traveling lightly," Peter answered, walking around the front to the passenger side. A round door opened. He slid into the plush red leather upholstered passenger seat.

"Very soft," he said, giving the door handle a slight tug. It swung back smoothly and soundlessly, save for a slight click as it locked back in place. "And this shade of red in leather is really unusual. Must be expensive."

"It's a Phantom 1," the woman said, focused on the road while reaching down to the floor and shifting the gearstick. The Rolls Royce sped off quickly, and Peter was jolted back into his seat. "It's not mine," the woman continued. "I work for a wealthy man in Bristol, Rhode Island, who owns a lot of factories. We call him 'the Captain' from his days in the Navy. I'm basically on errand duty. The Captain sent me out to the west coast where they took those moving pictures. I picked this up from some bigshots at the First National Studio in Burbank and am driving it back to Bristol."

"What do you do for 'the Captain?'" Peter inquired.

"This and that," she said. "Serve the food. Clean the manor. Watch the grandkids. Watch the adult children too. Whatever is needed. Technically I guess you'd call me the scullery maid."

Peter looked ahead at the road, but out of the corner of his eye he was studying the driver's unusual outfit. Robin hood boots, serge pattern knickers, and a black and yellow striped linen shirt. A touch of rouge on the cheeks. A white pearl necklace hung on her neck, not excessively opulent but clean and attractive. A French Beret was tucked between the seats.

"That's an interesting ensemble," Peter said. "Especially for a scullery maid. Reminds me of what the women making motion pictures out west are wearing."

The woman kept her gaze on the road but said, "Very good. That is exactly where I got this outfit. I like it for the same reason the girls on the set do. Crisp and clean. Nothing to get caught on."

Peter smiled again and said, "The perfect outfit for a quick getaway."

"The Captain trusts me with a lot of his personal errands. And he wants what he wants delivered on time."

Peter saw her lips spread into a little smile as she shifted the car and increased its speed. He paused when he saw a button on the steering column where the car key's ignition switch should be.

"Where the heck is the key?" he asked.

The woman patted a pocket on the blouse and said, "Right here. This is a new concept vehicle. The 'key' is a little battery you hold against the button, then press it. The car starts up. It comes on like that. Also, the doors lock, and no one gets in your car unless you put the key near the ignition to unlock the doors. Crazy what they are coming up with these days, isn't it?"

"Impressive," Peter said, shaking his head in actual admiration. Then, extending his right hand, he said, "I'm Peter. Peter Tenpenny."

"Fang Lin," the woman replied, giving his hand a playful slap and then regripping the wheel. "What brings you out tonight?"

Peter clasped his hands and stretched them out in front as he answered.

"Moving on. Headin' down to New Orleans. Figure my kind of people are there."

"What kind of people is that?" Fang Lin asked.

Peter paused several beats before speaking.

"The writing biz kind. I'm in publishing."

"Funnies?" Fang Lin asked. "Newspapers? Magazines?"

"A little bit of all," Peter said. "I used to work with my uncle, Talbert Tenpenny. He had a small press in Mystic. Published a bunch of stuff but mainly something called *The Tenpenny Dreadful*. Ever hear of it?"

"No, I'm not from around here. But Penny Dreadfuls? Oh, those are those terribly short scary stories, right?" Fang Lin asked.

"Well, yes, but we did news, and other stories too," Peter said. "Some people liked it, some didn't. Anyway, it doesn't matter. The press had a fire and, well, we ran into other issues, and we're not publishing anymore."

"Sounds sad," Fang Lin commented. "You know, those Penny Dreadful stories, a lot of them got printed in England. They scare the bejeesis out of me!" She laughed as she spoke.

Peter observed, "You don't seem like someone who would be scared easily. At least, not from anything on paper."

"Well," Fang Lin answered with a slight shift in her seat, "looks can be deceiving."

"That they can," Peter observed.

He kept his eyes forward. The car was moving very quickly.

"You drive pretty fast," Peter observed.

"When you move fast, not much can catch you," Fang Lin responded.

Peter relaxed in his seat. He watched the center strip of the road pass under the Rolls Royce as it sped down Route 129.

An hour passed, and neither one of them spoke, and there was no radio signal to pick up out here. The road had not changed, and nothing had gone by them, nor had they overtaken any drivers.

Peter sensed it was time.

"I'm really glad you picked me up," Peter said.

"Glad for the company," Fang Lin replied. "Can't get any radio out here. There was a small station I caught earlier tonight but can't get it now. I feel better having someone else in the car with me on a long night ride."

"Yeah, "Peter said, "Uh, I hate to ask you this, but can you pull over? I'm not used to being this long in so fast a car, and it makes me anxious. Nature calls."

Fang Lin giggled and said, "I suspect you've been in a few fast cars in your life. But I don't want this leather leaked on." She downshifted, and the car began to reduce speed.

The Rolls Royce's engine reverberated just a tad as it slowed.

Peter looked out the passenger-side window and observed, "Yeah, it's a lonely place. The view pretty much stays the same out here for a long time. The Ozarks to the left, this one straight road, and the Springfield Plateau, a barren plane as far as the eye can see."

"Except for us," Fang Lin said, pulling to a stop just off the road. "Speaking of eyes, mine are tired."

She pulled down the shade visor, which had a small mirror with a smaller light behind it and leaned forward. The full moon was shining into the car, and Peter saw her eyes reflected in the mirror.

"You know," Peter said, "this reminds me of a really bad joke."

"I've got time," Fang Lin said. "But please don't pee on the leather."

Peter laughed.

Fang Ling then put both hands in her pant pockets until she pulled out a small bottle of liquid which she shook in her right hand.

"Eye drops," she said. "Moisten the eyes."

"Well, it goes that there was a person driving down the road-"

"I like stories," Fang Lin interrupted. "Is the driver a man or a woman?"

"Doesn't matter. Call her a woman. Anyway, she picks up a hitchhiker. He seems like a nice guy. After a few miles, the hitchhiker asks the driver, 'Aren't you afraid I could be a mad serial killer?'"

"Hope this doesn't freak you out," Fang Lin said. Peter watched her lean towards the mirror on the shade visor. She pulled her right eyelids back and put eyedrops in the right eye with the bottle in her left hand.

Peter reached into his inner coat pocket with *his* right hand and clasped a wooden handle in a leather holster strap, which he kept hidden under his jacket.

He liked her. He really did. But he had things to do.

"And the driver says, 'I think the chances of two serial killers being in the same car tonight is really improbable.'"

Fang Lin shifted in her seat, tilting her left eye closer to the mirror which turned her left shoulder towards him.

Peter tightened his grip on the wooden handle and drew from the holster—a sterling silver straight barber's razor.

"You seem pretty interesting, I kind of like you, maybe you're someone I could be partners with," he said, focusing on her eyes' reflection in the mirror. "But for now, I need to travel by myself. Sorry."

Upon finishing his words, Peter grabbed the steering wheel with his left hand. With his right, he pressed the razor blade against Fang Lin's neck. For an instant, he saw her eyes widen in the mirror's reflection. Peter shoved her head against the back of the seat, made a deep slice with the blade across her neck, and sat back.

Blood splattered on the dashboard and the window. Fang Lin raised both of her hands to her neck and made gagging noises. She stamped her feet on the car's floorboards, blood spurting through her fingers and covering her black and yellow linen shirt. Her body convulsed forward, and she was propped up on the steering wheel.

Peter sat passively.

"Your carotid artery has been severed," he said. "You can't stop the bleeding. It's called a massive hemorrhage. You're going into shock. Then you'll pass unconsciousness. You won't feel a thing. So, try to relax, this will be over quickly." He paused before adding, "And I am sorry."

Peter saw the blood pooling over the driving wheel and onto the floor. The leather interior was so red, the blood did blend in. He might not have to worry about cleaning it.

Fang Lin coughed, then wretched blood and shuddered.

Her body shook some more.

Then she stopped shuddering.

Peter sat and watched Fang Lin's body for some time. The motor was still running. Then he realized he needed the keys to open the car door. He reached for the shoulder and pulled her up. Fang Lin's body flopped back, upright, into the seat. The yellow-and-black striped shirt was smeared with blood.

Her dead eyes were open, the pupils having shrunk, staring at him. She had said something about a battery starter. Peter started to reach into her shirt pockets, trying to find it.

He froze when Fang Lin grasped his hand in a tight vise. Another hand seized his wrist holding the blade and squeezed so hard that he dropped the barber's tool onto the car floor.

Peter gasped, and now it was his turn to tremble. He looked into Fang Lin's face—and saw the eyes may have been dead, but not lifeless. Fang Lin freed her grip on Peter's knife hand and rubbed her pearls against her neck. Peter lurched back and saw the blood had stopped spurting and—this could not be! As she continued stroking the pearls against her throat, her skin was coming together! Not perfect, there was a severe scar, but the wound was closing. She finally wiped her throat with her hand and licked off the blood. The wound was a dark scar, but it had sealed.

"I didn't see that coming," she said, taking a deep breath. Some blood dribbled out of her mouth. She reached for a tissue from her blouse and blotted her lips. She released Peter's other wrist and adjusted the rear-view mirror down. Rubbing her neck, she mused, "Damn. I loved this shirt. And I'm going to have my girl Mary stitch me up again."

Then turning back to Peter, she said, "Sorry. Anyway, your joke, it has a ring of truth to it."

Hey eyes. The pupils had grown large again. Peter also noticed when she spoke that her teeth were more prominent as if she'd been using her lips to hide them earlier.

He shoved the passenger door, but it would not move. Fang Lin raised a finger as she spoke.

"First, the story is true, that the odds of two serial killers randomly winding up in the same vehicle are highly unlikely."

She held up two fingers. "But there is a second part of that story. Suppose there are undead creatures who live among us. Not those poor mindless wandering souls you think of, but ones who can *think*. Suppose they *love* the taste of human flesh, but they learned to restrain their urges. Now not all could, but those with the mind to do so, they *might* adapt to live among living. They might even find it a better life, be able to blend in very well. Why, with that sort of mental discipline, a creature like that could even learn to heal itself."

Peter saw the teeth were sharp.

"But the odds are that no matter how well they assimilated among the normal living, such creatures would need real flesh and blood on occasion. Their checked cravings would sometimes have to be satisfied. They might drive around backroads at night, looking for the dregs of the world to satisfy their hunger."

Peter pushed on the handle of the passenger car door. It would not open.

"Automatic lock, nice feature of the Rolls Royce Company," Fang Lin said, leaning in towards Peter.

"Now the chances that, if such a creature did exist, that it would indeed wind up in a car with a serial killer. Well—"

She paused and coughed.

Peter shook his head and thought, "*This can't be happening to me!*"

"Sorry, needed to clear the throat. Takes a while to heal. As I was saying, if such a creature was out and about, the odds of a serial killer winding up in the same car with her would be very good."

Peter felt his bladder release.

"Aww, I asked you not to pee on the seats."

Peter cowered back and whimpered, "This—isn't—right."

"Oh, but it is. You see, in the scenario in my version, those odds are very good indeed."

Fang Lin crawled over Peter's body until her lips were just above his face, blood dripping from them.

"Believe me, I know."

42

THE EERIE ENCOUNTER AT CALIBAYAN

DEXTER AMOROSO

THE WARM SEA BREEZE greeted Sheryl and her friends as they embarked on a journey to the picturesque town of Pasacao for a life-changing seminar and an encounter they'd never forget. Little did they know the trip would lead them to a haunting experience that would test their courage and beliefs.

Sheryl was so busy with work that she didn't realize it was already nighttime. Only their office on the 2nd floor was open. She quickly packed up her things. Suddenly, she felt a chill as if someone was watching her. She looked towards the sliding door in front of their office, but she didn't see anyone. Fear and anxiety slowly engulfed her as she was alone in their office. She cautiously glanced at the door from time to time because she still felt someone's gaze on her. Sheryl is easily frightened by ghosts and supernatural beings since she has an open third eye, which makes her see various things.

"Why are you here?" Sheryl asked irritably.

"Oh, nothing, I was just checking, and you might be alone here again. You tend to get really scared," Jet replied, still chuckling.

The young man was delighted to see annoyance in the young woman's expression.

"Come on, I'll take you home. There's a story that a white lady supposedly appears here," the young man teased again, which annoyed his friend even more.

After a week, Sheryl traveled to Pasacao for the scheduled seminar in the barangay. She decided to bring her friends, Arvin and her sister Rhea, who are also her colleagues at work. They planned to go swimming after their purpose in that place. Pasacao is known for its numerous beach resorts, no matter where you go. Their schedule was on Saturday at 8 am, so on Friday afternoon after leaving the office, the group left and agreed to stay at Mae's downline's house to ensure they won't be late the next day.

The group was happy while traveling. They were all laughing and joking around, seeming like children who had just come together for the first time. Sheryl, on the other hand, remained quiet, nodding and observing her companions. The place they were heading to seemed to be quite far, as they had to take another tricycle after getting off the jeepney, and the journey was still quite long. As they approached Mae's residence, they noticed that the road was getting narrower and less populated. Until they reached the end of the road, where Mae was standing, waiting for their arrival. The sun was setting as they arrived. Mae waved at them, and they approached her to get off the vehicle.

As agreed, after eating, the group headed to the beach. They changed into their swimwear. Kevin, Mae's husband, accompanied them. On the way, the friends were making noise, laughing, and joking around. It was chaotic since there were six of them together. When they reached the spot where they got off earlier, they crossed the road and entered a small alley where a few houses were located, but beyond that, they saw a wide expanse of grass with some tied-up cows and carabaos. They continued walking until they reached a hanging bridge. There were no more houses in that area. The bridge was quite old, which made them nervous as they crossed. Menchie and Rhea went first, followed by Jessa and Kevin. Sheryl was left behind, and Arvin was supporting her since he knew she had a fear of heights and was easily scared. After crossing the bridge, they finally caught sight of the sea.

The rest of the group happily frolicked in the sea, while Sheryl and Arvin were left sitting on the sandy shore with Kevin. They talked about various family matters until the conversation shifted to topics about aswangs, ghosts, and supernatural beings.

"Many stories like that used to circulate here, ma'am. But I don't believe in those," said Kevin.

"For all my years, I haven't experienced or seen anything like that, ma'am," he added.

After Kevin left, Sheryl felt scared. The place they visited was isolated, and they couldn't see anyone else around except for their group. The surroundings were dark, and only the moonlight provided them with some illumination.

An hour later, Sheryl suggested that they should head back since they had an early event the next day. As they were on their way back, she couldn't get the conversation with Kevin out of her mind. It was quiet as they returned, and they seemed tired.

Their seminar in the barangay turned out to be successful. Many people tried their products, and some even signed up for registration. Instead of immediately going back to Naga City, the group decided to visit Sheryl's relatives in Calibayan, a distant barangay still within Pasacao, to offer their products and share the business opportunity with them. After leaving Mae's house, they headed to the pier where they would take a boat to Calibayan. They traveled for almost an hour before reaching their destination, where Sheryl's cousins happily welcomed them.

They spent time talking, catching up, and having a feast. In the afternoon, they also enjoyed drinking coconut juice brought by another cousin of Sheryl's. Time flew without them noticing.

After their dinner, the group went to the seaside. They set up a tent for the night and found their spots on the sand. Jessa and Rhea were sitting while Menchie was lying down. Sheryl and Arvin were making a bonfire not too far away. The three friends were engrossed in their conversation, and Sheryl occasionally joined in. Arvin eventually moved away from the group and walked towards a coconut grove to gather coconut husks and firewood for the bonfire. Sheryl watched him intently, and after a while, she noticed he suddenly hurried back. She asked him curiously about it, but Arvin reassured her that everything was fine.

As the night grew darker, they continued enjoying their conversation when suddenly, Sheryl felt something strange. It was like she heard a peculiar sound, resembling the heavy breathing of a fierce animal. She quickly sat up from lying on the sand, listening closely to the noise. It seemed to be getting louder and closer to their location. She initially thought she was the only one hearing it, but she soon realized that her companions also heard it. Menchie and Sheryl quickly stood up, and out of fear, Sheryl hugged Arvin tightly before they all ran back to their cousin's house.

Breathless, they arrived where Sheryl's cousins were drinking outside the house. Scared, they narrated what they experienced, and to their surprise, their cousins mentioned the presence of an aswang in that area. The group spent the rest of the night restless, despite the promises of their cousins to watch over them while they waited for the boat to leave for the sea.

The next day, while traveling back to Naga City, Sheryl felt a pain in her stomach. Upon arriving home, she noticed she was bleeding, so she immediately went to see a doctor for a checkup. That was when she learned she was pregnant for about a month. She thought about what happened in Calibayan, and she attributed it to her condition. Elders say that the smell of an unborn child is attractive to such beings.

Sheryl was grateful that nothing bad happened to her baby. A week later, she experienced bleeding again, so she decided to resign from her job to prioritize the safety of her and her child. Through this haunting experience, Sheryl not only discovered her vulnerability to the supernatural but also found the strength to protect what matters most in her life.

43

A DARK PAST

LAVENDER WALKER

SIA WOKE WITH A start to the sound of the chickens going cuckoo out back. She jumped out of bed and slipped her boots on before grabbing her rifle to go investigate, knowing full well the other farmers in the area have been having more problems with coyotes than in previous years.

"Of course, this happens when Jake's gone for the weekend." She muttered to herself before flinging the back door open. She was met with the sticky warmth of a humid, Missouri night.

It wasn't long before she stumbled upon a few chickens running around and squawking like crazy. "What the hell has gotten into you?" she asked, gingerly picking up one of the hens and stroking her feathers while feeling for any wounds. Once satisfied that she was fine, she repeated the process with the other two and led the trio back to the coup.

When the group got there, Sia was appalled to find the gate open. The hens scurried into the coup where their friends were still making a ruckus. The farmer followed closely and found the most gruesome slaughter she'd ever seen. Half a dozen hens were scattered in pieces among the hay, the ground was slick with fresh blood. One thing was for sure, it wasn't a coyote that had done this.

She ran back to the house, making sure to lock the gate up tight behind her and went straight for the phone to call the sheriff.

"Hello? Sheriff Binder?"

"Sia? What in blazes could be so urgent this time of night?" The sheriff was a kind man but didn't take too kindly to his sleep being interrupted.

"Yes, sir, I swear it." Sia choked the words out, trying to maintain some composure. "I woke up to the hens going crazy and I haven't a clue what done it, but half a dozen were slaughtered in the coup. It wasn't no coyote, I can tell you that for damn sure."

The sheriff took a pause before he answered, "I'm on my way. Sit tight, you hear? Whatever it was might still be around and I don't want you getting hurt."

"Yes, sir. Everything's locked tight."

While she was waiting for the sheriff, she sat in her cozy armchair and tried to relax, but every fiber of her being was on edge. She thought about calling her husband, but there was no guarantee he'd pick up, or be able to cut his rodeo weekend short. The only thing she was grateful for at that moment was that the kids didn't wake to that disaster. She could only imagine

Dolly's heartbreaking sobs if she'd seen those poor hens ripped to shreds that way.

After about an hour, a firm knock at the door ripped her from her thoughts. Glad to have a second set of eyes, she hurried and opened the door for the sheriff. He was a burly man with kind, blue eyes and just a bit of a 5 o'clock shadow grazing his chin.

"Sheriff!" Sia practically melted with relief. "Thank you so much for coming at such a late hour."

"Of course, Sia," the sheriff managed a warm smile. "Now, you mind taking me to see this mess?"

"Absolutely, just follow me." She led him out back, her cheeks warm with embarrassment as she realized she still was in her robe.

Arriving at the scene, Binder's face went pale. "You're right, darlin'. That sure wasn't no coyote." He took a deep breath before going in and examining the scene further, muttering to himself along the way.

Sia shifted on her feet as she waited for the sheriff to come back with his findings. She looked to the sky and saw that the morning sun was just starting to peek over the horizon. "I better get back inside in case the kids wake up, you know where to find me when you have something or if you need anything."

"Mhm," The sheriff gave a slight nod and continued his search while Sia headed back to the farmhouse.

Not wanting to wake her teenagers, she made a fresh pot of coffee and busied herself in the kitchen. Before she realized what she was doing, she had the fixings for a breakfast feast laid out and ready to cook.

"Mama, what's got you so busy this morning?" Dolly wondered as she shuffled into the kitchen and poured herself a cup of coffee.

"Oh, nothing much." Sia lied to her daughter and put on what she hoped was a reassuring smile. "Something got the chickens spooked late last night, so Sheriff Binder's out there having a look."

The young girl's face fell, darkening her delicate features. "It's not just a coyote?"

Sia shook her head. "It sure doesn't look like it, Hun."

"Another animal maybe?" Dolly twirled her caramel brown hair around her finger absentmindedly as if it could give the answers she was looking for.

"Dolly, Hun, I really don't know!" Sia set the knife down she was using to chop up some peppers and spun around to look at her daughter. "I truly hope that's all it is, but I've never seen anything like it before."

"Sorry, Mama, I was just thinking out loud." The girl was taken aback, her mother had always been so patient and understanding, it wasn't like her to raise her voice.

"I know, and I'm sorry, too." Sia softened. "Why don't you come help me with breakfast and we'll wake Caleb up when it's ready? Maybe the sheriff will have some answers for us by then."

"That sounds good." She answered her mom with a tentative smile and busied herself with breakfast.

As they finished getting the table set for a family breakfast feast, there was a firm knock on the front door. "Stay here, Hun. I'm sure it's the sheriff." Sia mustered a reassuring smile and made her way to the door.

"Sia," the sheriff's voice dripped with concern. "I'm afraid there wasn't much in the way of evidence, what I did find... well, I ain't ever seen a thing like it."

Sia gestured for him to come sit in the living room, hugging herself as if to protect her from the news to come.

"Would you like something to eat or some coffee?" Her voice was shaking.

"No, I'm fine." He answered, running his hand down his face, whether from exhaustion or something else, Sia couldn't tell. "Why don't you have a seat, Darlin'?"

Listening to the sheriff, she sat on the couch across from him and waited for the news. The sheriff placed an odd-looking feather on the table between them. It was garnet red tipped with black, like someone dipped the tip into oil. Sia reached for the specimen and found that it didn't feel like a feather, it wasn't soft, instead the feathery part was sharp. The stem still seemed normal, hollow on the inside, but the rest was like a thin sheet of metal painted to look like a feather, in explicit detail.

She let out a slow breath, trying to find the words to explain what this meant. "Sheriff... I'm afraid I know what this is, and the short version? This means big trouble."

Intrigued now, the man leaned forward and gestured for her to elaborate.

"Before I moved here from Dallas, there was this man... He participated in the rodeos and sold art whenever he could. At some point, he became mad with rage, coming after everyone who he perceived as a threat or who had bested him in any way.

"I was young and blind to his issues, I thought he was my forever partner. One day, I came home to find him painting dozens of these. When he laid them out to dry, he wrote a name above each one. At first, I thought he was symbolically giving up his rage. Soon after, I heard that a good friend had been murdered in his sleep, but only after every other person he cared about. The police report said that the killing started with his pet dog, moved to his kids, then his wife, and eventually the man himself.

"The police report also described a metal feather that had been left on the victim's nightstand. A feather just like this. I told the police what I knew as soon as I'd heard, but it was too late. The bastard had already fled. It wasn't long after that I packed up my stuff and moved out here.

"I always knew there was a chance that he'd find me, but after all this time, I'd been hopeful that the nightmare wouldn't come to reality."

The sheriff pondered Sia's story for a moment, it was a lot to take in. He'd been one of Sia's first friends when she'd moved to the town, and he never would've suspected such a dark past from the friendly woman sitting across from him. "Damn, Sia, I hadn't a clue! When's Jake due to come home? I don't want you and them kids here all by your lonesome with that wacko out there."

Sia took a sip of coffee and gave the sheriff a solemn glance. "He's not due back for a couple of days. I'll call him and see if he can cut his rodeo short, though. I know I'd feel a hell of a lot better if he were here."

The sheriff nodded and stood to leave. "In that case, I'll have a couple of the boys stationed out front, just in case. Now, don't hesitate to call if something else happens."

"I won't, Sheriff." Sia gave a soft smile as she stood to walk him to the door. "Thank you again for coming at such an early hour. I appreciate it more than you know."

After walking out the door, the sheriff took one more look back at his friend. "I mean it, Sia. You be careful. I don't want anything bad happening to ya, or your kids."

"I will, Sheriff," Sia tried to reassure him. "Now, go on home and get some rest before Hailey kills you and me both."

With a nod, the stout man headed back to his truck. Sia stood at the door and watched as he called the guys to keep watch and stayed until he was out of sight. With a deep sigh she headed upstairs to wake her son and have a family breakfast with a disturbing family meeting.

"Caleb, Hun." She shook the boy gently, ignoring his groans of resistance. "It's time to get up. Your sister helped me make a big breakfast, and we need a family meeting. I'm calling your father too."

"Can't I have five more minutes?" He groaned again, rolling over and wrapping his blanket tight.

"No, now!" Sia demanded a little more sternly than she meant to, but it worked. Caleb threw his blanket off and sat up.

"Okay, Ma, sorry." He rubbed some sleep from his eyes and watched his mom head out the door. He followed a second later wondering what could be so important this early in the morning.

Once everybody was at the table, Sia called Jake. Her kids set up plates and she watched in silence while the phone rang.

"Howdy, Beautiful," Jake's warm voice blasted through the speaker. "What are y'all up to this fine morning?"

Sia's cheeks warmed, and she had to clear her throat before explaining. "Hey, Hun, we're having a breakfast with a family meeting. Something's happened on the farm, and I'm afraid it might mean we're all in danger."

"Danger? What kind of danger?" She could hear the panic slip through her husband's voice and noted the worry on her kids' faces.

Sia relayed the entire story of her past to her family and waited for a response.

"I'll tell the rodeo manager I can't stay." Jake decided after taking a moment to let the news sink in.

A breath that she didn't realize she was holding escaped her lips before Sia could say anything. "Thank you, Jake. Sheriff has a couple cars stationed out front, too."

"Are we gonna die, Ma?" Caleb's bright green eyes grew wide with worry.

"Not if anyone can help it, Caleb." Sia grabbed his hand and squeezed tight. "We're gonna stick together, and we're gonna get through this." The fear was setting deep within her too, but she had to try and stay strong for her family.

The long drive back home gave Jake too much time to think. He knew Sia had a dark past but hadn't a clue that it could be this bad. He never thought that their family could be in danger because of some psychotic bastard she used to associate with, that's for damn sure. He'd gotten on the road as soon as he got off the phone with his family and only stopped for gas since.

Now, the sun was setting over the rolling hills, casting a dusty orange glow over everything in sight. Under different circumstances, he'd find a scenic spot to pull over and take some pictures. Sia had always loved sunsets and had passed the passion down to Dolly.

While he was lost in thought, something ran out in front of his pickup. Jake slammed on the brakes, heart beating fast. He took a deep breath before climbing out to make sure that whoever, or whatever, it was didn't get hurt. Trailing his hand along the cold steel as he inspected, he found a man standing not a foot in front of the vehicle.

He wore a shabby, oversized coat despite the heat of the day, not that it could add much warmth with the holes scattered throughout. The man was tall and bulky with greasy, black hair.

He smiled at Jake as if he hadn't almost gotten run over before reaching for his coat pocket.

"Crap!" Jake thought before thinking to pull his pistol out from the back of his belt. "Stay where you are!" He called out, mustering all the authority he could.

The other man ignored him and pulled out a pack of cigarettes. "You smoke?" He finally spoke, his voice was raspy, but purposefully so.

"No," Jake breathed a sigh of relief. "Where ya headed?"

"Oh, up yonder a ways." The man smiled again as he tucked a cigarette in his mouth and gave it a light.

"Climb in, I'll take you as far as I can." Without waiting for a response, Jake climbed back in behind the wheel and started his truck once again to finish the long drive home.

A split second later, the man from the road climbed in the other side and they were off. His name was Seth and he'd been hitchhiking across the country for the last few months, doing odd jobs for people whenever he could.

"You know anything about building fences?" Jake asked after a while. "Something happened back home, and I could use some help fixing the chicken coup."

"Sure, I could lend you a hand. Least I could do for you taking me all this way." Seth shrugged and tried to hide a smirk.

"Sia? Kids? I'm home, and I brought company!" Jake called as he let himself in the house, Seth following close behind.

"Oh, thank God!" Sia ran and hugged her husband tight, their kids close on her heels. "I've never been so happy to see you!"

"It's okay, Love." Jake stroked his wife's hair, trying to comfort her.

When she finally pulled away, tears were stinging the corner of her eyes as she remembered Jake had said something about company. Turning from her husband, she reached for the man's hand before a flash of recognition crossed her face forcing her to pull away.

"Howdy, I'm Seth," the strange man greeted with a smile, reaching out his hand.

"Sia, a pleasure to meet you."

Sia took his offered hand and gave it a shake. "Sorry, you remind me of someone I used to know."

"I'm sure I'd remember meeting a woman as beautiful as you." Seth chuckled. "Your husband was gracious enough to give me a ride from the middle o' nowhere in exchange for help fixing... what was it? The chicken coup?"

"I'm sure Jake will be grateful for the help." Sia admitted. "It's quite the disaster, but you two come on in and get settled. Seth, please make yourself at home as long as you're here."

Seth gave a gracious nod and mumbled under his breath as soon as the family was out of earshot. "My dear, Sia, I plan on it."

Throughout the rest of the day, Sia answered lots of questions from Jake and the kids about who the man was that could be after them. Seth stuck around through it all with concern riddling his face. By the time everybody was satisfied that they were as protected as could be and exhausted every question imaginable, it was already about dinner time.

"How about I order some pizza?" Jake suggested, thinking that Sia probably wouldn't be up for cooking.

"That sounds great!" Sia agreed with a wave of relief.

"Hawaiian?" Dolly asked hopefully.

"We can do Hawaiian." Jake rolled his eyes at his daughter. "Seth, what do you like?"

"Oh, anything's fine with me, thank you," Seth answered. "I haven't had a good pizza in a while."

"Okay, give me two shakes and I'll call up Henry's. They have the best pizza in the county and their breadsticks are to die for." Jake smiled at the group and wandered out of the room to make the call.

"Kids, why don't you head on upstairs and work on some homework until dinner's here?" Sia gave a very pointed look at each of them, who just nodded in response and went their way.

Once they were out of earshot, Sia whipped on Seth with fire in her eyes. "I know who you are. Give me one good reason why I shouldn't call the sheriff and his boys right now."

Dropping the innocent act, Seth's face took on a sinister shadow. "Well, if you come with me tonight and say not a word to this darlin' family of yours, nobody gets hurt." He leaned in so his face was mere centimeters in front of hers. "I know you recognized the feather, and you know I've always loved you. Be mine again, and it all goes away."

Sia set her jaw and glared at the man she once loved. "You have fallen so far from the man I loved Heath. I will never go with you." She reached behind the couch to grab something, but before she could, Heath had her arm pinned behind her back.

"Don't try anything funny. Come with me tonight. Or else."

"Everything okay here?" Jake asked as he came around the corner, forcing Seth/Heath back to his place.

"Just fine," Sia tried to sound sweet, but was sure her voice was shaking. "I was just getting to know our new friend."

"Not much to know, though." Seth feigned innocence once again.

Trying to maintain a cool exterior, Sia let out a slow breath and tried to sound chipper. "How long until the pizza gets here, Jake?"

"They said maybe twenty minutes," He answered as he came around and sat by his wife, throwing his arm over her shoulders. "Let's just take a breath and hope that psycho doesn't try anything."

Sia nodded and laid her head on her husband's shoulder. As much as she wanted to melt into him, she felt Heath's eyes on her and couldn't shake the feeling that she was about to lose everything.

After the kids were in bed and Jake was asleep, poor Sia was stuck awake staring at the ceiling, wrestling with herself. If she stayed, her kids could die, or Jake. The one thing she believed more than anything was that somewhere in the murderer's twisted mind, he did still love her.

She glanced at her sleeping husband who looked so peaceful, as if there had never been anything to worry about. Leaning over, Sia gave him a quick kiss on the forehead before getting out of bed and throwing some clothes on. Stepping out of their room, her heart was already aching, but she knew what she had to do.

Before she lost her nerve, she checked on Dolly who was sound asleep with a book hugged to her chest. Gently, Sia moved the book to the nightstand, clicked the lamp off, and kissed her daughter on the forehead. Continuing on to Caleb's disastrous room, she repeated the process before walking down the stairs.

"I knew you'd come around, Darlin'," Heath smirked.

"No harm comes to them?" Sia asked, holding back a sob.

"Not a hair will be harmed on any of their heads." Heath held up a weathered hand. "I only want you."

"Fine," Sia stalked up to the man and looked him dead in the eye. "Then where are we headed?"

"Anywhere we want to, Baby."

Sia rolled her eyes and followed Heath out the front door. All she could do now was hope that Jake called the sheriff in the morning when he noticed she was missing.

"There a hotel near here?" Heath asked as they made their way down the winding driveway, the trees casting eerie shadows in the moonlight.

"Yeah, not too far a walk." Sia shivered despite it being a hot, humid night.

"Lead the way."

The sun was already rising when they finally got a room. Sia laid down on the bed and wrapped herself up in the comforter as tight as possible, not wanting to feel Heath's touch as he climbed in bed after her.

"Us against the world, Baby," He whispered in her ear before kissing her on the back of the head, making her skin crawl. Sia didn't respond, just shut her eyes tight and tried to sleep.

Heath watched as the beautiful woman lying next to him drifted off to sleep.

"Good, now I can go about my business," he thought, sneaking out of bed. He meandered to the desk on the other side, pulled out three of his feathers and added some finishing touches.

He made it back to Sia's driveway before he heard sirens and saw cop cars coming in the dim morning light. *"Shit! This ain't good!"* He put on his warmest smile as the first car started to pull in.

"What seems to be the matter, Officer?" He asked as the sheriff stopped and rolled his window down.

"That's 'Sheriff' to you, Sir, and seems to be Sia went missin' in the night. You wouldn't know anything, there would ya?"

Heath hoped the sheriff couldn't sense his nervousness as he answered, "Not a thing, just an early riser. Thought I'd take a stroll and see what this town's about."

The sheriff looked him up and down with a furrowed brow. "Well, hop in and I'll give you a lift up the drive."

Heath nodded and climbed in the back seat, feeling sure that no one suspected a thing.

When they got to the house, the sheriff and his deputy looked around and asked the routine questions. Of course, nothing seemed out of the ordinary, and since no one heard anything, the best they could do was keep an eye out.

"Thanks, Sheriff. I'll call you first thing if she makes it home." Jake told him as they walked to the door.

"I'm sure she's fine, Jake. She's a tough one. Stay safe." With a tip of his hat, he and his deputies were off.

Jake slumped into the armchair in the living room and the kids sat on the couch, unsure of what to do or say. Heath took a look around and thought how easy it would be to take them all out right then and there, too easy for his taste.

"Dad, is Mom gonna be okay?" Caleb asked.

"I wish I knew, Son," Jake answered warily, running a hand down his face. "In the meantime, I'm sure you both have homework. Seth, ready to get workin' on that coup?"

"Sure, probably be good to get your mind on something else, anyway." Heath gave a smile of encouragement and followed Jake outside.

After grabbing what they'd needed from the shed, the pair made their way to the coup. Heath started in with the boards, following Jake's instructions. "Man, with your help, this will be done in no time!"

"Anything to help a kind soul." Heath smiled at him.

They worked and talked about different dreams and aspirations of their youth. Heath told Jake about his first love, and Jake didn't catch that he was describing a young, wild Sia. After a bit, it was getting close to lunchtime and Jake started packing up the tools to pick the job up again later.

Bent over his toolbox, putting loose screws in their place, he didn't notice Heath behind him with a hammer. A hard hit over the head and Jake was on the ground staring at his assailant.

"She's mine now!" Heath shouted before pounding Jake's head repeatedly until his face was barely recognizable. A crazed smile spread across his face as he dropped a feather by the lifeless body and whistled as he walked back up to the house.

Sia woke up to sunlight streaming through the hotel window and rolled over to realize Heath was gone. "No!" she screamed as she jumped out of bed and ran to the phone, dialing 911 as fast as she could.

"911, what is your emergency?" a female operator answered.

"Hi, my name is Sia Nimins. I was coerced to leave my house last night with my ex. I think he's trying to murder my family. 45682 Prancer Street. Please hurry."

"Alright, ma'am, we're sending units right away. Can you stay on the line?"

"No, ma'am. I have to get home. Thank you!" Sia hung up and ran as fast as she could from the hotel.

"Caleb? Dolly?" Heath called as he walked in the house. "Ready for lunch?"

The kids came downstairs and looked at the man, confused. "Where's Dad?" Dolly asked.

"Oh, he just wanted to finish up out there, but asked that I get you some lunch. That work for y'all?"

Caleb shrugged and walked to the table. Dolly gave him an inquisitive look, but nodded anyway and went to the table with her brother.

"Grilled cheese work? Tomato soup?" He waited a minute without a response before muttering to himself. "I guess that works, then."

He got the sandwiches and soup on the stove, keeping an eye on the kids for an opening. Unfortunately, Caleb was sitting in a clear line of sight. Heath sighed, realizing he'd have to make this messy.

He brought three plates over to the table. Set his where Jake would normally sit, set Dolly's in front of her and went around the table to set Caleb's in front of him from behind. As he set the plate, he used his other hand to pull a knife from his back pocket and slash the boy's throat.

Dolly screamed as she saw blood gushing from his brother's neck. "What the hell? Who are you?"

"Now, now, don't you see?" Heath grinned devilishly. "I'm the man your mother was worried about." He played with the bloody knife and stalked over behind the girl. "She was always meant to be mine, you see? You and your brother? Never supposed to have existed."

Dolly paled as she realized what he meant. He came behind her, leaning down to whisper in her ear. "Don't worry now, it'll only hurt for a second." Then he ripped the knife across her throat too. Her pretty face stuck in shock as the color drained from her body and her blood drizzled to the floor, forming a pool with her brother's.

Satisfied at a job well done, he got to cleaning up his mess when there was a knock on the door. He kept on cleaning and the knocking kept getting louder.

Eventually, he heard the door open and hid in the pantry. "What in blazes?"

The sheriff? How'd he know?

Heath tried to keep his breathing steady.

The sheriff noticed bloody footprints. Whoever this was wasn't very careful. They led straight to the pantry. He motioned for his deputy to watch his back and readied his gun as he opened the door.

The sheriff got a shot off to his shoulder before the criminal could do anything. Binder knocked him to the ground, shoved his knee in the man's back, and cuffed him.

At that moment, Sia walked in and saw the kids' bodies. "How dare you? You asshole! I was doing what you wanted!" She walked over and slapped Heath across the face as the sheriff was pulling him to his feet.

"The kids never should have existed." A maniacal laugh slipped from his lips as Binder handed him off to one of the deputies to take to the car.

"I'm so sorry, Sia. We weren't fast enough."

"Jake?" she called in a panic. "Where's Jake?"

The sheriff shrugged and shook his head. Sia barely noticed before she took off through the back door.

"The coup. The coup," she repeated it over and over until she got there and found her husband's decimated body. She fell to her knees in despair, hugging the man she loved. "Jake, I'm so sorry, Jake. This is all my fault."

The sheriff came up behind her and rubbed her shoulder. "I'm so sorry, Darlin'."

"Just make sure Heath goes away forever." Sia had a fire in her eyes when she finally looked up.

"I'll do my best. Hang in there, okay?"

Sia nodded and the sheriff went on his way, hoping she'd be alright.

Instead, Sia went straight to her bedroom, tied a noose from her bedsheet, and hung herself. They didn't find her body until a couple of days later when the sheriff came back to check on her.

44

THE EX BOX

MARY BETH NIX

WE'RE WALKING DOWN THE boardwalk, the pink neon spokes of the Ferris wheel ahead, when I stumble. I'm wearing my new silver stiletto sandals with the ankle straps. Inappropriate, I know, but the night started out as a dinner date. The toe catches on an uneven board, and I teeter off balance. Jeremy doesn't grab my arm. That's when I know. I already suspected—that's why we came to the Boardwalk—but that's when I *know*.

"Are you okay?"

The question is too late, and his voice holds guilt, not concern. We're breaking up, and he's probably counting the hours until he can say goodbye and go home to his Sherpa throws and subtitled anime. He doesn't know I know.

"I'm okay."

I will be. Jeremy isn't my first Mr. Wrong. The almost full cardboard box in my bedroom closet holds mementos of all my exes—the Mr. Wrongs I've dated, the lessons I've learned.

Tonight, I need to figure out the lesson I'm supposed to learn from Jeremy and the piece of him I need to keep with me. *The Goddess's Guide to Dating*, the book that changed my life, says so. I reread the chapter on breakups just this morning.

Rule Number 1: It's not you; it's him.

I've done the work on myself to be a good partner in a relationship. I learned gluten-free recipes for Charles, watched Peruvian soccer matches with Hector, and helped Benjamin through a career change after he lost his job as a chef. I'm available and supportive, and I deserve a guy who will appreciate me.

Jeremy gets in line to buy tickets to the Ferris wheel. We usually split expenses, but since the Boardwalk is my last request, relationship-wise, Jeremy can pay. We join the line to get in one of the cars for two. Jeremy fastens the bar across us, but he's sitting as far away from me as he can. He's afraid I'll think this ride is romantic.

The wheel starts to turn, and we lurch upwards. Pink neon light washes over Jeremy's face and reflects off the glasses that hide his beautiful brown eyes. He looks like a stranger, but I *know* him. He can't wear contacts because of a dry-eye condition, he still wears a retainer at night, and he never eats the crusts of his sandwiches.

We're together and separate as the wheel turns, swinging us upward. I look down at the crowd—couples who've made it, who are making it, who never will. Some of them know which direction they're headed, but most of them don't. I lean forward. The car tilts and Jeremy grabs the bar that's holding us in.

We reach the top and start downward. Jeremy doesn't say anything as we loop around, up and down, until the ride slows and stops to let couples off, one by one. Finally, we're at the bottom, the metaphor for our relationship complete, and the carnie lets us out.

Rule Number 2: Accept any gift he offers—you deserve it.

Jeremy isn't a giver. Our romance has consisted mostly of Netflix and chilling at his place. I haven't met his friends or gone anywhere special with him. We've done dinner or coffee out a few times, gone to a new bar that opened two streets from his apartment, but he doesn't invite me to his work events, and he wouldn't go to my cousin Arlene's wedding with me because "dressing up isn't really his thing." I bought him a vintage Captain America t-shirt and crocheted him a scarf. He thanked me, but I hadn't seen him wear either of them.

We're walking past the other rides. "Tilt-a-Whirl?" Jeremy asks.

"No, thanks. They make me dizzy."

We stop at a ring-toss game with a row of stuffed animals as prizes. I don't have a teddy bear in my ex box, so I point them out.

"Can you win me one of those?"

"Sure," he says.

He buys a ticket and tosses the rings. He misses. He tries again and again. Finally, we settle for the smallest prize: a little plastic duck. I pick one with a top hat and bow tie. It won't look impressive besides the malachite turtle Barry bought me from the park store when we went camping or the wooden owl Colin carved as a breakup gift, but it'll work.

"Thank you," I tell Jeremy. Now it's time for my gift to him. "Shall we walk?"

The wooden walkway continues past the carnival. Benches grow further apart, and the streetlamps give way to dim solar pathway lights. We pass a guy who's operating a small drone with lights on its wings. He's tall, with dark hair cut in short spikes. Drone Guy smiles and says hello, but Jeremy doesn't answer. We keep walking. The solar lights run out, and it's dark when we reach the end of the pier. It used to be a viewing area where families would sit and feed the fish that swam close to shore, but half the rails are missing, and no one comes here now.

Rule Number 3: Learn from what went wrong.

The bench is broken, but Jeremy sits on one end and pats the wood beside him. He looks out at the water, where the reflection of the carnival neon gives us just enough light to see each other. Now that the time has come, he's having trouble saying the words. That means he does care for me, at least a little. He's also weak.

"I'm really glad I met you," he says.

He tells me that I'm great, that I supported him through a period of depression, that I helped him adjust to life after the pandemic. Then he tells me we're not on the same page. He's not ready for commitment. He can't give me what I need.

"You deserve better," he says.

"I know," I tell him. "That's the lesson I've learned from you: never settle. You don't deserve me, Jeremy Compton."

Then I push him, hard, and he falls backward into the lake with a big splash, his mouth an "o" of surprise. One of Jeremy's secrets is that he never learned to swim. Another is that he never watches the news, so he doesn't know they've started dredging the old landing to build a boat pier. He thrashes in the water and calls my name again and again. The carnival music keeps playing, so no one else hears. I watch until he sinks under the dark water and the bubbles stop.

Rule 4: Keep a memento of the relationship.

I hold out the little plastic duck and squeeze it, just as Jeremy's spirit rises out of the water. I'm not greedy; I capture a tiny shred, barely enough to hold a few wisps of memory. The duck's painted black eye turns Jeremy's shade of brown and blinks. Its little body bulges, but the cheap molded plastic doesn't give.

"Looks like dressing up *is* your thing now," I tell him and tap the little plastic top hat.

Then I tuck Jeremy's rubber ducky into my pocket, to add to my box of exes when I get home. I start walking back to the carnival. When I reach the first of the streetlamps, I see Drone Guy again. He's holding the drone upside down and examining one of the wheels. When he sees me, he waves.

I wave back, and he jogs over to me. "Are you okay?"

"I'm fine," I tell him.

He looks towards the dark pier and then back at me. "You're all wet. You must be cold." He takes off his hoodie and drapes it over my shoulders.

I start walking again, and he joins me. "Aren't you flying your drone?"

He shrugs. "It's not working. I'll try again tomorrow."

The hoodie is still warm from his body, and I hug it against me.

Rule 5: Look for someone new.

We reach the main boardwalk, and I see the pink neon spokes of the Ferris wheel ahead. The heel of my sandal catches in a knothole, and Drone Guy grabs my arm.

"Thanks."

"No problem." He grins at me, and I can see the white of his teeth in the pink-lit shadows. "I'm Dexter."

"Nice to meet you," I say and smile at him as we walk on. His arm is strong, and he stays close to me.

Maybe this one's a keeper.

Or maybe I'll need a bigger box.

45

BLOOD DEEP

MINDI CARVER

"Awake. All is ready, my little nobody."

I fought my way through the brain fog. I didn't want to wake up. Opening my eyes would make the wrongness real. I felt trapped; like I was caught in a seaweed bed being dragged along by the currents, unable to lift my head above the water; to breathe. My limbs felt heavy as if I was again learning to shed my skin and move like humans do. But I had been given an order, and so I must wake up.

Gods, NO!

Instantly alert, I found myself unable to move. The clink of metal chains made me look up at each of my wrists in turn, secured to the corners of a slab. I tried to kick with my feet. They also were shackled to opposing corners, stretching my body taught. The prickle of splinters against my ass and shoulders was uncomfortable, but not nearly so painful as a bed of coral. I tried to move again, testing my inhibited range of motion.

"Don't worry, my dear. Your strength will return. At least, some of it. Can't have you dying on me before I've finished my book, now can I?"

That voice... I blinked into the face of the pale stranger from the inn. My gut reaction was to flee, same as last time. But that was impossible now. Then the rest of what he said sank in. *A book? Of what? For what?* I shivered.

Because of the stretched positions of my arms, I had a limited field of vision, but I started taking in what I could of my surroundings as fear settled like an anchor stone in the pit of my stomach. The first thing that caught my eye was my staff, belled skirt, drum, and... My pelt. Arranged and mounted together prominently over a messy writing desk, like a trophy.

"You, my dear, are so much more than you appeared last night."

Last night? Damn! My glamour must have faded off in due course, leaving my true form exposed to him. Somehow it made me feel more vulnerable than if I'd simply been naked. I looked down at myself and a little corner of my mind was grateful that he hadn't actually stripped me to my skin, but being tied down in one's undergarments wasn't much comfort either.

My physical skin... Almost every inch of me was covered in fine ink lines and symbols. I couldn't read them, but I found if I focused on one for too long it felt like ghost shrimp were crawling up and down my spine.

I attempted to work up some saliva to swallow and ease the parched feeling in my throat. I had been without water for too long. To distract myself, I continued taking in my surroundings.

One wall was covered in overflowing bookshelves and there were more worktables full of glass vials, odd apparatuses, and dead, dissected creatures. My pack was tossed carelessly on one of the tables, its contents scattered. A wooden podium stood near my feet, covered with books and scraps of notes. Anatomy charts of creatures both mundane and magical lined most of the remaining wall space.

"I know you can understand me, my dear." The pale man brushed some of my curls out of my eyes with a cold, bony hand that made me cringe. "Now, what would a pretty little selk like you be doing so far inland?"

Damn, damn, double-damn!

I tried to shrug as much as my bonds would allow but stayed silent, as he had not actually commanded me to answer his questions yet.

He stepped over to the desk and dipped a quill methodically, then looked at me expectantly as he held it, ready to write. "Answer me truthfully. Why are you are so far inland?"

Now I had no choice. He told me to. I mustered enough of myself to resist a full disclosure. Fey couldn't lie, but we were good at keeping secrets. "I gos where tha money flows best."

He barked a laugh. "So clever... For a selk!" I flinched at the vitriol in his tone when he practically spat the slur. "Tell me why you are so far inland."

"Adventuring. Why else would I leave home?" I huffed. It seemed to satisfy him, thankfully, and he moved on to the next question.

"What sorts of things can your magic do?" I could feel my eye twitching. "Typical fey magic." He scowled at me over his shoulder. "I need, specifics, Selk."

"Not my fault if you haven't done your research!" I hissed back.

He slammed his fist down into the middle of the desk, sending a few papers floating through the air. He quickly retrieved them before glaring at me and speaking with a monotone calmness that didn't match the rage in his eyes. "Are you a name collector?"

"Yes..." Shock ran through me. I had replied before I could think of a proper feyish answer.

He approached me and prodded the swirl tattoo on the ball of my shoulder with a ruler. "What is this?"

"A gods-mark." Again, the quick reply. I harshly reminded myself I was fey and I had to be more careful.

"So, you're a 'chosen one' are you?" he sneered.

I did my best to shrug again as his frown deepened.

"I had hoped for a clean slate..." He gave it one last poke, then muttered something to himself about the 'trickiness of fey' as he returned to the desk and finished writing in his notes. He set the ink well on the podium, then began to scoot it closer to my left side. I could now see a tool pack, tightly rolled in his hand. "When I'm finished, those totters in the college will never dare laugh at me again!" He dropped the tool kit onto the table next to my side before unrolling it. I didn't recognize anything inside, but most had sharp edges so to me, they were all implements of torture.

I shuddered, my joints already beginning to ache from the strain as he lifted the hem of my under-top to expose my midriff from ribs to hip bones. Struggling to continue my false bravado, I forced myself to meet his gaze. "An' how long will that take, you shark?"

He leaned over me, grinning hugely. "As long as possible. I need you alive for my work to succeed, after all." He started muttering to himself as he measured and double-checked his sigils. Then he moved to my shoulder where he drew on and around my gods-mark. He must have been satisfied then, because as soon as he corked the ink and set it aside, he began to weave magic over me, into me. It prickled and burned into my bones like a blanket of sea urchins.

"Wha—what're ya doin'?" I twitched and struggled in my bonds.

He flashed his crooked, yellowed teeth in a frightening grin. "Making history, of course. Now, my work requires precision. Do. Not. Move." He retrieved another ink bottle and set it almost reverently next to the open kit. "The key to all of this, you know... And the cost was dear." He picked up his tools; a needle bound to the end of a stick, and a small hammer.

I now realized that the marks already on my skin were placeholders and he intended to make them permanent. My gaze was drawn to the little glass jar and the oddly swirling pigment inside it. It almost seemed alive as it moved within its crystalline confines long after it should have stilled from being relocated. I hadn't thought my feelings of dread could deepen. I was wrong. He inked his needle from the pot and with no other words and began to rapidly tap the stick below the needle, driving the point deeply into the taught skin over the left side of my rib cage.

Two types of pain tore through me at once. The physical was localized, repetitive, sharp. It was unpleasant but I could've handled it. The other... The magic was worse. It burned its way into my blood as my magic was forcefully fused with the ink and image of the sigil; the dark, evil nature of the spell felt as if it were turning my blood into a hot, oily sludge in my veins; twisting my essence, extinguishing my fey-light, ripping my spirit to shreds...

tap tap tap tap

I wanted to struggle, but I could not. Cursed by my own nature, by what I am; inescapably bound to obey the possessor of my pelt. Gods Above, Mothers Below, hear this plea from your ocean-born child—Tears rolled down my temples and into my curls as I screamed.

"Hush!" he rasped grumpily. "You'll break my concentration. Not another sound!"

I had no choice now. Colorful spots floated in my vision as I lay obediently still and silent.

46

OVERLAND PARK

WILLIAM J. CONNELL

"A GREAT WHITE SHARK swimming around and eating people is NOT an elevated horror movie," Anabella said, kneeling to fill her bucket with water from the stream.

"That's rather smug of you to say," Jeannie replied, gathering more dry wood for the fire. She looked down at her camp-issued t-shirt. Though it was dark, she could see the lettering—LAKE WASSAMATTA PROGRAM STAFF—had been smeared with dirt.

"No, it's not," Anabella replied. "An unusually large mackerel shark swims off the coast of an island and starts feeding on people. We've overfished our waters, Jeannie. So naturally the animal, an apex predator, finding its natural food source diminished, will expand its territory, and seek prey where it can find it. There's no villainous or horrific element, it is just nature."

Jeannie sighed. "You're so right Anabella. But it is getting too dark. I want to be back at the fire."

Jeannie peered into the night and looked across the stream. It seemed shallow here. Although there was not much light from the crescent moon, she thought she saw a path over there. Plus, she had a feeling that—something —was observing them.

The inner monologue she heard (and relied on) in extreme duress, her *Jeannie sense* said, "Get out of here."

Her heart jumped.

"Let's go," Anabella said as she rose, holding onto the bucket handle with both hands.

On hearing these words, Jeannie dismissed her thoughts as night fright and her attention shifted.

Anabella swayed, almost losing her balance. "Woah," Anabella uttered, as she stabilized herself. "Nearly faltered there."

Jeannie said, "If you did, I am sure Steve would catch you before you hit the ground."

"Steve," Annabella replied nonchalantly. "Meh."

The camp counselors laughed and started back down the path to the others. Thick roots covered the ground.

"This trail was hard enough to walk with empty hands," Anabella spat. "Now I'm carrying this stupid bucket, and I can't hold my flashlight."

"I've got mine here," Jeannie said. She'd managed to hold the light in her right hand while still cradling the wood. After flicking the torch on, she instructed Anabella, "Stay behind me."

Anabella followed closely after Jeannie as they made their way along the path. Some water from Anabella's bucket splashed onto Jeannie's backside.

"Shit, Anabella, I have to sleep in these shorts and shirt you know."

"They'll dry off," Anabella replied. "Besides, that's what you get for not bringing any spare clothes."

They walked in silence. Well, at least without talking between them. Jeannie was until recently a city girl and not used to absolute quiet, so she thought being a summer camp counselor at Lake Wassamatta would be fun. The program's mission was to give younger children ages eight through fourteen two weeks in the woods. Jeannie had been told almost all the kids attending were referred by a social worker or agency and came from urban core communities in St. Louis and Kansas City.

When Jeannie had arrived at camp three days ago, the woods seemed quiet in daylight. Maybe that was because the counselors were always busy. Her days were spent in orientation, which consisted of cleaning, painting, repairing, and overall prepping of cabins, the large cafeteria complex, and the grounds for the campers' arrival. Night was different. Her first evening sleeping in one of the cabins on the girls' side did seem a little weird. After all, she'd lived in the Hyde Park part of St. Louis for most of her life, until her mother could no longer afford the rent and they wound up moving to her aunt's place in Mystic a few months back. Jeannie was accustomed to sirens, flashing lights, and neon signs after dusk. Out here, the night was darker.

When a few of the other counselors plotted to camp out the night before the campers arrived, she was happy to be invited. They went off the campgrounds, hiking to a nearby wooded area, specifically Overland Park. Overnight camping was prohibited in the two-thousand-acre state park, but there did not seem to be any rangers or guards on the grounds. Now that Jeannie was in Overland Park, she realized she was really IN a forest, and strange sounds surrounded her.

They came to a fork in the path and Jeannie thought to take the left one.

"You sure?" Anabella asked.

"I'm sure," Jeannie said, hoping she was correct.

In a few minutes, the two reached the camp. Anabella put the water bucket down and went to her tent. Jeannie dropped the wood next to the pail and sat down within the ring of counselors surrounding the campfire.

She looked at the grime on her top and mumbled, "I really do need a new shirt." If only she had another one to wear.

Jeannie scanned the group of her fellow counselors.

To Jeannie's right, Lawson, a bookish junior from Washington University, was opening a can of beans. He was sitting with his back against a log. Next to Lawson was Anabella, who had brought her sleeping bag out from a tent and had rolled herself up in it. She was a true preppie from the wealthy suburb of Hermosa Beach, just outside of Glendale, attending Missouri State. Beside her was William, who hailed from the Fairgrounds neighborhood in St. Louis, near where Jeannie had lived.

He was slightly older than the others and worked in a group home. He had also brought wood for the fire he was stoking. Off to the side was Steve, a jock on a partial athletic scholarship for lacrosse at the University of Missouri. He was picking up rocks at the edge of the camp.

On Jeannie's left was Eileen, a computer science major, also at Washington University. She was tending two pans over the fire, a skillet with hot dogs and a deeper pot with baked beans. Lawson poured more baked beans into this pan.

Then there was Jeannie herself. A month ago, she was working in a nursing facility, and taking night classes at Mystic Community College to become a certified nursing assistant. The home suddenly closed. No notice, no warning. Then a posting appeared on the college summer job board for a camp counselor, and she decided to take a chance. At the interview, the camp director liked that she had basic first-aid skills and had experience living in the city. So here Jeannie was. Sitting down by a campfire in Overland Park, just off Highway H, at the edge of Mystic, Missouri.

Anabella said, "This forest reminds me of that movie with the family who are thrown out of their puritanical home in the 1600s. They try to make a home in the woods. I forgot the movie's name. The way it is filmed, the forest looks friendly during the day. But at night the wilderness is a much - darker place."

Anabella made air quotes and laughed at her own joke.

"My favorite elevated horror film is the one set in that giant hotel, where the writer goes crazy," Lawson said.

"Correction, he doesn't go crazy," Anabella said. "The hotel doesn't make him do anything. It merely amplifies his already borderline psychotic personality."

William gave a little smirk and then asked, "That's the movie where the black guy gets killed with an axe, right? A horror movie where the black guy is the first to die. How unusual is that?"

Unlike Anabella's attempt, this comment brought laughter from the group. Jeannie smiled but picked up the slightest trace of pain in William's comment.

Anabella turned to Jeannie and asked, "Speaking of writers, Jeannie, since I got here, I've heard rumors about weird things going on in Mystic. Something about the local paper?"

Jeannie shrugged. "I don't know. It's a small town. I've only been there a few months. But you're talking about 'The Tenpenny Dreadful.'"

"That's its name?" William asked incredulously.

Jeannie laughed a little. "Yeah, it is. Anyway, the guy publishing it is called Talbert Tenpenny. Weird local guy. And he can't write at all. But in the last few weeks, he's been doing these crazy stories about people getting killed in really bad ways. And he names people in the area. The townsfolk want to shut him down, but he can't be found. The papers keep showing up. Weird."

Eileen kept the pans over the fire and commented, "Yeah, that does sound weird. Hand me some more dogs."

Jeannie reached into the plastic package and put a few more frankfurters onto the pan. She did not want to get into how she'd seen fewer and fewer people on the streets of Mystic, as of late.

Steve came over with an armful of stones and added them to the wall of rocks they had built around the fire. He sat on the log that was across from William, then announced, "I'm not into these newer horror movies. Give me the old splatter films with lots of kills."

Eileen was able to rest the pot of beans on a flat stone and hold the larger frier with both hands further over the flames. She said, "Hey, some of these are pretty done."

"I love burnt dogs," Steve said as he stabbed one of the plump frankfurters with a fork. Water sprayed from the hot dog. "Just like in a slasher movie."

"Hey!" Anabella yelled. "You almost got grease on me."

"Just flavored juices," Steve said.

Lawson passed out plastic plates and utensils. Everyone got a spoonful of beans and one or two hotdogs with buns, and if asked for, condiments.

Anabella regained her composure and continued.

"You are all way to old school. You want an elevated horror film? Five words. He—red—a—tea—ray."

Eileen, eating and cooking at the same time, chirped, "Anabella's playing her word games again."

"Heard that movie is overrated," said Steve.

"What movies do you like, William?" Jeannie asked.

"Well," William answered, "I'm not into horror movies but I really like true crime horror."

"Do tell," Eileen said.

"Well, like here. You all know about the Overland Ogre Massacre, right?"

Suddenly they all grew silent. Jeannie could sense everyone tighten up. The sounds from outside their campsite seemed amplified.

Anabella broke the hush and asked, "What, there was a masked killer in these woods at one time? That's original."

William shrugged and leaned closer to the fire.

"We've heard stories in the Fairgrounds about the Overland Ogre. Nobody's ever seen him and lived. He's supposed to be a giant who prowls the woods, looking for isolated campers and other people all alone. He just comes out after dark, grabs 'em while they sleep, and eats them."

Anabella chided, "Pu-leeez, William, can't you do better than that? Sounds like one of Steve's campground horror movies from the big eighties. We're talking about stories on a higher level here. For instance, anything made by Ari Aster is classic."

Steve looked over his shoulder and said, "Oooh, there's a boogie man out to get us camp counselors."

"You don't even merit being called a comic book," Anabella sneered.

While the others laughed, something made Jeannie look around.

Something was off.

The woods had grown silent.

The brush behind them parted. Out stepped a man. Or at least, a large figure who looked like a man. Though difficult to see in the firelight, Jeannie could determine the creature was well over six feet tall, dressed in blue jeans and a flannel shirt. It wore a potato sack over its head with a straw cowboy hat attached. The face was covered except for two holes for eyes and one where a mouth might be. He, or it, was clutching a butcher knife in its right hand.

Eileen screamed and dropped both pans into the fire. Steve fell off the log onto the ground. Everyone else was petrified into silence.

The figure looked around the campfire, taking in each person. When it came to Jeannie, they locked their eyes.

Jeannie's heart jumped, but she held the creature's stare. Either the being had no eyes, or she couldn't see them in the dark. Her *Jeannie sense* spoke loud and clear to her.

"*You are going to die unless you do something.*"

Out of the corner of her eye, Jeannie saw Steve shifting into a crouch like he was going to rush forward. The creature was still looking at Jeannie, then turned its gaze to Eileen. Steve launched himself at the figure's midsection. The creature grabbed Steve by the shoulder with its free left hand and clenched. Jeannie heard a popping sound. Steve yelled and his knees buckled, but he could not fall. The creature was holding him in mid-air with one hand, while still looking at Eileen. Then it dropped Steve to the ground. Steve was moaning and rubbing his shoulder joint.

The creature sat down on the log and stuck the butcher knife into it, then gestured for Eileen to come over to him.

"Nooooo," Eileen half-whimpered. Jeannie touched Eileen's knee and, with all the calm she could muster, said, "It's all right, he just wants to eat."

The figure nodded and motioned with both fingers.

"Give me a plate," Jeannie directed. William tentatively picked up one of the plastic plates with a shaky hand, but he could not move.

"Oh hell," Jeannie said and grabbed the plate from William. "Now Eileen, put some franks and beans on this."

Eileen was still frozen. Jeannie used her free hand to guide Eileen's arm to the pans. Eileen managed to put a spoonful of beans on the plate. She tried to grab a hot dog with her hands but burned her fingertips and uttered a yelp.

"I'll do it," Jeannie said, spearing a couple of dogs with a fork and placing them onto the plate. Then she tossed on a couple of buns and leaned over, shaking but not so much as Eileen, extending her arm to the figure. It took the plate from Jeannie and nodded.

"Fork?" Jeannie asked.

The figure shook its head but shifted the plate to its left hand, then grabbed the butcher knife and used it to spoon the food into its mouth.

Jeannie glanced over and saw Anabella had wiggled deep into her sleeping bag. Only her face was showing and that was icy still, but her bag was shaking.

The creature ate some more. Steve was groaning on the ground, still rubbing his shoulder.

The creature cocked his head at Steve, then turned to look again at Jeannie.

"*He's questioning me,*" Jeannie thought. "*What does he want?*"

Her *Jeannie sense* was working in overdrive. The creature aimed the point of the butcher knife at Jeannie, then pointed back to Steve's shoulder, and looked again at Jeannie. Jeannie emitted the words, "I think we have a first-aid kit."

The creature made a motion for her to go. Jeannie crawled over to her tent, fumbled in the dark for a minute before realizing she still had her flashlight, then used it to find the white plastic box with the red cross on it. She scurried back to the campfire and opened the first-aid kit. Inside were the expected contents. Jeannie instinctively grabbed a white pouch, twisted it in both hands, and got up carrying the ice pack and tape. She quietly walked behind the log and went to Steve. She slapped the ice pack on his shoulder, taped it in place, and placed Steve's free hand on it. Then she crawled back to her spot, where she took Eileen's hand and dabbed some bacitracin ointment where her fingers had been burned.

The creature held the plate forward.

Anabella, breathing heavily, whispered, "He's toying with us."

A trembling Eileen said, "Anabella's right."

"*Eileen's no use anymore,*" Jeannie thought. Then her *Jeannie sense* kicked in.

"*No, he's just hungry.*"

Jeannie took the plate and put more franks and beans on it, then handed it back to the creature, who took it with a nod. Again, it fed using the knife.

Jeannie heard Lawson ask weakly, "What does he want?"

"He wants—to—kill—" Anabella stammered.

Steve groaned.

"Keep that ice pack on tight," Jeannie ordered.

In the middle of eating, the creature pointed to the fire. No one moved. The creature shook his arm at the fire again.

The voice inside Jeannie said, "*He wants the fire fed.*"

"Lawson," Jeannie asked, "Can you add some more wood to the fire? Steve's a little indisposed."

Lawson murmured something unintelligible.

"*Lawson's gone too,*" Jeannie thought.

"William," Jeannie implored, "could *you* put some more wood on the fire?"

William reached for a stick of wood.

"More!" Jeannie ordered, feeling frustration. Then, in a gentler tone, she added, "And William, please hurry."

William tossed several large pieces of wood onto the fire, and the flames grew.

The creature made some more gestures to William.

"Wh—wha—What?" William stammered.

The creature slammed the knife into the log and looked back at Jeannie, then rolled its hands over each other.

Jeannie watched him. Inside her head, she thought, *"Hey Jeannie sense, I need some help here."*

After a moment, the inner monologue asked, *"What was happening just before our guest arrived?"*

Jeannie thought, then said, "William—he's rolling his hands because he wants you to continue. Tell us more about the Overland Ogre Massacre."

The creature slapped its hands together and pointed at Jeannie, then resumed eating.

"So please, William," Jeannie continued. "You were talking about the Overland Ogre. I am guessing he comes out on nights like this."

"Well," William said, "they say no one has ever lived to see the Ogre. But he eats people."

The creature initially seemed pleased with this, but when William stopped, the potato-sack head turned and stared in William's direction.

"William, was there ever a camp here—in the park grounds?" Jeannie prompted.

She saw William nod.

"Then tell us about it."

"It was run by a small college that used to be here as well, Overland State or something. It was in that old mansion in the northern part of the park. They ran a camp in the summer for kids called Overland State College Camp. Well, it went on one summer and there were a lot of counselors getting the camp ready."

"Just like us," Anabella whimpered.

Jeannie quickly interjected, "Please don't interrupt, Anabella. William, please continue."

"The night before the campers were supposed to arrive, a lot of the counselors went into town. But a few stayed behind. The Overland Ogre came and killed seven - "

The creature tapped its knife on the stones surrounding the fire.

"Uh," William said, "he killed eight?"

The creature tapped its knife again.

"Uh, nine?"

The creature sat back, and Jeannie thought it looked satisfied.

"Nine counselors. And the mansion burned. And the school closed. And that's all I know. "

The creature continued to eat.

An instant later a second large figure burst into the campsite, wielding an axe in one hand, and wearing a football helmet. The being, clearly a male, grabbed Anabella's sleeping bag by the back and lifted her into the air with one free hand and held her above its head. Then he cocked his elbow and Jeannie knew he was going to slam Anabella to the ground.

It seemed like the football-helmeted figure had not noticed they already had a guest. But their guest had seen the new interloper. Then Jeannie saw their potato-sack-mask-wearing friend rise to his feet, gripping his butcher knife. His cowboy hat fell off.

The two behemoths stood on opposite sides of the campfire, staring at each other. Anabella was screaming and twitching in the football-helmeted figure's hand.

"Anabella." Jeannie uttered as a breathy whisper, finding something deep within her gut. "Please. Try to be still."

The swinging in the bag slowed a little, but Anabelle could not stop heaving heavy breaths. The two large figures were motionless.

"*A standoff*," Jeannie thought.

The football-helmeted figure turned his head just enough to look at the others cowering around the campfire, pausing for a moment to lock eyes with Jeannie. She could not see any face; it was all dark in that helmet. He continued till he gazed at their knife-wielding "guest." Then Jeannie saw the helmet dip - the slightest, most barely perceptible of nods. He tossed Anabella into the air and caught her with the same hand, and then slowly lowered her to the ground.

The football-helmeted figure stepped backward and receded into the darkness. No one spoke.

The potato-sacked creature sat back down on the log, picked up its hat, and continued to eat. After a while, he stopped, tossed the paper plate onto the fire, and laid the knife in his lap. The creature stared at the campfire, motionless, silent, as the fire consumed the plate.

Again, no one spoke.

After a length of time Jeannie could not measure, the creature stood up and walked out of the campsite. Jeannie felt her companions' relief, with some gulping for air while others cried.

Eileen touched Jeannie's shoulder and observed, "Now you're the one who can't stop shaking."

Jeannie hadn't been aware of it, but Eileen was right. Both uttered nervous laughs.

"Yeah, you're right Eileen."

Lawson asked, "Jeannie, how did you understand what he wanted?"

"I don't know. I really don't. Just my *Jeannie sense* I guess."

Anabella said, "Someone should check on Steve,"

Steve was lying against the log, groggy, nearly unconscious. Jeannie went over to check his shoulder.

"It's bruised pretty bad. But you'll live."

Steve managed to get out, "Thanks, Dr. Jean- ouch!"

Jeannie adjusted the ice pack. "That'll teach you to wander into an elevated horror story. You know—"

The woods parted, and the potato-sacked figure reentered the clearing, knife in his right hand, something else in the left. He pointed his knife to the path Jeannie and Anabella had been on to get the water.

And spoke in a refined Gaelic accent. "That path leads to a stream where you can cross. You recall, where I saw you two earlier."

He aimed his knife at Anabella and Jeanne, then continued.

"On the other side of the stream, there is a footpath. It's difficult to see. But you," and he pointed his knife right at Jeanne, "you noticed it. If you get on it and keep moving, it will lead you out of the park. Nothing should bother you, at least, not for the next hour. I would get going if I were you. Now." He sheathed his knife and started to turn but stopped and looked back at Jeannie.

"You're right. Talbert Tenpenny cannot write. And you do need a new shirt." He tossed what was in his left hand at Jeannie. Expecting the worst, but with no time to react otherwise, she caught it.

Then the creature returned to the forest.

William went up to Jeannie and asked, "Are you ok?"

"Yeah," Jeannie said. Then she felt the package that was thrown at her. Some type of clothing, wrapped in plastic.

"Hey, this is actually pretty soft."

She unwrapped the plastic and held up the contents. It was a long-sleeved heavy-weight sweatshirt. Light green, with yellow lettering on the front that read "Overland State College."

Anabella started to say, "This is like that movie—"

Jeannie cut her off with, "Shut up, Anabella. We're leaving!"

And with Jeannie leading the way, using her flashlight (and wearing her new Overland State College gear, of course), the Lake Wassamatta Program Staff counselors hurried down the path pointed out to them. Steve needed a little help.

Though I'm not positive, I think they made it out alive.

47

Cosmopolitan: A New Orleans Ghost Story

Amy Nielsen

THE TAXI TURNED FROM Tchoupitoulas onto Iberville Street and an ivory building plunged into the heavens. The monstrosity, flanked on each side by smaller boutique-style establishments, looked out of place and magnificent.

Janie squealed with delight. "The Easton is incredible!"

James checked his watch. "Damn, I'm gonna be late for the first meeting. Can you handle the check-in so I can get my projector set up?"

"Fine. I got it." But she wasn't fine.

"Listen, I said if you and Michael came you'd mostly be on your own."

"I know. It's just hard to check in with him by myself." Janie hung Michael's Autism Badge around his neck. This usually gained sympathy help from strangers.

"Daddy, look. Boats!" The boy's plump finger pointed toward a river full of paddle-wheelers hauling tourists and barges hauling shipping containers.

"That's the Mississippi River, Son. Runs clear from Lake Itasca in Minnesota through the Gulf of Mexico. Over 2,000 miles."

The driver pulled under the covered entry. He opened the door for Janie. "Ma'am, welcome to New Orleans."

"Thank you." She walked around the other side of the taxi and unbuckled Michael out of his car seat.

A bellman pushed over a rolling cart and started loading the rich brown leather luggage from the back of the taxi—far more than a family needed for a three-day trip. But Janie insisted Michael had all his favorite things when they traveled, including food. She planned to eat her weight in gumbo, but Michael wouldn't deviate from his mac and cheese and oatmeal.

"Here." James passed Janie a handful of bills to tip the hotel attendants, then disappeared toward a conference room on the other side of the hotel.

She shoved the cash into her Louis Vuitton cross-body bag and pulled out Michael's harness.

"I don't wike it, Mummy."

"I'm sorry, Bud. When I'm by myself, I gotta keep you safe." She locked the chest clip and slipped the other end of the tether onto her wrist.

She pulled him close, and they entered through a revolving door that deposited them into a chandelier-adorned lobby. An aroma of white tea and jasmine welcomed them. Marble-veined floors guided them to a mahogany desk.

A blonde in a dark burgundy suit beckoned them to *come here* with an equally burgundy long-nailed finger.

Three days of single parenting in this place would be worth it. "Follow me, Bud." Janie tugged gently at Michael as he tried to wander toward a cooler of cucumber water that sat atop a golden tree-branchy-looking table.

"Good afternoon. What's the last name?"

"Williamson. James and Janie."

"Great news for you, Mrs. Williamson. Due to your husband's Titanium status, we've upgraded you to a suite facing the Mississippi." She scanned room keys through a machine.

"Here you go. Take that elevator to the 25th floor. You are in Room 2525. The bellman will meet you there. Any questions?"

Janie took the room keys from the young woman. "No. Thank you."

"Come on, Michael. Let's go check out the room!"

As she and Michael headed toward the hallway of elevators, an out-of-place photo of an old building hung on the wall. It didn't fit Easton's elegance.

Janie peeked as they walked by. A placard read that it was an old hotel that sat in the same location. A fire destroyed it back in the early 1900s. It would be another 30 years before Thurston Dupar purchased the land and built a new hotel. She knew the hotel was recently remodeled. But had no idea something sat here before it.

"Mummy, let's go." Michael had slipped from the grip of her hand and was pulling her via his harness toward the elevator.

"Coming."

Inside the elevator, Janie asked Michael, "Can you find floor 25?"

"It's the top one!" He shouted as he pressed the button.

A long hallway carpeted in gold and burgundy and lined with statues and oversized artwork led to room 2525.

"Can I open it?" Michael asked.

"Sure, press the key card right here."

Michael's eyes lit up when the keypad dinged and flashed a green light, allowing the pair entry.

"Holy shit." The words escaped Janie's lips faster than her brain could stop them.

"Mummy! You're not supposed to say the s-h-i-t word."

"Sorry, Bud." Wall-to-wall glass faced the mighty Mississippi. Holy shit hardly captured the beauty of the scene before her.

The bellman entered with the luggage.

As he emptied his cart, Janie placed a few bucks in Michael's hand and whispered, "When he's done, give him this."

"Have a nice stay, Ma'am."

Michael smiled and handed over the bills.

After the bellman left, she unbuckled Michael's harness.

He pounced on the living room's fluffy pillow-topped blue velvet couch.

She didn't stop him.

Janie's gaze gravitated to the right to a huge round bar—topped with a sparkling granite countertop—equipped with a minifridge, microwave, and sink.

She rolled her suitcase through a set of double doors to an expansive master suite with a sitting area and floor-to-ceiling marble ensuite bath with a free-standing tub. Then she rolled Michael's suitcase through another door into an equally impressive double-bed guest suite with its own bath.

"Michael, you hungry?" When she walked back into the living room, Michael was standing atop the ledge of the windows facing the river."

"Ten boats, Mummy!"

"That's unsafe. Bud, you can see from the floor."

"I'm a big boy. I'm not unsafe." He held his ground.

This was when she needed James. Michael didn't fight him as much as he did her.

"I have an idea. Let's go check out the pool."

"Pool!" Distraction to the rescue.

She hustled and got him into his swimsuit and sunscreen, and they were out the door in five minutes, even though she didn't want to leave that room. *Ever.*

Back on floor one, they followed signs to the pool. A winding tube waterslide sat in the middle. Afternoon swimmers and sunbathers created the laidback vibe she was after.

A pool bar caught Janie's attention. "Let Mommy get a drink, then you can swim."

Michael fussed a little but eventually complied.

Janie ordered a Cosmopolitan—because she felt that fancy.

"Thanks for waiting. You can go but stay where I can see you."

"Okay, Mummy."

She took off the harness, and off he went. Years of swim lessons meant he was a good swimmer. Janie could relax—kind of. She kicked off her flip flips, pushed up her Lulu Lemons, and sat on the pool's edge while Michael swam.

An hour later, her drink was empty, and he was done. She toweled him dry then they made their way back inside.

She assumed James would wrap up his conference and head out for elbow rubbing with the Elder Law Section. For herself, Janie envisioned room service, a bottle of wine, and curling up to read her airport Romcom.

Back in the room, she microwaved Michael's mac and cheese while he watched cartoons on the large screen. Then she dialed room service and ordered a cup of gumbo and a bottle of Kim Crawford.

After they'd both eaten, she showered Michael and slipped him into his favorite train pajamas.

Tucked in one of the cozy guest beds between crisp, white sheets, Michael asked, "Mummy, tell me a bedtime story about the little boy who died in the fire here at the old hotel."

She gripped the stem of her wine glass. "I don't know that story."

"You saw his picture downstairs. Tell me his story, or I won't go to sleep."

Janie remembered the photo of the old hotel she'd seen, but she'd not seen a boy in it. But, if Michael asked for a request, she did her best to fill it. It kept the autistic meltdowns at bay.

"Okay. Once upon a time, there was an old hotel here. It was called"—she stumbled to come up with a name—" The Oldest Hotel in New Orleans. And one night, a family was spending the weekend here to take a ride on a ferry boat up the Mississippi. But because the hotel was old, the electrical wiring sparked. A fire broke out. The family then became friendly ghosts. And when the hotel was rebuilt, instead of going to the afterlife, they decided to stay here and spend the rest of eternity keeping families like ours safe. The End."

"The boy—his name was Bobby," Michael said.

Janie laughed. "How do you know his name if I made up the story?"

"He told me." Michael had always had a vivid imagination. "Goodnight, Mummy." He clutched his dinosaur plushie and closed his eyes.

"Goodnight." Janie plugged in, turned on Michael's sound machine, and turned off the light. "If you wake up, come straight to my room." She left his door slightly cracked.

She poured the last of the Sauvignon Blanc into her glass and plopped onto the plush sofa. Her phone buzzed—a text from James.

—*Sorry, babe. Networking. Cigars & whiskey on Bourbon Street. Don't wait up*—

Such was the life of the wife of a rising law partner.

—It's fine. Michael's asleep. I'm drowning my loneliness in the last of a bottle of Kim—

Three dots flickered. Then stopped. He probably got distracted by one of his voluptuous associates. She trusted James. But his associates worshipped him. She hoped the attention never went to his head.

She pushed the thoughts out of her mind, determined to enjoy her evening in luxury. There were some perks to being married to a lawyer.

She read for a bit, but her head kept nodding. Even though she hated most television shows, especially anything super popular like epic fantasy and *not reality* reality shows, she pressed the remote. Eventually, she settled in on a local station highlighting cozy NOLA ghost stories.

One by one, stories of ghosts in graveyards and old hotels lulled her to sleep. The mixture of wine and jet lag was the perfect cocktail to keep her there.

After what only seemed like seconds, a siren sobered her up. A smoke alarm! Michael! Lights flashed in the room.

She darted into the guest room. The unmade bed was empty. The door to the suite was open. She grabbed her phone and texted James.

—Where are you? The smoke alarms are going off, and Michael is missing—

Three dots then

—I'm on my way—

Janie sprinted into the hallway. What looked like female apparitions floated near housekeeping carts. The sirens were SO loud. Janie screamed, "What's going on? Have you seen my son? He's about this tall and was wearing train pajamas."

They smiled and pushed their carts into rooms. They weren't real. This wasn't real. I'm dreaming. Janie tried to convince herself. But it was real. The sirens screamed into her ears.

Smoke filled the hallway. Janie dropped to the floor. The door to a stairwell was ajar. Coughing and gagging, she crawled to it.

"Michael! Michael!" she screamed into the smoky vacuum of the stairwell.

"Mummy!" Small arms wrapped around her neck.

"Michael. Are you okay?" Janie cried as she embraced her son.

"Mummy, I'm okay. Bobby kept me safe. See."

Janie looked over and saw a foggy apparition of a child near the stairwell.

"Michael, we gotta get outta here. Follow me." Twenty-five flights of stairs later, they fell onto the street.

"Janie, Michael." James scooped his family and moved them away from the burning building. "I'm so glad you're okay."

First responders and firefighters ascended. "They're gonna be okay," an EMT told James as he strapped an oxygen mask on Michael.

The EMTs hoisted Janie and Michael onto stretchers and pushed them toward an ambulance. James climbed in.

Before the EMT wheeled Janie in, she saw three apparitions. A small one in the middle and two larger ones on either side.

"Thank you," Janie muttered to them.

Michael waved. The small one in the middle waved back.

The ghost family disappeared into the Canal Street fog.

48

Sleepwalker

Jinxie R. Thorne

HAVE YOU EVER HAD a dream feel so real, that you couldn't distinguish reality from fantasy? I have. Maybe you'd first dismiss it thinking it's only a dream, but for me vivid imaginings, have consequences. I've never figured out how to call it forward, but when it happens— my life becomes a *freak show* It's run in my family for generations... so I've been told. There's been nights where I wished to God, it'd just stop. In my opinion, this gift is a blessing and a curse.

Sulfurous fumes overpowered the air. Wild flames danced as they scorched the earth beneath it. Orange smoke billowed, limiting visibility next to none. Ray knew his family was running out of time. His wife Diana had gone ahead of him. Their daughter Alex was hiding. Ray had one mission: Get Alex and himself out safely.

A young child clutched her lion stuffy. Heat seared her skin, and soot smudged her cherub face. Flickering embers crept

across the floor. Alex did the only thing she could think to do—
HIDE. Her gaze darted around the room. The closet seemed
to be her only option. Alex lowered herself down, and crawled.
"Stop, drop, and roll," she said to herself.

Creeeak! The closet door squeaked. A void lurked just beyond the rickety frame. Voices whispered incoherently from the
darkness. Alex's choices were: One, being eaten by Mr. Boogeyman, or two, the fires. *Well, Mr. Boogeyman would just have
to eat her!* Alex cracked open the door to squeeze passed. She
closed the door behind her. Alex let out an ear-piercing scream
as she huddled in the corner. With luck, someone would hear
her.

Violet-red embers flew in every direction. Ray dodged a
falling beam as he trudged through the smoke.

"Alex!" he called.

Faint sobbing caught his attention. Based on the direction of
the sound, Ray knew Alex was in her room. He followed the
sound of his daughter's voice and veered to the right.

"Alex! I'm here honey!" Ray hollered over the roaring flames.

Ray rushed into the room. The faintest touch disintegrated
the wooden door. He found his daughter and scooped her up.
"Daddy's gotcha! We're ok!" he said, holding his daughter close.

Young Alex nestled into her father's arms. He smelled like
smoke and burning wood, but she didn't care. Alex knew that
she was safe. Falling ash clouded her vision. Her lungs felt like

weighted lead. She coughed and buried her face into her father's shoulder.

Freedom was just beyond their reach. Blistering heat rushed past them as they bolted for the door. The only door leading out— was made of stained glass and wood. Neon embers trailed their path. Rays' steps ignited into flame. Scarlet gold engulfed the door, causing Alex to wince.

Ray patted his daughter's back. "It's ok, baby! We're gonna make it!"

The stained glass glowed incandescent gold. He'd have to smash their way out– if the door didn't explode first. Ray gritted his teeth. He used the brunt force of his strength to burst through the flaming door. Iridescent shards shattered into thousands. Glass crunched underfoot. Ray staggered away from their home. He choked back, coughing, although his lungs burned like hell. Once they were safe, Ray set his daughter down onto a clear patch of lawn.

Spiky grass crunched under her butt. Alex playfully curled her fingers into the mud. She giggled as it squelched and squished into her hands. Coolness brushed her cheek, soothing the burns. She extended her muddied hands outward, forming 'grabby hands'. Alex hoped Daddy would pick her up and hold her.

Ray knelt down. He glanced protectively over Alex, checking for any clear injuries. Other than a few smudges, she seemed to be ok. He hugged her close.

"It's ok baby girl we're out," he said. "Now we just need to find momma."

Momma. The word rang like a bullet from a gun. His hazel hues darted around the property. Diana was nowhere to be found. A blood-curdling scream pierced the air. As he gazed at the fire, Ray realized Diana was still trapped.

Ray turned to face his daughter. "I love you Alex," he said, placing a kiss on her forehead.

A tear rolled down Alex's cheek. "Daddy, No!" The child sobbed as her father pulled away.

Ray mustered his courage and bolted into the jaws of Hell.

"Daddy, Noooo!" The words echoed in her ears. Alex jolted upright, screaming from her desk. Cold sweat dampened her forehead. Her eyes watered, and tears rolled down her cheek. "Huh? wha-" she muttered. Reality wavered from a misty haze. Her hands trembled as she lifted them to eye view. The familiarity of Alex's soft hoodie brought her peace. Relief washed over her. "It's only a nightmare," she mumbled.

Her weary gaze drifted over the rest of her body. She had no feeling in her ass from sitting so long. Pinpricks traveled from the base of her feet upward into her calves. Acute pain shot into the core of her knees. *Snap, crack, and Pop.* Her bones cracked. Rampant popping ricocheted from her tailbone into her vertebrate. Alex cringed through gritted teeth.

Snap, crack, pop! That's all her body did since she turned thirty. Fuck it, adulting was overrated. She didn't want to 'adult' anymore.

Alex found herself hunched over an open laptop. The laptop screen displayed two ladies smiling brightly. A medieval backdrop played against their glitzy fairy attire. Alex dressed in Earthy forest green. The woman was named Willow. She glittered in pastel blue. The two ladies had been friends for—ages. A smile curled on Alex's lips. 'Renaissance Day.' She remembered it well. Playing fairy at Ren Fest was the perfect 'girls' day'.

Imaginary hammers split her nerves. Alex rubbed her temples as pain brought her back to reality. Her momentary happiness was shattered.

"Well, that's another one to tell the therapist." She sarcastically muttered.

An exasperated sigh fell on her lips... She hated therapy–hated it with a passion. Therapy sessions were supposed to help, but it only made her feel crazier. When your family dies in a house fire...what did people expect? Happy go-fuckin' lucky?

The good doctor also mentioned that writing 'Health Reports' would help her heal. Alex laughed. Health reports, HA! *More like a glorified diary.* Her experiences, emotions, inner thoughts— it sounded like a diary to her! She opened a document on Word pad. The blinking cursor greeted her, bouncing on screen. Her fingers danced across the keys:

Health Report- Document: ???

I'm feeling fine, I guess? Nightmares suck ass.

Emotionally, I'm confused. Maybe aggravated?

Physically: I'm tired as fuck. WHY. CAN'T. I. SLEEP!

She jotted down the blurb and then closed the document. There wasn't much to these reports that she hadn't written a thousand times. When she first began writing—many, *many* moons ago—Alex would describe every detail per doctor's orders. Now, a blurb sufficed; she was tired of writing elaborate paragraphs.

How could she write exactly how she felt? Everything written always paled in comparison to her thoughts. Alex would never forget when her world burned. The sight, the smell– It wasn't enough that guilt ate her alive. She was scarred for life.

What's worse? Night terrors kicked her ass on a nightly basis. Night terrors, nightmares? Alex knew there was a difference, but it didn't matter. The fact was– she didn't sleep for days at a time. Her baggy eyes and dark circles made Alex look like the living dead. As for the cherry on top of the dumpster fire? *A demon was stalking her.* The demon appeared when her old house burned– or maybe that was the lack of sleep talking.

She hit the save button, then clicked over to another file. Alex kept three files. Health Doc, Night Terrors, and Ink works. Their titles were respective of their contents. The terror files were fucked up to say the least. Alex could write a book on the crazy shit that her brain made up. Staccato clicking sounded as she jotted the details of her dream. Admittedly, they sounded like pure fiction works. Maybe she'd turn her work into a book— who knows. Only time would tell. The working hour passed, and a full-page document stared at her.

"Looks good," Alex said. She hit the save button and closed the file.

The third file was last for the night. Alex opened <u>Ink Works.</u> Ink work files were strictly work-related. The cursor blinked over a single manuscript file. She clicked the yellow folder. Several tiles rapidly cascaded across her laptop screen.

"God, how I wish these edits were done!" Alex groaned. She'd been working for months on this manuscript, and she *always* found something to edit. Alex changed her mind every time she turned around! 'Over-critical pain in the ass much?' she thought. Blame the perfectionist side of her. It made her want to spit nails!

Edits were another circle of hell in their own right. There were no shortcuts with them either. Rewrites, typos— GOD FUCKIN' FORBID TYPOS. Typos were enough to drive someone insane. The process was worth the stress, though. No matter how grouchy Alex became, the work was always worth it.

Alex slowly rose and stretched. Her jaw sleepily dropped into a yawn. If she was gonna stay awake through the next lines, she needed coffee— preferably in an IV. The author drug her heels into the kitchen. The countertops were clean, save for the basic essentials. A jar of Maxwell House sat neatly beside the coffee pot. '*Maybe*' she thought. 'Some cartoons would help—or maybe not?' Alex debated this as water rushed from the sink. She patiently waited for the coffee pot to fill.

"I need a muse," she whispered.

Water droplets always sounded unique, when falling against a surface. She listened intently. When the time was right, she poured the coffee pot contents into the reservoir. Alex's wrists turned off the faucet. The on switch glowed red as she flipped it over. *Ding!* the metaphorical bell rang in her ear. Lightbulb moment, *that's it!*

"It's not procrastinating if I watch T.V. for inspiration's sake," Alex said slyly. She quickly grabbed the remote and flipped through her Amazon Prime list. "Where is it?" She asked.

Grave Keeper's Chronicles was among her favorite binge-worthy series! Granted, she'd seen every episode, but they never got old. Rapid clicking zipped through her options. "Damn, it's buried deep into the content," she said.

A wolf's cry broke the clicking trail. Translucent clouds sifted across a moonlit sky. The scene panned out, overlooking a desolate graveyard. A gremlin lunged from the shadows. The creature was frail and grey. He looked like a tiny skeleton, with its skin pulled taut over the bones. His pointed devil ears, larger than Dumbo, flapped in the howling wind. The monster carried a lantern in his spindly hand. As he brought the light closer, bug-eyed oculars came into view.

Alex chuckled. When she was a child, that jump scare always caught her off guard. Now, it only made her smile. She remembered Mogul the Gremlin fondly. The monster would always do his little jump scare, then announce the story for the evening.

"Good evening, Darklings!" the nasally gremlin chimed. Mogul slobbered as he spoke. Needle fine teeth protruded from his underbite.

Joy radiated through Alex's tired features. She loved this show so much! The T.V. glitched, scrambling the signal. The picture froze on Mogul's ghoulish face. Low-key Alex had to admit, he was a little creepy. Moguls' eyes stared her down as if peering through to her soul. Alex turned the TV off, feeling uncomfortable. The TV flashed. Mogul reappeared, but this time perched atop a tombstone. He crouched low as an impish grin curled on his grimy lips.

"Hello, Alex." the little monster cackled.

Alex's eyes went wide. "Uhm, I don't remember this being part of the show," she said.

The official creep factor was a ten for her. Enough was enough. *Beep beep.* The coffee pot sputtered and steamed. Perfect timing! Alex tossed the remote onto the sofa and walked into the kitchen. Columbian roast wafted through the air, drawing her in. '*Ahhh,* 'Alex sighed contently. She grabbed a bag of marshmallows from the pantry and then fixed her coffee.

Alex trudged to her desk with midnight spoils in hand. Her eyes briefly drifted to the T.V. Thankfully, the screen was dark. "Must've been my imagination," Alex said. She opened her recent manuscript titled Autumnfell Draft and settled back into work. Distant rumbling echoed across the horizon. Spiderweb flashes streaked across a starless sky. The author peeked over her laptop screen. Heat Lightning. It'd be nice if they got some rain. Hmm, *Oh well*. Alex thought. Her gaze drifted back to the document. Three cups of coffee and an entire bag of marshmallows later, any other person would be wired from sugary caffeine overload. Not Alex! Her jaw dropped into a yawn. The clock read 3:00 A.M. *Damn time flew by.* Last time she looked, it read 10:00 p.m.

"Time to call it a night," she said.

Alex lazily crawled into bed. In the back of her mind, she hoped that her sleep wasn't disrupted again. The wind began to howl, scraping the nearby trees across her window; Twisted shadows trailed greedy claws across the wall. Alex tossed and turned through the symphony of thunder. ***KAPOW***! Lightning flashed, illuminating the eastern sky. Between flashes, ominous figures slithered through the darkness. Icy wind seeped through her window. Goosebumps pricked her skin. Why did her body choose to do this? Acute pin pricks crept down her right shoulder blade, creating tension along her back.

Her stomach began to wrench as if twisting into a thousand knots. Something *wasn't* right. "I'm just being paranoid." she tried to reason with herself. Alex clutched her pillow and shut her eyes. She took a few slow, deep breaths. At first, she felt her body drift.

"Alex...." a sinister voice hissed through the cold air.

A crimson sea flooded Alex's vision. The sea ebbed. The rolling waters darkened into tar. She tossed and turned. Alex grumbled, pulling the blanket tightly over her head.

The creature neared Alex. It reached out and curled its bony fingers in her hair. Alex's shifting startled it, causing it to retreat for now.

☐Both hands instinctively flew to the back of her head. *'tink, plunk'* metal clinked against the nightstand. Someone tried to grab her! Alex felt around her tangled mess of umber curls. 'Nothing, thank God.' She breathed a sigh of relief.

Alex rubbed her eyes, then reached for her glasses. Smooth oak brushed against her fingers where her glasses should've been.

"Great, just *fucking* great." she groaned sarcastically. Alex was blind as a bat, and her glasses fell on the floor.

She scooted to the bed's edge. The linoleum was cool from the night air. Alex gingerly stepped around, feeling for the frames. Knowing her luck, they probably got swatted across the room. The glasses lay miraculously unscathed beside the closet door. Alex cleaned the lenses with her shirt, then pushed them back onto the bridge of her nose. She glanced at the clock again.

4:20 am.

"So much for sleeping." she huffed.

Something was bothering her though; Alex knew she heard a voice. It made her question if she really *had* fallen asleep. Going batshit crazy was out of the question.

"Might as well get back to work." She said.

The apartment was eerily still. Alex dismissed this at first before feeling eyes on her again. She didn't like the feeling of being watched. Paranoia crept along her spine.

I'll see the killer in the window soon." The voice in her head remarked.

That's what happened in books. If the killer wasn't in the house, they were in the window. Alex shook her head. 'No.' she thought. She knew better than to joke about that. The author sat at her desk and opened her laptop.

The dinosaur technology took its sweet time rebooting. Alex swore under her breath. while thrumming her fingers on the desktop. That's what she got for using outdated software. She checked the charger outlet, seeing it was still plugged in. "It's plugged in; it should be working," she said. The laptop froze. Dozens of files unpromptedly opened. Windows cascaded in layers until the monitor was completely covered.

"What the *hell*?" She exclaimed. What kind of sick joke was this?! Those files were sealed tight in a zip file like Fort- fuckin-Knox. Alex hastily pulled her work file from the pile windows. "Please don't let my work be gone." she pleaded.

Alex clicked the manuscript file. She felt her jaw instantly drop. The screen glowed white, and a blinking cursor glared back at her.

"Mother fucker!" she exclaimed.

Alex wanted to throw her laptop! *A blank document?!* The damned file had at *least* three chapters written! A week's worth of progress was *gone*!

"Fuck a duck!" she snapped.

The editor wasn't going to be happy about this. Alex angrily slammed down on the keys. Straining to remember a portion of her work was half the battle. She didn't care if the shit didn't make sense or not. Some work was better than no work.

Zzipp, the laptop suddenly discharged, sending a jolt of shock through my fingers. Sharp pains surged upward into her hands and ricocheted into her wrists that were riddled with carpal tunnel. In the mirror reflection of the darkened screen, Alex caught glimpses of a towering, lanky figure. It lurked behind her, appearing farther away than it actually was. Its eyes were devoid of life. Alex stiffened immediately when their eyes met, unable to move as its cheshire grin widened from ear to ear. In her screen, she could see seeping caliginous blood between its jagged rotted teeth, and it's as if the creature were scrutinizing her from afar.

"It's not real," she whispered.

Maybe the creature would disappear. That's what all nightmares did, right? Fade away? Alex squeezed her eyes shut to avoid a face-on encounter. If her theory was correct, the creature would disappear.

"Remember me, Alex?" It shrilled.

Wrong! Ignoring the creature only provoked it. Alex was in deep shit. Her heart pattered. She felt her anxiety creep like stalkers in the night.

"Their blood is on your hands." It taunted. The creature crept forward and curled its bony fingers around her shoulders.

Conflicted memories derived from guilt piled onto her chest like cement bricks. As much as Alex tried to ignore it, she knew the creature was right. It *was* her fault. The fires took everything from her, and she did nothing to stop it. Alex watched her family reduce to ash. The stench of charred flesh was still ripe in her nose, same as the day it happened. The more Alex remembered, the weaker she felt. Her body felt frail under the monster's grip. Years slowly dwindled her youthful features, like sand in an hourglass.

The creature *reveled* in Alex's fear. It slowly siphoned off her life force. Sweet fear nourished its starving form. Alex would be easy pickings at this rate. The creature watched her through the years. It knew she was strong-willed. A strong host in its prime meant survival. This woman wouldn't be taken without a fight...but a fight was *exactly* what it expected.

Alex bit her lip. The creature's grip felt like sludge, slowly poisoning her veins. Silver strands began to lace throughout Alex's hair. Deep age lines slowly etched along her cheeks. 'I have. to. be. asleep.'Alex thought. 'It's not real.'It was too freaky *to be real*. 'It's not real.' The mantra repeated in her mind. "FUCK OFF ASSHOLE!" Alex screamed at the demon.

The creature cackled. Oh, the chaos it would wreak with Alex as its host! The sheer thought made the monster ravenous. It could've taken her now, but where was the fun in that? The creature was patient and loved toying with its meals. Fear nourished it; slowly, it would siphon her life force away. The creature could sense Alex's healthy aura. It *needed* her to live. Body and soul, the creature would have her tonight.

Lurking shadows cast illusions, manipulating Alex's peripheral vision. She noticed the creature's face distort from menacing to *scared shitless.* — that caught her attention. An Earth-shattering screech rattled the walls. Alex felt the creature loosen its grip and fade away. She sighed in relief. She was glad the creature was gone. On the other hand, Alex wondered *what* frightened the creature so much.... that it ran for cover.

A faceless spirit materialized before her. The ethereal figure kept themselves concealed, shrouded by black robes. They stood solemn and silent. The guardian scrutinized Alex too. This spirit, however, was unlike any other that she had encountered.

"Who are you?" Alex asked the spirit.

Silence.

"Can you speak?" She asked again.

Static buzzed as the WIFI signal scrambled. A blank Word document opened. Keys sparked with life. The keys typed two gibberish lines, then stopped.

Alex locked her emerald gaze onto the spirit

"W- what's happening?" She asked, struggling with her words.

The spirit nodded, and the document cleared. Clicking keys slowly typed:

H.E.L.P.

Alex considered her next question carefully. "You need help?" she asked.

Gentle tapping followed:

Y.O.U.

"Me?!" she clarified. This was going to be a *long* night. Alex remembered having dreams as a kid. They were like another world. The family always called her crazy, but in these worlds– the monsters were always real.

Clashing broke her train of thought. She knew she wasn't alone anymore. Something was in the kitchen. Alex quickly averted her gaze, feeling ice seep into her spine. No telling what monsters lurked in the shadows tonight. She discreetly walked down the corridor. The walls tapered the further Alex walked. What was this? Some fucked up escape room? Well, while in Wonderland– or in this case.... Borderland.

Acrid fumes overpowered the air. Alex struggled to hold her head up. Her vision began to blur, distorting the world around her. *Tick tick tick.* 'Did the stove get turned on?' She thought. The odor smelled like rotted eggs. She lumbered across the threshold. Her steps felt like weights dragging her down. High-pitched ringing deafened her hearing.

Ssss, the gas stove hissed. Alex could barely see straight. Reality split into two identical lenses. Double vision was a bitch! In one lens, Alex saw her apartment; the second lens blurred into hazy waves. Shadows blurred the line of focus. Both lenses completely dissolved. Alex reached to turn the dial before being cast into darkness.

The overbearing absence of feeling drove Alex into madness. Coldness wrapped her weakened frame in an icy sheet. A sharp pain erupted through her skull, shooting down into her spine. When Alex regained consciousness, she found herself inside a grim lapse of time past: *her childhood home*. Her chest tightened. She staggered to her feet.

The house was preserved *exactly* how she remembered before the fire. A large area opened to a country kitchen with two doorways. Alex could still smell the warm butter bread fresh from the oven. It made her mouth water just thinking of it! Momma made the *best*-baked bread here! The neighbors called her the best baker in town.

A slender hallway led to the back of the house. From the second door frame, there were four rooms – five if someone counted the children's hideaway. Alex's old room and a guest bed on the right, Straight down the center hall, lead into a small bathroom. The left side was reserved for her parents and the half-bath.

Overstuffed beanbag chairs welcomed weary visitors. Anime movies lined the walls, stacked in the shelves. To the left, directly across the den, a small children's hideaway lay cluttered with an overfilled toybox, rocks, odd 'n end trinkets, and broken toys.

The guardian reappeared, huddled in the corner. A delicate finger raised to their lips —motioning for silence.

Alex tip-toed further down the hall. Pungent florals led directly into her parents' room, 'Momma's perfume.' She thought. Alex twisted the doorknob and entered the room. A queen-sized bed was pristinely made. The light panel had two switches: One for the half bath and one for the bedroom itself... She flipped the bedroom switch on.

An eerie glow illuminated from the half-bath. Dreary hymns alarmed her. When Alex turned the corner, she found... Momma standing in front of the mirror? Momma hummed as she fixed her makeup. Alex wanted to bolt. Momma was always beautiful with her deep auburn curls and emerald eyes— but this creature in front of Alex– wasn't momma. Residual energy oozed from the spirit like tar. Alex's stomach churned. It made her want to vomit.

Air escaped from her chest, followed by her thundering heart. Memories of early Saturday mornings flooded back to memory. She'd spend most of the early morning watching '*Scooby-Doo*' while Momma nagged Alex to prepare for Mass.

Alex was rendered speechless as she witnessed her past.

"Pumpkin," Momma spoke softly. "Why aren't you ready for church? We'll be late." Alex slowly backed away, causing Momma to turn around

"Dear?" Momma asked. "What's wrong? You look like you've seen a ghost."

She shook her head while attempting to contain her composure. Momma was *dead*. *How* was this possible?! Cold tears streamed down her face.

"Oh, pumpkin.... Don't blame yourself," Momma casually dismissed.

Alex trembled. Her knees began to buckle. The true 'Momma' reflected in the mirror. Cracking bones protruded through pasty flesh. Murky blood oozed from open wounds lined along its back. Maggots squirmed with life as they feasted upon the creatures' rotted muscle.

"Their blood is on your hands." it hissed. Momma's once angelic voice now distorted, and manic laughing.

Light in the room dispersed, shattering the creature's facade. Alex had no reaction time. Unearthly speed propelled it forward. They collided on the floor with a resounding *THUD.* The creature snatched Alex by the left ankle. Bones crushed under its grip, causing Alex to scream. Skin broke as shattered bone sliced through the muscle like butter. Alex felt woozy. Stars hovered above her head as the room spun like mad. Deranged eyes locked onto Alex's throat. Razor talons kept the creature anchored as it slithered up Alex's body. The demon hissed in wicked delight– the host was theirs for the taking.

'That's it!' Alex thought through the haze. It was do or die, and she'd be damned if this asshole was gonna win! Blood pooled around her. The sticky matter stained her flesh. Die by demon, or die by blood loss– blood loss was better than soul loss. Adrenaline coursed through her veins. She thrashed wildly. The creature clung on for dear life. Alex's counter-attack deterred the demon, causing it to shimmy further down her leg.

Alex watched the creature slither. Now was her chance! Hell, or high water, kick until the fucker went down! Alex's body shifted, and she rolled on her side. She targeted the creature between its' beady eyes. *CRUNCH, SNAP.* ***"SCREEEEEE!"*** Her foot landed, nailing her target.

The creature wailed in agony. Its skull caved inward, and cerebral matter splattered the wall. Tarry goo squished under Alex's foot, oozing between her toes. The creature's body lifelessly collapsed onto the floor.

Freedom was within her reach. Alex staggered and dragged herself up. Excruciating pain surged through her ankle as her weight pressed down. Weak as a ragdoll, she fumbled face first. Her fingers clawed their way across the floor.

"Almost there! You can make it!" She panically said to herself. The kitchen was in sight. Alex drug herself down the hall. Sweat beaded down her forehead. The front door was just beyond the kitchen. If Alex could make it there, then this nightmare would be over.

Sssss. Sickeningly sweet fumes filled the air. Alex felt pressure building in her chest. Ominous cackles pierced the shadows. *"See you in Hell Alex..."*

Tick Tick Tick. the gas stove clicked. Flames instantly combusted. Golden Red paved a war path across the floor. Alex had no more fight left in her. Blood-curdling screams echoed as the fire consumed her. The sacrifice of body fueled the ravenous blaze. Smoke pervaded her lungs, as Alex withered away, her lungs collapsed, and body slumped. Blistering heat broiled her flesh layer by layer.

Alex's vision slowly dimmed. The spirit in black materialized on scene. They mulled over their next move. As the hooded figure glided across the burning floor, the flames forged a path.

The spirit attended Alex's side, then knelt down. A gloved hand reached out to brush over her eyes.

"Sleep," the mysterious figure soothed.

The spirit vanished, and the world faded away.

An unforgiving void encompassed her, leaving nothing in its wake. She felt weightless, floating in the abyss. Alex's attempts of movement were futile. Her limbs felt bound by unseen chains. Her skin was cold and clammy. Was she dead? Was it finally over? She opened her mouth to scream, yet nothing sounded. 'What is this place?' Alex wondered. There were so many questions that she wanted to ask. A sinister voice broke the silence.

"You're mine now.". It sneered

Alex's arms and legs drooped. 'What the fuck?' She thought. Every fiber in her body felt weighted down. There was a sudden stillness, yet her body hovered in place. Disembodied screams riddled the atmosphere. There was an instant drop as her body plummeted. She fell faster and faster. Alex could've sworn she was falling at warp speed. A light glinted in the distance. She didn't know what it was– but she was headed right for it

Warmth wrapped around her like a blanket. ***SLAM.*** She landed flat on her back. Scratchy cotton made her itch. The air smelled clean, riddled with antiseptic. Alex was brought into a misty haze. "Huh?" she barely managed to whisper.

As her conscience returned, Alex felt leather straps tightened around her ankles and wrists. Her emerald hues drifted over to a metal door. A distorted figure stood peeking through plated glass.

An ear-splitting crackle buzzed as a female's voice shrilled through an intercom. "Where did your mind go this time, Alex?"

49

SOMETHING IN THE WATER

BRUCE BUCHANAN

MARC DODSON PULLED ON the vape pen and spewed a cloud of electrically generated nicotine into the still-cool morning air. From the porch swing on the side of the small cabin, the cedars, firs, and pines seemed to stretch straight into the sky.

I'm going to buy a fucking mountain, he thought. Technically, that was incorrect. Marc actually stood on 400 acres of undeveloped forest land deep in North Carolina's Blue Ridge Mountains.

At least they were undeveloped for now. But as he looked across the dark green panorama, he envisioned timeshare condos, pickleball courts, valet parking lots, and whatever else the hipsters, reverse snowbirds, and parents-and-brats vacationers dreamed of in a mountain getaway.

This all-in attitude toward commercial real estate development had made Marc a multi-millionaire before his 35th birthday. But the Charlotte market, where he had made that fortune, had gotten too crowded and competitive. Bigger sharks than Marc patrolled those waters. Which is why he had looked to this patch of forest in Bear Creek, a rural community left of Asheville. Here, he could be Jaws.

All at such a good price, too. Almost too good to be true. Currently, the cabin, built in the 1930s, and a small work building were the only two structures on the entire property. Marc got the land after its previous owner died unexpectedly, leaving no will and no heirs.

Guy has lived here all his life and one day, for no apparent reason, he hangs himself from the stairway banister. The local yokel cops found him dangling above his living room after he didn't show up for the weekly pancake breakfast with his buddies. Their loss, my gain, I suppose.

Still, being in the cabin gave Marc the creeps, which was why he chose to wait for the local real estate agent on the porch.

Within a few minutes, an older Subaru Outback pulled into the gravel driveway and up to the porch. A black-haired woman in her mid-twenties, wearing an off-the-rack business ensemble, stepped out and waved. Marc returned the greeting, then leered as the young woman leaned into the backseat to grab an attaché case.

A bit thicker than the spin-class-sculpted honeys I normally encounter at the office. But cute all the same. And definitely on Sir Mix-A-Lot's approved list.

He chuckled at his own joke as he exhaled another plume of cinnamon vanilla vape.

"Mr. Dodson? Hi—I'm Emily Crow from Conley Realty in Bear Creek," she said.

"Call me Marc, Emily... Crow, you said...?"

"Yes. I'm Cherokee," she said, with the exasperation generated by an intrusive question answered hundreds of times. "I've brought the contract for your review. I know you'll want a day to look it over, but in the meantime, I'd be happy to provide any additional information you may need."

Then riddle me this: What are the chances of you staying over tonight?

"Oh, I'll look it over a bit later. But come have a seat and enjoy a celebratory toast with me." Marc pulled a bottle of single malt scotch from a tote bag beside the swing and poured a dram into a crystal glass. He held the glass up to Emily, who waved her hand.

"No thank you. I've got driving to do. Now, you'll see on page thirty-seven that the surveyor completed—"

"Yeah, I'll look over tonight. I'm spending the night here, so we've got plenty of time. But c'mon—show me what I'm about to buy." Marc stood, set the glass of scotch on the swing, and gestured for Emily to follow him into the yard. He had made sure to wear this year's pair of Air Jordans for the hike–still an expensive pair of shoes, but not nearly as valuable as the fifty or so vintage pairs of high-top sneakers in his closet back in Charlotte.

Not that they had many yards to explore. The rhododen-drons, honeysuckle, and blackberry vines aggressively pushed the border of the woods closer toward the house every summer.

Not for much longer. Once we pave all this over, we can put the entrance gate here. $20 to park.

"This workshop comes with the property," Emily said, ges-turing to a pine plank shed with a rusty tin roof. "The previous owner was a woodworker by trade. He doesn't have any family, so all his tools are part of the sale."

Marc stuck his head in the shack. Specks of dust hung in the beam of sunlight from the open door. Stacks of wood—oak, ash, and hickory—had been piled at the far end, and tools hung from racks on each side. In the middle stood a workbench with a table saw mounted on its edge.

No, thank you. Too sharp for my liking. But hauling this junk away won't be a problem.

Besides, he was more interested in the barely visible worn path leading into the woods. "So where does this go?" he asked.

Emily changed into some comfortable walking shoes and traded her suit jacket for a zip-up hoodie. They then tromped through dense forest for a half hour, the narrow trail providing little distance from the bramble. They moved slowly and single file until they emerged into a clearing. Marc squinted when he stepped into the sunlit field.

Good spot for the swimming pool. He stepped into the knee-high grass.

"Be careful. There probably are snakes out here," Emily said, but Marc was determined to explore the clearing and ignored her.

In the far corner of the field, where the forest resumed, he spotted a small, algae-clogged pond. A black cloud of gnats hung over the still water, and Marc could practically smell the brackish pond's stench from a hundred yards away.

Emily stopped. "What's wrong? Is there something in the water?" Marc joked.

"I... it's nothing. I just... my grandfather always warned me about this pond. I haven't thought about it in years. But coming back here again...."

"What? Is there something going on here? Someone dump chemicals in it or something?" *If so, that was a big problem. My lawyer would be on the Conley Agency so hard they'll regret the day they hung their shingle.*

Emily waved him off. "No, it's nothing like that...."

"What then? A flesh-eating amoeba?"

Geez. Imagine if that got around. This place would be worthless. And I would be worthless! That can't happen.

"No... it's not that. It's just... my grandfather used to say this pond had a bad vibe. Everyone in Bear Creek knows it."

"So that's it?" Marc sneered. "You're weirded out because of some backwoods superstition?"

"My grandfather was no superstitious old Indian, Mr. Dodson," Emily hissed. "He served in the infantry in Vietnam—said what he saw there cured him of believing in luck or karma or anything supernatural. It's a perspective I share.

"But he learned another lesson in Vietnam—always trust your gut. If something feels wrong, it probably is. I subscribe to that belief as well."

She exhaled and reapplied her real estate agent's smile. "But listen to me—you would think I'm trying to talk you out of a sale! Let's go back to the house and we can look over that contract."

They did, but other than closing terms and tax considerations, Emily said little more to Marc. "You have my office number, so please call me if you have any questions. Otherwise, I'll be by in the morning, and we can finalize the sale."

Marc watched the Outback wind down the two-lane road away from the cabin. *Guess she won't be staying over. Oh, well—no biggie.* He tossed the stack of paperwork on the porch. *Heh. How dumb do you have to be to get so worked up about a damn pond?*

As planned, Marc rode into town, spending the next few hours working and web-surfing at Bear Creek's lone coffee shop. His laptop dinged, notifying him that he had won an online auction for a pair of rare Adidas sneakers. *At least that's one bid that's gone my way lately.*

He also found an admittedly good cheeseburger at the local diner, then tapped into the library's free Wi-Fi to make a round of Zoom calls. The chairs were cushy and comfortable, and the internet speed was much faster than he expected in an out-of-the-way mountain town. But just as he thought his luck might be turning around, his business manager, Susan, delivered the latest bad news.

"I'm sorry, Marc—we weren't able to close that South End redevelopment. I thought we had it, but Joyner & Co. swooped in at the last minute with a low bid," she said, from his computer screen. "Can we regroup for the next round of projects? I'll plan to work through the weekend to make sure we're ready."

"See that you do that," Marc said, then clicked the "LEAVE" button. This would have been a lucrative deal. And it was the third project in a row they had lost. This was the type of work the Marc Dodson Company used to land with regularity, but lately, bigger competitors had been edging him out.

Ah, well—it won't matter once this project closes and that sweet vacation home money rolls in. Increasingly, Marc's future depended on the Bear Creek development, and he was well aware of that reality. *Good thing I've got a winner.*

That evening, he sat on the cabin's pale green sofa, a relic of the Reagan era, and clicked on the TV. Nothing but static. *Damn—the cable company must've already shut off service after the old owner croaked.*

He already knew he couldn't get any internet coverage this far up in the mountains–that would be the first thing his team would address when he signed the contract sitting beside his $200 sneakers on the coffee table.

Might as well get started. Nothing else to do around here.

He grabbed the ream of documents and started reading. Or at least he intended to read. Instead, he looked at the same page a half-dozen times before throwing the stack down on the couch.

Why the hell was she so squirrelly about that pond? Was there something she didn't tell me? The environmental nerds gave the land a thorough probe and didn't find any contaminants. But still... if this deal goes south, I'm ruined. The whole company—everything I've built—is gone. Forget collecting vintage sneakers—I'll be lucky to buy off the rack at Walmart.

He sipped a can of energy drink, puffed on his vape, and leaned forward. *Only one way to find out.*

———

Marc shined a flashlight across the pond. Sweat dripped from his forehead, and he pretended the summer humidity was the sole culprit.

The water looked... different. The sickly green water bubbled like the contents of a witch's cauldron. And the area around the pond was devoid of wildlife. Not even a frog's croak or cricket's chirp interrupted the silence. Marc Dodson hadn't been hiking since his Cub Scout days, but even he knew that wasn't normal. His breathing was short and rapid; even Marc couldn't pretend he was just winded from the walk.

He broke a branch off a dead pine tree nearby and dipped it into the water. It came out wet and a little slimy, but nothing unusual.

What did you expect, you idiot? This... whatever. It's all in your head. And you have to prove that to yourself so you can get past this.

He carefully unlaced his left shoe and placed it in the grass well back from the water. He then stripped off his sock and walked to the edge of the pond.

Here goes nothing. And he dipped his foot into the dark water.

Marc flinched, half expecting his toes to be bitten off. But nothing happened. Other than the water being a little cooler than he expected on a June night, it felt like...water.

He stepped out of the water and looked at his foot. W*ait, is that a leech on my big toe? Some type of spider?* No, it was just a piece of moss. Marc exhaled and laughed. Even though he knew he was miles away from his nearest neighbor, he still felt the need to stifle his laughter and he looked around to make sure no one was watching.

Get a hold of yourself, Dodson. Keep this up and you'll sound as wacky as that dumb hick. He defiantly stomped his barefoot back into the dark pond, splashing water all over his khaki shorts.

Telling himself he had made this point, Marc dried his toes on the grass as much as he could, then slipped his still-damp foot back into his expensive sneaker.

He stayed on the couch reading the contract until nearly 2 a.m., at which point he stretched his stiff arms and yawned. He had finished most of the document, and at this point, he was too tired to read any longer.

He stood up, intending to lay down for the night. *Is it my imagination, or is my foot... tingling? Don't tell me I stepped in poison ivy down at that stupid pond...*

Marc pushed the shoe off his left foot with the toe of his right. When he looked down, he screamed as though his soul was in peril. And perhaps it was. For each of his five left toes had grown tiny demonic faces.

Each gruesome face varied from its neighbor. The middle toe's visage, for example, had hooked horns protruding from its forehead, while the face on his index toe had a goatee, like a Halloween devil costume. Long fangs hung over the lip of the face now occupying his fourth toe. His big toe's face was bulbous and warty, while a serpentine tongue drooped out of the mouth of the face on his little toe.

But none of the sinister faces moved independently of Marc's foot. Instead, they all appeared to be... sleeping.

"AEIIIEEE!!" he shrieked again. He mindlessly tried to run backward, as if to flee his own foot. In doing so, he tripped over the coffee table, landing ass-over-teakettle on the linoleum floor.

Marc sat up, hyperventilating, He peered over his knees. The faces were gone.

Wha...? But I know I saw... Man, you must be tired. Or that chick's crazy story has your imagination working overtime. His breathing slowed a little and he looked at his foot again, more carefully this time. *There's nothing there. Just your mind playing tricks on you.*

Marc took some deep breaths and laid down on the bed. His heart thumped too fast for him to sleep, but he thought he could at least calm himself by getting horizontal.

Surely, that wasn't real... right? He leaned up off his pillow and checked his foot again. Still normal, no demon faces to be found.

While Marc's panic had subsided, he still was too keyed up to sleep. He put his left shoe back on and went to the porch swing, vape pen in hand.

The night air was a bit chilly at 2,800 feet above sea level, even in June. Marc wished he had brought more than short-sleeved shirts.

First thing in the morning, I'm heading down the mountain. I'll drop the contract by the real estate office on my way out of town. Getting the hell out of this awful place. He exhaled a big cloud of scented vapor. The nicotine rush didn't soothe him the way it usually did, and the forest's night sounds unnerved him. He wished he hadn't come to Bear Creek, and had never even heard of this "once-in-a-lifetime" opportunity.

After an indeterminate period of sitting on the porch and staring into the blackness, Marc got up to go back inside. He knew he still couldn't sleep, but he didn't want to stay outside for another second.

When he stood, he felt an intense pain in his left foot. *Did I stretch a tendon? Crack a bone?* No—the pain was a burning sensation. And how his foot burned.

He plopped down on the floor, just inside the front door, and tore off his left shoe. The faces were back. And now, they were awake and angry.

All five faces leered at Marc and squirmed in place, as if they were trying to break free from the confines of his body. He could hear their hisses and snarls from the ends of his toes.

The bulbous face even whispered, "Mar-cus! Mar-cus!", causing the goateed face to snicker and nod its chin.

Marc looked away again, hoping that once again, the faces would vanish, and he would realize they were merely hallucinations. But no such luck. The faces remained, alert and agitated.

If anything, his obvious panic emboldened the demonic heads. The fanged face chortled, and the rotund one doubled down on his schoolyard chant of "Mar-cus! Mar-cus!" The face on his smallest toe then started flicking its forked tongue in the direction of Marc's face, daring him to do something.

What the hell—?!? How is this...? The pond! The water in the pond truly is cursed! Oh God, why didn't I listen to Emily? He looked out into the dark front yard, hoping for help that would not be coming.

And then he spotted the woodworking shop.

Only one chance... With one shoe on and one foot bare, Marc half-ran, half-crawled toward the small outbuilding.

Marc pressed his palms into the edge of the woodworking table as if to steel himself for what was to follow. *That damn pond has infected me! But I can save myself–get those demons out! I can cut them out!* He flipped the power switch and the circular saw growled to life.

Ha! You thought you could get me. But nobody gets one over on me! I'm too smart for you. You'll see.

Marc threw his foot up onto the table. No one heard his screams, nor did anyone see him grab his left foot off of the sawdust-strewn concrete floor and hurl it out into the yard.

There! Tol' you I was... gonna... gonna get rid of you. Marc quickly became light-headed. He slumped down to the workshop floor and rested his head against his arm.

I'll... get back up... Just lemme... relax a sec...

———————

"Sheriff Thomas! You won't believe what we found!"

The deputy ducked under the yellow tape blocking off the workshop and cabin, carrying a zipped clear plastic bag under his arm. He handed it to the sheriff, who, upon seeing its contents, pushed his brimmed hat off his forehead and shook his head.

"Spatter trail shows it was thrown from the workshop," the deputy said, after pausing to catch his breath. "And there's only one set of footprints—"

"Don't you mean 'footprint' singular?" the sheriff joked.

"Well... good point," the young deputy conceded. "What I mean is that only one person walked into that workshop, and it was Dodson. You don't see many Air Jordans around here, and that's what made prints in the sawdust–both right and left. So, he had two feet when he went into that shed."

"Well, I'll be damned! What kind of fool cuts off his own foot and throws it in the grass?"

"Beats me, Sheriff," the deputy continued. "And here's the crazy thing—as far as the Medical Examiner can tell, there's nothing wrong with this foot. Nothing but a mild touch of poison ivy."

Sheriff Thomas rolled his eyes and snorted. "City folk. Who the hell can figure them out?"

50

────⟨⟨⟩⟩────

LOVED

DAVID RYDENBACKER

EVERY YEAR, ON THE same day, I still feel the pain.

In the beginning, he made sure each time to tell me how much he loved me. How much he needed and wanted me. We would sit on the sofa, and we would remember how we had met. Later, when he fell asleep, I would drape myself over him and keep him company, feeling the warmth of his body and the vulnerability of his soul. We remembered differently. He remembered the love he had for me. I remembered when he made the pain finally go away, before he took me in his arms and caressed me.

As the years passed by, I came to accept more and more how he was able to show me his love and his affection. I had finally admitted to myself that I had come to him; asking him to take me in, protect me and love me. I don't know why I sometimes had this elusive feeling that I should hate him, but it always passed quickly when he talked to me. It faded more and more over the years as I accepted his love for me.

He started to talk to me more and more during the days, but especially in the nights. It felt good when he noticed me. Whenever he came home, I made sure to be close to him. The closer we became, the more empty bottles filled the house. But the bottles also brought him closer to me, lowering the barrier between us. The more bottles piled up, the more time he spent with me instead of at work or with his friends. So, I welcomed them. His friends still came over from time to time to sit with him on our sofa. I didn't like that, so I didn't make them feel welcome. Soon, they stopped coming.

I remember the night he had dared to bring home that whore, saying she was just a friend. I knew him, I knew what his intentions were, and I had been furious. He never did that again. Ever. He had made me his and I would not be replaced.

The last year we spent most of our time together, only us. Sitting on the sofa, watching TV, talking. He often fell asleep there with an empty bottle on the floor, not bothering to go to bed; just so he could be closer to me.

We were going to be together like this, forever. Just me and him.

Then one day, he didn't wake up. His body lying still on the sofa like he was still sleeping. On the sofa where he had made love to me; where he had made the pain go away. His head resting on the bundle that had been my clothes. The colours had faded over the years, and they had become frail and threadbare from his touch. He had never washed them after he had taken them off my body and I appreciated it. He had wanted to keep my scent on them so he could better remember me.

He is gone. Only his body remains, and I am alone.

I cannot leave. I am bound to this place where he had buried my body in the shallow grave underneath the basement floor all those long years ago.

He had made me his in life, I was his in death. Why wasn't he mine?

Authors

Tom Elmquist

Tom Elmquist has always been what you would call a jack of all trades. He has worked in many fields starting with his career with the US Navy straight out of high school to IT support. From a young age he dreamt of having his work published. So much so that he spent his time filling spiral notebooks with stories and poetry, never giving up.

His stories range from fantasy to horror, drawing inspiration from his favorite authors Stephen King, JRR Tolkien, and many more. He was first published in *I'm Not The Villian I'm Misunderstood* and hasn't stopped since.

In his downtime, he enjoys movies, gaming, and being a self-proclaimed geek. He lives in a small apartment in Pennsylvania with his four pet lizards, enjoying a simple and quiet life.

Nedan Rambo

Nedan Rambo fell in love with the art of storytelling at an early age. He wanted to become a filmmaker, but his parents gave him a typewriter instead of a camera, and he's been writing ever since. After graduating from CSULB, he continued writing and submitting short horror, science fiction, and fantasy stories to various publications and podcasts. Believing that genre fiction can be unapologetically honest through its storytelling, he continues to write to this day from his home in California. He frequently posts updates about work on his social media. Twitter(X): @Nedan8 Instagram: @nedanrambo

S.E. Reed

S.E. has spent the last 20 years of her life moving around all five-regions of the United States which gives her a unique American perspective. Many of her pieces have a strong Southern theme, but she also dabbles in the strange, bizarre and fantastical.

Her work has been featured by Wild Ink Publishing, Parhelion Lit, The Writer's Workout, Tempered Rune's Press and Survival Guide for the 21st Century. She has won several YA writing contests and actively participates as a delegate for YA Hub on Twitter.

S.E. resides in Florida with her family– nestled between the swamps of the Everglades and the salt of the Atlantic Ocean. This summer she'll be sitting in a lawn chair, working on her next novel and listening to EDM... (Ask her about her days as a DJ). Or she'll be in the pool begging her kids not to get her hair wet.

S.E. won the Florida Book Awards and the Paterson Prize for Young People for her novel *My Heart is Hurting*, through Wild Ink Publishing, she has also published Old Palmetto Drive through Wild Ink Publishing, and The Darkness of Dying in the Light through Conquest Publishing.

You can find S.E. Reed in the following places:

www.writingwithreed.com

Amy Nielsen

Amy Nielsen spent nearly twenty years on the other side of the writing aisle as a children's librarian, sharing her love of books with young readers. Daily immersion in story took root, and she started penning her YA debut, *Worth It*, behind her checkout desk. When her youngest son was diagnosed with Autism Spectrum Disorder, life shifted. She used her love of writing to help other families and started the Big Abilities blog.

She is the author of *It Takes a Village: How to Build A Support System for your Exceptional Needs Family* and the picture book, *Goldilocks and the Three Bears: Understanding Autism Spectrum Disorder*. She recently had a piece featured in the Writer's Workout *Our Pandemic* anthology. Amy also freelances for The Autism Helper, Playground Magazine, and other online publications.

When not writing, she and her family can be found boating in Tampa Bay. You can find Amy at http://www.bigabilities.com or http://www.amynielsenauthor.com.

David Rydenbacker

David currently lives in France, enjoying the wine, but was born elsewhere and lived for a long time in Australia. He loves telling stories and likes a challenge. Sometimes, he wakes up with a story in his head that wants to be explored.

When he is not a slave to his writing urges, he likes to run a game of DnD, leisurely ride his bike, rough it up with some sword fighting or Krav Maga, or chill out reading or listening to books about history, archaeology and anthropology. Basically, he is a giant nerd and enjoys it.

Kim Plasket

Kim Plasket is a Jersey girl in Florida. She enjoys writing horror and paranormal. She has several stories in various anthologies such as :

Holiday Horror Collection:

Dark Halloween: A Flash Fiction Anthology

Supernatural Drabbles of Dread: A Horror Anthology

Extreme Drabbles of Dread: A Horror Anthology

Forgotten Ones: Drabbles of Myth and Legend

The Thrill of the Hunt: Cabin Fever (Thrill of the Hunt An-
thology Book 6)
Scary Snippets: A Halloween Microfiction Anthology
Blood From a Tombstone Volume 2: Fear
The Thrill of the Hunt: Urban Legends Re-Imagined
The Gathering
And more.....
https://www.amazon.com/-/e/B074YCLRCF

Adele Liles

Adele Liles has been a high school English teacher for 24
years. She has been a finalist in the Writer's Workout Fiction Potluck contest and her work has been published in
the *North Carolina Bards Poetry Anthology.* Her young adult
novel, *Among the Whisperings,* debuts with Wild Ink in 2026.
She lives with her husband and their "tiny panther" in Virginia,
where she can be found working on her next YA contemporary
novel or watching a ridiculous amount of reality TV.

Raven Ellis

Raven Ellis is a queer demigirl who is passionate about storytelling and loves to experiment and expand the boundaries of
stories and the truths they tell. Writing has always been a way
to find solace for them, and they use it to create art and spark

meaningful connection. They are also a parent and hold kindness and mental health close to their heart as they understand what is to be an outcast. Through their work, Raven hopes to bring love and understanding to their readers.

Trevor Atkins

Trevor Atkins lives with his family on the west coast of Canada and has been working with words for much of his life. Nowadays, he is writing historical fiction & designing educational tabletop games for young humans to help #MakeLearningFun.

Trevor is currently working on the sequel to The Day the Pirates Went Mad, an entertaining tale of pirate-ty adventure written for his daughter and other middle grade readers. Over the course of the story, many nuggets of knowledge about real-life during the Age of Sail and the Golden Age of Piracy in particular are shared.

Glenda Darusow

Glenda was born at St. Joseph's Hospital on February 29, 1960. She grew up in Hampton, Maryland and graduated from Notre Dame Preparatory School in 1978. She received her B.S. in Education from the University Of Maryland in 1982 and taught English at various high schools within the Baltimore County School System. In 2013 she retired and married her longtime partner Belinda Deets. The couple now reside in New Market, Maryland. Glenda enjoys reading, writing, yoga, camping, and gardening.

J.K. Raymond

J.K. Raymond received her Bachelor of Fine Arts from Fontbonne University in St. Louis in 1995 where she fell in love with everything in St. Louis and under it! Additionally, she obtained Missouri teacher certification in 1995 for art K-12. J.K. continued her education at Fontbonne University in 2005, adding an additional teacher certification for elementary education for grades 1-6.

J.K. became an author when chronic illness made her very active life become very sedentary. An artist at heart, she channeled that passion from the canvas to the written word and has never looked back. J.K. has an amazing safety net in her tiny world, who selflessly help her to heal, write, love and live out loud. Her husband of twenty years, Matt Houser, her two sons, Aidan and Jace, her mother JoAnn, and her grumble of pugs, Lollie, RueRue, and TukTuk

---

Leta Hawk

Leta Hawk grew up in Millersburg, Pennsylvania, where she spent her summers reading, stargazing, and walking along the Susquehanna River. She currently lives in Dillsburg, Pennsylvania with her husband, two teenage sons, and a black lab, too far away from the river to enjoy walking along its banks, but still able to enjoy books and stars.

She is the author of the Kyrie Carter: Supernatural Sleuth series, which includes The Newbie, School Spirits, The Witch of Willow Lake, An Uneasy Inheritance, and Dandelion Souls. The sixth book, Outwalk the Light, Outrun the Darkness, is expected to release in Spring 2024.

Rebecca Linam

Rebecca Linam lives in Alabama and teaches German at the University of North Alabama by day. At night, she turns into the author of several short stories for children, teenagers, and young adults. She's also written a series of Open Educational Resource textbooks in German. Find her on Twitter @rebecca_linam or on her website: www.rebeccalinam.com.

Melissa Rotert

Melissa Rotert is a nurturer and logophile who combines these passions to write stories that capture the joys and struggles of life. She's found freedom in writing micro and flash fiction, helping to hone her craft. Her stories can be found in INKbabies literary magazine, OxMag, and National Flash Fiction Day (Flash Flood). She is also the fiction EIC for Epistemic Literary. Melissa's MG debut, SUE B AND THE RIDDERS is available now. Follow @OnPunsnNeedles (X) and @melruthwrites (IG) or melruthwrites.com.

Nicole Smith

Nicole Smith is an advocate for mental health and body acceptance. She lives just outside of Pittsburgh with her husband and daughters. Recently she was published in the Pennsylvania Bards Western PA Poetry Review 2023. If Nicole isn't writing poetry, you can find her with her nose in a book.

Jessica Scott

Jessica works with best-selling, award-winning authors on character and plot development and as a proofreader. She is a silver alum of 12x12, a Courage to Create scholar and a founding member of Query Help, Etc., an editorial services company. She, her children, and cats live in north Georgia.

Christopher DeWitt

Christopher DeWitt lives in Phoenix, Arizona with his wife Christine, son Alex, three dopey but lovable dogs, and a weird, vegan cat. When he isn't writing and reading, he is exploring the beautiful and sometimes eerie Superstition Mountains and the haunts of Tombstone. He also occupies his free time trying to figure out if his house, built practically on top of old western mines, is as haunted as The Copper Queen Hotel in Bisbee, Arizona. (It is.) A United States Air Force veteran and licensed pilot, he loves anything that flies and earth-bound racing machines that go very, very fast. He is an incorrigible and unapologetic Godzilla and Star Wars geek and loves to read history, historical fiction, westerns, sci-fi, and horror.

Sheelagh Aston

Writing since she could hold a pen or tap a keyboard, Sheelagh is the author of Natural Talent, a YA novel with several short stories and articles published. She seeks to bring stories that enthrall, entertain, and inspire readers. When not writing you can find Sheelagh being taking for walks by her dog in the beautiful Lancashire countryside or listening to Siouxsie & the Banshees and Lindisfarne.

Lindsay Schraad Keeling

As the cliche goes, Lindsay has been writing her entire life. She graduated from Mustang High School in Oklahoma in 2010, then went on to obtain her Bachelor of Science in Funeral Services in 2016 from the University of Central Oklahoma. In her twenties, she created a website that featured articles written about homicide victims and missing persons with assistance and permission directly from their families.

In 2020 - after moving across the country to Virginia - she co-authored the memoir *Where the Trail Ends: The Kenny Suttner Story* with her friend Angela Suttner, which won Honorable Mention in Writer's Digest 30th Annual Self-Published Book Awards.

In September of 2021, Lindsay won a Curator's Choice Award along with third place from Something or Other Publishing's 1st Annual Short Story Contest for her nonfiction piece, *Divorce in the Time of Social Media*.

In 2022, Lindsay graduated with her Master of Fine Arts in Creative Writing from Southern New Hampshire University. While her thesis novel was shelved for a time period, she was intrigued with a new story idea about a clandestine relationship from a unique perspective in addition to the complexities and dangers of social media, which turned into *The Funeral Director's Wife*.

Raised in Oklahoma, Lindsay wants to give back to those who've been affected by senseless crime. All of the author's proceeds, she is blessed with from the sales of The Funeral Director's Wife, will be donated to the nonprofit organization Oklahoma Homicide Survivors Support Group.

N.M. Lambert

N.M. Lambert is a part-time writer, editor, avid reader and gamer, and a heavy metal enthusiast. She graduated from Northern Arizona University with a bachelor's in both criminology and anthropology and with minors in both French and psychology. When not writing, she can be seen surfing the web, singing and sometimes trying to perfect her metal growls, and spending way too much time on Oblivion and Skyrim. She currently lives in Pollock Pines, California with her family and a menagerie of dogs, birds, and a cat.

Riley Kilmore

Kilmore is the author of the award-nominated middle-grade fantasy adventure *Shay the Brave*. Her short fiction and poetry have appeared in numerous anthologies, including three volumes of *The Anthology of Appalachian Writers*, *Like Sun-*

shine After Rain (Raw Dog Screaming Press), *Beacons of To-morrow* (Tyrannosaurus Press), all three volumes of Wild Ink Publishing's *Magical Muse* anthology series, as well as *UnCensored Ink* and *I'm Not The Villain; I'm Misunderstood* (both also from Wild Ink Publishing).

Kilmore, a 20-year veteran of the fire service and one of the first women police officers in Lancaster County, PA, earned an MFA in Writing Popular Fiction from Seton Hill University in 2022 and went on to win the 2023 West Virginia Fiction Competition.

You can learn more about Kilmore at her website: www.rileykilmore.com.

Alex Herod

Alex is a writer, therapist, and marketer from Manchester, UK. An avid horror fan, book hoarder, and one-time theatre maker, Alex is also a PhD researcher at the University of Salford, exploring the therapeutic benefits of reading and writing in recovery from alcohol addiction.

LindaAnn LoSchiavo

A native New Yorker, Elgin Award winner LindaAnn LoSchiavo is a member of British Fantasy Society, HWA, SFPA, and The Dramatists Guild. Current books: "Messengers of the Macabre," "Apprenticed to the Night," "Vampire Ventures."

Forthcoming: "Cancer Courts My Mother" (Penumbra, May 2024) and "Always Haunted: Hallowe'en Poems" (Wild Ink Publishing, coming soon).

Danielle Ruess

With a 25-year career that includes leadership roles across pharma, tech, and chemical coatings, Danielle Ruess has always incorporated storytelling in her work and life. An avid reader from a young age, she had a preference for horror and fantasy/sci-fi. She wrote her first self-published novel, FaerEarth, in 2010, and enjoys writing in her spare time. She's also passionate about F1 racing, sports cars and her family.

Binod Dawadi

Binod Dawadi, the author of The Power of Words, is a master's degree holder in Major English. He has worked on more than 1000 anthologies published in various renowned magazines. His vision is to change society through knowledge, so he wants to provide enlightenment to people through his writing.

Lorie Wackwitz

Lorie Wackwitz is an author, editor, publisher, and filmmaker with lead editor responsibilities at two micro-presses. She writes from her island cottage in northern Michigan where her family maintains a private nature reserve.

Emilia Thornrose

Emilia Thonrose was born in December of the year 2000 in southeastern Kentucky. She grew up with a love of romance and fantasy. She began writing at thirteen and never looked back. She has written "Hope" in The Carnation Collection, and "The Imposters Game" in Tenpenny Dreadfuls: Tales as Hard as Nails. She is also the author of "There's This Girl". Her work is an extension of herself and serves the purpose of connection, to resonate with others. Everyone knows the feeling of being alone, misunderstood, or unappreciated.

Emilia's work talks about the good days and the bad to remind readers they aren't alone and that no matter where they come from, they're seen and they matter.

Jinxie R. Thorne

Thoughts and words hold more power than we realize. Life is an unwritten book, and we are the characters. Every chapter holds unlimited possibilities.

Hidden within the misty mountains, a witchy woman remains huddled in her library weaving thoughts into words through creative writing. Jinxie has always enjoyed reading, anything fantasy, paranormal, and Halloween. She is a librarian, a beloved wife to her husband of eight years, and a caring mother to precious furbaby, Nova, whom she affectionately calls 'Baby Fluff'. Family is her everything, and she loves supporting her friends, and family.

William J. Connell

William J. Connell is currently a practicing attorney in the great states of Rhode Island and Massachusetts. He has also worked as a public-school teacher in the areas of Special Education and History in the same states. He enjoys writing on a wide variety of topics. Most of his non-fiction material is in the legal field, and his work has been published in many law journals, most frequently in The Rhode Island Bar Journal. His fiction tends to run to historical adventure, which reflects his love of teaching history, mixed with elements of sci-fi, classic literature, and horror thrown in for good measure!

Besides being a member of the Wild Ink Writing Family, for which he is most grateful, he has had fiction pieces published by The Ravens Quoth Press, Godless Publishers, Culture Cult Press, and Underland Press. He likes to spend time with his family and Lulu, the family's green-cheeked conure. His author/writer website continues to be a leading example of why you should not do one yourself unless and until you know what you are doing.

Dexter Amoroso

Meet the gentle warrior, a poetic samurai with a panther heart. Caressing petals and kissing flowers, he finds solace in nature's sanctuary, crafting Haikus that dance upon the winds. As a devoted father, he nurtures his two boys with boundless love, embracing the chaos of parenthood. Founder of McKinley Publishing Hub, he empowers authors, offering solace, support, and a haven for dreams to take flight. With a pen in one hand and a world of possibilities in the other, he ignites creativity, cultivating growth, and painting stories that enchant hearts. His legacy, enduring as the ancient cherry blossoms, leaves an indelible mark on the literary landscape.

Lavender Walker

Lavender Walker is a full-time mom with a certificate in culinary arts working toward her BS in psychology and finishing her first novel. Her debut short story "Silver Wolf" can be found in Wild Ink Publishing's anthology Calliope's Collection of Mystical Mayhem. With the goal of raising intellectual, creative children, she hopes to be a shining example of working hard to make dreams come true.

Mary Beth Nix

Mary Beth Nix has just completed her MFA in Creative Writing at Southern New Hampshire University. She loves reading, playing with her two dogs, and traveling, both to real and imaginary places. She has published a story and essay in the anthology Into the Mirror, and she is currently working on a science fiction novel.

Mindi Carver

Mindi was born and raised in West Virginia, but now call upstate South Carolina her home. She's been a storyteller since she could talk and a writer since she could understand the concept. So, when Mindi couldn't find the kinds of adult (and spicy content) stories she wanted to read, she decided it was time to try writing them for myself.

When not fighting with her muse, Mindi enjoys reading other people's hard work, cooking, small-scale gardening, singing, dancing in the kitchen when she thinks nobody's looking, cuddling her miniature, fluffy house-panther, handicraft making, playing D&D, doing cosplay photo shoots, and participating in historical re-enactments.

Bruce Buchanan

Bruce Buchanan is the communications writer for an international law firm and a former journalist. But he's been a fan of fantasy and heroic fiction for most of his life. His influences range from the novels of Margaret Weis & Tracy Hickman and Terry Brooks to the Marvel Comics stories of Stan Lee, Jack Kirby, and Steve Ditko. Bruce has short stories appearing in the upcoming Wild Ink Publishing anthologies *Tenpenny Dreadfuls*, *Clio's Curious Dash Through Time*, and *UnCensored Ink*. He lives in Greensboro, N.C. with his wife, Amy Joyner Buchanan (a blogger and the author of five non-fiction books), and their 17-year-old son, Jackson.